There would simply be no more kissing!

*S*he'd not make that same mistake twice. *You've already made that mistake twice*, her inner voice reminded her.

Fine. She'd not make that same mistake *three* times.

She forced her feet to move away, pulling her hand free from his. He nodded slowly, regarding her through serious eyes.

"Yes," he said. "This is neither the time nor place."

"Actually, there is *no* proper time or place, my lord. A single kiss was one thing, but repeating it today was . . ." *Delightful . . . incredible . . . unforgettable . . .* ". . . not wise. Doing it again would be foolhardy indeed."

"Why?"

Because with only two kisses you've made me want things I shouldn't. Things I can't have. "Surely you don't need to ask."

"No, I don't," he said quietly. "I feel the deep attraction between us. The question is what are we going to do about it?"

"Nothing," she said quickly. "We'll simply ignore it."

"I don't believe that's going to be an option."

By Jacquie D'Alessandro

NEVER A LADY
NOT QUITE A GENTLEMAN
LOVE AND THE SINGLE HEIRESS
WHO WILL TAKE THIS MAN?

Jacquie D'Alessandro

Never A Lady

AVON BOOKS
An Imprint of HarperCollinsPublishers

This is a work of fiction. Names, characters, places, and incidents are products of the author's imagination or are used fictitiously and are not to be construed as real. Any resemblance to actual events, locales, organizations, or persons, living or dead, is entirely coincidental.

AVON BOOKS
An Imprint of HarperCollins*Publishers*
10 East 53rd Street
New York, New York 10022-5299

Copyright © 2006 by Jacquie D'Alessandro
The Care and Feeding of Unmarried Men copyright © 2006 by Christie Ridgway; *Her Officer and Gentleman* copyright © 2006 by Karen Hawkins; *A Bite to Remember* copyright © 2006 by Lynsay Sands; *Never A Lady* copyright © 2006 by Jacquie D'Alessandro
ISBN-13: 978-0-06-077941-2
ISBN-10: 0-06-077941-1
www.avonromance.com

First Avon Books paperback printing: August 2006

Avon Trademark Reg. U.S. Pat. Off. and in Other Countries, Marca Registrada, Hecho en U.S.A.
HarperCollins® is a registered trademark of HarperCollins Publishers Inc.

Printed in the U.S.A.

10 9 8 7 6 5 4 3 2 1

This book is dedicated with love to my son, Christopher. Thank you for filling my life with music, for making me laugh, and for making every day a Big Adventure—even those days that don't include Zodiac rides or ATVs. Love you, honey. Best Friends. xox

And as always, to my wonderful, encouraging husband Joe. If there was an award for Most Patient Man Alive, you'd win it, hands down. Thank you for always being so supportive and kind. Have I told you today how much I love you? xox

Acknowledgments

I would like to thank the following people for their invaluable help and support:

My editor, Erika Tsang, and all the wonderful people at Avon/HarperCollins for their kindness, cheerleading and for helping make my dreams come true.

My agent, Damaris Rowland, for her faith and wisdom.

Jenni Grizzle and Wendy Etherington for keeping me going and always being up for champagne and cheesecake.

Thanks also to Sue Grimshaw, Kathy Baker, Kay and Jim Johnson, Kathy and Dick Guse, Lea and Art D'Alessandro, and Michelle, Steve, and Lindsey Grossman.

A cyber hug to my Looney Loopies Connie Brockway, Marsha Canham, Virginia Henley, Jill Gregory, Sandy Hingston, Julia London, Kathleen Givens, Sherri Browning, and Julie Ortolon, and also to the Temptresses.

A very special thank-you to the members of Georgia Romance Writers.

And finally, thank you to all the wonderful readers who have taken the time to write or e-mail me. I love hearing from you!

One

Alexandra Larchmont pinned Lady Miranda with the intense stare she knew lent her predictions extra credence. As Lady Miranda was a distant cousin to Alex's hostess, Lady Malloran, she wanted to make certain the young woman was pleased with her card reading.

"While I divine from your card reading and aura that you suffered pain in your past, your present is filled with bright promise—parties, jewels, fabulous gowns."

Lady Miranda's eyes glittered with delight. "Excellent." She leaned closer to Alex. "What about my future?" she whispered.

She was about to look down to consult the cards when the crowd of milling party guests separated a bit and her attention was caught by the sight of a tall, dark-haired man.

Panic rippled along her nerve endings, and her muscles tensed, for in spite of the fact that four years had passed since she'd last seen him, she recognized him instantly. Under the best of circumstances, he wouldn't be a man easily forgotten—and the circumstances of their last encounter could never be described as "best." While she didn't know his name, his image was permanently etched in her memory.

She dearly wished that's where he'd remained—not standing a mere dozen feet away. Dear God, if he recognized *her*, everything she'd worked so long and hard for would be destroyed.

Her every instinct screamed at her to flee, but she remained frozen in place. As if trapped in a horrible, slow-moving nightmare, her gaze wandered down his form. Impeccably dressed in formal black attire, his dark hair gleamed under the glow of the dozens of candles flickering in the overhead chandelier. He held a crystal champagne glass, and she involuntarily shivered, rubbing her damp palms over her upper arms, recalling in vivid detail the strength in those large hands as they'd gripped her, preventing her escape. Out of necessity, she'd learned at a young age how to master her fears, but this man had alarmed and unnerved her as no one else ever had, before or since their single encounter.

The cards had repeatedly warned her about him—the

dark-haired stranger with the vivid green eyes who would wreak havoc with her existence—years before she'd ever seen him that first time. The cards had also predicted she'd someday see him again. Unfortunately, the cards hadn't prepared her for someday being *now*.

Looking up, she noted with a sickening sense of alarm that his gaze moved slowly over the crowd. In a matter of seconds that gaze would fall upon her.

"Are you all right, Madame Larchmont? You've gone completely pale."

Lady Miranda's voice jerked Alex's attention away from the man, and she found herself the subject of the young woman's narrow-eyed scrutiny.

Digging deep to locate the well-practiced inscrutable mien that had always served her well, Alex said, "I'm a bit overheated, which sadly disrupts my psychic energies." The well-modulated, even-toned voice she'd perfected long ago gave no indication of her inner turmoil. "A bit of air will set me to rights and allow me once again to commune with the spirits. If you'll excuse me . . ."

Her gaze flicked back to the man. A stunning young woman she recognized as Lord Ralstrom's daughter Lady Margaret approached him, smiling in unmistakable greeting. Surely a beauty like that would keep his interest engaged long enough for her to escape.

She quickly wrapped up her cards in a square of bronze silk, slipped the deck into the deep pocket of her gown, and hastily rose. Apprehension shivered down her spine, and she felt the weight of someone's stare upon her. Her gaze snapped up, and her breath stalled.

Vivid green eyes assessed her with a piercing intensity that simultaneously chilled and heated her. And rendered her as immobile as his hands had four years ago. Her heart seemed to stutter and it flashed through her mind that there were undoubtedly dozens of women who would go to great lengths to be on the receiving end of this man's attention. She, however, was not one of them.

Did he recognize her? She couldn't tell, as his expression gave nothing away. But she did not intend to wait to find out. "The spirits are calling, I must go," she said to Lady Miranda, then executed a quick turn and melted into the crowd with an expertise born of years of practice.

Unfortunately, she didn't know where she was going, her entire being consumed with only one thought: escape. The very same thought the stranger had implanted in her the last time they'd met.

After navigating her way to the edge of the room, she halted, and frustrated dismay filled her. Damnation, in her panic, she'd fled the wrong way. Her fortune-telling table had been set up near the French windows leading outside and was, therefore, now on the opposite side of the large, crowded room. And dozens of party guests stood between her and the corridor leading to the front door—a situation made all the more vexing, as succumbing to panic was simply not like her. Yet she couldn't deny the agitation gripping her.

She quickly scanned the crowd. Her heart stuttered when her gaze settled on the green-eyed man. His features were set in a dark scowl as he, too, scanned the crowd. Looking for her?

Spurred by the desperation she couldn't control, she slipped into the nearest corridor. Heart pounding, she forced herself not to run, not to show any outward signs of alarm in case she met someone. An open door on the left offered the hope of sanctuary, but as she drew closer, she heard masculine voices coming from within and moved on. She passed other doorways, but didn't pause, determined to put as much distance between herself and the man as possible. Surely he wouldn't search the house for her, if indeed he looked for her at all.

Her mind raced. All she needed to do was find a room . . . preferably one at the back of the house. She'd slip out the window into the garden, then disappear into the mews. Lady Malloran would most assuredly be annoyed, and Alex would no doubt lose the entire evening's wages, a troubling prospect as she badly needed the money. She'd have to plead her case, claiming a loss of the spirits or deep psychic fatigue or some such so her reputation wasn't damaged. Of course, her efforts might well be for naught, thanks to the stranger. The ramifications of what running into her past might mean for her future—

She sliced off the disturbing thought. The future she needed to worry about right now encompassed the next few minutes. Once she escaped here, she'd worry about tomorrow.

The corridor made a series of turns, and the light dimmed to near darkness. The sounds of the party—laughter, chatter, the tinkling of crystal—faded to a dim, indistinguishable murmur. After rounding another corner, she noted a closed door. Excellent. Based on what she knew of Mayfair town houses, the room was most likely a library or study, and clearly wasn't being used for the party. Moving swiftly, she pressed her ear against the wood door panel, then dropped to her knees and peered through the keyhole. Satisfied the room was empty, she turned the brass knob, eased the door open just enough to slip through, then closed the door behind her.

Leaning back against the polished oak panel, she sucked in a deep, calming breath and conducted a quick survey of the room, which was, as she'd suspected, a study. Based on the dark, wood paneling, and masculine maroon leather sofa and chairs, clearly Lord Malloran's domain. Her gaze riveted on the window on the opposite side of the room through which silvery moonlight glowed—the room's only illumination, and she allowed herself to relish an instant of relief. Escape beckoned, no more than twenty feet away.

Just as she was about to push off from the door, however, a noise stilled her. Relief vanished, and tension gripped her anew, and she pressed her ear to the crack between the door and the jamb.

"The study is just ahead," came a low, deep voice. "We can talk there without interruption."

Dear God, could her luck this night get any worse? Spurred to action, Alex raced across the room. With no time to escape out the window, she dashed behind the heavy velvet drapes, simultaneously blessing the darkness of the room and cursing her foolishness for hesitating even a second to catch her breath. She pressed her back against the cool glass windowpanes. Her escape hatch.

For all the good it did her.

The soft *swish* of the door opening was followed seconds later by a *click* as it closed. Then a louder *click*, indicating the door was now locked. She went perfectly still and reminded herself that over the years she'd successfully escaped tougher spots than this. More times than she cared to recall. *Just remain calm, quiet, and patient.*

"The date and place are set." She instantly recognized the rough, masculine voice as the same one she'd heard seconds ago through the door crack.

"When?" came another voice, this one a barely audible raspy whisper.

"Wexhall's party. On the twentieth."

"All the arrangements are in place?"

"Yes. No one will suspect it were more than a tragic accident."

"Make certain of that," came the soft, raspy whisper. The person's real voice—or an attempt at a disguise? Most likely a disguise, she decided. One never knew when one might be inadvertently overheard in a house swarming with guests and servants. *Or fortune-tellers hiding behind draperies.* "No mistakes. His death will assuredly give rise to inquiries."

"No need fer worry. Ye've hired the best."

"You'll be compensated as such. Provided all goes as planned."

"It will. And speakin' of compensation . . . I'll be havin' another bit of blunt now that the arrangements are made. As we agreed."

"I'll see that it's delivered tomorrow. There's to be no further contact between us after this."

"Understood. Now I've got to get back to servin' the fancy folks drinks 'fore I'm missed."

"With the money I'm paying you, soon you'll be the one throwing the fancy parties."

A sound of disgust filled the air. "Bah, I won't be wastin' no blunt on parties. Soon as this is over, you'll never see me in London again."

"That is, undoubtedly, for the best," came the silky, whispered reply.

"Gonna get my own place. By the sea. Hire myself a servant. Be the one gettin' waited on fer once in my life."

No reply other than the sound of muffled footfalls came, and Alex, scarcely daring to breathe, visualized the pair crossing the room. Seconds later the *click* of the door being unlocked sounded. Even while her strong sense of self-preservation screamed at her not to move, she peeked around the edge of the curtain and for an instant caught sight of the back of a tall, dark-haired man who was dressed in the unmistakable elaborately gold-trimmed Malloran livery. Obviously the rougher, less-educated speaker. To whom had he been talking? She craned her neck, but the door shut, ensconcing her in tomblike silence.

She remained behind the curtain, pulling in slow, careful breaths in an effort to quell the sick dread snaking through her. Someone was going to be killed . . . on the twentieth. But who?

It's not your problem, the inner voice that had successfully helped her survive the mean streets of London warned. *You have your own problems to worry about.*

Yes, she did. And she well knew what happened to people who stuck their noses where they didn't belong— they tended to lose their noses. Or worse.

She squeezed her eyes shut and cursed herself for wondering if this evening could get any worse, for clearly it could. Everything inside her screamed at her to forget what she'd overheard. Ignore it. Flee. Now. While she had the chance. Before the Malloran servant or the person who'd clearly hired him to kill discovered her absence from the party and wondered to where the entertainment had disappeared. Then looked for and found her. Hiding in this room. Where they'd just discussed their murderous plot.

But she knew that no matter how hard she tried, she'd never be able to forget what she'd heard. Her conscience, that inconvenient inner voice that plagued her when she most wished it not to, would eat at her.

Yet what to do with this information? Clearly the intended target was someone important. *His death will assuredly give rise to inquiries.* Someone had to be told. Someone who could stop this crime before it took place. Someone who wasn't her.

But who? A magistrate? She swallowed the bitter sound that rose in her throat. She'd spent her life avoiding magistrates and Runners and anyone of that ilk, and given her past, she definitely preferred to keep it that way. Besides, who would believe her? A woman who barely scraped together a living telling fortunes? The instant the murder of this important person was committed, they'd believe her guilty—of something. Didn't matter what. They'd hunt her down like a fox. Toss her in a cell. Her stomach turned over. *Never again.*

Yet she'd be forced into her own private prison if she didn't at least *try* to warn whoever was in danger. With a wistful glance at the window that beckoned with the sweet temptation of freedom, she moved from behind the curtain and walked swiftly to the elegant polished wood desk. Quickly extracting a piece of vellum, she dipped the quill into the inkpot and penned a swift note, then folded the vellum in quarters and wrote "Lord Malloran—urgent and private" on the outside. She set it on the desk, securing it by placing an egg-shaped crystal paperweight on the corner, then blew out a long breath and told her conscience to cease grumbling.

She'd done what she could to save the intended victim. Now she needed to save herself.

Moving to the window, she looked through the glass at the small garden, which was thankfully empty, no doubt because of the unseasonably chilly weather. Finally, something was going right. Noting the fifteen-foot drop to the ground, she grimaced. Last time she'd made such a jump, she'd slipped and strained her ankle. She briefly considered retracing her steps and exiting through the front door, but a sore ankle held infinitely more appeal than running into either the green-eyed man or the murderous duo roaming the party. No, the window offered the only way out of this mess.

After one last look to ensure the garden below remained free of partygoers, Alex opened the window and nimbly swung her legs over the sash. Bracing her palms on the ledge, she gave her body a deft twist, then carefully lowered herself until she held on, her fingers curled over the sill, facing the rough stone exterior. Drawing a deep breath, she pressed the toes of her soft leather boots against the stone wall, kicked off, and let go.

Her stomach rushed upward. For the space of a heartbeat she felt as if she were flying, then she landed lightly, bending her knees and touching her palms to the cool, moist earth. When she stood, she nearly laughed from the sheer exhilaration of her feat as she brushed off her hands. She was free. All she had to do was melt into the shadows. She turned, intending to head toward the mews.

And found herself staring at a snowy white cravat.

A snowy white cravat that was mere inches from her nose. She sucked in a startled breath and caught the scent of freshly starched linen mixed with a whiff of sandalwood. She took a hasty step back but halted when her shoulders hit the rough stone of the town house. Strong hands gripped her upper arms.

"Steady," came a deep, masculine voice.

Dear God, when had her luck turned so horrendously . . . unlucky? This night just went from bad to worse.

Fingers flexed against her skin left bare by her gown's short, puffed sleeves, and she noted he wasn't wearing gloves. A heated tingle that was surely nothing more than annoyance skidded through her. Determined to talk her way out of this irritating further cog in her escape plans quickly, Alex lifted her chin.

And looked into the hauntingly familiar eyes of the stranger.

Two

Alex's annoyance evaporated and alarm roared through her with such force she actually felt light-headed. A tiny inner voice commanded that she step away from him, but she couldn't move. Could only stare into those fathomless eyes, which regarded her with an unreadable expression. Every muscle tensed, gripping her with the strangling fear she thought she'd long ago conquered.

Tense silence that seemed to last an eternity swelled between them while Alex fought to master her dread and appear outwardly calm.

Something flickered in his gaze . . . something that disappeared before she could decipher it. Something she prayed wasn't recognition. Yet what else could it be? Surely it was no coincidence that this particular man appeared just below this particular window at this particular time.

The years she'd spent running from her past had finally caught up with her. In the form of this stranger who continued to hold her in a firm grip. Drawing on all her reserves, she bludgeoned aside her apprehension, and grasped her aplomb. She knew how to bluff her way out of difficult spots—although nothing about his demeanor labeled him an easy mark, an observation she'd foolishly chosen to ignore four years ago.

"Are you all right, Madame Larchmont?"

Any tiny flicker of hope that he didn't know her identity vanished with his question. Straightening her spine, she lifted her chin. "You know who I am."

One dark brow jutted upward. "Did you think I wouldn't?"

A girl can dream . . . "I wondered since you've obviously forgotten yourself." She flicked a pointed glance down at his hands, which still held her in place. "You may release me, sir."

His grip instantly loosened, and he stepped back. Alex fancied that his fingers trailed for a fraction of a heartbeat over her bare skin before he released her. A tremor ran through her, surely the result of the brisk night air brushing over the spot his palms had warmed.

"Did you hurt yourself when you stumbled?" he asked, his voice laced with unmistakable concern as his gaze ran down her form.

"Stumbled?"

"Yes. I was walking in the garden and heard a sound. When I turned the corner, I saw you rising and brushing off your hands. You are not injured, I hope."

"N . . . no, thank you. I'm fine." Alex's mind whirled, and she studied him carefully. She prided herself on her ability to read people, and his expression, easily visible in the full moon's glow, revealed nothing more than polite concern, with perhaps a touch of curiosity. It seemed he didn't know she'd jumped from the window.

She looked at him again. Not the slightest flicker of recognition flared in his eyes. Was it possible he didn't remember their previous encounter? That he only knew her from tonight? Relief rushed through her, only to halt. The intensity with which he'd stared at her in the drawing room had to mean something. If he didn't remember her, then what?

He moved, and her muscles tensed, but he only pulled a handkerchief from inside his waistcoat. Presenting the white linen square to her with a flourish, he said, "To wipe your hands."

With her composure now fully collected, she concealed her wary suspicions of his motives with the skill of a seasoned actress and shook her head. "Thank you, but my gloves protected my hands. I'm quite all right." She then favored him with her most imperious look. "What are you doing in the garden?"

He smiled, and she fought the urge to blink. Under other circumstances, she might well have been dazzled by that devastatingly attractive flash of even, white teeth, as she imagined most females were. Luckily, she was immune to this man's allure.

"Like you, just getting a much-needed bit of air," he said. "Along with a desire to get away from the crowds for a moment . . . although coming upon Madame Larchmont is an unexpected pleasure."

Still suspicious, but willing to play out the game, she inclined her head in silent acknowledgment of his compliment. "You have the advantage over me, sir, in that I do not know *your* name."

A sheepish look too genuine to be feigned passed over his handsome features and he tucked away his handkerchief. "Forgive me. I am Colin Oliver, Viscount Sutton." He made her a formal bow. "At your service."

Alex swallowed the lump of dread in her throat. Of course she recognized the name. Lord Sutton was one of the Season's most eligible bachelors, made even more so by the news that he was actually looking for a wife and wouldn't have to be dragged to the altar. A well-respected peer with power to wield. If he were to remember her from before . . . a shudder ran through her.

He could ruin everything she'd worked and fought so hard to achieve.

He flashed her another grin. "It appears by your expression that my name is not unfamiliar to you. Perhaps you read the snippet in today's *Times*?"

Her relief at not being instantly recognized was tempered by an unreasonable prickle of pique that he didn't recall her—especially since she recalled him in such vivid detail. Was she so unmemorable?

She shoved the ridiculous question aside. Good God, she should be kicking up her heels at his faulty memory. And really, why *would* he remember her? Their encounter had been so brief. A lofty member of the peerage would hardly focus on the face of a dirty street urchin.

The cloud of disaster that loomed over her livelihood, all her plans for her future, receded . . . slightly. She couldn't dispel the odd feeling that, contrary to all appearances, he was somehow toying with her. She needed to stay on her guard, and to do so, she needed information. The cards had predicted this stranger's reappearance in her life—and that he'd somehow figure prominently. But what she didn't know, and needed to know, was *why*.

Offering him her best mysterious Madame Larchmont smile, she said, "I did indeed read the snippet in the *Times*. I believe half of London hopes I'll be able to predict whom you will marry."

He chuckled, a deep, rich sound. "I'm hoping so myself. It would certainly save me a great deal of time." He extended his elbow. "May I escort you back inside? I'm looking forward to my turn at your fortune-telling table."

Alex paused. She had no desire to return to the house where the murderous Malloran servant and his unseen cohort she'd overheard moved amongst the guests.

"Thank you, but I was on my way home."

"So early?"

She spread her hands. "When the spirits call me home, I must obey."

"Has your carriage been called?"

She hid her grimace of distaste. Typical spoiled aristocrat, assuming everyone had a carriage at their disposal. She lifted her chin a notch. "I intended to hire a hack."

He·waved her intention aside with a dismissive gesture. "Nonsense. It's far too late for a lady to be traveling alone. I'll have my carriage brought 'round immediately and escort you home."

"I appreciate the offer, Lord Sutton, however, I'm well accustomed to seeing myself home from these soirees."

"Perhaps. But it is not necessary for you to do so *this* evening."

"I wouldn't dream of dragging you away from the party where you might well meet your future wife."

"I've already seen this evening's offerings, and I'm quite certain the woman of my dreams is not in Lady Malloran's drawing room. Indeed, by far the most interesting woman I've met tonight is standing in front of me." His smile was warm, friendly, and tinged with a hint of flirtatious mischief. "Believe me, you'd be doing me a great favor by allowing me to escort you home."

Was he playing games with her? Perhaps. But if so, she needed to know. Since she found herself inexorably curious about this man who, she was convinced, was the one who'd figured so prominently in her card readings for years and because she couldn't think up any reason to refuse his offer that wouldn't sound churlish, she nodded. "Very well."

He extended his arm at the perfectly proper angle. "Careful where you step. I wouldn't want you to stumble again."

Was that a glint of dry humor in his voice? She studied him, but his expression didn't waver. "No, I wouldn't wish to stumble again," she agreed. She wrapped her gloved fingers around the crook of his elbow, and they made their way over the narrow strip of grass running along the side of the house toward the front. The hard muscles of his forearm flexed beneath her fingers, indicating a likely love of riding. She noted with surprise that he walked with a slight limp, favoring his left leg. He hadn't suffered from any such affliction four years ago. In fact, he'd been extraordinarily fleet of foot. Frighteningly so.

When they reached the front steps, a footman appeared, and Alex stiffened, fearing the tall, dark-haired servant was the person she'd heard in the study.

"Your carriage, Lord Sutton?"

She let out a long breath and forced her muscles to relax. Not his voice. Not the same man.

"Please," Lord Sutton replied. He then turned to her. "Do you have a wrap or any belongings that require fetching?"

Heavens, in all the confusion, she forgotten about that. "Yes. My bonnet and green velvet cloak." She eyed the wide double doors leading into the foyer. She supposed she should go back inside and say good night to Lady Malloran, but the mere thought of doing so edged unease down her spine.

"Why don't you wait here while I see to our belongings and bid our hostess good evening?"

She hoped her relief didn't show. "Thank you," she said in her most regal tone.

He entered the house, and she drew her first easy breath since she'd first seen him in the drawing room. Perhaps he wasn't the man who the cards repeatedly predicted would reenter her life, but her instincts, which had always served her well, told her he was. If she were able to read his cards, she might be able to discern more. Yet in order to do that, she'd need to spend more time in his company. If she did, would she run the risk of his remembering her?

Now that she could think clearly, she realized she could simply deny any previous encounter. Claim she must just resemble someone he'd once briefly met. Obviously his memory didn't ring with the crystal-clear vividness of her recollection of him. He'd rendered himself unforgettable in the course of several frantic heartbeats.

Clearly she was not made of such memorable stuff—something for which she again inexplicably found herself miffed. She looked skyward. Miffed? She was a candidate for Bedlam. The fact that he didn't remember her could only be described as a miraculous blessing.

Her thoughts were interrupted when an elegant black lacquer carriage, a coat of arms decorating the door, pulled by a handsome pair of matching grays halted in front of the town house.

"Perfect timing," came Lord Sutton's deep voice from behind her. Before she could turn around, he settled her cloak around her shoulders. When she reached up to grab the ties, her fingers brushed against his. She felt him go perfectly still, and realized that he stood very close to her. Scandalously close. So close the warmth of his breath caressed her nape. The heat of his hands penetrated her thin lace gloves, and her skin tingled at the contact. Before she could react in any way other than simply to stand there and absorb this unsettling reaction to him, he stepped back.

Irritated at herself, she jerked on the ribbons at her collar, but to her further annoyance, her fingers weren't quite steady as she tied the long strings, resulting in a sloppy mess of a bow.

Lord Sutton moved to her side. Appearing completely

composed and unruffled, he handed her her bonnet, which, given her current poor ribbon-tying abilities, she opted not to don.

"Lady Malloran is bereft at your departure," he said, "so I took the liberty of explaining that when the spirits speak to you, you have no choice but to heed, and they'd expressly told you it was time to go home. I hope that meets with your approval?"

She searched his countenance for any indication he was mocking her, but his voice and expression were perfectly serious. Light spilled from the town house's tall windows, highlighting his handsome features, and she instantly recalled how she'd been unable to tear her gaze from him when she'd first spied him in the crowd at Vauxhall four years ago. Tall and devastatingly attractive, he'd stood alone, under a tree, his back propped against the sturdy trunk, watching people walk by him, and she'd immediately felt a kinship. She knew exactly how it felt to be alone. To watch people pass you by. One look at him, and every impossible fantasy she'd ever secretly dreamed of being whisked away by a handsome, dashing hero had converged in her mind, casting him as her knight in shining armor. The one who would keep her safe, slay her dragons, and make the aching loneliness, the always present fear, go away. Silly, impossible dreams as her mind well knew but that her foolish heart clung to just the same.

Over the years she'd observed countless aristocrats and dismissed them without a thought, but something about him had captured her imagination and stirred her in a way she'd never before experienced. A disturbing, exciting, heart-pounding way that had simultaneously confused and intrigued her. In spite of his outward gentlemanly mien, he'd exuded a contradictory aura of wistfulness mixed with danger and mystery that had drawn her like a thief to a cache of jewels.

He clearly belonged with the members of the *ton* wandering the grounds, yet he remained apart from them. Every aspect of his appearance, from those compelling eyes to the slash of his high cheekbones and straight, classic nose to his firm, square jaw to his very bearing marked him as a highborn gentleman. Not the sort she'd ever fancied, and certainly not the sort who'd ever fancy her.

She now found herself studying him, and her gaze rested on his perfectly shaped upper lip, then his fuller lower lip. How did his mouth manage to look soft and firm at the same time? Surely a man blessed with such extraordinary good looks would have no trouble finding a wife. Indeed, he'd no doubt require a broom to sweep the dozens of willing young women from his steps. Hmmm . . . was there any truth to the rumor that a full lower lip on a man indicated he possessed a sensuous—?

"Does what I told Lady Malloran meet with your approval, Madame Larchmont?"

The softly spoken question jerked her gaze upward. Lord Sutton was regarding her with an unreadable expression that made it impossible for her to know if he'd noticed her fascination with his mouth, but regardless, she sent up a silent prayer of thanks that she'd long ago lost her ability to blush. If he *had* noticed, the knowledge obviously hadn't elicited any sort of reaction in him, with the possible exception of boredom—something that shouldn't have, but nonetheless surprisingly pricked at her feminine vanity.

Good heavens, perhaps she *was* a candidate for Bedlam. This man, in less than an hour's time, had ruffled her normally never-out-of-place feathers more than any other man ever had over any period of time. Indeed, the only other man who had ever ruffled her so was . . . him. Four years ago. *Yes, and look at how disastrously that encounter went.*

He must be well accustomed to gawking females. An overwhelming desire to assure him that her gawking had been a completely uncharacteristic, inexplicable aberration assaulted her, but she managed to swallow the urge. Instead, she looked him straight in the eye, and said, "As what you explained to Lady Malloran is perfectly true, yes, it meets with my approval. Thank you."

"You're welcome." He nodded toward the carriage. "Shall we?"

Waving off the footman, he helped her step up, then asked, "What is your direction?"

She named a part of the city that, while not the most fashionable, was certainly respectable. After repeating her words to his coachman, Lord Sutton joined her, settling his long frame on the soft, gray velvet squabs opposite her. Seconds after the door closed, the vehicle jerked into motion.

The confines of the luxurious carriage made Lord Sutton's large, robust frame appear even larger, his shoulders wider, his muscular legs longer. Unsettled in a manner she neither liked nor could explain, she pulled her attention away from him and looked down, but found no relief as her gaze riveted on the hem of her cloak resting across the toe of one of his polished black boots. An odd feeling rippled through her at the sight of her clothing touching his. It somehow looked too . . . intimate, and she shifted in her seat so the green velvet would slide from his boot.

Refusing to examine her relief too closely, she drew a breath, and any sense of inner calm vanished like a puff of steam as her senses filled with the pleasing scents of freshly starched linen and sandalwood she'd smelled when her nose had nearly been buried in his cravat. He smelled . . . *clean*. In a way she normally did not think of men smelling. In her experience, they reeked either of perfumes or of unwashed body odor.

"How long have you lived in London, Madame Larchmont?"

She gave herself a mental shake and refocused her attention on him. He appeared perfectly relaxed, but he'd stretched out his left leg, the one he favored, and she wondered if it pained him. Although his face was cast in shadows, she could see he regarded her with polite interest.

"I've lived in the city for several years," she said, then adroitly changed the subject. "According to what I've heard, you haven't been to London recently, but rather have been living at your family's estate in Cornwall."

He nodded. "Yes. I much prefer it there. Have you ever been?"

"To Cornwall? No. What is it like?"

His expression turned thoughtful. "Beautiful, although if I had to choose only one word to describe it, I'd pick 'peaceful.' The smell and sound and sight of the sea are things I miss deeply whenever I leave." He spread his arm across the back of his seat in a nonchalant gesture and regarded her with another of his inscrutable expressions—something she found both frustrating and oddly fascinating, as she could normally read people easily.

"Tell me, my lord, did you mean what you said earlier about wanting me to read your cards?"

His grin flashed. "Of course. I am always happy to indulge in a harmless diversion."

She hiked up a brow. "You do not believe in the power or accuracy of card readings?"

"I cannot say that I've ever given the matter a great deal of thought. But I must admit that my initial reaction is one of skepticism in giving any credence to a deck of cards."

"You present me with a challenge, my lord, to change your mind."

"I assure you that changing my mind will indeed be a challenge. I fear things of a mystical nature go against my pragmatic temperament."

"Yet you are willing to give me an opportunity to convince you?"

"Convince me of what, exactly?"

"That the cards can tell of your past, present, and accurately predict your future. In the hands of the right fortune-teller."

"Which would be you."

"Of course."

"Then let us say I am willing to allow you to read my cards. Whether you can convince me"—he shrugged—"remains to be seen."

"I must warn you, it may require a fair amount of time for me to do so, as skeptics always take more effort."

He smiled. "You say that as if I should I be alarmed."

"Perhaps you should." She returned his smile. "I'm paid for my readings in quarter-hour increments."

"I see. And your fee?"

Without batting an eye, she named a figure triple her normal rate.

His brows shot upward. "With fees like that, Madame, one might be tempted to call you a . . ."

"Fortune-teller second to none?" she supplied helpfully when he hesitated.

He leaned forward and braced his forearms on his knees. His eyes glittered in the semidarkness as they stared into hers. "A thief."

Thank goodness for the lack of light, for she actually felt the blood drain from her face. Her heart stuttered, and it suddenly felt as if all the air inside the carriage had disappeared.

Before she could recover, he leaned back and smiled. "But I suppose that when your services are in high demand, as I understand yours are, one must expect exorbitant prices."

His expression appeared perfectly innocent, yet she could not dismiss the uncomfortable sensation that she was a mouse to his cat. She moistened her dry lips, then arranged her features into a haughty expression. "Yes, one must expect exorbitant prices under those circumstances."

"For that much money, I'll expect a great deal of information."

"I'll tell you everything about yourself, Lord Sutton. Even things you may not wish to know."

"Excellent. I truly would like nothing better than for you to inform me whom I am destined to marry so I can begin courting the young lady. I'd like the entire process to be concluded as quickly as possible so I can return to Cornwall."

"How overly romantic of you," she said in a dust-dry tone.

"I fear there is nothing romantic about a man in my position looking for a wife. It's really nothing more than a business arrangement. Which is why I suspect there are so many unhappy marriages amongst my peers."

She studied him for several seconds then said, "You sound almost . . . wistful."

"Do I? I suppose because my father recently remarried and my younger brother wed. Both are deliriously happy." A ghost of a smile flashed across his lips. "And I'm happy for them. But I cannot deny that there's a part of me that is envious. They both married for love."

"And you wish to do the same?" She couldn't keep the surprise from her voice.

"It doesn't matter if I wish to or not, as I do not have the luxury of basing my choice for a wife on the whims of the heart." He turned to look out the window, and a muscle ticked in his jaw. She saw his face reflected in the window and was struck by his bleak expression. "Nor do I have the time to do so," he murmured.

Intriguing words she would have liked to question him about, but before she could do so, he returned his attention to her. His lips curved upward in a slow smile that curled unwanted awareness of him through her. Awareness that bathed her in an unaccustomed warmth, which had her fighting the urge to fidget in her seat.

"But now I can hope that you will tell me that my future bride is a paragon," he continued. "A diamond of the first water. A highborn lady of impeccable breeding who is not only the perfect candidate for my wife, but with whom I shall fall insanely, ridiculously in love."

While she wasn't certain about *his* capacity for falling in love, she didn't doubt for an instant that female hearts littered the paths he'd walked upon. "Is falling insanely, ridiculously in love your fondest wish?"

"Actually, if my bride were tolerable and didn't resemble a carp, I'd be quite satisfied."

"Hmmm. So long as she is wealthy and from an aristocratic family whose holdings mesh nicely with yours, she'll do nicely?"

"A rather blunt way of putting it, but yes."

"I would think that a man of your—how did you describe it?—oh, yes, your pragmatic temperament would appreciate plain speaking."

"I do. I'm simply not accustomed to receiving it from a lady. It's been my experience that women tend to speak in riddles rather than simply saying what they mean outright."

"Really? How interesting as I've found *gentlemen* to be far less forthcoming than women."

He shook his head. "Impossible. Men are by nature straightforward creatures. Women are so much more—"

"Clever?"

"I was going to say devious."

His expression gave nothing away, and she again experienced that unsettling sensation that he was toying with her. Well, if he was, he was doomed to disappointment, as she had no intention of allowing him to be successful. "For a man who wishes to win a wife, you do not appear to hold my gender in very high esteem, my lord."

"On the contrary, I greatly admire the feminine art of cunning, evasive conversation." He smiled. "I just wish I were more adept at translating the hidden meanings."

Alex adopted her most innocent expression. "I'm afraid I have no idea to what you're referring."

"Then allow me to give you an example. When a lady says she *isn't* upset, I've found she is more often than not, not only angry, but furious. Why not simply say, as a gentleman would, when asked, 'Yes, I am upset'?"

"At which time you gentlemen would drink an excess of brandy, then resort to fisticuffs or pistols at dawn." She gave an elegant sniff. "Yes, that is much more civilized."

"At least it is honest."

"Really? Clearly, my lord, you've formed this opinion without benefit of engaging in enough conversations with gentlemen. In my experience, nearly everything that comes out of their mouths is fraught with hidden meaning, and that other meaning nearly always has to do with things of an . . . amorous nature."

"Oh? Such as?"

"For example," she said, "when a gentleman compliments a woman on her gown, his gaze, invariably is riveted to her chest. Therefore, while he is *saying* 'I like your gown' what he *means* is 'I like your décolletage.' "

He nodded slowly. "Interesting. What does he mean if he says, 'Would you care to dance?'?"

"Surely you would know better than I, my lord."

A smile played at the corners of his lips. "Perhaps. But I am curiosity itself at this theory of yours that everything a man says means something else. What do *you* think he is saying?"

" 'Would you care to dance?' really means 'I want to touch you.' "

"I see. And 'You look lovely' means . . . ?"

" 'I wish to kiss you.' "

"How about 'Would you care for a stroll in the garden?' "

" 'I hope to ravish you.' " She smiled and spread her hands. "You see? All merely polite euphemisms for what he really wants. Which is to—"

"Bed her."

His softly spoken words hung in the air between them, reverberating through Alex's mind, skittering heat to her every nerve ending. Clearly Lord Sutton wasn't averse to plain speaking either. She inclined her head. "Yes."

"You are very cynical for one so young."

"Perhaps I am older than you think I am. And besides, I have the opportunity to observe a great deal of human nature in my work."

"And you've concluded that everything men say has a hidden meaning of a sensual nature."

"Yes."

"I must confess I've not found that to be the case."

Her lips twitched. "Most likely because you are not telling other gentlemen that you wish to dance with them, nor are they telling you that they like your gown."

"Ah. I see. So you're saying that men are honest with other men—that it's when we speak to women that the deceptions begin."

"I've no idea if you're honest with each other, but when it comes to conversing with women, you most definitely speak in circles."

"And women most definitely speak in riddles, the majority of their words merely polite euphemisms for what they really want."

"And what do you imagine women want?"

"A man's money, his protection, and his heart—the latter on a diamond-encrusted platter, if you please."

She hiked up a brow. "Now who's being cynical?"

"Actually, I rather thought I was agreeing with you, only from the point of view of my own gender."

"So you're saying that women are honest with other women—that it's when we speak to men that the deceptions begin," she said, playing upon his earlier words.

"So it would seem. Makes one wonder if perhaps men and women should only speak of the weather."

She laughed. "You wish to remove all the nuances and sophistication from conversation, my lord?"

"No. Just the deception." He leaned his head back and regarded her through hooded eyes. "Which begs the question, have you and I been the victims of such deceptions tonight?"

Her amusement faded, and she fought the urge to pluck nervously at the velvet of her cloak. "Since I have no need of your protection or your heart, and you are in search of an aristocratic wife, there is no need for deception between us."

He studied her for several seconds, and she found herself holding her breath. "I notice you did not say you've no need of my money," he said softly.

She slowly released her pent-up breath, then gifted him with a half smile. "Because I intend to see you part with a healthy bit of it in return for my fortune-telling services."

A clearly reluctant smile tugged at his lips. "I certainly cannot fault you on your honesty, Madame. Indeed, your candor is downright frightening."

"You do not strike me as a man who is easily scared off, Lord Sutton."

"No, Madame. I most certainly am not."

His gaze bored into hers, and once again Alex found herself trapped in his compelling stare, unable to look away. Her mind went completely blank of anything to say, and he'd fallen silent as well. She was saved from trying to think of a new topic of conversation when the carriage slowed then stopped. He looked out the window.

"We've arrived," he said. He opened the door, stepped down, then held out his hand to help her alight. His strong fingers wrapped around hers, and heat sizzled up her arm. When her boots touched the cobblestones, he released her, and her fingers involuntarily curled inward, as if trying to retain that unsettling heat.

"Thank you for the ride, Lord Sutton."

"You're welcome. Regarding my card reading . . . are you free tomorrow afternoon? Say around three o'clock at my Park Lane town house?"

Alex hesitated, torn between the urge to end this association, which felt fraught with undercurrents, and her desire not only to find out more about him, but also for the outrageous sum of money he'd agreed to pay her. She desperately needed that money. . . .

"I'm afraid I'm already engaged at three. Does four o'clock suit you?" She said the words quickly, before she could change her mind.

"That's fine. Shall I send my carriage?"

"Thank you, but I'll see to my own transportation. And there's no need to walk me to the door."

He inclined his head. "As you wish."

"Good evening, Lord Sutton."

She purposely did not extend her hand, but to her surprise, he extended his. Not wishing to appear rude, she held out her hand. With his gaze steady on hers, he lightly clasped her fingers and raised them. Her gaze flicked to his fascinating mouth, her entire body quickening in anticipation of his lips touching the backs of her fingers. Instead, he turned her hand and pressed his lips to the sensitive skin of her inner wrist. The warmth of his breath penetrated the delicate lace of her gloves and heat, shocking and fierce, bolted through her. How was it possible that such a brief touch could make her knees shake?

The contact of his lips against her skin lasted only a few seconds, yet nothing about it felt in the least bit proper. Clearly she needed to disabuse him of any notions he harbored regarding her availability for anything more than card reading.

Slipping her hand from his and with her fingers feeling as if he'd whispered fire over them, she raised her chin. "In case you are not aware, Lord Sutton, my title of *Madame* is not merely for effect or part of my fortune-telling mystique. There *is* a Monsieur Larchmont."

He said nothing for several seconds, and she had to fight to hold his steady, penetrating gaze, which somehow seemed to bore straight through to her soul, laying bare every lie she'd ever told.

Finally, he made her a formal bow, then murmured, "He is a lucky man. Until tomorrow, Madame Larchmont."

Not trusting her voice, she jerked her head in a nod, then hurried around the corner toward the side entrance of the modest brick building. The instant she turned the corner, she hurried forward and turned into an alleyway where she ducked into a shadowed alcove and pressed her back against the rough stone. Heart pounding, she strained her ears, listening for the sounds of his carriage departing. She didn't move until the echo of the horses' hooves against the cobblestones faded away. After they did, she slipped from the alcove and headed swiftly toward the less fashionable part of town, closer to St. Giles, moving like smoke amongst the dirty, narrow alleyways she knew so well.

It was time to go home.

Three

Colin opened the wrought-iron gate leading to his town house. The moon had slipped behind a cloud, eliminating the silvery glow that had shimmered over Mayfair only moments ago. Tendrils of smoky fog danced around his boots, but the hazy vapor wasn't nearly as thick here, across from Hyde Park, as it had been on the other side of the city where he'd left Madame Larchmont an hour earlier.

He climbed the brick steps, wincing at the pain throbbing in his left leg. As his boot hit the final step, the oak door swung open, and he was greeted by a tall figure holding an ornate candelabra. He immediately wiped all expression from his face, although he wasn't certain how much good it would do against the ever-observant Ellis.

"Good evening, my lord," intoned Ellis in the same sonorous voice Colin had known since childhood. "A message was delivered for you shortly after you left this evening. It awaits you on the desk in the library, along with your usual repast. Will you be wanting a cup of chocolate?"

Ellis knew everything that occurred inside the town house, down to the smallest detail, including Colin's boyhood predilection for sliding down the polished banisters and pilfering sweets from the kitchen. Colin had eventually outgrown his fondness for banister sliding, but his love of sweets hadn't abated one bit—as Ellis well knew. Along with Colin's habit of not retiring immediately upon arriving home.

He shook his head. "Thank you, but I'm afraid brandy is called for tonight."

Ellis's gaze filled with concern and flicked down to Colin's leg. "Shall I warm a blanket for you?"

"No, thank you, Ellis. The brandy will suffice. I'll see you in the morning."

"Good night, my lord."

After bidding the butler good night, Colin waved off the candelabra and headed down the dark corridor leading to the library. God knows he knew his way around this house well enough, and he was grateful that the deep shadows prevented him from having to look at the elaborately framed portraits of his ancestors adorning the silk-covered walls. Even as a child he hadn't liked looking at them, always feeling that their forbidding gazes followed him, as if they knew he was up to some mischief or another, all chanting admonitions of the importance of duty and his obligations to his title. As if the words *duty* and *obligation* weren't drummed into him every waking moment.

After entering the library, he closed the door behind him and immediately strode across the maroon Axminster rug toward the decanters, ignoring the aching pull his long strides caused in his leg. He poured himself a generous splash of the potent liquor, frowning at the unsteadiness in his hands. He would have liked to blame that bit of tottering on exhaustion or hunger or anything other than what he knew it to be, but he'd learned long ago that while lying to others went hand in hand with how he'd chosen to live his life, lying to himself was a fruitless waste of time.

He tossed back the brandy in a single gulp, closing his eyes to absorb and savor the heat easing down his throat. If he'd been able to summon up anything resembling amusement, he would have laughed at himself for being so bloody unsettled. Opening his eyes, he poured another drink, then moved with jerky steps to the fireplace. After easing himself onto the overstuffed brocade settee, he leaned forward and rested his elbows on his spread knees. The cut-crystal snifter dangled from his fingers, and he stared into the dancing flames.

Immediately an image of her rose in his mind, accompanied by the gut-clenching shock he'd experienced when he'd seen her in Lady Malloran's drawing room.

Madame Larchmont. Alexandra, as he'd learned from Lady Malloran. Finally, a name to go with the face that had haunted him for the past four years.

He'd recognized her instantly, with a visceral punch that had staggered him. Stolen his breath. He'd been surveying Lady Malloran's guests without much interest when his gaze had happened upon the fortune-teller he'd heard several people discussing. Although she'd been hired for the evening's entertainment, he hadn't paid particular attention as card reading was of no interest to him.

Then she'd looked up. And his gaze had riveted on her face . . . those unforgettable features that had been branded in his memory from the first instant he'd seen them in Vauxhall that long-ago summer evening. He'd stared in disbelief, and for several seconds it had seemed as if his entire being had stilled—his heart, his breath, his blood. And as it had that first time, everything else, the crowd, the noise, the laughter, had faded away, leaving only the two of them. As he'd stared at her, the words *Thank God you're alive* pounded through him.

She was no longer dressed in rags as she'd been in Vauxhall, no dirt marred her complexion, but there was no mistaking those dark eyes. That stubborn, square chin, which bore a shallow indent, as if the gods had pressed a finger there. The small, straight nose above those impossibly full, plush lips that were entirely too large for her heart-shaped face. She wasn't beautiful in any conventional manner . . . her features were too mismatched, too nonsymmetrical. Still he'd found her unusual looks compelling. Captivating. In a way that had stunned him. Yet what had flummoxed him most, even more than the fact that she'd attempted to pick his pocket, was the way she'd looked at him.

He hadn't expected to find himself face-to-face with a female, but there was no mistaking the dirty urchin he held for a boy. The play of emotions that shifted across her face as he'd clutched her arms were quick, fleeting, yet utterly unmistakable. First shock. Even though he'd caught her in the act of relieving him of his gold watch, he'd only been able to do so because of his own razor-sharp skills in that particular area. She was talented and clearly not accustomed to being caught.

Her shock had given way to unmistakable fear. The sort that made it clear she believed he'd hurt her. Both of those reactions were understandable. But then she'd blinked and stared at him for the space of several heartbeats, her eyes widening with what he could only describe as recognition. And whispered the words, *It's you.*

Before he could question her, she'd jerked from his grasp and ran as if the devil pursued her. He'd given chase, but she vanished like vapor in the crowd. He'd kept up his search until mauve streaks of dawn had painted the sky, even venturing into the dark, dirty alleyways of St. Giles and the rookery, compelled by reasons he didn't understand to find her. Talk to her.

What had her cryptic words meant? He knew he'd never seen *her* before—he prided himself on never forgetting a face, and hers was not a countenance he would forget. Something about her beckoned him, tugged at him in an unprecedented way he couldn't comprehend. When he'd held her for those few unnerving seconds, he'd felt her desperation. Her despair. They, along with hunger and poverty, had rolled off her in waves. And then that fear. He could almost smell it pumping from her, and his heart had filled with pity. *She'd* been robbing *him*, yet somehow *he'd* inexplicably wanted to reassure *her* that he meant her no harm. And wanted to help her. Damn it, after he'd seen her profound desperation and fear, he'd wished he'd let her have the damn watch.

His fingers clenched on the cut-glass snifter, and he pulled his gaze from the crackling flames to look into the amber liquid. How many times over the past four years had he thought of her? More than he could count. Those eyes had haunted him, while his conscience berated him for denying her something that was an easily replaced trinket to him but could have meant the difference between survival or death to her. He well knew the various dire fates that awaited women in her position, who earned their livings as thieves, and his gut clenched every time he thought about her, which was far too frequently.

He thought about her most often when he lay awake at night, wondering if she were still alive. Or if she'd been caught and hanged. Or killed in the rough underbelly of London where thieves and pickpockets dwelled. Or been forced into the nightmare of prostitution. The thought of her hurt—or worse—ate at him, as did the confusing yet undeniable fact that she'd seemed to know him. And he'd done nothing to help her. He'd traveled to London three times since that night, and on each occasion had spent long hours strolling Vauxhall and the seedier parts of town, alternately making himself an easy target, then hiding himself to covertly observe the crowds, hoping to see her, or be her victim once again. But his efforts had proven unsuccessful.

Even on this trip, he'd spent his first two nights in Town not at Almack's or the opera or private soirees in search of his future bride, but combing the underbelly of the city and wandering through the poorly lit sections of Vauxhall and Covent Garden in an effort to locate her. He'd been spectacularly unsuccessful, and had arrived home both nights disturbed and saddened by the abject poverty and unrelieved suffering and violence he'd witnessed. The second night he'd barely avoided an altercation with a giant of a man who'd made it plain he wouldn't hesitate to gut Colin in order to relieve him of his money. Fortunately, the giant's gutting abilities were severely curtailed after Colin relieved him of his knife. By the time he'd arrived home, he'd realized his search was pointless and had finally given up, believing he'd never see her again.

He sure as hell hadn't expected to see her in Lady Malloran's drawing room.

There was no doubt in his mind that she'd recognized him, which filled him with a grim satisfaction as he sure as hell hadn't forgotten her. Still, she was clearly adept at hiding her emotions—a trait he easily recognized, as he himself had perfected it long ago. He'd seen the flicker of stunned recognition in her eyes, eyes which, thanks to the light cast by the dozens of lit candles, he realized were the same shade as rich, melted chocolate. The glimmer of recognition passed so quickly it was nearly indiscernible. But his years in service to the Crown had made him keenly observant, especially in regard to reading people. She'd recovered well, he'd give her that, but then, just as she had in Vauxhall, she'd disappeared into the crowd. He'd searched for her, yet, as she had four years ago, she escaped him. Determined not to lose her, he'd gone outside, knowing she would have to exit the house eventually. And she had—through that window.

He'd seen her hanging from the sill and his heart had leapt into his throat while his worst suspicions were confirmed. Clearly she was up to something and clearly that something wasn't anything good. Before he could so much as move, she'd jumped to the ground. Not wanting to reveal his hand, he'd pretended she'd stumbled.

And so their game had begun.

Leaning back, he took a deep swallow of brandy. He had to admire the way she'd regained her aplomb and gone along with the game. Clearly she felt safe in the belief that he hadn't recognized her, and he intended to keep it that way. At least until he determined what she was up to.

He stared into the flames, wishing their flickering red-and-gold depths could provide the answers he sought. Her appearance at tonight's soiree both intrigued and alarmed him. Even though he'd only been in London four days, he'd already heard about the wildly popular Madame Larchmont. How in demand her fortune-telling services were at parties and for private readings. But how many of Society's finest, into whose homes she was invited, knew that four years ago Madame Larchmont had been picking pockets in Vauxhall's dimly lit pathways?

"Not many, I'd wager," he murmured.

So, the question was, had she turned over a new leaf or was her fortune-telling just a ruse to bilk the wealthy partygoers of money? Or worse, pick their pockets? He didn't believe for a minute that she could actually tell fortunes. Didn't believe anyone could predict the future, with or without the aid of a deck of cards.

Still, fortune-telling was an entertainment, and entertainers were paid for their services, and he'd certainly not begrudge her or anyone the opportunity or means to make an honest living. Yet in his experience, people engaged in honest activities didn't normally exit homes through windows—and courtesy of his work for the Crown, he'd certainly escaped enough homes through windows to know. At any rate, he was determined to find out if mere entertainment was the only activity in which Madame Larchmont was engaged. Because he knew damn well she had secrets. Like where she lived.

He'd suspected she had not given him her correct direction, a suspicion that had proven true. He'd exited his carriage the instant she'd disappeared around the corner of the brick building where she'd claimed to live and followed her. While she clearly knew her way around the twisting narrow streets, so did he. She'd moved swiftly, and the effort of keeping up had strained his leg, but he'd managed to stay with her. He'd watched her enter a building in a section of town populated by merchants and small stores. Not fashionable by any means, certainly not as fashionable as where she'd claimed to live, but respectable just the same. Still, a woman who would lie about where she lived was certainly capable of lying about other things.

And he intended to find out what those other things might be.

Given the fact that she was so popular, she no doubt was scheduled to attend more parties over the upcoming days . . . parties where he would also be a guest in his search for a wife. Surely their paths would cross regularly.

And, of course, she would be giving him a private reading tomorrow. Here. At his home. Where he'd be able to observe her closely, and in the light of day, for the first time.

Heat that had nothing to do with his proximity to the fireplace or the brandy he'd drank rippled through him at the thought, and his brows yanked down in a frown at the reaction. The same reaction he'd experienced walking with her in Malloran's garden, with her hand resting in the crook of his arm, her shoulder brushing his. Then again while sitting across from her in the confines of his carriage. It was an almost painful, heated awareness that made him notice details about her he wished he hadn't. Such as the generous feminine curves highlighted by her bronze gown. The way the skeins of moonlight glinted on her dark, shiny hair. The smattering of freckles that marched across her nose. The way her plump lips regained their fullness after she pressed them together.

The way she smelled so deliciously of sweet oranges. His favorite fruit.

With a groan, his eyes slid closed, and he breathed in, as if to capture her fragrance. Her delicate scent had teased his senses during the entire carriage ride. When he'd said good night, he'd been unable to resist touching his lips to her skin to see if she tasted as delicious as she smelled. She had. And during that brief kiss to her wrist, he'd felt her rapid pulse against his lips—the only indication that she was not as calm as she outwardly appeared. Which pleased him, as he hated the thought of being the only one unsettled. The only thing that had kept him from giving in to the overwhelming urge to touch his lips to her skin again was her assertion that she had a husband—a statement that had resulted in an unpleasant sensation much like a cramp.

What sort of man was her husband? How long had they been married? Was he an honest merchant—or a thief? Did he know of his wife's pickpocketing abilities? Did he possess them himself? More questions to which he was determined to find the answers. And he needed to do so quickly because the sense of impending doom that had first gripped him in its unrelenting grasp last month, was growing steadily stronger—even more so since he'd arrived in London.

He opened his eyes, tossed back the last of his brandy, then rose to pour another. Swirling the amber liquid in the snifter, he stared into the golden depths and asked himself the question that had plagued him ever since the recurring dream of his own death had settled upon him.

How much longer did he have?

Blowing out an impatient breath, he dragged a hand through his hair. He'd tried to convince himself that the sense of growing doom was his imagination run amok, or merely the result of weariness. Nothing more than the melancholy that always struck him at the approaching anniversary of his mother's death. But even after that sad day passed, he still couldn't shake the feeling.

Then the dream had started. Nightmare, actually. Trapped in a dark, narrow space, heart pounding, lungs burning, everything in him knowing danger was near. Death imminent. Waking up, bathed in cold sweat, unable to fall back to sleep, his throat tight with the inexplicable fear of closed-in places he'd suffered since childhood.

He'd learned long ago to listen to his gut feelings and trust his instincts. Indeed, during his years of service to the Crown, his instincts had saved his life on more than one occasion. Which was why he couldn't ignore the disturbing message they'd been whispering to him for the past month: Something bad was going to happen to him. Something he wouldn't be able to walk away from. Something he most likely wouldn't survive. The feeling had become more pronounced since his arrival in London, one that hadn't in any way been averted by his run-in with that knife-wielding giant. He'd managed to escape disaster there, but would he be so lucky next time? His gut told him no, he would not. And that further danger awaited him.

He'd considered that perhaps part of this deep foreboding stemmed from the fact that he was now the same age his mother was when she died, but had dismissed that as superstition. No, he wasn't a superstitious man. But he was a man who listened to his instincts.

The undeniable sense of his own mortality, of time running out, weighed on him heavily, thus his driving need to fulfill his duties and obligations—immediately. Before it was too late. The most pressing of which were finding a bride and producing an heir.

His common sense tried to tell him he was wrong—that he'd be fine and live to a ripe old age. Certainly that was his hope. But there was no denying the sense of doom he couldn't shake off, and it wasn't a risk he was willing to take. Especially since, should he meet with an untimely demise, Nathan would inherit the title and all that went with it. And that, he knew, was the last thing his younger brother would ever want, and therefore was the last thing Colin would want for him. Nathan had always eschewed the trappings of Society, preferring to focus his attentions and talents on medicine, and he was a fine doctor. He wanted the title as much as he'd want his internal organs ripped out with a rusty blade.

No, the responsibility of providing an heir was Colin's. He now only wished he'd set about meeting that obligation earlier. Before this sense of urgency had grabbed him by the throat. While there'd still been time. Of course, until a month ago, he'd always believed he had all the time in the world. . . .

Looking up, his gaze fell on the cherrywood desk, and he recalled Ellis's saying a letter had arrived for him. After setting his empty snifter on the end table, he crossed the room and picked up the folded ivory vellum sealed with a bit of red wax. His brows lifted at the sight of his name written on the outside in Nathan's unmistakable bold scrawl. Amazing that his brother would find the time to write a letter, what with him being a newlywed of only seven months and all that. Certainly, if Colin were lucky enough to have a wife like the very beautiful Victoria, with whom Nathan was passionately in love, God knows he wouldn't spend time writing letters.

After breaking the wax seal, he perused the short note:

> *Arriving in town the day after tomorrow rather than next week with Victoria and several friends in tow. Will stay at the Wexhall town house, as she's assisting her father with his party preparations. Will plan to call on you after we arrive.*
>
> Nathan

The same sense of lingering guilt that thoughts of Nathan always brought pushed at him, but he shoved them aside, instead focusing on how good it would be to see his brother again. He folded the note, then turned his attention to the small blue-and-white Sèvres dish resting on the corner of the desk. A smile curved his lips at the sight of the trio of exquisite marzipan candies, each a miniature work of art fashioned to perfectly resemble a fruit. He looked over tonight's choices—a strawberry, a pear, and . . .

An orange.

There was no question as to which one he wanted.

He reached out and plucked the luscious orange from the dish then popped the morsel in his mouth. He closed his eyes and savored the sweet taste of citrus and almond coasting over his tongue, while an image of the mysterious Madame Larchmont filled his mind.

Yes, she was mysterious, her motives unclear. But if there was one thing he excelled at, it was unraveling a mystery; and he'd never yet failed at solving one that came his way. He was determined to have the answers to a good many of his questions about her before she ever arrived at his home tomorrow.

The fact that she had not only survived but appeared to be prospering indicated she possessed a great deal of cleverness and an abundance of luck. But this time, Colin vowed, she'd met her match. And if she were engaged in any sort of thievery, her luck was about to end.

Alex made her way swiftly through a series of back alleys, then hurried up the worn stairs to the second floor of the building where she lived. After glancing around the dark corridor to ensure she was alone, she inserted the key and silently opened the door to her rooms. Slipping inside, she quickly locked the door behind her, then leaned back against the rough wood panel and closed her eyes. Her ragged breaths burned her lungs, and her heart pounded—not only from her haste but from the unsettling feeling that someone had been watching her. Following her as she'd made her way home after leaving Lord Sutton's carriage. She was accustomed to the presence of thieves and footpads and knew how to avoid them. Her fingers brushed over the bump on her skirt from the sheathed knife tucked into her garter. And she knew how to defend herself if she couldn't.

But what she'd experienced tonight was different. An overwhelming sense of being watched, stalked, had plagued her the entire way home, slithering unease down her spine. Unease that was especially acute after the conversation she'd overheard tonight in Lord Malloran's study. Whoever had her in their sights was very good at remaining hidden, but she'd lived in the mean streets of London too long not to know when she was being observed.

"Are ye all right, Alex?"

Her eyes popped open at the softly spoken question, and she found herself being regarded by Emma's concern-filled blue eyes.

Even though, at seventeen, Emma Bagwell was six years younger than Alex, she was, thanks to her acquaintance with London's underbelly, very resourceful and perceptive. They'd found each other three years ago and, together, had managed to survive and rise above where they'd come from.

Realizing it was not only useless to try to keep a secret from her tenacious friend, but needing to confide the details of her unsettling evening, Alex said, "Actually, there *is* something troubling me, but before I tell you . . ." She nodded toward the faded blue velvet curtain that separated a third of the room. "How many have we tonight?"

Emma's gaze shifted to the curtain. "Eight."

Eight. Last night there'd been six, the night before that, twelve. Last Tuesday they'd made room for seventeen. "Is Robbie here?"

Emma nodded. "He were the last to arrive, about an hour ago. Filthy and exhausted. Could barely stay awake long enough to eat." Anger flared in Emma's eyes. "He were more than filthy, Alex. He'd been beaten."

Alex's hands clenched her cloak. "How badly?"

"Swollen eye, busted lip. I cleaned him up, but ye should check on him. He asked for ye."

"All right," she murmured. "I'll do it now, because he'll be gone before we awaken."

"Like a ghost he is," Emma agreed, nodding. "All of

'em are. I'll add more water to the kettle and make us some tea."

"Thank you." She crossed the room and hung her cloak in the battered wardrobe she shared with Emma. Even with both their clothes combined, there was room to spare. Knowing Robbie and the others were already asleep, she took a few extra minutes to remove her gown, then quickly dress in her plain cotton nightrail. She knotted her robe's sash around her waist, then walked to the velvet curtain. After doing this for the past two years, she knew what to expect; still, she pulled in a bracing breath before pulling aside the heavy material.

She waited a moment for her eyes to adjust to the dark, and slowly they became more visible. Eight of them tonight, each wrapped in the only comfort they'd ever known—a blanket. Her gaze touched their sleeping forms, and no matter how many nights she saw them here, each night they tore at her heart.

She recognized Will and Kenneth. Dobbs, Johnny, and Douglas. And there, in the corner, lay Mary, and next to her, Lilith. All sleeping on the pallets that were kept rolled in the corner, ready for them, each child looking like a small, broken angel. Which in Alex's mind they were, as none of them was older than twelve. All safe for a few hours in the shelter her meager home provided, but all too soon dawn would arrive, and they'd leave this sanctuary for the hell that awaited them on the unfriendly streets and back alleys where they spent their days.

Her gaze fell last on Robbie and, as it did every time she saw him, her heart clenched, more so now as the soft light from the low-burning fire in the main room touched on his bruised eye and busted lower lip. All these children, and the scores of others like them, who were orphans or abandoned, victims of severe poverty and abuse and horrible living conditions tore at her heart, but something about Robbie touched her even deeper. Perhaps because he so reminded her of herself at his age. A bundle of trembling fear wrapped in layers of false bravado.

Tears of anger and frustration and utter pity pushed at the backs of her eyes. Dear God, he was barely six years old.

A lock of his pale hair, darkened with soot, fell across his forehead, and her fingers ached to brush it aside. But she knew if she touched him, he would most likely awaken. Out of necessity, because of where they lived and how they lived, all the children were light sleepers. If one slept too deeply, any manner of horror could sneak up upon them. To this day, Alex slept lightly, and never for more than a few hours at a time. The children slept more soundly here, knowing they were free, for a few hours, from harm. So although she ached to go to him, Robbie needed sleep more than Alex needed to touch him and risk frightening him.

After one last lingering look, she let the curtain close, then made her way toward the kitchen area, where Emma poured tea into thick ceramic mugs. She sat at the long wooden bench, suddenly bone-weary, drained of all her energy. The scent of oranges and fresh-baked muffins lingered in the room.

"Thank you for doing the baking this evening," she said with a tired smile, keeping her voice low so as to not awaken the children.

"Ye're welcome." With a flourish, Emma produced a plate upon which sat a single biscuit. "I saved ye one."

Alex's throat tightened at the thoughtful gesture. Emma well knew her weakness for sweets—a weakness Emma shared. Reaching out, she broke the biscuit in half and gave the bigger piece to her friend. "I'm sorry to leave all the chores to you."

"Nonsense," Emma said, setting a steaming mug before her. " 'Tis a labor of love for me, and is more important for Madame Larchmont to ply her fortune-tellin' wares on the rich, fancy folks. With the extra money yer earnin', we'll be able to move to a bigger, better, safer place. And sooner than we'd thought possible. Then you can start educatin' them."

Yes, a bigger, better, safer place for herself and Emma and the children who trusted them, came to them for protection, was what she'd worked so hard for. What she was determined to have. What she'd finally been able to hope, with the recent success of her Madame Larchmont persona, to achieve.

"That is my hope," she said, "but you know how fickle Society can be, how easily bored, how quickly they move on to the next entertainment. I'm in demand now, but I have no illusions that my current popularity will last more than the length of the Season."

"Then let's make certain ye make a killin' this Season," Emma said, looking at her over the rim of her steaming mug.

"Again, that is my hope ... but ... well, we both know that Madame Larchmont's career would be over if the elite of Society now clamoring for her services were to discover her past."

Emma's gaze sharpened. "Ye say that as if there's reason to think they might."

She wrapped her hands around her mug, absorbing the warmth into her suddenly cold fingers. "Emma, tonight I met a man. It's ... *him*."

Emma blinked twice in clear confusion, but then her eyes widened with realization. "*Him?* The man from yer card readings?"

She nodded. "Yes."

"Yer certain?"

"I am."

Emma didn't question how Alex knew this was the

man who'd figured so prominently in her readings over the years, which didn't surprise her. Her friend was well accustomed to Alex's "intuition." Instead, she nodded thoughtfully, then said, "Well, now. He's been a long time in comin'. Who is he?"

"His name is Colin Oliver." She refused to acknowledge the tingle that rippled through her at saying his name aloud. "His title is Viscount Sutton."

Emma's jaw dropped. "A *viscount*?" She shook her head. "Ye must have the wrong bloke. Yer cards said the man would figure prominently in yer future. Would have a great impact on ye. How could that apply to a viscount?" Her mouth rounded into an O and she touched her fingertips to her lips. "Oh. Unless he's wantin' ye to be . . . unless ye're plannin' to be his . . . ladybird."

Heat flashed through her, which she immediately blamed on the steam rising from the hot tea. Pushing her cup aside, she whispered, "No, of course not."

"Then how else could such a man figure into yer future? Anyway, the man from the cards is supposed to be someone ye've already met. Years ago." She gave her head a decisive shake, prying loose a dark red curl from her braid. "No, he's not the man, Alex."

"He is. I . . . I've met him before. I picked his pocket."

"How can ye be sure it's same bloke? All look the same in the dark, those rich toffs do. Always full of themselves and of drink. Easy marks, that's what they are."

"*Were*," Alex stressed. "That was our former profession. And I remember him distinctly because he caught me."

"Caught ye?" Emma repeated in an incredulous whisper. "But ye never got caught! Ye were the best!"

"While I appreciate your assessment of my *former* talents, I assure you, he caught me. I managed to escape and never saw him again. Until tonight."

The ramifications hit Emma instantly. "Lord above. Did he recognize you?"

Unable to sit still, she rose and paced in front of the table. "I don't know. I don't think so, but . . ." She shook her head, then told Emma the entire events of the evening, including the conversation she'd overheard and the note she'd left for Lord Malloran. The only details she left out were the way Lord Sutton had made her feel and the way he'd kissed her wrist. She concluded with, "I'm giving him a private reading at his home tomorrow afternoon. Or rather, later today."

Emma looked at her with troubled eyes. "I'm not sure which worries me more, Alex. The fact that ye're seein' this viscount again—that smacks of pullin' a tiger's tail—or the conversation ye overheard. What if someone finds out you did? That you were the one who wrote the note?"

"How could anyone find out? I deliberately disguised my handwriting. No one will waste time trying to discover who wrote the note. They'll be too occupied trying to figure out who's going to be killed at Lord Wexhall's party and preventing it from happening."

In spite of her assurances, Emma still looked troubled. "I hope ye're right."

So do I, Alex thought. *So do I.*

Four

Colin stood in the shadows provided by a door-way across the narrow, cobblestone street from the building he'd followed Madame Larchmont to last night. In the light of day, the soot-covered brick looked uninviting, made all the more ominous by the gray clouds hanging low in the slate-colored sky.

From his observations last night after she'd entered the building, the shadows moving across the window in the third room on the second floor indicated that was her destination. Two people had exited the building in the last quarter hour, but so far no sign of Madame Larchmont. He withdrew his pocket watch and checked the time. Half past two. Was it possible she'd already left for her three o'clock appointment?

A red-haired young woman emerged from the building, and Colin's eyes narrowed. Not his prey. Dressed in a plain brown gown, she carried a shallow box, which rode low on her midsection, strapped to her front. The sort of carrier orange girls used to sell their wares, although from what he could see, whatever she carried wasn't oranges. They appeared to be tarts or muffins.

Another ten minutes passed, and he patiently waited, biding his time. He'd just checked his watch again when he saw her exit the building. Although a wide-brimmed bonnet shaded her face, there was no mistaking her. She carried a bag that resembled a knapsack. His breathing hitched, and his heart executed a strange maneuver when he saw her, pulling his brows down in a frown. She hesitated for several seconds, her gaze quickly scanning the area, and he melted farther into the shadows. Then she took off at a brisk pace, heading in the opposite direction of his town house.

As she had last night, she moved with the surefootedness of someone well familiar with the area. After approximately ten minutes, she approached a battered building just outside the fringes of the rookery. Four shop fronts, three of them boarded up, lined the ground floor. A stained sign with a poorly painted mug of ale advertising The Broken Barrel marked the fourth door. She entered the pub, then exited five minutes later, no longer carrying the knapsack. Before starting off, she again glanced around, and he wondered if she normally did so or if she'd sensed his presence. Might just be the unsavory area, however, as he, too, felt the weight of eyes upon him. After his own quick look around and detecting no one, he followed her for a few more minutes. Once it became clear she was not heading back to her rooms but in the direction of Mayfair, he retraced his steps. He paused around the corner from the building where she lived to rub his thigh, which pulled with a dull ache.

After ascertaining he wasn't observed, Colin entered the building. The scents of cabbage and stale bodies clung in the air as he made his way silently up the stairs. Muffled voices and the sound of a baby crying floated downward. Once he'd arrived on the second floor, he stopped outside the third door, pressing his ear to the crack to listen for voices within while his nimble fingers played with the lock. Hearing nothing, and satisfied the room was empty, he opened the door and slipped silently inside.

Leaning back against the door, he stood perfectly still for several long seconds, noting details. The room was larger than he would have imagined, although not spacious by any stretch. And scrupulously clean. He sniffed the air, noting the pleasant scents of oranges and fresh-baked muffins. The wooden floors were covered with rugs made from what appeared to be braided strips of material. A single wardrobe stood in the corner, flanked by two narrow, neatly made beds. A gray-striped cat lay curled up on the end of the bed nearest the window. An end table stood next to each bed, a hip bath occupied the corner, and a single dresser sat against the wall. On the opposite side of the room was the kitchen area, with a table and two bench chairs. A faded blue velvet curtain cordoned off a portion of the room. Another sleeping area?

Colin walked on silent feet toward the wardrobe. Opening the door, his senses were immediately hit with a delicate, citrusy scent. An image of Madame Larchmont, her chocolate brown eyes assessing him, her full lips poised to speak, slammed into his mind. His gaze riveted on a familiar bronze gown. Reaching out, he ran his fingers over the material, vividly recalling how it had appeared to glow against her pale skin. Before he could stop himself, he leaned forward, and brought the material up to his face and breathed in.

Oranges. And something else, something pleasing he couldn't name other than to call it *fresh*. The remnants of her soap, most likely. He closed his eyes and another image of her materialized in his mind, rising from the bath, a trail of soap bubbles meandering down her wet, glistening form. Heat shot through him and his eyes popped open. A sound of self-disgust rose in his throat, and he dropped the material as if it had burned him.

A quick search through the wardrobe revealed one other gown in a deep green that looked like something Madame Larchmont would wear, then a plain brown day gown showing signs of age, but meticulously cared for. At the other end of the wardrobe he saw two gray gowns. Like the others, these were old yet neatly mended, but were at least four inches in length shorter than the other gowns. Not a single masculine item anywhere.

Tucking away that interesting bit of information, he turned his attention to the end tables. Both held tallow candles on chipped plates. The table closest to the window had a book resting next to the candle. Colin noted the title: *Pride and Prejudice*. The other table also contained a book, one that appeared more of a tablet similar to what students used. He picked it up and flipped through the pages of carefully copied letters and numbers made in a childish scrawl. After replacing the book, he glanced toward the cat who'd awakened and was treating him to a suspicious glare.

"Good afternoon," Colin murmured, taking a slow step toward the animal. In a flash, the cat darted under the bed.

Not wishing to frighten the beast, Colin moved on, crossing the handmade rug to look over the kitchen area. Oranges were stacked in a pyramid shape, the top one missing. A slight sound caught his attention, and his head whipped around to look at the blue velvet curtain. The cat? Moving silently, cautiously, he approached the curtain, then with lightning speed, whipped it back. To reveal a small area empty except for a stack of rolled-up pallets in the corner.

And a child attempting to escape down a trapdoor opened in the floor.

Their gazes met, and, for an instant, pure terror

flashed in the child's eyes. Colin ran forward and grabbed the door before it closed, then plucked up the youngster by the back of the collar.

"Let me go, ye bloody bastard," came a voice that throbbed with outrage and unmistakable fear. Scrawny arms encased in a filthy coat swung wildly while thin legs in ragged pants and deplorable, hole-filled shoes tried to connect with anything. "Let me go, or I'll slice open yer bloody gut I will."

In spite of the brave words, Colin could see that the child, who appeared to be a boy of perhaps five or six, although it was difficult to tell, was terrified. "No need to slice me open," Colin said mildly, setting the boy on his feet. The child tried mightily to get away from him, but Colin held him firmly by the shoulders. The boy went still and glared up at him with narrowed eyes in a dirty face. The area surrounding Colin's heart went hollow, then his jaw clenched when he saw the bruises under the dirt. Bloody hell, someone had beaten this boy.

"Who are ye and wot are ye doin' here?" the boy demanded. "If ye think I'll let ye steal from Miss Alex and Miss Emmie, ye're dead wrong."

He wrested his gaze from the sickening sight of the purple bruise surrounding the child's eye and found himself staring at the round lump in the boy's pocket. "You mean the way you stole their orange?"

The boy flushed under the dirt and bruises. "Ain't stealin'. They leave 'em for me. 'Sides, I only took one." The boy's gaze flicked to Colin's hands gripping his upper arms and undeniable fear flickered in his dark eyes. He swallowed, then said, "I'm allowed here. You ain't."

That flicker of fear tugged on something deep inside Colin. "I'm not going to hurt you," he said softly.

"Whys don't ye prove that by takin' yer hands off me," the boy said, with a sneer Colin couldn't help but admire.

"If I do, I'll expect you to answer a few questions."

"Why should I?"

"Because there's a shilling in it for you if you do."

The boy's eyes widened a fraction, then took on a sly look. His gaze slid over Colin's tailored clothing. "Bloke like you can do better than a bob."

Letting go with one hand, Colin reached into his waistcoat pocket and pulled out a gold coin. The boy's eyes widened. "Very well," he agreed, holding up the coin between his fingers. "A sovereign for your answers."

"Just fer answers?" he asked, eyeing the coin. "Nuthin' else?"

Colin's stomach tightened at the horrific implications of the boy's suspicious question. "Just for answers. You have my word."

It was plain that a man's word meant little to this child. "I won't let ye hurt Miss Alex or Miss Emmie."

"I have no intention of hurting them. Again, you have my word."

The boy considered for several seconds, then jerked his head and held out his grimy hand. "Coin first."

"One question first, as a show of good faith, then I'll give you the coin."

The boy pressed his lips together, then nodded.

"How do you know Miss Alex?"

"She's my friend." He jabbed out his hand. "My coin."

Colin tossed the gold piece lightly in the air. The boy plucked it from midair, then, like a lightning bolt, he shot toward the door. Colin watched him go, not giving chase. Deeply troubled, he walked slowly to the door, closed and locked it, pushing back the dozens of questions bombarding him regarding the child and "Miss Alex and Miss Emmie." Later. He'd have time to reflect later.

He returned to the room behind the velvet curtain. After lifting the trapdoor, he slowly descended a rough wood ladder. The air was cool, dark, and musty. When he reached the end of the ladder, he carefully felt his way along a narrow passageway guided only by a thin sliver of light peeking through a hole about thirty feet in front of him. When he reached the sliver, he realized it came through a door which appeared boarded over. Applying his eye to the crack, he saw what appeared to be a deserted alleyway. He tried to open the door, but failed. Clearly there was a way in, which meant there had to be a way out.

He felt carefully around and after a few minutes located a length of rope near the top of the door. When he pulled it, he heard a muffled scraping sound, as if something on the other side of the door were lifting, and he realized that a bit more light had flooded into the passageway near the floor. Bending down, he saw an opening. He lowered the rope a bit and the opening was covered over. An opening small enough for a child to fit through, but not a man.

He slowly released the rope, watching the ray of outside light lessen to a sliver, then made his way back along the passageway and up the ladder. After a cautious peek through the trapdoor to ensure no one had entered the rooms, he quickly exited, then made use of the skills that had come in so handy during his spying days to lock the door from the outside. Less than a minute later, he stepped outside and began walking quickly in the direction of Hyde Park.

Without breaking stride, he consulted his pocket watch. Madame Larchmont was due at his home right about now. While his brief look into her life had answered a few of his questions, it had spawned dozens more. Who was that child? He'd said Miss Alex was his "friend." Did he live there? Other than the child himself, he'd found no evidence of a child's presence—no clothing or trinkets. Just as he'd found no evidence of a man's presence. Who was this "Miss Emmie" the child had mentioned? Just another piece of the mysterious puzzle that made up Madame Larchmont.

He arrived home twenty minutes later and was greeted by Ellis. "Is she here?" Colin asked.

"Yes, my lord. Arrived at precisely four o'clock. As you instructed, I gave your apologies for not being readily available and offered her tea in the drawing room. She awaits you there."

"Thank you." Colin strode down the paneled corridor, tugging his cuffs and jacket into place. He paused in the open doorway of the drawing room and went still at the sight of her.

She stood in front of the fireplace, gazing up at the portrait hanging above the white marble mantel. A cheery fire burned in the grate, dispelling the gloomy gray spilling into the room from the wall of windows behind her. He studied her profile, noting the slight tilt of her nose, the graceful arch of her neck as she looked upward. Her midnight hair was arranged in a simple chignon, with a pair of loose, glossy dark curls curving over her shoulder. Her pale green day gown highlighted the creamy texture of her skin, and lace gloves, similar to the ones she'd worn last evening, covered her hands. Everything about her looked soft and feminine, and his fingers twitched with a sudden, powerful urge to touch her, to discover if she felt as soft as she looked.

His gaze ran down her form, and although her gown was perfectly modest, his imagination conjured up lush, feminine curves. She shifted slightly, tilting her head to the left, pulling his attention upward. Her tongue peeked out to moisten her lips, and his body tightened with an unmistakable grip of lust. As if in a trance, he found himself mimicking the action, his imagination ignited, burning with a mental picture of his tongue brushing over her plump lower lip while his hands explored the lush curves hinted at by her gown.

A tiny part of his rational brain coughed to life and hissed out a warning that such thoughts about this woman—a woman who at *best* used to be a thief, and most likely still was—were totally inappropriate, but there was no stopping the sensual images bombarding him.

Just then, she turned, and their gazes met. He tried to blank his expression, but suspected some remnants of his thoughts must have remained when her eyes widened slightly. As on each occasion their gazes locked, he felt slightly off-balance, a puzzling phenomenon he neither understood nor liked.

Her expression smoothed and, appearing completely unruffled, she inclined her head. "Lord Sutton. Good afternoon."

When he opened his mouth to speak, he realized with a jolt of annoyance his mouth was already opened. And he'd been holding his breath. Bloody hell. This woman's effect on him was simply . . . out of the question. He'd never allowed his passions to enslave him—he controlled them, not the other way around—and he wasn't about to start now. Snapping his lips together, he arranged his features into a mask of regret and walked toward her.

"Madame Larchmont. Forgive me for keeping you waiting. I was unavoidably detained." He paused in front of her and made a formal bow, irrationally disappointed when she did not offer him her hand.

"As I was provided with such lovely surroundings and delicious refreshments while I waited, I'm not likely to complain, my lord." Her lips twitched. "At least not overly much."

He glanced at the silver tea service set up on the cherrywood table in front of the settee, noting her empty tea-cup and the tiny crumbs left on her plate. "Would you care for another cup of tea? Some more tea cakes?"

"An offer I fear I cannot refuse. The tea cakes were heavenly." Again her lips twitched, drawing his attention to their ripe fullness, fascinating him. "I'm afraid I harbor a tremendous affection for sweets."

Good God, he was gawking as if he'd never seen lips before. Thoroughly irked at himself, he jerked his gaze back to her eyes, only to find himself distracted by the realization that her irises were flecked with shades of paler brown. As if cinnamon had been sprinkled over rich chocolate. Damn. He had a particular fondness for cinnamon sprinkled over rich chocolate.

He cleared his throat. "A tremendous affection for sweets . . . something we have in common." He indicated the settee with his hand. "Please sit."

She turned and moved past him, leaving a scent of oranges in her wake that had him all but salivating. "What are your favorites?" she asked, settling herself on the brocade cushion.

"Favorites?"

"Sweets. I've a fondness for frosted cakes and a dreadful weakness for chocolate."

"I wouldn't say no to either of those." *Or anything else for which you might have a fondness . . .*

Swallowing a sound of self-directed disgust at his wayward thoughts, he settled himself in the leather chair opposite her. Six feet and a table now separated them. Excellent. "I also have a weakness for marzipan."

Her eyes slid closed and a sound that could only be described as a purr came from her. "Marzipan," she said softly, reverently. He watched her lips form the word, and found himself transfixed. And in need of shifting in his seat. Did she have any idea how bloody aroused she looked? Her eyes slowly opened and fixed on his. "Yes, that is lovely," she murmured in a husky voice that did nothing to dispel the discomfort occurring in his breeches. "Especially with a cup of chocolate."

"I agree. That happens to be my favorite before-bed snack."

She raised her brows. "Indeed? Not brandy or port and a cheroot?"

"No, I'm afraid it's chocolate and marzipan for me."

She smiled. "How very unfashionable, my lord." She inclined her head toward the tea service. "Shall I pour?"

"Please." He sat back and watched her serve with a deft skill that gave no indication she'd spent time picking pockets rather than taking deportment lessons. She appeared perfectly calm and relaxed, completely at ease in his presence, a fact that irritated him more than he'd like to admit since he had to struggle to maintain his outward calm. Indeed, in spite of his suspicions regarding her motives, he couldn't help but admire her cool exterior. But then, it was an excellent, and much-needed, trait for a thief.

"Sugar?" she asked.

"Two, please."

After passing him the cup and saucer, she picked up the delicate silver tongs. "Tea cake?"

He smiled. "Is that a rhetorical question?"

She smiled in return, revealing a pair of shallow dimples that flanked her lips. They formed a perfect triangle with the indentation on her chin, a shape he felt an overwhelming desire to explore. "No, as I wasn't so much asking *if* you wanted one, my lord, but rather how many you wanted."

"Hmmm. It seems I made a tactical error in revealing my weakness for sweets."

"Surely a man in your position would know that

revealing *any* weakness is a tactical error." She placed two of the tiny frosted cakes on the plate, then raised her brows in a questioning manner.

"I'll take three."

She added another confection to the plate and passed it to him. Watching her carefully, he deliberately brushed his fingers against hers when he accepted the plate. If she experienced the same heated tingle as he at the brief contact, she gave no indication of it.

Pushing back the unreasonable irritation that rippled through him, he asked, "What do you mean 'a man in your position'?"

It took Alex several seconds to answer because in spite of the barrier of her lace gloves, the brush of his fingers had seriously undermined her concentration. How could a mere touch affect her so? After clearing her throat, she said, "A titled gentleman looking for a wife. I imagine if the young, eligible Society misses were to learn of your penchant for sweets, you would be overrun with offerings of confections."

"Now why didn't I think of that? I believe I'll take out an advertisement in the *Times* proclaiming my love of all things sweet."

She laughed and deftly served herself a tea cake.

"Only one, Madame Larchmont?"

"I've already had two."

"I hope that won't stop you from indulging further."

"It would be a social *faux pas* of the first order if I were to eat more than my host."

His gaze slid to the silver platter on the tea tray where a trio of cakes remained. "Well, I do not intend to leave this room until that tray is empty. I hope you won't be shy in helping me eat those."

"I have many faults, my lord, but believe me, shyness is not one of them."

A slow smile curved his lovely mouth, coiling warmth

in secret places she had no desire to feel warm and making her wonder what that lovely mouth would feel like brushing over hers.

"A fascinating tidbit of information, Madame Larchmont, although perhaps a tactical error on your part to admit it."

"It wasn't so much an admission as a warning, my lord. So as to prepare you for when I dispense with polite conversation and move on to the topic of your paying me for reading your cards." When he raised his brows, she added, "I thought it best to be straightforward, given our conversation of last evening. I wouldn't want you to think I was saying one thing and meaning another."

"In this instance, I don't believe anyone could accuse you of such. Are you normally paid before your services are rendered?"

"Yes. Based on my experience, that is best. I've found that if I tell someone something they don't particularly like—"

"They don't wish to pay."

"Precisely."

"Are you planning to tell me something I won't like?"

She lifted her chin. "I don't *plan* to tell anyone anything, Lord Sutton. I only relay what the cards themselves indicate."

He made no comment, instead raising his teacup to his lips to sip, watching her over the rim. She forced herself to hold his gaze, feeling as if they were locked in some silent battle of the wills that she refused to lose by looking away first. After lowering his cup to the saucer, he rose and crossed to the mahogany desk by the window. He opened the top drawer and removed a leather pouch from which he spilled coins into his palm. After counting out the amount he wanted, he withdrew another, smaller pouch and placed the coins in it. He then placed the larger pouch back in the drawer and returned to stand next to her.

Holding out the pouch, he said, "I believe this is the amount we agreed upon."

She took the bundle then set down her teacup. "If you don't mind, I'll count it. Just to make certain."

He resumed his seat and picked up one of his tea cakes. She felt the weight of his stare while she quickly counted the coins.

"All's in order?" he asked, when she finished.

"Yes."

"You're not a very trusting sort."

She met his gaze squarely. "I meant no offense, Lord Sutton. I just find it is better not to leave anything to chance."

"No offense taken, I assure you. I was merely making an observation. Indeed, I admire your caution, especially where money is concerned. A shocking number of thieves wander about our fair city, you know."

"Sadly, I'm aware of that," she said, keeping her voice even, despite the quickening of her heart rate. She tried to read his expression, but his features gave away absolutely nothing, making her feel once again a mouse to his cat.

"Oh? You haven't been the victim of footpads I hope?"

"Not recently no. But I meant that it is impossible to live in London and not be aware of the sad state of poverty in which so many citizens live. And sadly, poverty can drive good people to do bad, desperate things."

"Such as steal."

"Yes."

His green gaze rested on hers. "But some people, Madame Larchmont, are simply bad."

"Yes, I know." God help her, she knew only too well.

Wanting to change the subject, she nodded toward the huge portrait over the fireplace. "Your mother?"

His gaze shifted to the painting, and Alex turned to look at the image of a stunningly beautiful woman dressed in an ivory gown. She stood in a garden filled with pastel blooms, an invisible breeze touching her skirts and glossy dark hair. A faint smile played around her lips and a hint of mischief glittered in her green eyes. She shifted her attention back to Lord Sutton. A muscle ticked in his jaw, and his throat moved as he swallowed.

"Yes," he said softly. "That is my mother."

"She's beautiful." In a way she'd always imagined her own mother looking. Happy. Healthy. Well dressed. Cared for. Certainly cared for by more than a scraggly, hungry, frightened child who hadn't known how to make her well once the illness came upon her.

He pressed his lips together for several seconds then nodded. "Beautiful . . . yes, she was. On the inside as well. The portrait was finished just before she died." Deep sorrow edged his voice, and when he looked at Alex, she was struck by the bleakness in his eyes.

"I'm sorry," she said, not sure how to respond, yet understanding all too well the agony of losing a mother. "She was very young."

A frown shadowed across his face. "The same age as I am now."

"You have her eyes."

His gaze wandered back to the painting. "Yes. I inherited her love of sweets as well." Silence swelled for several long seconds, then his eyes took on a faraway look. "She used to bring my brother and me to Maximillian's Confectionary on Bond Street. We'd spend forever making our selections, acting very serious and proper." The hint of a smile whispered over his lips. "But the moment we entered the carriage to go home, we'd tear into the packages and eat and laugh until our sides ached. Her laughter was magical. Contagious . . ."

His voice trailed off, and Alex remained perfectly still, struck by his quiet, wistful tone. She wasn't sure he was even aware he'd spoken that last sentence aloud. Clearly he'd loved his mother very much, and she him. A pang of envy hit her. How lovely it would be to have such memories of happy outings. An odd, unsettling ache she couldn't quite name flooded her. Sympathy for his loss? Self-pity for her own—although how could she mourn something she'd never had?

"What of your father?" she asked.

He blinked, seeming to recall himself, then shifted his attention back to her. "As I mentioned last night, he recently remarried. His wife is the aunt of my brother's bride. A pity that Lady Victoria—my brother's wife—doesn't have a sister. If she did, I'd marry her like that," he snapped his fingers, "and I wouldn't have to waste my time looking for a suitable bride."

"I believe you would be well served to keep the phrase 'waste my time looking for a suitable bride' to yourself. Even the most pragmatic of women like a bit of romance."

"Oh? And do you consider yourself pragmatic?"

"Of course."

His gaze bored into hers in a way that made her feel as if she sat too close to the fire. "Yet you still like romance."

"Of course. But I wasn't talking about me, Lord Sutton. I was speaking of the Society misses you'll be considering for your future wife."

"Is that how Monsieur Larchmont won your affection? With romance?"

"Naturally." She picked up her teacup and regarded him pointedly over the rim. "That and his natural reticence."

"Ah. He is a man of few words."

"Very few."

"He is more a man of . . . action."

"That describes him perfectly, yes."

"He does not possess this habit that you find males have of saying one thing and meaning another?"

"No, he does not. When he says 'I'm hungry,' he means 'I'm hungry.' "

"I see." His gaze slipped to her lips, lingering for several seconds and halting Alex in the act of reaching for her tea cake. "And therefore I take it that when he says 'I'm hungry' he is referring only to food . . . and not to any other sort of hunger his wife would inspire?"

A flash of heat sizzled through her, flooding her with an awareness of her darkly attractive host she did not wish to feel. She forced herself to continue reaching for her cake, noting with annoyance that her movements appeared jerky. "Yes. He is refreshingly straightforward." She curved her lips into a smile. "We're very much two of a kind."

"You consider yourself straightforward?"

Not in the least. "Very much so."

"That is . . . refreshing. Not many people are." Before she could decide if there was any hidden meaning behind his words, he reached out to pick up a tea cake, and asked, "He enjoys living with you here in London?"

She frowned. "He?"

He cocked his head and peered at her with a quizzical expression. "Your husband."

Good God, what on earth was wrong with her? Annoyed at herself for losing track of the conversation, and at him for persisting in his questions, she said briskly, "Of course. Why do you ask?"

He shrugged. "I only wondered if he missed his native France."

"Oh. Sometimes. However, he's adapted very well."

"How long have you been married?"

"Three years. About your reading—"

"Do you have any children?"

"No. Your reading—"

"He doesn't accompany you to the soirees you attend?"

If he hoped to provoke a reaction from her, she refused to oblige him. "No. He does not enjoy crowds."

"Is he a fortune-teller as well?"

"No. Tell me, Lord Sutton, once you choose a wife, do you intend to remain in London?"

"No. What is his occupation?"

"Who?"

"Monsieur Larchmont."

She set down her teacup and lifted her chin a notch. "He is a ratcatcher, my lord." Her tone dared him to cast aspersions upon such a lowly occupation. Indeed, she dearly hoped he would so as to incite her anger, so she felt something, *anything* other than this almost painful awareness of him. She'd lambaste him with the fact that if not for ratcatchers, the homes of lofty peers such as himself would be overrun with the vermin. But he merely nodded, his gaze never leaving hers.

"He's been a ratcatcher for a long time?"

"For as long as I've known him." Botheration, why did he ask so many questions? None of the other members of the peerage showed such curiosity. And how had he managed to turn the conversation back to her? Determined to regain—and this time retain—the upper hand, she said firmly, "The hour grows late, Lord Sutton. We'd best begin your reading as I must soon leave."

"You've another engagement this evening?"

"Yes."

"Lady Newtrebble's soiree?"

She nodded, and realization dawned, bringing a jolt

of alarm, followed immediately by a wash of tingling warmth. "You'll be attending as well?"

"Yes. Must keep looking for my bride, you know." His grin flashed—mischievous and far, far too attractive. "I'm hopeful you'll be able to tell me who she is during our reading."

Whoever she was, Alex wished her luck in resisting this dangerously attractive man. "Yes. To cut down on all that time wasting. Shall we get started then?"

"By all means."

Colin slid his chair closer to the table, then moved the tea service to one end, forcing himself to concentrate on the matter at hand and not the delicate whiff of oranges he had just breathed in. "Do we have sufficient room here?"

"This is fine." She opened the drawstring on her reticule and pulled out a rectangular bundle wrapped in a bronze silk.

"Who taught you how to read cards?"

Staring at the bundle in her hands, she said, "My mother."

"Do you see her often?"

"No. She's dead."

He heard the hurt, the pain in her brusque words—hurt and pain with which he was intimately acquainted—and he couldn't stop the sympathy that welled in him. "I'm sorry. I understand how deeply that loss cuts."

"These cards are all I have left of her," she said softly.

She looked up, and their gazes met. And he found himself holding his breath. Her expression was frustratingly unreadable, but something in her eyes, something he fancied was vulnerability, beckoned him. In an unprecedented way that confounded and confused him.

Silence swelled between them. Did she feel this thick, unsettling tension, or was it just him? Her gaze lowered to rest on his lips. Bloody hell, he felt the impact of that look like a caress. To his utter irritation, he swelled behind his breeches, and it took all his concentration to keep from shifting in his seat to relieve the unwanted ache.

Damn it, after only a few years out of the spying game, he'd obviously lost his touch. His control. And in such an inexplicable way. Why, this woman wasn't even in the least bit beautiful in any conventional sense. Nor was she a lady of his class. _And_ she was a _thief._

She was a thief four years ago, his conscience broke in. _People can, and do, change._

He mentally cursed his annoying inner voice. Fine. _Four years ago_ she was a thief. Most likely she still was. _That's_ what he was supposed to discover—not that his wayward body found the mere sight and scent of her irrationally and intensely arousing.

He clenched his jaw, and she blinked rapidly, as if recalling herself. Swiftly setting the bronze-wrapped bundle on the table, she said in a brisk tone, "In order for me to focus my psychic energy and maintain my concentration, it would be best if we refrain from further unnecessary conversation until your reading is finished. Your role here is that of inquirer. While I shuffle, I want you to think of the question you would most like for me to answer."

He realized with no small amount of chagrin that he still held his breath. After pulling in a lungful of air, he said, "All right."

With the room silent except for the ticking of the mantel clock and the snap of the burning fire, Colin watched her unwrap her cards, then carefully fold the square of bronze silk. She didn't remove her lace gloves, and he wondered why, but decided not to ask at the moment as she'd no doubt deem his question "unnecessary conversation." Heaven knew he wouldn't want to disrupt her "psychic energy."

She closed her eyes and drew slow, deep breaths. His gaze wandered down, lingering on the delicate hollow of her throat, which deepened with each inhalation. Her chest slowly rose and fell, and he found himself matching the rhythm, waiting for the creamy skin above her bodice to swell with her next breath. Damn it all, she truly did have the oddest effect on his breathing.

Looking up, his gaze riveted on her slightly parted lips, and he pressed his own lips together to tamp down the coil of lust snaking through him with growing intensity. Unfortunately, his effort proved supremely unsuccessful. Especially when he was hit with the overpowering urge to trace the fullness of her lush mouth with his fingers. Then with his tongue—

She opened her eyes and looked directly at him. Once again, the impact of that clear, chocolate brown gaze hit him like a heated wallop.

"What is your question, my lord?"

A frown bunched his brows. "Question?"

"Have you decided what you wish to ask me?"

May I kiss you? Touch you? Make love—

He clamped his jaw tight. Bloody hell. Not *that sort* of question. Some other question. One that didn't involve her lips and his tongue and naked bodies and indulging in ridiculous, inappropriate fantasies.

"Er, I wish to know who will become my bride?" Yes. Perfect question. Concentrate on some other woman. Some beautiful, young, nubile, wellborn, nonthief.

She nodded, then briskly shuffled and cut the cards. Setting the deck on the table, she said, "Cut the cards. Once. Using your left hand."

He made a mental note to ask her later why he had to use his left hand. After he completed the task, she picked up the deck in her left hand and began turning over cards.

The cards appeared old, their colors faded, and they depicted people and things completely unfamiliar to Colin. After she finished, she looked over the spread. And went completely still. Colin looked up. Something flickered in her eyes, then she frowned. He barely resisted the urge to look toward the ceiling. Clearly she intended to play this charade out to the fullest and give him his money's worth. Relieved to have something other than her to concentrate on, he focused his attention on the cards and prepared to be entertained.

"Is something wrong?" he asked, when she remained silent, trying not to sound amused.

"N . . . no." She drew several slow breaths, then indicated a grouping of cards. "These represent your past." She studied them, then said, "You enjoyed a privileged childhood and a close relationship with someone younger than you. A brother."

Again Colin had to force himself not to look heavenward. He'd told her he had a brother—

"But in spite of your closeness," she continued, "you felt . . . lonely. Weighted down by responsibility." She brushed her gloved fingers over the cards. "Responsibility first to your family, your title, but then to something else. Something that meant a great deal to you but caused a deep, hurtful rift with someone you cared for very much. You experienced profound pain and guilt because of this rift and blamed yourself. I see betrayal. Lies. Your actions shamed you, and you're still experiencing guilt because of them."

An uncomfortable sensation washed over him, as if his cravat were suddenly too tight. He forced his features to remain impassive, his fingers loosely knitted between his spread knees. Her attention remained fixated on the cards, and her hands indicated the next grouping.

"These represent your present," she said, her voice low and serious. "They strongly indicate inner turmoil. You're deeply troubled . . . concerned about your future. These concerns weigh heavily on your mind. Your spirit is at war with itself, with your mind telling you one thing, your instincts insisting something else. Important decisions must be made, yet while you're worried about choosing wisely, you also feel a need for urgency. To make these decisions quickly. A sense of dread surrounds you, pushing you to act—perhaps in ways you might not wish to."

Ignoring the odd prickling sensation slithering over his skin, he remained perfectly still, watching her carefully as her gaze slid to the final grouping. Her frown deepened, and she pressed her lips together. Finally, she said, "These show your immediate future."

Silence stretched between them, during which she appeared increasingly troubled. Something about her demeanor rushed a chill down his spine and he inwardly frowned. Good God, what was wrong with him? Finally, forcing a note of lazy amusement into his voice, he prompted, "I do hope you intend to tell me before we creep into the next outrageously expensive quarter-hour increment of your time, Madame."

She raised her gaze, and he stilled at her troubled expression. "The things the cards are indicating . . . I don't wish to alarm you."

He waved his hand. "Fear not. I'm made of very stern stuff, I assure you."

"Very well." She looked distinctly uncomfortable. "I see danger."

He nodded encouragingly. "Marriage is considered a dangerous pursuit by most men. What else?"

She shook her head. "This danger is not related to

marriage, at least not strongly. It's something else. Something that isn't clear. There is a woman . . ."

"But surely that's good news. My future wife? Have you divined her name? Her hair color at least? Is she blond or dark?"

Again she shook her head, her eyes intent on his. "No. This woman isn't what she appears to be. You need to beware. Of her, and your surroundings as well. The cards strongly indicate treachery. Betrayal. Illness." Her voice dropped to a whisper. "Death."

Silence descended once again. An uneasiness he refused to acknowledge crept over him, irritating him. And his irritation snapped him back to his senses.

"Well done," he said, nodding approvingly. "I must say you're very good. Very gypsylike and atmospheric. I'd think such dire predictions might cast a pall upon the festivities at one of the elegant parties at which you're hired to entertain, but then again, I suppose one cannot ignore the bloodthirsty side of human nature."

Unmistakable anger flashed in her eyes before she retreated behind the mask she wore so well. It was the first hint of true emotion she'd shown, and he found himself fascinated.

"You're mocking me, my lord." Her voice throbbed with a hint of the same anger he'd detected in her eyes.

"I'm simply not taking an entertaining pastime too seriously. You told me nothing that you couldn't have gleaned from conversations with any of my acquaintances, or indeed from your own conversations with me. Your statements were vague and could apply to anyone. And to any number of situations. You did some research, embellished a bit, and acted your part flawlessly. I applaud you."

Her expression chilled and she lifted her chin. "I had no such conversations about you. With anyone.

I conducted no research. And I embellished nothing. I only interpreted what the cards themselves told me."

"I mean no offense, Madame. I'm not disputing your talent at providing an entertaining quarter hour. I'm merely stating no 'psychic energy' was required to divine that I enjoyed a privileged childhood. My position in Society would indicate as much. I'd also mentioned that I had a brother."

He leaned back and regarded her steadily, forcing himself to swallow the urge to inform her that the woman who "isn't what she appears to be" of whom he needed to be wary was sitting directly across from him. "As for your other statements, I'd be hard-pressed to name a person who reaches adulthood without experiencing some form of loneliness, hurt, guilt, lies, and betrayal. Thanks to the *Times,* you and everyone else in London know perfectly well that my future is very much on my mind. My duty to my title, finding a wife so as to produce heirs, is the precise reason I'm here. As for illness and death, sadly, they eventually touch us all."

"I was not speaking about 'eventually' but rather of your immediate future," she said stiffly. "I take no pleasure in delivering dire predictions, Lord Sutton. I wish I had better news, but everything in your reading points to your need to be wary. On guard. And mindful of your health. *Now.* I hope you will heed and take care."

"Duly noted. Luckily my brother is a physician. Should I fall victim to the headache or a stomach ailment, he'll put me back to rights."

It appeared she wished to belabor the point, but she said nothing, just jerked her head in a nod, then quickly wrapped up her cards in the square of silk and replaced the bundle in her reticule. Then she stood and looked at him with her usual calm, unreadable expression.

"I'd like to read your cards again, my lord, if you'd

permit it. Here, at your house, but in a different room. Using different cards. To see if the readings are the same."

He rose and crossed his arms over his chest. "And why would you want to do that?" He barely refrained from adding *other than to relieve me of another outrageous reading fee*.

"Because I want to make certain that the reading is true. Be positive that I'm correct. And perhaps gain some further insight as to what danger awaits you."

"I'd much prefer to concentrate on discovering the identity of the woman I'm destined to marry," he said dryly, "but by all means, let us schedule another appointment. Shall we say tomorrow, at three o'clock?" he said, deliberately choosing the same time he'd originally suggested for today's meeting.

"I'm afraid I'm already engaged at three. However, I'm available for four o'clock."

"Excellent. I shall look forward to it. As I told you, I'm always delighted to indulge in diverting pastimes."

Keeping his gaze steady on hers, he moved around the table to stand directly in front of her. A mere arm's length separated them, and he found himself staring at her. The creamy texture of her skin looked so incredibly soft, he had to clench his hands to keep from reaching out to brush his fingers over her cheek.

The firelight coaxed subtle highlights from her shiny hair, and his palms itched with the urge to pull the pins from her carefully arranged chignon and run his fingers through the glossy tresses.

When he realized to his chagrin that he was once again holding his breath, he pulled in a slow lungful of air. The subtle scent of oranges filled his head, mixed with something else that, God help him, smelled like sugar. He barely suppressed a groan. Bloody hell, how could a woman smell like *sugar*? He instantly imagined leaning forward to brush his tongue up the length of her graceful neck, to see if she tasted as sweet as she smelled. His pulse quickened at the thought, and as much as it galled him to admit, there was no getting away from the fact that he desired this woman. Badly.

More galling, however, was the realization that she apparently suffered from no such affliction. She looked at him with her perfectly calm expression from those huge chocolate brown eyes. How was it that she appeared so composed while he felt so . . . not composed?

Annoyed at himself, and determined to put them on a more equal footing, he lightly grasped her hand and raised it. "I'm especially delighted to indulge in any pastime that includes the company of a beautiful woman." His gaze locked with hers, he lightly kissed her lace-covered fingertips, then, as he had last evening, turned her hand and pressed his lips to the pale, silky skin of her inner wrist.

Her eyes widened, and her lips parted with a quick intake of breath. A beguiling wash of rose stained her cheeks. Her gaze dropped to where his mouth rested against her fragrant skin, and the tip of her tongue peeked out to moisten her lips.

Grim satisfaction filled him. So . . . it wasn't just him. She felt it, too. This heat sizzling between them. Now the only remaining question was what were they going to do about it?

A knock sounded at the door. She gasped and pulled her hand away, and he silently cursed the interruption. By God, she looked flushed and aroused, and he'd barely touched her. Keeping his gaze on her, he called out, "Come in."

His voice sounded husky even to his own ears, and he cleared his throat as the door opened. Ellis entered bearing a silver salver, a frown puckering his normally impassive countenance.

"This message just arrived from Lord Wexhall. His messenger said it was urgent and that he would wait for your reply."

Urgent? During his service to the Crown, Colin had reported directly to Wexhall and knew *urgent* wasn't a word the man tossed about lightly. A finger of cold dread ran down Colin's spine. Nathan and Victoria were due to arrive tomorrow. Had some accident befallen one or both of them?

Stomach tight, he broke the seal, unfolded the thick vellum, and quickly scanned the brief note.

"Doctor Nathan and Lady Victoria," Ellis said. "Are they—?"

"They're fine, Ellis," Colin said. The man's shoulders drooped with relief that matched Colin's own that his brother and sister-in-law were not the subject of this urgent missive.

He returned his attention to Madame Larchmont, whose inscrutable mask was firmly in place. "Sadly," Colin said, "the same cannot be said for Lord Malloran. Or one of his footmen, a young man named William Walters. They were both discovered dead in Lord Malloran's study this morning."

Six

The blood drained from Alex's head. Her knees wobbled, and she grasped the back of the settee to steady herself. Lord Malloran—the man in whose study she'd overhead a murder plot—the man to whom she'd written a letter detailing that plot—*dead*? Along with his footman? An image of the back of a tall, dark-haired man dressed in the elaborately gold-trimmed Malloran livery leaving Lord Malloran's study last night flashed in her mind. Her stomach cramped with the sickening suspicion that the dead footman was the same man she'd seen.

Everything inside her stilled. Then turned to ice. Dear God. Was it possible that the note she'd left had somehow precipitated this tragic turn of events? She pressed her hand to her midsection in a futile attempt to calm her inner turmoil. Certainly the fact that the person to whom her note had been written *and* the man who'd most likely prompted her to write it were both dead couldn't be a mere coincidence. Her survival instincts screamed it wasn't.

But what of the other person whom she'd overheard in

the study? That person had most definitely not been Lord Malloran, whose deep voice boomed. Even if he'd attempted to disguise his voice, she doubted him capable of the whispery rasp she'd heard. Besides, it had been the footman's voice that suggested they speak in Lord Malloran's study for privacy. Such a suggestion wouldn't be necessary to make to Lord Malloran himself.

Questions clicked rapidly through her mind. What had become of her note? Had Lord Malloran read it? If so, had he burned it—or was it still in his study? A chill raced down her spine. If the note had something to do with the men's deaths . . .

The murderer would be looking for the person who'd written the note.

"Are you all right, Madame Larchmont?"

Startled, she turned toward the deep voice. Lord Sutton's sharp gaze bored into hers.

"Y . . . yes. I'm merely stunned at the news."

Without taking his gaze from her, he said to his butler, "Ellis, tell the messenger that Lord Wexhall may expect me within the hour."

"Yes, my lord." The butler quit the room, quietly closing the door behind him.

Lord Sutton's gaze pinned her in place, and the all-too-familiar and much-hated sensation of feeling like a trapped animal crawled through her. Damn it all, she'd sworn never to allow herself to feel that way again.

"You're very pale," he murmured, walking toward her. "Would you like to sit down?"

She licked her dry lips and shook her head. "I must be going." And she would. As soon as her knees firmed up.

He nodded, his gaze never leaving hers. "Before you leave, tell me, did you speak to Lord Malloran last evening?"

Dear God, she was trembling. "Briefly. When I first

arrived." She licked her lips again. "How did he . . . they . . . die?"

"I don't know. But given the fact that there were two deaths, I'd guess it wasn't from natural causes. The note I received indicated there might have been a robbery, as the study was in some disarray."

Clutching her reticule, she forced herself to move. "A tragedy," she murmured, moving stiffly toward the door. "If you'll excuse me, my lord, I'm afraid I must leave."

"Of course," he said, falling into step beside her. "I'll have my carriage brought 'round to take you home."

She opened her mouth to protest, but before she could say a word, he said, "I insist." As she had no desire to prolong her exit by arguing, she nodded. "Very well. Thank you."

Five minutes later she found herself ensconced in his well-sprung, luxuriously appointed carriage. Sitting back against the soft pale gray velvet squabs, Alex buried her face in her hands.

Dear God, what had she done?

And what was she going to do next?

When he arrived that evening at the Newtrebble soiree, Colin accepted a brandy from a passing footman, then slowly made his way around the perimeter of the crowded drawing room. Rather than a subdued atmosphere given the untimely deaths of Lord Malloran and William Walters, a sense of excitement seemed to hover in the air. The soiree was in full swing, with footmen bearing silver trays of drinks and hors d'oeuvres. As he moved along, he listened intently to the snippets of conversation buzzing around him. The deaths were the main topic of conversation, with speculation running rampant as to how and why they'd died and who—or what—had killed them. A robber? His lordship's study had reportedly been searched. Or perhaps canapés gone bad? The latest *on dit* was that the Malloran servants claimed a nearly empty plate of seafood tarts had been found on his lordship's desk.

"Good heavens, I ate a prawn tart myself last night," exclaimed a woman, who stood in the center of a small group of ladies. "It smelled a bit 'off' if you know what I mean, and I felt decidedly queasy afterward. Why, I'm lucky I didn't meet the same horrible fate as Malloran and that poor young man—although why a *footman* was eating prawn tarts . . ." She made a tsking sound and shook her head.

"Servants," said another lady with a sniff, while the rest of the group nodded in clear commiseration of the foibles of the lower class. "Makes one wonder if he deliberately served tainted food to Malloran in order to rob him, but was foiled when he fell victim to his own treachery."

Moving on, Colin slipped into a shadowed alcove set behind a huge potted palm. His vantage point afforded him a good view of the room. Leaning back into the shadows, he swirled his snifter of brandy and frowned at the gently whirling amber depths.

His earlier conversation with Lord Wexhall, who, although recently retired from his service to the Crown, had gone at the magistrate's request to the Malloran town house along with the magistrate and doctor, echoed in Colin's mind. *Appears to be a robbery,* Lord Wexhall had said, *with both men having head wounds, the fireplace poker out of its holder, and the room in shambles. But my gut . . . and nose . . . tell me Malloran and Walters didn't die from blows to the head. They both smelled faintly of bitter almonds, as did the dregs in the decanter. And you know what that means.*

Colin took a deep swallow of brandy. Yes, he knew what that meant. Prussic acid. Malloran and Walters had most likely been poisoned. By a substance frequently used to kill rodents.

By ratcatchers.

His fingers tightened on the cut-glass snifter, and he scanned the crowd, until his gaze riveted on the table in the far corner of the room. His stomach executed an odd maneuver, and his breath hitched. Madame Larchmont, dressed in the deep emerald gown he'd seen in her wardrobe this afternoon, sat with her cards spread before her, talking to the matron seated opposite her.

Alexandra... Her name whispered through his mind, while his far-too-eager gaze roamed over her. Her hair, arranged in an attractive Grecian knot entwined with gold and green ribbons, gleamed under the soft light cast by the candle-filled chandeliers. She smiled, momentarily drawing his attention to her lush mouth.

Everything about her appeared perfectly innocent and straightforward. Just the evening's entertainment, cheerfully providing what she'd been hired to do. She'd clearly regained the composure she'd allowed to slip earlier ... or had she? For just an instant, her gaze shifted sideways, as if searching the nearby crowd, and a ghost of a frown whispered across her face. Indeed, the change in her expression was so fleeting, Colin wondered if he'd imagined it. But his gut told him he hadn't. And that her perfectly innocent and straightforward appearance was just that—an appearance.

For there was nothing innocent and straightforward about the fact that two men were found dead in the room from which he'd witnessed her emerging through the window only hours earlier—in all probability killed by a substance she would, by her own admission that her husband was a ratcatcher, have easy access to. Although he had strong doubts as to the veracity of her admission.

Nor was there anything innocent or straightforward

in the fact that he'd neglected to share that information with Wexhall and the magistrate.

Resting his head against the wall, he tossed back a generous swallow of brandy and closed his eyes, savoring the burn down his chest, hoping it would singe away the guilt eating at him. Bloody hell, what was wrong with him? He'd never before shirked his duty, his responsibilities. Not toward his family and title, and not once during his years of service to the Crown under Wexhall's command. During that service, he'd committed several acts, one in particular, that had resulted in much soul-searching afterward, but his duty had been clear and he'd done what he'd had to do. He should have told Wexhall, for whom he had the greatest respect, and the magistrate what he knew of Madame Larchmont's nocturnal window-escaping. Yet he'd remained silent. And damn it, he didn't understand *why*.

He opened his eyes, and as it had every time his gaze found her since that first time four years ago at Vauxhall, his breath hitched. Which confused and unsettled and severely irritated him. Damn it, in addition to having been a thief, everything he knew of her pointed to her *still* being a schemer. Or worse. Certainly a liar. She'd been untruthful about where she lived, and Monsieur Larchmont, if he even existed outside her imagination which, based on his search of her rooms he strongly doubted, did not reside with her as she'd claimed. No, instead she apparently lived with someone called "Miss Emmie" and had a trapdoor leading into her rooms with which an urchin child was familiar. Secretive, mysterious . . . she most certainly was both. Yet neither trait was illegal. Murder, however, was.

Still, in spite of his suspicions regarding her motives and honesty, he couldn't cast her in the role of murderess. Someone who would, without feeling, poison two men. She'd been visibly shaken when he'd announced the contents of his note from Wexhall. Was that shock or guilt? Or finely honed acting skills? Had she added something to the decanter, perhaps at the behest or demand of someone else, not realizing it was poison and would result in death?

A sound of disgust pushed past his lips. *Listen to yourself, you dolt. Making excuses, grasping at explanations, inventing rationalizations to explain away what you saw with your own eyes—a known thief exiting the now-dead Lord Malloran's window.*

He shook his head and frowned, feeling uncharacteristically out of sorts. *Was* he making excuses for her? Or was he simply trying to avoid making the same mistake he'd made with Nathan—a mistake that had damn near cost him his relationship with his brother? Then, as now, all the evidence pointed one way—toward guilt—and four years ago he'd accepted damning evidence without question, refusing to listen to his heart's suggestion there might be another explanation. Now his heart was making that same suggestion in regard to Madame Larchmont, and he found it impossible not to listen this time.

Time. He needed time. To find out more information about her. Her life. He had no doubt that she was up to something, but until he found out what that something was, he was reluctant to turn her over to the authorities for questioning. His common sense told him he was being a bloody idiot. But his instincts . . . those bloody instincts . . . warned him to wait.

One thing was for certain: He was more determined than ever to discover Madame Larchmont's secrets. But his sense of honor, his ethics, balked at withholding information from Wexhall and the magistrate.

Three days, he bargained with his conscience. He'd give himself three days to watch her. Follow her. Spend time with her. Find out as much as he could about her.

With the goal being to firmly establish either her guilt or innocence. But regardless of his success, on the fourth day, he'd tell Wexhall everything.

Although his conscience no longer screamed outrage, it did continue to glare at him; but he forced aside any second thoughts. He'd made a decision, and he planned to abide by it. Now it was time for action.

After swallowing his last sip of brandy, he exited the alcove, preparing to make his way toward his quarry. Before he could take so much as a step, however, a female voice directly behind him said, "*There* you are, Lord Sutton!"

Biting back his irritation at this delay in his plans, he turned and found himself facing his hostess, whose ample figure was shown to dubious advantage in a dark blue gown, while a spray of peacock feathers fanned out around her head in a complicated coiffure. If her goal had been to resemble a satin-clad bird, she'd succeeded in an admirable, if rather frightening, way.

"Good evening, Lady Newtrebble," he said, making her a bow.

"I've been looking for you everywhere. Whatever are you doing hiding here in the shadows?"

"I'm not hiding. I only just arrived." He held up his empty snifter. "Thought I'd enjoy a bit of your excellent brandy before jumping into the fray."

"Well, you're here now, that's all that matters." She leaned in closer, and he barely evaded a jab with her feathers. "And a bit of revivification is probably wise given the task before you. Tell me, how goes the search?"

"Search?"

She tapped his upper arm with her folded fan and laughed. "For your bride, silly man!"

Bride? He blinked. Bloody hell, he'd completely forgotten.

"There are at least two dozen eligible young ladies

here this evening, including my very own niece, Lady Gwendolyn." She batted her eyelashes. "I introduced you last evening at Lady Malloran's soiree."

An image materialized in his mind's eye of a stunningly beautiful young woman who, during their brief conversation, had done nothing but complain—about everything from the weather (too warm), to her family's servants (too nosy), to the hors d'oeuvres she'd just eaten (too salty). All that beauty, wasted on such an unpleasant, petulant person.

"Ah, yes. Lady Gwendolyn." A shudder of distaste he couldn't entirely contain rippled through him.

Lady Newtrebble clearly didn't notice. "The Season's barely begun, and already she's been declared an Incomparable." She slipped her hand through his arm in a manner that could only be described as commandeering. "Come along, now," she said, giving him a tug. "There is much to be done."

He smoothly disentangled himself under the pretext of placing his empty snifter on a passing footman's tray, then stepped back and raised his brows. "Done?"

"Yes. I must introduce you to the fortune-teller, Madame Larchmont. Everyone is agog to know if she'll predict who your future wife is." Her eyes glittered with unmistakable greed, and Colin could almost hear her thinking, *Such an amazing coup that she'll read your cards at* my *soiree.*

"After that," Lady Newtrebble continued, "my niece shall give you an extended tour of the gallery."

"Very kind," Colin murmured. "However, I wouldn't dream of monopolizing her time." He favored her with his most charming smile. "If I attempted to keep such a rare beauty all to myself, I'm certain half the men in this room would challenge me to pistols at dawn."

"But—"

"Now about that card reading . . . a fascinating offer.

I'd very much like to speak to this Madame Larchmont, and I've no wish to keep you from your other guests." He made her a quick bow. "If you'll excuse me?"

Without waiting for her answer, he moved into the sea of revelers. He deliberately took more than an hour to work his way across the room, stopping to chat with friends and renew acquaintances, many of whom then presented to him a marriage-minded daughter or sister or niece, or in one instance, aunt. Through all the conversations and introductions, Colin remained outwardly attentive and polite, chatting easily, interjecting smiles or thoughtful nods as the conversation called for, yet he remained constantly aware of Madame Larchmont. Knew every time she smiled, which she'd done three times while he spoke to Lady Miranda, and twice while he conversed with Lady Margaret, both of whom were very beautiful and clearly interested in him. Knew every time she frowned, which she'd done twice while he listened to Lord Paisler, whose daughters Lady Penelope and Lady Rachel laughed like hyenas and were also clearly interested in him. Noted every person who sat at her table. Who spoke to her. For investigative purposes only, of course.

By the time he stood only a dozen feet from her table, he'd concluded that something was troubling the inscrutable fortune-teller. Whenever she believed herself unobserved, her gaze swept over the people standing near her. At first he'd thought that she perhaps might be looking for him, but abandoned the idea, scolding his own conceit, when he realized her quick, furtive peeks took in only the immediate area around her table—not the entire room. Also, her posture appeared extraordinarily alert. Rigid. Tense. Several times he'd noticed her imperceptibly straining forward, as if trying to hear the conversations buzzing around her. If he hadn't been watching her so carefully, he wouldn't have detected the nuances. But there was no denying them, or the fact that her nervousness was very . . . interesting.

He was listening to Lady Whitemore and her very attractive daughter, Lady Alicia, who was in her second Season, pontificate on the shocking deaths with an enthusiasm Colin found very off-putting, when a low, throaty laugh captured his attention. His senses tingled, instantly recognizing the smoky sound as belonging to Madame Larchmont. His gaze swiveled toward her table.

She was smiling at the man sitting opposite her, her dimples winking. The man leaned forward, as if to impart something he wanted no one else to hear. Colin's gaze flicked over the man's broad back, the perfect fit of his midnight blue jacket, and his well-cut dark hair. His jaw clenched. Who the hell was he? He craned his neck a bit to catch a glimpse of his profile. Whoever he was, Colin didn't recognize him.

Returning his attention to Madame Larchmont, he watched as she cast her gaze demurely downward and chuckled once again at the man's obvious wit. His insides tightened in a way he neither liked nor wished to examine too closely. When she looked up, her eyes glittered with unmistakable mischief. She said something that made her companion laugh, and Colin cursed his inability to read lips. Possibly she felt the weight of his stare, for just then her gaze shifted and collided with his.

Her eyes instantly lost their whiff of mischief, and she regarded him for several seconds with nothing more than a long, cool stare. She acknowledged him with a barely noticeable tilt of her head, then returned her attention to the man, at whom she smiled. Annoyance, and something else, which felt exactly like jealousy but couldn't possibly be, coiled through him.

"—don't you agree, Lord Sutton?"

Lady Whitemore's imperious voice yanked him from his reverie and jerked his attention back to his companions, both of whom were staring at him with expectant looks. Bloody hell, he'd dropped the conversational ball. Before he could speak, Lady Whitemore snapped her quizzing glass to her eye and peered at him.

"I say, Lord Sutton, are you all right? Your countenance resembles a thundercloud."

Colin instantly smoothed out his features and forced a smile. "I'm fine. Tell me, Lady Whitemore, who is the man having his fortune read?"

Lady Whitemore glanced toward the corner, then leaned in closer to confide, "That's Mr. Logan Jennsen. The *American*." She wrinkled her nose. "Have you not met him?"

"No."

"He arrived in England only about six months ago, but has already caused a bit of a stir."

"How so?"

"Rich as Croesus," Lady Whitemore stated, clearly relishing her role of informer, "but it's *new* money, of course. Owns an entire fleet of ships and is looking to purchase more, as well as start some other sort of business. He's very abrupt and brash in that manner of upstart Colonials. No one particularly likes him, but he's so wealthy, no one is yet prepared to give him the cut direct."

"He's quite handsome," Lady Alicia offered in a rather breathless tone. At her mother's fiercely disapproving scowl, she hastily added, "for someone who's in *trade*."

"Yes, tradesmen are normally notoriously unattractive," Colin said in a dust-dry tone. "Ah, it appears Mr. Jennsen is finished, which means it is my turn at the table. Please excuse me, ladies."

After a brief bow, he moved toward the fortune-telling

table, watching as Jennsen rose. His jaw clenched when the man brought Madame Larchmont's gloved hand to his lips and kissed her fingers.

"Thank you for the delightful reading," he heard Jennsen say in an unmistakable American accent as he approached. "And for your delightful company. I look forward to seeing you again tomorrow."

"And I you, Mr. Jennsen."

The man moved off, and Colin found himself staring down at Madame Larchmont, whose lips were parted and who gazed at Jennsen's retreating back for several seconds with a rapt expression that set his teeth on edge. Then she turned toward Colin. And as it had earlier, a mask of cool indifference instantly fell over her features. Irritation prickled his skin, and he made a mental vow to somehow erase that lack of interest from her gaze.

"Lord Sutton. Good evening."

"Madame Larchmont." Without waiting for an invitation, he slid into the chair opposite her. And stared. Damn it, he felt as if the breath had been knocked from him. Golden candlelight cast from the overhead chandelier and the single votive glowing from a cut-glass bowl on the corner of her table glimmered on her dark hair and highlighted her unusual features with an intriguing array of dancing shadows. He detected none of the nervousness he'd observed over the past hour. No, she looked perfectly composed and . . . amazing. Beguiling and mysterious. And tempting in a way that he bloody well wished she didn't.

His gaze wandered downward, lingering on her mouth before continuing. Her emerald green bodice, while still modest in comparison to what most of the other women in the room wore, was cut lower than the one she'd worn last evening, exposing creamy skin and the generous curve of her breasts. His jaw clenched at the spectacular view—the same spectacular view that bastard Jennsen had just enjoyed.

He tried to offer her a smile, but his facial muscles felt oddly stiff and puckered. As if he'd bitten into a lemon.

"Are you all right, my lord?" she asked, not sounding as if she truly cared if he were or not. "You seem . . . tense."

"I'm fine. How did Jennsen's reading go?"

"You are acquainted with Mr. Jennsen?"

"Isn't everyone? Clearly *you* are."

"We were introduced at a party several weeks ago. He attends many Society functions."

Several weeks . . . Bloody hell, Jennsen had been enjoying her company all that time. "Didn't appear as if you told him dire things such as you told me today."

"I don't discuss a client's reading with anyone else."

"Excellent. I wouldn't want any potential brides scared off with the gloom and doom you predicted for me. You're seeing Jennsen tomorrow?" Damn it, he hadn't meant to blurt that out, especially in a tone that sounded far less casual as he'd have liked.

She raised her brows. "Are you normally in the habit of eavesdropping?"

Actually, yes. "Actually, no. I am not, however, deaf."

"I fail to see how whether or not I'm seeing Mr. Jennsen tomorrow is any of your concern, Lord Sutton."

"And I fail to see why you're so prickly about answering a simple question, Madame Larchmont."

She pursed her lips in obvious annoyance, and his gaze flicked down to her mouth. "Very well, yes, I have an appointment with him tomorrow for a private reading."

He forced a smile that he knew didn't reach his eyes and managed not to ask if this was the first time she'd arranged such an appointment with the man. "There now. Was that so difficult? Tell me, is he the victim of the same exorbitant fees you're charging me?"

Instead of taking offense at his brusque question, amusement kindled in her eyes. "Now, Lord Sutton, how can I be expected to answer that question? If I say *he* is paying more, you will brag about the bargain you are receiving, and thus I risk Mr. Jennsen's wrath. If I say *you* are paying more, I risk your wrath. As I find neither scenario appealing, I must decline to answer."

His heart performed the most ridiculous maneuver at the hint of a smile tugging at her lips. He moved his chair a bit closer to her and was rewarded with the barest whiff of oranges. "If *he* is paying more, I promise not to brag."

"A kind offer; however, it is my strict policy not to discuss a client's fee with anyone other than that client."

"Your strict policy," he repeated softly. "Do you have many of those?"

"Strict policies? As a matter of fact, I do. Such as I don't spend time at my fortune-telling table indulging in idle chatter."

"Excellent. Then let us begin." He indicated her cards spread out on the table. "Shouldn't you be shuffling or something?"

"Another strict policy is that I don't shuffle until my next inquirer is seated across from me."

He spread his arms. "And here I sit."

All traces of amusement left her eyes. She leaned forward slightly, and he found himself doing the same while taking a slow, deep breath, basking in the delicate scent of oranges that teased his senses. "Given the outcome of our reading this afternoon," she said quietly, "I'd prefer not to read your cards in such a public forum."

"I see. You'd rather be alone with me."

"Yes." Her brows jerked downward. "No. I mean—"

"Ooooh, how exciting you're about to have your cards read, Lord Sutton," came Lady Newtrebble's unmistakable voice from directly next to Colin. He turned and looked up at her. She waved her fan vigorously, setting her peacock feathers in motion, making her look as if her head were encircled by flapping wings. "My niece Lady Gwendolyn and I shall be *very* interested to hear Madame's predictions regarding your future wife, my lord." She waved her hand at Madame Larchmont. "Carry on. Do not mind me."

"Now, Lady Newtrebble, you know my strict policy," she said with a smile that to Colin appeared forced. "I cannot read Lord Sutton's cards with you standing right there—"

"I have no objection," Colin said.

Lady Newtrebble beamed at him. "Excellent." Then she frowned at Madame Larchmont. "Carry on."

"Although, before we begin," Colin said, smiling at his hostess, "I'd dearly love another bit of your outstanding brandy. Could you possibly arrange that?" When she hesitated, he added solemnly, "We won't begin without you."

"Very well," Lady Newtrebble said, looking none too pleased. "Botheration, where on earth is a footman when you need him?"

The instant she moved away, Colin leaned forward and said in an undertone, "I'll pay you a half crown to say that the woman I'm to marry has dark hair."

She blinked. "I beg your pardon?"

"All right, fine. A crown. It will be worth it to squash her hopes of my choosing her blond niece for my bride."

"You do not like her niece? Lady Gwendolyn is very beautiful."

"Yes. However, I'm afraid I harbor a freakish intolerance for petulant, supercilious complainers, regardless of their hair color."

"I see." Her lips twitched—very faintly, but enough to let him know she was amused. "But what if the cards predict that you *are* to marry a blond woman? You'll be eliminating all other potential blondes as well as Lady Gwendolyn."

"Given my dubious belief in fortune-telling, it's a chance I'm willing to take."

"Still, if the cards do indicate a blond woman"—she shook her head and sighed—"that would require me to *lie*."

"Are you implying that you've *never* told a lie, Madame Larchmont?"

"Have you?"

More than I can count. "Yes. You?"

She hesitated, then said, "I don't like to lie."

"Very admirable. Neither do I. However, sometimes circumstances force us to do things we don't like."

"You sound as if you speak from experience, my lord."

"I do. And surely you have not reached the age of . . . ?" His voice trailed off, waiting for her to provide her age.

"Three-and-twenty."

"The age of three-and-twenty without doing something you haven't particularly liked."

"Indeed. This conversation being a perfect example." The glint of amusement twinkling in her eyes belied her words.

He leaned closer and filled his head with her sweet, citrusy scent and upped his offer. "A half sovereign."

She heaved a sigh. "Lies, I fear, are . . . expensive."

"More expensive than *a half sovereign*?"

"I'm afraid so. Especially lies that will most likely

result in my losing a wealthy client such as Lady Newtrebble."

"If you think a renowned miser such as Lady Newtrebble would part with a half sovereign to have her cards read, you've gone mad."

For an answer she merely smiled.

"There's a word for what you're doing, Madame Larchmont."

"Yes. It's called *payment*."

"No. It's called *extortion*." For some insane reason, this exchange—which should have utterly aggravated him—inexplicably exhilarated him. In a manner he hadn't experienced in a very long time. Heaving his own put-upon sigh, he asked, "Very well, what is your price for one small lie?"

"A sovereign."

"You realize that's utterly ridiculous."

She shrugged. "The decision is yours."

"An outrageous sum to charge a friend."

She raised an eloquent brow. "I hardly think our brief acquaintance could be described as friendship, my lord."

"I suppose that's true." Keeping his gaze steady on hers, he said, "A circumstance I'd like to remedy."

"In the next three seconds, I'm certain," she said with a smile.

He smiled in return. "Yes, that would be most helpful."

"Actually it wouldn't. I charge friends the same rate as mere acquaintances."

"Ah. So it really does no good at all to know you."

"I'm afraid not." She looked over his shoulder. "Lady Newtrebble is approaching with your brandy, my lord."

"Very well," he grumbled. "A sovereign it is—but I'll pay only if you give a convincing performance."

"Agreed. And fear not, my lord. I'm very good at what I do."

"Yes, I'm certain you are."

The question remains, however, what exactly is it that you're doing?

Seven

Alex briskly shuffled the cards. As if she weren't already distracted enough this evening with her attempts to detect the raspy whisper she'd heard in Lord Malloran's study last night, now she was further unsettled by Lord Sutton's nearness. Lady Newtrebble, who hovered nearby, all but quivering with anticipation, only added to her discomfort.

Still shuffling, she asked, "What question would you like answered, Lord Sutton?"

"The one that is clearly on everyone's mind. Who am I going to marry?"

With a nod, she set the deck on the table. "Cut the deck, once, with your left hand."

As he did so, he asked, "Why my left hand?"

"It helps impart your personal energy to the deck." Without another word, she turned over the cards that would predict his immediate future. And caught her breath.

Deceit. Betrayal. Treachery. Illness. Danger. Death. All the same things she'd seen during their reading that afternoon. And the last card, which denoted the single entity around which all the others revolved, indicated . . .

A dark-haired woman.

If she'd been capable of doing so, she would have laughed at the irony. At least she wouldn't have to lie about seeing a blonde in his future. Of course, the bad news was that the brunette would most likely be the death of him.

"What do you see?"

Her first impulse was to immediately tell him, warn him, but given their lack of privacy, this was neither the time nor place. Especially since his skepticism regarding her reading's veracity meant he'd require some convincing. But convince him she must, for based on this reading, she had no doubt danger awaited him.

Later. She would tell him later. Right now she had that much-needed sovereign to earn.

"I see a woman in your future," she said.

He spread his hands and smiled. "Well, that sounds promising. Can you tell me her name?"

"The spirits, the cards, they are not indicating a name, but . . ." She paused for dramatic effect.

"But what?" Lady Newtrebble interjected. "Who is the chit?"

"She is considered beautiful—"

"Of course she is," Lady Newtrebble said in a triumphant tone.

"—Intelligent—"

"Naturally," Lady Newtrebble said, making a rolling motion with her hand. "Continue."

"I believe it is *my* fortune that's being told, Lady Newtrebble," Lord Sutton said in a dry voice.

"Oh. Yes. Of course. Carry on, Madame Larchmont."

"And she is a brunette," Alex said. "With brown eyes."

A deafening silence engulfed the trio, broken by Lady

Newtrebble's *harrumph*. "What nonsense is this? She is nothing of the kind. She is a blue-eyed blonde."

Alex shook her head. "I'm afraid the cards indicate— very clearly and most emphatically—that the woman destined for Lord Sutton is a brown-eyed brunette." She looked at him across the table. "Do you know anyone of that description, my lord?"

"Half the women in England answer that description, as do half the women attending this party." He studied her intently for several long seconds, then said, "Yourself included, Madame."

Her insides fluttered, and if she hadn't been rendered speechless by his words and the compelling look in his eyes, she would have laughed. She was the last woman in the entire kingdom who would be destined for this man.

Before she could think of a reply, Lady Newtrebble said, "Well, I hope you'll remember that this fortune-telling is merely a harmless amusement, my lord."

"I'll keep that in mind every moment I'm searching for my brown-eyed brunette future wife," he said solemnly. "You have my deepest gratitude, Lady Newtrebble, for allowing Madame Larchmont to bring me this news during your soiree. I'm certain if the story appears in the *Times*, your name and this delightful party will be prominently mentioned."

Lady Newtrebble blinked, then her eyes narrowed with unmistakable avarice. "The *Times*. Yes. They'll certainly want to know all about this." She excused herself, and Alex heaved an inward sigh of relief.

"Nicely done," Lord Sutton said in an undertone.

"Thank you. I trust my performance was acceptable?"

"Yes. I'll pay your fee tomorrow when you come to the town house for my reading." He rose, but rather than leaving, he set his palms on the table and leaned toward her. "May I escort you home after the party?"

His voice was low, compelling, and his eyes appeared

impossibly green and gave away nothing of his thoughts. The prospect of being alone with him, in the privacy of his carriage, sitting close, in the dark, sent an unwanted tingle down her spine—a tingle she wished she could say was apprehension but could only be called what it was. Anticipation.

She should refuse, wanted to refuse, and surely she would have, except she needed to tell him what she'd actually read in the cards. Grasping on to that excuse, yet refusing to appear eager, she said, "It is not necessary—"

"I know it is not necessary, Madame. But as a gentleman, I cannot, in good conscience, allow you to take a hack home, especially so late at night. A lady should not be out without a proper escort in a city so rife with crime."

A lady. Alex swallowed the humorless sound that rose in her throat, barely refraining from pointing out that she was not now, nor would she ever be, a lady.

"You're very gallant, my lord."

"And very accustomed to getting what I want."

She raised a brow. "Which tempts me to refuse on those grounds alone."

"I hope you'll fight that particular temptation."

Something in his voice, in the way he said *temptation*, in the way he was looking at her . . . her heart stuttered. "It is necessary to fight temptation, my lord."

"In some cases, yes."

"Not all?" Dear God, was that breathless sound her voice?

His gaze flicked to her lips, halting her breath. With his gaze once again steady on hers, he said, "No, Madame. Not in all cases. May I escort you home?"

"Very well." Her pride forced her to add, "I'll accept your offer, as there is something I wish to discuss with you."

He smiled. "Not a raise in your rates, I hope."

"No, but that is an excellent idea."

"No, it most emphatically is not. However, I *do* have an idea that *is* excellent."

When he didn't elaborate, she prompted, "And what would that excellent idea be?"

His lips curved slowly upward, and he smiled into her eyes. She barely resisted the urge to fan herself with her gloved hand. Good Lord, the man was . . . potent. And seemingly without trying. Heaven help the woman who attempted to resist him should he actually put any effort into charming her.

"I thought you'd never ask, Madame. I shall answer your question during the carriage ride home."

"And what am I supposed to do until then? Wither away from curiosity?"

"No." He leaned closer and she was treated to a hint of freshly laundered linen. "You are to think of me," he said softly. "And wonder what my excellent idea is."

Before she could so much as breathe, let alone fashion a reply, he turned and walked away, melting into the crowd.

You are to think of me.

She blew out a long, slow breath. Most likely that would not present a problem. Indeed, since she'd seen him last night at the Malloran soiree, she'd found it nearly impossible to think of anything *but* him.

Three hours later, after giving her final reading of the night, Alex was, as she had been since he'd left her, thinking about Lord Sutton. Just as she had been while conducting her readings for more than a dozen guests. And while listening carefully to all the voices floating around her, wondering if she'd again hear the husky rasp from Lord Malloran's study, not at all certain she wished to hear that voice again. For if she did, then what would she do?

Since he'd melted into the crowd, she'd forcibly kept her attention focused on the parade of inquirers who'd sat opposite her, not allowing her gaze to stray and seek him out. Still, he'd occupied every corner of her mind, which in itself was disturbing enough. But even more unsettling was the *way* he occupied her mind. The disconcerting direction of her thoughts.

His hair . . . it looked so thick and shiny, beckoning her to touch. How would it feel to sift her fingers through those silky, dark strands?

And his eyes. So deeply green. So frustratingly unreadable. Yet so devastatingly attractive when they glittered with a hint of humor. What would they look like filled with desire?

Filled with desire for *her*?

A dangerous thought she'd pushed aside more times than she cared to contemplate.

Yet no sooner did she push away thoughts of his eyes than she found herself dwelling on his broad shoulders, the fascinating way he filled out his formal black jacket and breeches. His arms looked so strong . . . what would they feel like wrapped around her, holding her close against him?

And then there was his mouth . . . that beautiful, masculine mouth whose lips drew her gaze like a starving man to a feast. How would those lips feel beneath her fingertips—soft? Firm? Both? How would his mouth feel brushing over hers? God help her, she wanted to know. Desperately. And she greatly feared that if given the opportunity to know, she wouldn't be able to resist.

All the feminine urges and yearnings and curiosity she'd ruthlessly suppressed in the past now felt about to burst from their confines, like an overripe fruit rupturing its skin. For the first time, she longed to shed her *Madame* title, to indulge in her fantasies with the man who'd inspired them since the moment she'd seen him at Vauxhall four years ago.

A sound of self-disgust rose in her throat, and she pressed her lips together to suppress it. As she must suppress these torturous, ridiculous thoughts. And inappropriate, impossible questions to which she'd never know the answers. Yet even as her common sense told her that, sensual images of him continued to bombard her, which thoroughly irked her. She had no wish to harbor such thoughts about *any* man, but if she was going to, why, oh why, did it have to be *this* man? A man she could never have? Who was wrong for her in every conceivable way? Whom she would never be able to touch or kiss?

Thoroughly annoyed at herself, she gathered up her cards. Her last inquirer had left the table several minutes ago, and she'd sat here like a dolt, idiotically mooning over a man so far above her social strata it was laughable.

After wrapping her cards in their square of bronze silk, she reached down and felt beneath the long white damask tablecloth to locate her reticule. When she couldn't find it, she leaned lower, lifting the cloth to peer beneath the table. Spying the bag just out of reach, she stretched lower still. Her fingers had just brushed the velvet drawstring when she heard a raspy whisper say, "I'm afraid that's impossible."

Alex froze. All the tiny hairs on the back of her neck jumped to attention, and an icy finger raced down her spine. She recognized that voice. Dear God, she'd never forget it. Heart pounding, she shot upright. A group of people were passing by the table, presumably toward the foyer to depart. Four men, two women, all of whom she recognized, all well-known members of Society. As they passed, she noticed another group consisting of three men standing about ten feet away. And a trio of women next to them. Again, all respected members of the aristocracy. Two footmen stood nearby as well, relieving the departing guests of their empty glasses. She strained her ears, listening, but none of the voices were the raspy whisper. Whoever had spoken was either now silent—or had resumed a normal speaking voice.

From which group had the voice come? God help her, she wasn't certain she wanted to know. That person planned to see someone dead next week, and most likely was responsible for Lord Malloran's and his footman's deaths. Most likely because of the note she'd written. She had no desire to become a corpse. But the only way to stop this was to find out who the killer was. Before someone else died. Namely her.

Cold fear gripped her, but she had to find out who had spoken. She stood and quickly shoved her cards into her bag. Then she turned to hurry around the table. And walked into something solid. Something solid that smelled of clean linen with a hint of sandalwood. Something that gripped her upper arms and said in an amused voice, "If bumping into me is going to be a habit, I must say that I prefer the seclusion of the garden to the crowded drawing room."

Alex's heart thumped, and, to her horror, instead of pulling back, or even remaining perfectly still, she moved her nose closer to his shirtfront and drew in another Lord-Sutton-scented breath. For the space of several rapid heartbeats she felt safe, for the first time in her life. As if she were wrapped in strong, protective arms. An utterly insane notion she instantly shoved aside.

Light-headed from the combination of his scent and the warmth from his hands easing down her arms, she had to force her feet to step backwards. When she did, their gazes met. He still held her upper arms, and she found it difficult to breathe while they continued to stare at each other. Then he frowned.

"What's wrong?" he asked.

"N . . . Nothing."

His fingers tightened, and he leaned closer, lowering his voice. "*Something* is wrong. You're pale and trembling."

The weight of a stare other than his pressed upon her, again raising the fine hairs on the back of her neck. She scanned the people standing near the table, yet no one was looking at her.

He cast his own quick look around, his gaze raking over the group standing nearby before returning his attention to her. "Did someone say something to upset you?"

There was no missing the ice lurking beneath his calmly spoken words, and for an insane instant she experienced a feminine thrill such as she'd never known. He looked as if he were prepared to do battle with anyone who'd dare say anything untoward to her. As if he intended to protect her against harm—

A shot of annoyance, at her herself, cut off the ridiculous thought. He wouldn't do any such thing. Why would he risk so much as wrinkling his jacket for her? And even if he did, she didn't need anyone to protect her or do battle for her. She'd done fine on her own all these years. More irritation flooded her for allowing her distress to show so plainly. Gathering her self-possession, she lifted her chin and stepped back. His fingers slipped from her arms, but his sharp gaze never strayed from hers.

"No one said anything to me, my lord. But even if someone had, I don't see why you would concern yourself."

"You don't?"

"No. I'm perfectly capable of issuing a set-down should the occasion call for it. If I'm pale, it's merely because I'm fatigued. I find it draining to conduct so many readings in one sitting."

"Communing with the spirits is exhausting?"

She ignored his dry tone. "Yes, as a matter of fact, it is."

"Then, by all means, let's get you home."

Less than five minutes later Alex sat across from him in the confines of his luxurious coach. The thick, velvet squabs ensconced her in delicious softness, and her eyes slid closed as a sigh of pleasure escaped her.

"Better than a hack?" came his deep voice, laced with amusement.

Her eyes popped open. He leaned back in the seat opposite her, watching her through hooded eyes, a half smile curving one corner of his mouth.

"A bit," she said, matching his light tone. Even though she sternly reminded herself that this glimpse into luxury was fleeting, she was determined to enjoy her few moments of comfort.

Except it was difficult to feel completely comfortable with Lord Sutton's unsettling gaze resting upon her, not to mention the lingering doom predicted by his card reading and the possible threat to her from the raspy-voiced killer.

Silence stretched between them. Did he feel this same undercurrent of tension as she? She needed to warn him about what she'd read in his cards, but he looked preoccupied. Troubled. Deciding to fill the noiseless void before broaching the subject uppermost on her mind, she asked, "How was your evening?"

Instead of tossing off a reply, he appeared to seriously consider her question. Finally, he said, "Tiring. Forgettable. Yours?"

She was tempted merely to echo his sentiments, but while her evening had been tiring, it hadn't been forgettable, for which she blamed him entirely. Well, that and the fact that someone who'd surely like to see her with her toes cocked up had only moments ago stood close enough to touch.

"My evening was . . . interesting," she said.

"How so?"

"I enjoy meeting people. Learning about them through their readings."

"I'm envious. Perhaps I should take up card reading. I'm afraid I do not find fending off matchmaking mothers or attempting to converse with their vapid nitwit daughters in the least bit interesting." He leaned forward, and Alex's breath caught at his sudden nearness. Less than three feet separated his face from hers, a distance that simultaneously felt much too close and not nearly close enough.

Resting his elbows on his spread knees, he loosely clasped his hands and looked at her through eyes that glittered with a hint of deviltry. "While I appreciate your very convincing claim—for which I paid a fortune, by the way—that the woman destined for me has dark hair, I really would have preferred something a bit more exact. Something, *anything*, that would save me the pains of discussing the weather with another gaggle of giggling girls." He shook his head. "Can none of them carry on an even remotely intelligent conversation?"

"Most likely they are merely nervous in your presence, my lord."

"Nervous?"

"Surely you can understand that a young, inexperienced woman might find a man like you intimidating."

One dark brow shot up. "Actually, no. And what, exactly, is a man like me?"

"You're being deliberately obtuse, my lord. Your position in Society alone is enough to render many people tongue-tied, let alone a young woman. Especially one who is accompanied by a matchmaking mother and who wishes to impress you."

"*You* do not appear to find me intimidating, nor are

you tongue-tied in my presence. A fact that cost me a great deal of money this evening."

"But I am not a young, inexperienced girl bent on impressing you, my lord."

"From the standpoint of my rapidly diminishing funds, that is a pity indeed." He bent his head and appeared to study her gloved hands, filling her with the urge to bury her hands beneath the folds of her gown. Then he looked up, pinning her with a serious gaze. "So a man like me is one who is titled?"

"Yes."

"I see. And that's it? Nothing else?"

Colin waited for her answer, every muscle inexplicably tense, telling himself that he didn't care a jot what she said. That if she only saw him as a title and nothing more, it didn't matter at all.

A glimmer of mischief kindled in her eyes. "You're casting about for compliments, my lord. And in an entirely shameless manner."

Was he? Bloody hell, he didn't know. It wasn't something he normally did, but then he normally never felt this thrown off-balance in a woman's presence.

"Not compliments," he said after considering, "but simply your meaning. Of course, if your meaning happens to be complimentary, so much the better."

"And if it doesn't happen to be complimentary?"

"I'd still like to know. Of course, it could lessen your chances of bilking me out of another sovereign anytime soon."

Her lips twitched. "In that case, I meant a man of your commanding bearing, superior intelligence, and passable good looks."

His brows shot up. *"Passable?"*

"I, of course, meant your *superior* good looks."

"I thought it was my intelligence you found superior."

"As well as your looks."

"Two seconds ago, you found my looks only passable."

She smiled. "But in a most superior way."

His gaze dropped to her curved lips, and the carriage suddenly seemed bereft of air. The urge to give in to the longing to touch her that had clawed at him all evening threatened to overwhelm him. He gripped his hands together, fighting the need, because he strongly suspected that if he gave in, a single touch wouldn't be enough.

Deciding his best recourse was to change the subject, he said, "You told me you accepted my offer to escort you home because you wished to discuss something with me."

The amusement faded from her eyes, and he instantly missed it. Although he should be happy it was gone as he found it far too attractive and tempting. But bloody hell, she was no less attractive or tempting without it. Perhaps if he tossed a sack over her head . . . but no, he'd still be able to see her luscious curves. A full-body sack—that's what he needed. To cover her from head to toe. And if the sack happened to mask her alluring orangey scent, so much the better.

"I wished to discuss your card reading."

Her words yanked him from his brown study. "Oh? Which one? This afternoon's, which cost a small fortune, this evening's which cost a larger fortune, or tomorrow's, which I suspect will somehow end up costing me a larger fortune still?"

"This evening's. Because of Lady Newtrebble's presence, I did not tell you everything I saw." Her gloved fingers plucked at the folds in her gown. "I'm afraid the cards revealed all the same distressing things I saw earlier today, my lord. The deceit, betrayal, and treachery." Her voice dropped to a whisper. "The illness, danger, and death."

"I see." He studied her for several seconds, and while her expression gave nothing away, her manner seemed genuinely distressed. A fissure of unease crept down his spine. His gut had been telling him that he faced the same things she'd seen in his cards. Could there be any truth to what she read, or was it merely a parlor trick and coincidence?

He shook his head. Bloody hell, he was turning into a fanciful nodcock. This woman was clever, and he'd be a fool to underestimate her. If she predicted a rosy future for him, their sessions would end. By predicting doom and gloom, she no doubt hoped to keep him interested—enough to continue paying her outrageous fees.

"Given how we've agreed that women say one thing and mean another, am I to take it that 'deceit, betrayal, and treachery' actually means I'm going to come into large sums of money and find the woman of my dreams?"

"This is no joking matter, my lord."

"Don't disarrange yourself, Madame. I've no wish to insult you, but as I told you from the outset, I hold little belief in card readings."

She frowned and leaned forward. "You must be wary. Careful—"

"I always am, so please do not distress yourself further on my account. Now, tell me. Did you do as I suggested?"

"Suggested?"

"Yes. I told you to think of me." When she appeared completely nonplussed, he added softly, "And wonder what my excellent idea is."

She blinked then lifted her chin. "I was so occupied with my readings, I'm afraid I didn't give the matter any thought."

He shook his head. "Pity. As I'd hoped to tempt you.

But clearly you are not a woman who gives in to temptation."

"No, I'm not. Most definitely not."

Reaching into the darkened corner of his seat, he lifted a small, linen-wrapped bundle. "An admirable virtue, Madame. I applaud your resolve. However, I am not made of such stern stuff." He unwrapped the bundle then watched her eyes widen.

"What are those?" she asked, leaning closer.

"Miniature cakes. The insides are layers of chocolate cake and raspberry cream. Each creation is then dipped in chocolate and topped with a dab of creamy frosting."

"Oh . . . my." Her tongue peeked out to wet her lips, a pink flick that stilled him. "How did such lovely things come to be in your carriage?"

"My cook prepared them. I pilfered these four and hid them in the carriage so I could eat them on the way home. My excellent idea was to enjoy them with someone who shares my weakness for sweets." He blew out an exaggerated breath. "Alas, as you gave the matter no thought, 'tis clear you're not interested."

"Oh, but—"

"Nor are you a woman who gives in to temptation." He reached out and waved the bundle beneath her nose. "Pity."

Her nostrils flared, and her eyes closed briefly. Her lips parted, drawing his attention to her lush mouth. Then she cleared her throat. "My lord, I believe we'd agreed that it isn't necessary to fight temptation in all cases."

"Actually, while I recall saying as much, I've no recollection that you agreed."

"Certainly I meant to. Especially as frosted cakes are involved." Her gaze flicked down to the treats he held. "Lovely, delicious-looking, sweet-smelling frosted cakes. I think your idea to enjoy them with someone who shares your weakness for sweets is beyond excellent. Indeed, I'm tempted to call it genius."

He smiled. "Then I *have* managed to tempt you."

"I fear I've folded like a house of fortune-telling cards."

"My dear Madame Larchmont, given these cakes, even *I* could have predicted that outcome." He picked up one of the treats and held it out. When she reached for it, he pulled back his hand and shook his head. "You'll stain your gloves. Allow me." He extended his hand and held the morsel in front of her lips.

Her startled gaze met his, and he could almost see her internal struggle as she debated propriety over longing for the treat. Finally, she leaned forward and took a delicate bite.

Her lips brushed his fingertips, shooting heat up his arm. But that heat seemed cool compared to the inferno she ignited when her eyes slid slowly closed, and a low moan of pleasure rumbled in her throat. Transfixed, he watched her lips slowly move as she savored the bite of cake. When she finished, she ran the tip of her tongue over her lips to capture any remaining flavor. His entire body tightened, and he had to press his own lips together to stifle a groan.

She expelled a long sigh that sounded like a contented purr. Then her eyes opened, and she looked at him with a glazed expression through half-closed lids.

"Ooooooh, my," she whispered. "That was ... lovely."

Bloody hell. Lovely didn't even begin to describe it. With her lips parted and moist and her eyelids drooping, she looked aroused and more delicious than any sweet he'd ever seen. And by God, he wanted to taste her more than he'd ever desired any sweet.

He wasn't certain how long he sat there, simply

gaping at her, but finally she blinked, and said, "You're staring, my lord."

He had to swallow twice to locate his voice. "No, I'm . . . admiring." Without taking his gaze from her, he moved to sit on the seat next to her. Raising the uneaten half to her lips, he said, "For you."

"You don't want it?"

God help him, at the moment his entire existence boiled down to the word *want*. "I want you to have it," he said in a husky rasp he barely recognized.

He touched the morsel to her mouth, and she parted her lips. After slowly sliding the bite-sized portion into her mouth, he withdrew his hand, dragging the tip of his index finger across her lower lip, leaving a glistening film of melted chocolate behind.

Her pupils flared, and she pressed her lips together, catching his fingertip. The erotic sight and breath-stealing sensation of her lips surrounding his fingertip rendered him immobile. Heat engulfed him, and his heart pounded, pumping fire to every nerve ending. His finger slowly slid free, and he watched every nuance of her expression as she ate the offering, growing more aroused with each passing second. Damn it, when had watching someone eat become so sensual? So sexually charged?

Her eyes slid closed, and her jaw slowly moved as she chewed, eliciting a low growl of delight as she swallowed. Then her tongue slowly swept across her bottom lip, erasing the thin gloss of chocolate he'd left there.

Then she opened her eyes. "That was marvelous."

"For me as well." His voice sounded as if he'd swallowed gravel.

"But you didn't have any."

"I'd prefer to taste yours." Angling his head, he brushed his lips over hers. She drew in quick breath, then went perfectly still. "Sweet," he murmured, touching his lips to hers again. "Delicious." *More. Must have more.*

Cupping her face in his hands, he kissed each corner of her mouth, then lightly ran his tongue over her full bottom lip. Her lips parted on a tiny, breathless sound, and he instantly took advantage, settling his mouth on hers. And was immediately lost.

Had any woman ever tasted this luscious? This warm and delectable? No . . . only this woman. This woman who'd haunted him for four years. This woman whom he'd never expected to see again, touch again, anywhere other than in his dreams. This woman whom he'd somehow known, in his heart, would taste like this. Utterly perfect.

With a groan, he slipped one hand into her soft hair and the other around her waist, pressing her closer while his tongue explored the velvety sweetness of her mouth. Urgency pumped through him, overwhelming him with need, a need that multiplied when she rubbed her tongue against his, tentatively at first, then with a responsiveness that shaved away another layer of his rapidly vanishing control.

Bloody hell, he wanted to simply devour her. A searing, raw desperation unlike anything he'd ever experienced gripped him, forcing him to battle back the overpowering urge to unceremoniously lift her skirts and bury himself inside her—a humbling, confusing reaction as he'd always considered himself in command of his actions. His reactions. And certainly a man of some finesse. But with a single kiss, she stripped away his control, leaving him all but trembling, burning with a desire, a lust, unlike anything he'd ever before known, and one he wasn't certain how long he'd be able to contain.

Still, he couldn't stop . . . not yet. Not while his fingers still explored the silk of her hair. Not while the captivating scent of oranges rose from her skin. Not while her enticing mouth fitted so perfectly against his.

Closer . . . damn it, he needed her closer. Now. Without breaking their kiss, he lifted her, settling her across his lap. A deep groan vibrated in his throat when her curves settled against him, her hip pressing against his erection. He spread his legs, hoping to relieve the throbbing ache, but the movement only served to inflame him more.

All concept of time and place fled, leaving only hot want and desperate, clawing need in its wake. Mindless, his fingers plucked the pins from her hair, tossing them carelessly onto the carriage floor. He sifted his fingers through the long, silky skeins, releasing the faint scent of oranges as the locks fell down her back and over her shoulders to envelop them in a silken cloud of fragrant curls.

She moaned and shifted against him, her hip sliding against his straining erection, and another groan rose in his throat. Bloody hell. He felt as if he were unraveling. At a frantic pace that gained momentum with each passing second.

A small voice of reason worked its way through the fog of lust engulfing him, warning him to slow down, to cease this madness, but he shoved the admonition aside, and instead ran one hand down her back to her buttocks, pressing her more firmly against him, while his other hand explored the satiny length of her neck. His fingers skimmed over the delicate hollow of her throat, then dipped lower to explore the swells of her breasts where they met the material of her gown. Soft . . . she was so incredibly soft. And damn it, he was so incredibly hard, and he wanted her so very badly—

The carriage jerked to a jarring halt, jolting him from his sensual haze. He slowly lifted his head and looked at her. And bit back a groan. With her eyes closed, shallow breaths coming from between her parted lips, moist and swollen from his kiss, and her hair in complete disarray from his impatient hands, she looked wanton and aroused and more desirable than any woman he'd ever seen. His gaze dipped lower, riveting on the sight of his hand resting on her chest. Slowly he splayed his fingers, captivated by how dark and rough his skin looked against the pale delicateness of hers. Her heartbeat thumped, hard and frantic against his palm, a rhythm that matched his own.

His gaze wandered slowly back up to her face, roaming over each imperfect feature that somehow looked so . . . perfect. Unable to stop himself from touching her, his fingers, still not quite steady, followed the same path as his gaze, brushing along her jaw, over her smooth cheeks, down the short slope of her nose, then tracing the lush shape of her mouth. Her eyelids fluttered open, and he found himself looking directly into her dazed eyes.

Desire speared him low and hard, along with something else that felt suspiciously like possessiveness. Something that whispered *this woman belongs to me* through his mind. She lifted her hand from where it rested on his chest and slowly, hesitantly, feathered her fingertips over his forehead, brushing back a stray lock of hair. The simple gesture, combined with the look of utter wonder glowing in her eyes, made his heart roll over.

Taking her hand, he pressed a quick kiss against her gloved palm. "We've arrived."

She blinked several times, then, as if a bucket of cold water had been tossed on her, she shot upright, a look of sheer panic filling her eyes. "Oh, dear. I . . . oh, what have I done?" She pushed away from him, then her hands flew to her hair, which tumbled over her shoulders. She began frantically looking about, clearly for her hairpins, and he grasped her hands.

"Calm yourself," he said gently. "I'll help you gather

your hairpins." But before he could do so, she snatched her hands from his as if he'd burned her and grabbed her reticule.

"I must go," she said, reaching for the door.

"Wait," he said, stilling her hand.

She turned to him, her eyes filled with distress and unmistakable anger. Whether that anger was directed toward herself or him, or both of them, he didn't know. "Wait? For what, my lord? So I can further shame myself?"

"You've done nothing to be ashamed of."

A bitter sound passed her lips. "Haven't I? Haven't we both?"

"I don't see how."

She lifted her chin. "Are you in the habit of passionately kissing married women?"

"No. I've never kissed a married woman." His gaze probed hers, willing her to tell him he still hadn't. When she remained silent, he added, "Are you in the habit of passionately kissing other men?"

A stricken look filled her eyes, then her gaze hardened. "No. I . . . I never have. I don't know what came over me. I only know it will not, cannot happen again. I beg your most sincere pardon. I intend to forget this ever happened, and I suggest you do the same."

Without another word, she jerked open the carriage door, then exited as if pursued by the devil. As he had last night, he waited for her to round the corner, then left the coach, instructing his coachman to return to the town house. He followed her through the dark streets, wincing at the pain pulling in his thigh at keeping up with her swift pace. After making certain she arrived at her building, he stood in the shadows, watching the window of the third room on the second floor. Less than a minute later he saw the glow of a candle flare, and he knew she was safe.

He watched for several more minutes, then was about to depart when he sensed he was being observed. He quickly retrieved his knife from his boot. Palming the blade, his gaze swept the area, but he noted nothing out of the ordinary. The sensation faded and his instincts told him that whoever had been silently watching him was gone. Still palming his blade, senses on alert, he walked quickly home.

He arrived at his town house without incident, and the minute he closed the door behind him, he leaned back against the oak panel and rubbed his aching thigh while her words echoed in his ears. *I intend to forget this ever happened, and I suggest you do the same . . . it will not, cannot happen again.*

He was no fortune-teller, but he knew she was wrong in every respect. She wouldn't forget that kiss any more than he would. Bloody hell, he now knew what it felt like to be struck by lightning. The taste and feel of her was permanently imprinted in his mind, as was her response to him. And as unwise as it might be, it most certainly would happen again.

He intended to see to it.

Eight

FROM *THE LONDON TIMES* SOCIETY PAGE:

Brunettes of England rejoice! At Lord and Lady Newtrebble's soiree, the ever-popular and always right Madame Larchmont read the cards of a certain viscount who is looking for a bride, and the fortune-teller predicted that the woman destined for the very eligible Lord Sutton will be a dark-haired beauty. A crushing disappointment for the blond beauties out this Season, but clearly they'll need to set their caps elsewhere. Now, the only question remaining is who is this dark-haired lady Lord Sutton will marry?

She walked slowly toward him, her footfalls silenced by the thick Axminster rug in his bedchamber, her hips swaying with a sinuous rhythm that quickened his breath and riveted him in place. Her expression was no longer unreadable, and there was no mistaking her intent. Dark eyes the color of melted chocolate glittered with a wickedly sensual light, and a siren's half smile touched the corners of her plump lips. Her filmy aqua dressing gown floated around her—a shimmering silk column edged with ivory lace that provided teasing hints of the luscious curves beneath with every step. Her hair fell over her shoulders and down her back to her waist, a shiny waterfall of thick, shiny dark curls.

She halted when less than an arm's length separated them. Reaching out, she settled her hands on his bare chest, dragging a low groan of pleasure from him.

"Alexandra . . ."

He tried to reach for her, but it felt as if a weight sat upon him, and he couldn't move. With a seductive smile, she rose on her toes and lifted her face and . . .

Licked his cheek.

Frustrated, he tried again to move, desperate to touch her, kiss her, but his shoulders were held immobile by invisible hands. She rewarded him with another wet lick on the cheek. Clearly she required a few lessons in the art of kissing. His entire face was wet and by God, slimy as well—

With a groan, he opened his eyes. And found himself staring up into a black, jowly muzzle and wide-set dark brown eyes.

"What the hell—?" His words were cut off by the swipe of a large, wet, canine tongue across his chin.

"*Blech!*" He grimaced and tried to lift his arm to wipe his face, but the weight of the monstrous dog lying across his chest rendered him immobile. Paws the size of plates held his shoulders pinned to the bed.

Recognition hit him, and he narrowed his eyes, then shifted his head on the pillow to avoid another enthusiastic doggie kiss. Instead, he was pelted with a barrage of hot doggie breath followed by a deep, gravelly *woof*.

"B.C.," he muttered, glaring at Nathan's mastiff, who could easily be dubbed the Largest Dog in the Kingdom. "How the bloody hell did you get in here?"

"He came in with me," came Nathan's deep, familiar voice near the window. "In case you haven't noticed, he's ecstatic to see you."

Colin turned his head—the only part of his upper body he could move—and blinked at the bright sunlight pouring in through the window. The initial wave of happiness at seeing his brother was severely curtailed by the lung-crushing load pinning him to the mattress.

"In case you haven't noticed," he said through gritted teeth, "this beast weighs at least twelve stone." His words were rewarded with another swipe of canine tongue against his neck. He swiveled his attention back to B.C. and glowered. "Stop that!" B.C. shot him a reproachful look, then appeared to grin at him.

"Fourteen stone, actually," Nathan said.

Another doggie kiss dampened Colin's jaw. "Devil take it, stop that!" With a mighty heave, he managed to roll from beneath the dog's crushing weight and sit up. He then transferred his glower to his brother. "His breath is not exactly flower fresh, you know. What on earth are you feeding him?"

"His last snack was that boot," Nathan said, nodding toward the desk.

Colin followed his brother's gaze, and his jaw tightened at the sight of the mangled leather. "Those were my favorite pair."

"Not to worry, he only nibbled on one of them."

"How bloody delightful."

"You'll recall that B.C. does stand for 'Boot Chewer.' "

"I'm not likely to forget, seeing the souvenir he left of my new Hessian."

Nathan pushed off from the windowsill, where he'd rested his hips, and approached the bed. "About time you woke up. I wrote in my letter that I planned to arrive today, and I've been waiting for half an hour."

"Did it not occur to you to wait in the drawing room?"

"My, my, I'd forgotten how grumpy you are when you first awaken."

"I'm not grumpy, I'm . . . surprised. And slathered with wet doggie boot-scented slime." He stabbed his fingers through his hair. "What time is it?"

"Nearly two o'clock. Makes one wonder what you were doing last night to exhaust yourself so." Nathan grinned. "Aren't you happy to see me?"

Colin tried to maintain his scowl, but couldn't quite pull it off. "Actually I am. I just would have been happier to see you about an hour from now. When I was awake. And coherent. And dressed." After snatching his silk robe from the end of the bed—barely avoiding another swipe of B.C.'s tongue—he shrugged into the garment, tied the sash, then rose. Holding out his hand, he said, "Good to see you, brother."

Nathan clasped his hand, and for several seconds Colin stared into his brother's eyes while an unstoppable wealth of emotion swamped him. In spite of their different interests, they'd always been close growing up, a bond that had grown even stronger when they'd taken on the hazardous duty of spying on the French for the Crown. Or had grown stronger until Colin had made a terrible mistake and nearly lost Nathan.

The same guilt and remorse that struck Colin every time he thought of it hit him now, followed first by a swell of gratitude that Nathan had forgiven him for believing he'd betray his country, then by the shame he still experienced because Nathan had never doubted *him*—even when he'd had good reason to. No, unlike him, when his trustworthiness had come into question, Nathan's faith in him had been absolute. Unwavering. Unconditional.

Colin had always considered himself an intelligent man. A man of honor, integrity, and loyalty. But on that horrible night four years ago, the night he'd been shot, those qualities upon which he most prided himself had been put to the test, and he'd failed every one of them. Nine months ago, Nathan had returned to Cornwall for the first time since that night, giving Colin the chance to mend their fractured relationship. Even though Colin had atoned for his mistake, and they'd repaired the rift, part of him still didn't feel as if he'd done enough. Didn't feel as if he were worthy and deserving of his brother's forgiveness. One thing was for certain—he had no intention of ever repeating that mistake.

They both moved at the same time, pulling each other into a back-thumping embrace. He blinked several times to rid his eyes of the inexplicable moisture gathering there. By God, he needed to inform Ellis that his bedchamber needed a good airing. Damn it, he could barely swallow for all the dust clogging his throat.

When they stepped apart, Colin studied his brother—who appeared equally affected by the dust—for several seconds. Then he cleared his throat and, in an attempt to lighten the emotion-tinged air, grinned. "Anyone would think that you'd missed me."

In a blink, the old camaraderie between them returned, as if only seven minutes rather than seven months had past since they'd last seen each other.

Nathan shrugged. "Perhaps a bit."

"You look happy," he said.

"I am. A condition I entirely blame on Victoria."

"Clearly married life agrees with you."

An expression filled Nathan's eyes that Colin could only call besotted. His chest tightened with a combination of happiness and envy for his brother.

"Very much," Nathan agreed. His gaze flicked over Colin in an assessing way that made Colin feel like one of his brother's medical patients. "*You* look . . . tired."

"Why, thank you," he said dryly. "Perhaps because I was sound asleep a mere thirty seconds ago." A familiar scent caught his attention, and he sniffed the air just as his stomach rumbled in response. His glance shifted to the oval cherrywood table near the window where Nathan had stood and noted the china cup and plate. Nathan followed his gaze, then said, "I brought you a cup of chocolate and a plate of biscuits."

Colin walked to the table and stared into the cup, which held only the dregs of a dark beverage, then at the half dozen pale crumbs dotting the royal blue Sèvres plate. Blast. Some things never changed between brothers. "So I see. No doubt I'd thank you if you'd actually managed to save me a bit of either."

"You could have enjoyed both had you actually been awake." With an unrepentant grin, Nathan pinched one of the tiny crumbs between his fingers and popped it into his mouth. "Don't forget that famous saying Cook taught us as children: He who snoozes always loses."

"Apparently," Colin muttered darkly. "Which makes me greatly anticipate the time when you next doze off. I suggest you sleep with one eye open."

Nathan muttered something that sounded less than complimentary, then said, "As you showed no signs of rousing, and the chocolate was getting cold, I felt it my duty to make certain Cook's hard work did not go to waste. You know how dutiful I am."

"Yes, you are nothing if not full of duty."

"And naturally one cannot properly enjoy chocolate without dunking biscuits—which were fresh from the oven, by the way." He circled his hand over his stomach and made exaggerated *mmmmmming* noises. "They were *delicious*. I'd intended to save you the last one, but you'll be glad to know I gave it to B.C."

"And why would I be glad to know that?"

"Because the biscuit is the only thing that kept him from gnawing on your other boot."

"Excellent. Because *one* ungnawed boot is very useful to me. Why did it not occur to you to give him the biscuit *before* he made a snack of the first boot?"

"I was occupied."

"Oh? Doing what—besides drinking my chocolate and eating my biscuits?"

"Listening to you." Nathan smiled. "Who is Alexandra?"

Colin's insides tensed, but after years of practice he had no trouble keeping his features impassive. "I've no idea." Which was true. He didn't *really* know who she was. Yet.

Nathan raised one brow. "Surely you must as she inspired quite the lusty moan in you." He clasped his hands to his chest in a dramatic gesture and batted his eyes. "Alexaaaandraaaaa," he cooed in a falsetto voice.

Good God, had he actually believed he'd missed his irritating younger brother? "I'm certain I was merely snoring," he said in a frosty tone. "Or perhaps the noise came from your dog. Who was destroying my boot."

B.C. made a snuffling noise from the bed, where he reclined across the counterpane in all his enormous canine glory. He met Colin's gaze and licked his chops, and inexplicably Colin was hard-pressed not to smile. Then he sighed. The dog was a hazard to footwear, but he was undeniably lovable. Not that he'd ever admit that to Nathan. God no. If he did, he'd find himself saddled with a dozen boot-chewing puppies.

"No, it was you," Nathan insisted. "Maybe you weren't snoring, but you certainly were dead to the world. Late night?"

"As a matter of fact, yes."

"Because of Alexandra?"

An image of her looking aroused and thoroughly kissed flashed through his mind, leaving a trail of heat in its wake. "I don't know what you're talking about." Knowing how observant Nathan was, he strode to his washbasin to cleanse away B.C.'s greeting. "Where is Victoria?" he asked, yanking a hand towel from the brass rod. He shot a pointed look at the door. "Surely your wife is missing your company. And your dog's company as well."

"Not at all," Nathan said, blithely ignoring the hint. "Victoria is off to Bond Street with her father in tow. They're shopping while his household is being polished to within an inch of its life in preparation for the upcoming party he's hosting. As I mentioned in my note, Victoria plans to help him. Act as hostess. They've probably visited every millinery and jewel shop on Bond Street by now." He pulled a comical face and shuddered. "Better him than me. Even watching you snore is preferable to a visit to the shops. And now that you're finally awake, I cannot wait to find out what has precipitated this sudden desire for a wife—a quest, by the way, in which Victoria is determined to help."

Colin lifted his shoulders in a casual shrug. "I'd hardly call it sudden. I've known my entire life that it is my duty to marry and produce an heir. I'd think you would be particularly glad that I'm finally getting around to it."

"Oh, I am. It's about time you decided to settle down and produce those heirs that guarantee the damn title won't get foisted upon me should you kick off early."

Yes, which unfortunately is exactly what my gut keeps warning me about. Nathan was teasing, of course, but he'd unintentionally hit upon the truth—something he had an uncanny knack of doing. Colin briefly considered taking Nathan into his confidence right now, but discarded the idea as a case of poor timing. While he had every intention of discussing his concerns with Nathan— who would understand better than anyone the need to listen to his gut—this was neither the time nor place, especially as he was now pressed for time due to sleeping so late.

"I suppose I'm just curious as to what prompted you finally to get your arse moving," Nathan said. "Why now?"

"Why not now?"

"You're answering a question with a question."

"One of *your* annoying habits as I recall."

"*And* you're attempting to change the subject. So again, I ask—why now?" Nathan's gaze searched his. "Are you all right?"

Colin raked back his hair with an impatient hand. "I'm fine. My decision was partially prompted by you."

"Me?"

"Yes. You and Father. Both basking in marital bliss. Made me realize I wasn't getting any younger, and it was high time I saw to my duty."

"I see. So, have you chosen your bride yet?"

"Hardly. I only arrived in London a few days ago."

"More than enough time to at least whittle down the list of candidates to a manageable number. Any lady in particular standing out in your mind?"

Another image of chocolate-colored eyes and glossy dark hair flashed in his mind. "There are any number of possible candidates," he said vaguely. "I'll have more opportunities tomorrow evening, as I'm attending Lord and Lady Ralstrom's fete."

"So are Victoria and I."

"Looking forward to it, are you?" Colin asked with an inward smirk, knowing how much Nathan deplored Society functions.

"Normally I'd rather be nibbled to death by ducks, but I admit I'm quite looking forward to watching you mull over bridal candidates."

"Speaking of ducks, how are yours?"

"Very happy, thank you for asking."

"They're not *here*, are they?"

Nathan looked like innocence itself, something that instantly rose Colin's suspicions. "Of course not," he answered with an injured sniff.

"Thank God."

"I can only be grateful they didn't hear you say that. They're very fond of *you*, you know. You *are* their uncle."

"I am not an uncle to those ducks. Or your button-eating goat, or the pig or lamb or whatever other beasts you've taken on since I saw you last. Show me a *child*, and I'll happily take the title of doting uncle."

"We're working on it."

"Hmmm, yes, I imagine you are." He heaved an exaggerated sigh. "You know, if you hadn't married Lady Victoria, *I* could have wed her and saved myself all this infernal bride hunting."

Nathan smirked. "She liked me better. She's thinks I'm very clever and unsurpassedly handsome."

"Poor chit must have led a very sheltered life. And clearly she needs spectacles. But still, she's very charming. The least she could have done was have a sister."

"I believe there's a distant cousin in Yorkshire who isn't *too* terribly old and has almost all her teeth. Shall I arrange an introduction?"

"There are privet hedges two stories down, right below that window behind you. Shall I arrange an introduction?"

Nathan laughed, then reached out and clamped a hand on his shoulder. "Never fear, your brother is here.

I'll make it my personal mission to assist you in finding the perfect bride."

"Dear God."

"Not necessary to call upon help from above while I'm here. Not to worry, I've much experience in these matters."

"Indeed? I don't recall that you were actually looking for a bride when Victoria came along."

"And yet I still found her. You see how good I am?"

"You couldn't find your own arse with both hands and the benefit of a detailed map. I'll find my own bride, thank you very much."

Nathan nodded slowly, then stepped back and folded his arms across his chest. "Since you clearly don't wish to discuss your bride search or the mysterious Alexandra whom you claim not to know, why don't you tell me what's bothering you?"

Damn, he was clearly losing his touch if he could be read so easily. He strode to his wardrobe and yanked out a clean shirt. "I'm bothered I slept much later than I intended and am now pressed for time for an appointment."

"Not to worry. I'm sure no one other than I—who knows you so well—would guess you're troubled about something. What is it?"

Colin turned, and their gazes met, Nathan's filled with unmistakable concern. "Let me help," Nathan said quietly.

Guilt grabbed Colin by the throat. Such a simple offer, but one that cut straight to his heart. Because even though they'd made their peace and mended their rift, he still didn't feel he deserved such unconditional consideration. Nathan freely offered to him what he'd withheld four years ago—help with no questions asked. Because he believed in him. Ironic and humbling, as Colin had not doled out a similar offer four years ago.

"I appreciate the offer," he said, then cleared his throat to rid his voice of its oddly husky timbre. "And I would like to discuss something with you—"

"I sense a 'but' coming."

"But unfortunately I have an appointment I must get ready for now."

"Why don't you join us for dinner this evening?"

"All right. But I'd prefer not to discuss this at Wexhall's. Come for breakfast tomorrow, and I'll tell you everything."

Nathan studied him for several more seconds, then asked, "Does whatever's on your mind have something to do with Malloran and his footman turning up dead?"

I sincerely hope not. "Wexhall told you about that?"

"Yes. But even if he hadn't, it's the main topic of conversation no matter where you turn. Are the deaths troubling you?"

"I find them . . . puzzling. I hope I'll know more by the time we talk tomorrow, at which time I'll tell you everything."

While it was clear Nathan wished to ask him more questions, he merely nodded. "Very well. I'll be here for breakfast tomorrow morning. See to it that you're awake."

"See to it that you save me some biscuits and chocolate. Meanwhile, I'll see you tonight at dinner."

"Agreed." Nathan whistled for B.C., who'd clearly heard the word biscuit and, believing a treat was in his immediate future, jumped off the bed to trot after his master. The instant the door closed behind them, Colin hastily dressed. He had a great deal more to find out about Madame Alexandra Larchmont and not much time to do so before she arrived. His heart rate quickened at the thought of seeing her again. Touching her again.

Kissing her again.

But before that happened, there were things they needed to discuss. Certainly things she needed to tell him. And he intended to see to it that she didn't leave here today until she'd done so.

Seated in Logan Jennsen's richly appointed drawing room, Alex studied the cards spread on the table before her. She lifted her gaze to find him regarding her through his intense, dark eyes, with an expression that stilled her. Unlike Colin, there was nothing unreadable or inscrutable in the way this man was looking at her. The desire was unmistakable.

"What do my cards indicate for my future, Madame?" he asked, leaning forward.

She drew a deep breath, noting the pleasant scent of his shaving soap.

"I continue to see a wish for retribution, a deep need to right wrongs done against you. A need to prove yourself. To show people, one person from your past in particular, that you're a force to be reckoned with. I predict more wealth in your future, but also great sorrow. And profound loneliness."

"I see. Tell me, do you think there is a chance that I can change my future? Do something now that will prevent this profound loneliness you predict?"

"I'm certain that if you want companionship, you've only to say so, and you'll be surrounded by people."

"True. But I'm more interested in quality than quantity. For example, I'd prefer to spend my time with one woman who interests me than with a dozen who bore me." With his gaze steady on hers, he said softly, "*You* interest me, Madame."

Before she could reply, he reached out and lightly brushed a single fingertip across her cheek. His touch was warm and gentle, and although unexpected, not at all unpleasant. "Mr. Jennsen—"

"Logan."

"I'm very flattered," she said, meaning it sincerely. "But—"

"No buts," he said, shaking his head. "I just want you to know that I find you . . . refreshing. Much more so than these Society diamonds I'm surrounded by. You don't put on false airs. I come from dirt-poor beginnings and am far more attracted to someone like you, whose nose isn't in the clouds and hasn't had everything handed to her by a butler."

"You barely know me."

"And you barely know me, which is something I'd like, very much, to rectify."

"Some of those Society diamonds are actually very nice."

He shrugged. "Perhaps. But that doesn't change the fact that I still want to get to know you better."

"Logan," she said gently, "I'm married."

His dark gaze narrowed. "Are you? I've some experience with women, and you don't have the 'look' of a married woman about you."

Her heart skipped a beat, and she struggled to remain outwardly poised. "I beg your pardon?"

He leaned forward, pinning her with his compelling gaze. "I think you use 'Madame' for effect in your fortune-telling. And because it affords you freedoms you wouldn't have as an unmarried woman—such as coming to my home unescorted—as well as a buffer between you and any unwanted suitors. I admire your ingenuity. It's precisely what I would do in your position."

Nonplussed, she managed to hold his gaze while debating how to best answer his allegation. Before she could decide however, he continued, "I also suspect you're not married because I cannot imagine a man being fortunate to have you yet allowing another man to see you home from the soirees you attend. If you were mine, I'd damn well escort you home myself and not leave the job to Lord Sutton or anyone else."

Her insides fluttered at the mention of Lord Sutton, a reaction she hid by hoisting a brow. "Perhaps not all men are as possessive as you."

"When it comes to their women, *all* men are possessive. Unless, of course, the relationship is an unsatisfying or unhappy one. So, Madame, am I right? Allow me to assure you that if you confirm my suspicions, I will tell no one."

Part of her warned that to admit the truth was very unwise, that once a secret was told it was no longer a secret. Also, telling him would only serve to encourage his attentions. And she didn't want that.

Did she?

The attentions of a fabulously wealthy, incredibly handsome, intelligent man? her inner voice whispered, incredulous. *Are you mad? What woman* wouldn't *want such a man's attention?*

Yet how could she take such a risk?

"Please know," he said, when she continued to hesitate, "that I'll allow you to dictate how far our relationship does or does not progress. And keep in mind that I've neither a strong desire to remain a bachelor nor a lofty title that must be protected from anyone not of the upper echelons of English Society." Reaching out, he lightly clasped her hand. "At the very least, I would like to offer you my friendship and have yours in return."

An image of Lord Sutton flashed in her mind . . . a man who could never, would never be hers. Logan Jennsen was not only extremely attractive, he was available. And perhaps just what she needed to help her forget Lord Sutton.

"I don't know what to say. I'm . . . intrigued."

A slow, half smile curved his lips. "And hopefully tempted."

Unable to deny it, she nodded. Then reached a compromise with her conscience. "I am. Enough to admit that I can think of no one who would object to me forming a *friendship* with you."

He smiled with genuine pleasure. "Not an admission that you're not married, but still, the best news I've heard in a long time." He lifted her hand to press a kiss to her fingertips, and heat kindled in his eyes. "Friendship is a very good place to start."

After returning home from her extraordinary meeting with Logan, Alex locked the door, then, with her heart pounding, peered out the window at the street below. She couldn't shake the feeling that someone had been watching her, yet nothing appeared amiss.

Moving away from the window, she removed her spencer and bonnet, then paced, willing herself to focus on Logan, a man who wanted her and was free to do so, but her mind stubbornly kept drifting back to Lord Sutton. And the extraordinary kiss they'd shared.

Nothing in her experience had prepared her for him and that devastating kiss. Everything she knew of what occurred between men and women she'd observed on London's streets. Secretive assignations in back alleys, marked by animal grunts and rough sounds, grasping hands and harsh language. Such sights and sounds were impossible to escape, and they'd left her certain that in spite of her natural curiosity and the whispered yearnings of her own body, the actual act—or anything leading up to it—was nothing of which she wanted to partake.

But those few glorious minutes in his arms had stunned and delighted yet confused her. What she'd felt in no way resembled the hastily performed lewd acts she'd witnessed. With that single kiss, he'd opened up floodgates she hadn't fully realized were closed. She'd tasted and touched. And now she wanted more.

Why, oh why, if she were going to have such feelings, such yearnings, couldn't they be directed toward someone who didn't orbit in a social class so far above hers as to be completely out of reach? Someone who wasn't looking for a wife—a fine lady of impeccable breeding. A woman who could never be her.

For her own peace of mind, she should avoid seeing him, stay far away, not put herself close to a temptation she wasn't certain she could resist. Concentrate on someone else, perhaps like Logan Jennsen. But how could she, when Lord Sutton occupied every corner of her mind?

Unfortunately, avoiding him, at least at present, was impossible. She couldn't give up her fortune-telling income from the parties he'd doubtless be attending while searching for his wife—she needed the money too badly. She and Emma had plans for Robbie and all the other children—children whose lives were as wretched as hers had once been. She wanted, needed to help them, and she couldn't just throw away everything she'd worked for, everything that was finally within her reach because of some ridiculous infatuation with a man who next week undoubtedly wouldn't recall her name.

Of course, Logan Jennsen was a rich man—

She cut off the thought before it could take root. Damnation, pursuing a man because of his money was no better than stealing, and she was no longer a thief. And neither was she for sale. There was no doubt in her mind that if she secured funds from Logan for her cause, he'd expect payment—of a sort she wasn't willing to give. No, she would earn her money telling fortunes and retain her soul and dignity in the process.

But as for Lord Sutton . . . there was also the matter

of the danger she'd read in his cards. She couldn't simply walk away from that without trying to determine if she was correct. If today's reading didn't indicate the danger and betrayal she'd previously seen, she'd avoid further temptation and not schedule any more private readings with him, regardless of how much he offered to pay. But if the readings were the same, she'd at least have to try to help him. Attempt to figure out the who, where, and when of whatever threatened him. If she didn't, she wouldn't be able to live with herself.

Hopefully today's reading would show nothing but a bright sunny future filled with a lovely wife and scads of children. Then she could walk away and forget she'd ever met him. Rededicate her energies to building a future for the lost, broken angels of London's mean streets. Allowing Lord Sutton to kiss her had been a mistake. An aberration. One she would no longer dwell upon and one that she certainly wouldn't repeat.

Filled with resolve, she checked the time. Noting it was after two o'clock, she quickly refreshed herself. Emma had already filled the knapsack Alex was to deliver before she'd left to sell her oranges hours ago. After slipping on her gloves, Alex was about to reach for the knapsack when she heard the familiar muffled squeak of the trapdoor opening. Moving across the room, she pushed back the curtain and watched Robbie climb into the room. Relief swamped her. The child hadn't slept here last night, and even though he didn't come every night, she'd still been concerned.

After closing the trapdoor, he stood and looked at her through grave eyes. "Miss Alex," he said. His bottom lip trembled, then he dashed across the room and wrapped his arms around her waist, burying his face in her skirt.

She hugged him tightly, then crouched so she could look him in the eyes. "Are you all right, Robbie?" she asked, her gaze sweeping over him, afraid to hear his answer. His bruises had faded to a dull yellowish green, and she saw no evidence of new ones. Thank God.

He wiped his nose on his sleeve and nodded. "Are ye and Miss Emmie all right?"

"Of course. Except for being worried about you." She brushed back a lock of unkempt hair from his forehead and offered him a smile that she prayed hid the ache in her heart he always inspired. "We missed you last night."

"I tried to come, but I couldn't."

Alex's jaw tightened. She knew what that meant. His father hadn't been drunk enough to pass out and not notice the child's absence.

He hung his head and scuffed the toe of his dirty, worn shoe. "Couldn't get here 'til now to see if ye were all right." He lifted his head. "Ye swear ye're fine?"

"I swear. Miss Emmie, too. Why would you think we weren't?"

" 'Cause o' the man wot were here when I came yesterday. Right in this room, Miss Alex. Caught 'im, I did, when I came fer an orange." His expression turned fierce. "Told 'im I'd gut 'im if he hurt ye."

She stilled. "A man? Here? What did he want?"

"He asked about ye. Gave me a bob, 'e did, but don't worry, I outsmarted 'im and didn't tell him nuthin'."

"A *bob*? That's a grand amount," she said lightly, trying to hide her alarm. Dear God, had Lord Malloran's killer somehow discovered she'd written the note and tracked her down? "Did you recognize this man?"

Robbie shook his head. "Fancy bloke, he were. Rich. Tried to give me less, but I knew he could afford more." He reached into his pocket and pulled out a small bundle wrapped in a dirty piece of cloth, which he held out to her. "Bought meself a sweet roll. I saved half for ye and Miss Emmie. To say thanks fer"—he scuffed the toe of his shoe again—"well, ye know. I know how ye like sweets."

A lump tightened Alex's throat, and it felt as if her chest caved in. There was no mistaking the pride in his voice. Since refusing his gift—one he could ill afford to give—would crush him, she solemnly accepted the bundle, understanding his need to show gratitude. "Thank you, Robbie. This is the finest gift I've ever received. Miss Emmie and I will eat it with our tea." She carefully set down the precious bundle, then rested her hands on his thin shoulders. "Tell me more about this man. What did he look like?"

Robbie scrunched up his face to consider. "Bloke had fine clothes and dark hair. Tall, he was, and wide." He spread his arms to demonstrate. "But not fat, mind ye. Just . . . big. Strong. Picked me right up by me collar he did."

Anger jolted through her. "He hurt you?"

"Nah. Fought him off I did. He was scary, but not half as scary as my pa. Tried to stare me down, but I didn't let him." His face puckered again. "Bloke had real green eyes. Greener than I've ever seen before."

Alex froze. Green eyes? Realization clicked into place, and anger erupted inside her, leaving her feeling like a teakettle about to spew steam. There was no doubt in her mind as to the identity of this green-eyed rich bloke. No wonder she'd sensed someone watching her! He'd followed her. Then invaded her home. Her privacy. Her sanctuary. The children's sanctuary. The ramifications made her head spin.

"He saw me come up through the trapdoor, Miss Alex," Robbie said in a small, watery voice, jerking her attention back to him. In spite of all he'd gone through, she'd never once seen him cry, but he appeared on the verge of doing so now. "I'm sorry. I didn't mean—"

She stopped his words with a gentle finger to his quivering lips. "There's nothing to be sorry about, Robbie. I'm certain that, thanks to your description, I know who the man is."

"Is he a . . . bad man?"

She forced a smile. "No. So you're not to worry. I'll take care of everything. I promise."

Colin watched her building from the same shadowed doorway where he'd stood yesterday. When his quarry finally appeared, she held a knapsack that looked identical to the one she'd carried yesterday.

He followed her to the same building as yesterday, where she entered The Broken Barrel and emerged shortly afterward without the knapsack. She then walked in the direction of Mayfair, presumably to his town house for their appointment.

"What's the plan?" came a deep whisper from directly behind him.

He whipped around and found himself staring at Nathan. "Bloody hell," he hissed. "Where did you come from?"

Nathan cocked a brow. "Our mother's womb, same as you. Do you require a lesson on where babies come from?"

Damn. How had he managed to forget what a bloody pest Nathan could be? Or how light on his feet. Still, it unsettled him that Nathan had been able to sneak up on him so effectively. Didn't bode well for his success. "What are you doing here?"

"The exact question I was about to ask you."

"If I'd wanted you to know, I would have bloody well told you."

"Which you clearly weren't going to do, which is why I was forced to take matters into my own hands and follow you." A smug look crossed his face. "Seems I haven't lost my touch for covert dealings. You, on the other hand, are apparently a bit rusty."

Colin didn't bother to answer. He wasn't certain if he were more annoyed at himself for not detecting Nathan's presence or Nathan for his interference. "We'll discuss this later. Go home."

"Yes, we most certainly shall discuss this later. As for going home, if you think I'm going to leave, you're sadly mistaken. So just tell me the plan. Who was that woman and why are you following her?"

Damn it, why couldn't he have been an only child? Realizing there was no escaping his brother, he said in a terse undertone, "Later. Right now, time is short. I want to find out what she did in that building. I'm not expecting her to return, but as long as you're here, you can make yourself useful and be a lookout. If you see her approaching, give me the clear-out signal."

"All right."

Colin approached the building, noting the shabby exterior, the façade missing a number of bricks. The three abandoned storefronts looked deserted, but he suspected that life teemed behind the rough boards barring the entrances.

He opened The Broken Barrel's scarred wooden door and entered the dim interior. The sour smell of stale drink and unwashed bodies assailed him. Standing just inside the doorway, he looked around, noting the warped benches and worn tables. Two men hunched over mugs in the far corner looked at him through narrowed eyes, clearly assessing their chances of relieving him of his purse. With his gaze steady on the duo, he slowly reached down and pulled the knife secreted in his boot up several inches, so the gleaming silver hilt was plainly visible. The men exchanged a look with each other, then shrugged and went back to their drinks.

Satisfied, he approached the bar, behind which stood

a bald-headed giant of a man who wiped the dull wooden surface with a dirty-looking rag and regarded him with a suspicious glare. "Ale?" the giant asked.

"Information."

"I don't know nuthin'."

Colin reached into his pocket and laid a gold sovereign on the bar.

"Might know sumthin'," the barkeep muttered with a shrug of his massive shoulders.

Resting one elbow on the edge of the bar, Colin leaned closer, ostensibly to talk confidentially, but his gaze swept over the area behind the bar. A knapsack sat in the corner. "The woman who was just here—what did she give you?"

The man's eyes narrowed to slits. Setting his ham-sized fists on the bar, he leaned forward until his nose, which had clearly been broken at least once, nearly touched Colin's. "I don't know nuthin'." He then leaned back and stared at Colin with a frosty glare clearly meant to freeze him where he stood.

Keeping his gaze steady on the man's mud-colored eyes, Colin nodded toward the corner behind the bar. "That knapsack tells me otherwise."

"Who the hell are ye, and why do ye want to know?"

"I'm a . . . friend who's concerned about her."

"Yeah? Well, now *I'm* concerned—that a fancy toff like you is askin' about her and sumthin' that's none o' yer business."

Colin set another gold coin on the bar. "Why was she here? What's in that bag?"

The man picked up the two coins then reached out and slipped them back into Colin's pocket. "Yer money's no good here. But let me give ye a bit o' advice—for free. Stay away from her. If I find out ye've been botherin' her, ye'll have Jack Wallace to deal with." He made a fist and thumped it into his open palm. "And ye won't find it a pleasant experience, m'lord."

Colin cocked a brow upward. "Is she yours?"

The giant's eyes narrowed to slits. "All ye need to know is she ain't yers." He jerked his head toward the door. "Now get out. Before I forget my fancy manners and kick yer fancy arse out the door."

"Very well." He walked to door and opened it. Before stepping over the threshold, however, he turned and met the giant's gaze. "Since my money was no good here, I concluded my pocket watch wouldn't be either, so I retrieved it from you. I must commend you, Mr. Wallace. For a man with such large hands, your technique is quite good."

Surprise flashed in Wallace's eyes, and his hand flew to his apron pocket. Without another word, Colin exited the pub, heading swiftly in the direction of Mayfair. He'd only taken half a dozen strides when Nathan fell into step beside him. "Did you find out what you wished to know?" his brother asked.

"No."

"I was relieved the barkeep didn't decide to make an hors d'oeuvre of you. Even with both of us, I'm not certain we could have taken him."

"You were supposed to wait across the street."

"No, I was supposed be a lookout. Can I help it if during the course of performing my duty I happened to see the giant barkeep?"

Before he could reply, Nathan continued, "And speaking of what we're *supposed* to do, you're *supposed* to tell me what the devil is going on."

"And I shall. Tomorrow." He winced and rubbed his hand over the pull in his thigh as he walked. He turned to look at Nathan, noting his brother's tight jaw as he stared at Colin's massaging fingers. He immediately stopped rubbing, cursing his carelessness. "It's fine. Just a bit stiff."

Nathan's gaze met his and he easily read the guilt and regret in his brother's eyes. "I'm fine, Nathan. And if you apologize—again—for something that wasn't your fault, I swear I'll toss you into the Thames."

"As your being shot was *entirely* my fault, I'll apologize for it as many times as I damn well please."

"As it was entirely *my* fault, I refuse to listen to any further unnecessary apologies."

"I suppose we shall simply have to agree to disagree. And as for tossing me into the Thames, you'd have one hell of a time doing so, considering I can easily outrun you."

A bark of relieved laughter rose in his throat, and he coughed to cover it, grateful that the awkward moment had passed. "You may be faster, but I'm smarter."

"Debatable, but even if you were a bloody genius, I'm certainly not stupid enough to end up in the Thames."

"You'll look very silly repeating those words with river water dripping from you. But I've no time to debate the point any longer, as I have an appointment for which I'm already late. It is my hope that this appointment will result in me having even more to tell you tomorrow."

"I see. Well, then, I believe I'll depart your company at the corner as I have affairs of my own to see to. I'll see you at dinner? Eight o'clock?"

"Yes."

When they reached the corner, Colin continued straight, toward home, while Nathan turned right. Out of his brother's sight, he rubbed his sore leg, cursing the worsening pain that prevented him from moving as quickly as he would have liked.

Madame Larchmont awaited him, which was good since the questions just kept piling up. What had she given Wallace? Why hadn't the man accepted the bribe? What was it about her that inspired such loyalty? He'd have his answers. And by damn after he did, he intended to find out if the kiss they'd shared was as magnificent the second time around.

Nine

The instant Lord Sutton's butler closed the door to his elegant drawing room, leaving Alex alone, she swiftly crossed to the desk near the window. She wasn't certain how much time she had before Lord Sutton—or, as she now preferred to think of him, the green-eyed rich bloke—joined her for their appointment, and she intended to make the most of every minute.

With an effort, she swallowed the anger bubbling so close to the surface and quickly sifted through the pile of correspondence neatly stacked on a silver salver resting on the corner of the polished mahogany surface. A half dozen party invitations, a note from his brother, another from Lord Wexhall, several more invitations, the last one a single line which read *Looking forward to seeing you again soon.* It was signed with only the letter "M" and . . . she drew the vellum to her nose . . . scented with rosewater.

An unpleasant sensation she refused to examine too closely lest she be forced to admit its resemblance to jealousy rippled through her. Then she frowned in utter irritation. Damnation, what did she care if he had assignations with this "M" woman, or a dozen women? She didn't.

Still, the thought of him touching another woman, kissing another woman . . . she squeezed her eyes shut to banish the heated memory of him touching *her*, kissing *her*, but the effort failed completely. Which was ridiculous. And utterly vexatious. She was angry with him. Furious. Why, if he attempted to kiss her again, she'd blacken both his eyes.

If she'd known what he'd done, how he'd invaded her home, her privacy, before their kiss, she certainly wouldn't have allowed him such liberties.

Would she?

Dear God, she wanted, needed to believe she wouldn't have. But the fact that she didn't know frightened her—nearly as much as her wanton reaction to him and the fire he'd ignited in her body. Opening her eyes, she pressed her lips together and embraced her anger, an emotion much safer than the other unsettling feelings he provoked. And one she intended to cling to when she confronted him with his deception.

Forcing her attention back to the task at hand, she replaced the correspondence, then slid open the top drawer. She instantly saw the leather pouch from which he'd paid her yesterday. She lifted the bag, bouncing its weight in her palm, listening to the jangle of coins.

Judging by the weight of the bundle, she held a small fortune, and her fingers prickled with temptation. Not so very long ago she would have slipped the pouch into her pocket. Given what he'd done to her, it was certainly no less than he deserved. But she wasn't that person any longer. And didn't ever want to be that person again. After one last squeeze, she replaced the pouch, then quickly searched the remainder of the drawers, none of which yielded anything of interest.

Until she reached the bottom drawer, which was

locked. Without hesitation she dropped to her knees, yanked off her gloves, then pulled a hairpin from her chignon and set to work. The ticking of the mantel clock was the only sound as she concentrated on her task. It took less than a minute before she felt the lock begin to give way, and a smile of satisfaction curved her lips. Just one more little jiggle—

"This might perhaps help you," came a deep voice from directly behind her.

She gasped and turned. Lord Sutton leaned against the wall, ankles casually crossed, looking down at her with his usual unreadable expression. A silver key, suspended from a black ribbon, dangled from his outstretched hand.

Damnation. How had he managed to sneak up on her like that? He must move like smoke. And good Lord, he certainly managed to look extremely good while doing so. His midnight blue jacket, silver waistcoat, and cream breeches, which were tucked into black boots polished to a mirrorlike shine, fit his masculine form to perfection.

Her gaze traveled over him, pausing on the fascinating fit of his snug breeches. Her kneeling position left her on eye level with his groin—a riveting view that captured her interest in a way that certainly should have appalled her. And surely would, the instant she could tear her gaze away.

A wave of heat engulfed her, and her hand involuntarily drifted to her hip, to rest on the exact spot where his hard flesh had pressed against her last night.

"You're staring, Madame. In a most distracting way."

Another wave of heat, this one born of acute mortification, swamped her, and her gaze snapped upward. His green gaze seemed to burn into her, jolting her from her humiliating stupor.

She jumped to her feet, planted her hands on her hips, and glared at him. "You startled me half to death.

Are you normally in the habit of sneaking up on people, my lord?"

One dark brow inched upward. "Well, I certainly must give you marks for audacity. I think the more pertinent question, Madame, is: Are you normally in the habit of picking the locks on other people's drawers?"

"You could provide lessons on audacity, my lord. My presence before your desk is no less than you deserve, considering that you picked the lock to enter my rooms."

She'd expected him to deny it, but instead he merely inclined his head. "Clearly my lock picking proved more successful than yours." He jiggled the dangling key. "Since your skills are so severely lacking, please allow me to offer you this."

Lacking? *Lacking?* Of all the arrogance! Never had her skills been questioned—yet she couldn't deny the utterly chafing and humbling fact that this was the second time he'd caught her in the act, leaving her to question whether she was more irritated at herself or him.

Without sparing his offering a glance, she said in her best disdainful tone, "If only you'd been delayed another minute or two, I'd now bloody well know what you're up to. I don't suppose you'd consider toddling on off to one of your clubs for a while?"

"I don't suppose I would. And such language, Madame." He made a *tsk*ing sound. "I must say, you're not being very ladylike about this matter."

"Make no mistake, my lord. I never claimed to be a lady. You, on the other hand, *are* a gentleman. One can only wonder where and why a gentleman would acquire lock-picking skills."

"Obviously from a superior teacher than whoever taught you. What precisely were you looking for? Money? If so, I'd have preferred if you'd simply asked." His voice and expression turned cold. "Or did you already help yourself to the coins you know from yesterday's visit are in the top drawer?"

Humiliation scorched her. "I didn't take your money. I'm not a thief." *Anymore.*

He looked far from convinced. "Then what were you looking for?"

"What were *you* looking for when you broke into my rooms?"

Horrible man, he didn't even have the grace to appear the least bit abashed. "Information."

"Regarding?"

"You."

"Why did you not simply ask me?"

"I didn't believe you would be forthcoming in your answers."

She raised her brows. "A possibility—if you asked about topics which are none of your business."

"Annoying, but understandable. Which is why I took matters into my own hands to find out what I wanted to know. Would you like to hear what I discovered?"

"I know what you discovered." An image of Robbie's face, his bottom lip trembling, flashed in her mind, fueling her anger. She stepped closer to him and fisted her hands at her side. "Do you know how badly you frightened that child? A child who spends every day living with fear? A child whose only safe haven you invaded?"

A muscle jerked in his jaw. "I didn't mean to frighten him."

"Yet you did. Do you have any idea of the damage you've caused?" Her anger boiled over, and suddenly she couldn't stand still. She paced in front of him with jerky steps. "Robbie has nowhere else that's safe. None of them do. If he fears coming to my rooms . . ." She halted in front of him, unable to stop the words. "His father makes him steal. To earn his keep. If he doesn't bring home enough, he's beaten. That child spends his days struggling to survive and praying for the nights when his father drinks enough to pass out. Those are the nights he comes to me. To rest. To eat. To heal. To feel safe. And it's the only time he *does* feel safe. Seeing a strange man in my rooms, someone he thinks might harm him or me—it could keep him from coming. If he tells any of the others, it might keep them from coming as well."

"Others? How many are there?"

She drew a shaky breath. "More than I can hope to help. I'm all they have. Emma and I, my friend who lives with me. What little bit of trust they possess, they give to us. And none of them deserve more fear in their lives. Or to have their one safe place violated. You had no right—"

He reached out and laid his fingers over her lips, cutting off her words. "I'm sorry. I didn't know. If I had—"

"You would have done the exact same thing," she said in an accusatory tone, jerking away from his hand.

"Yes."

"Why?"

"I wanted to know more about you."

"Again, I must ask, why?"

He studied her for several long seconds, then asked, "Are you casting about for compliments?"

A humorless sound of disbelief escaped her. "*Compliments?* How you would arrive at such a far-fetched conclusion is a mystery to me. But to answer your question, no. Now I ask you to answer mine. Why would you be interested in finding out more about me?"

"What if I told you it's because I find you . . . fascinating?"

"I'd say there clearly must be another reason."

His gaze roamed her face with an intensity that curled her toes inside her shoes. "I wonder . . . are you that modest, or are you truly so bereft of vanity?"

"I've nothing to be vain about, my lord, as anyone

with eyes can easily discern; therefore, I demand you cease this nonsense at once and tell me the truth."

"Very well." He indicated the sitting area in front of the fireplace. "Let us sit."

"I prefer to stand."

"As you please." Colin settled his shoulders against the wall and loosely crossed his arms over his chest, his deliberately nonchalant posture at complete odds with the tension gripping him. "I wanted to know more about you for a number of reasons, one of which was my burning curiosity regarding your unique method of leaving Lord Malloran's house."

He caught the barest flicker in her eyes, one he would have missed if he hadn't been watching her so closely, and reluctant admiration filled him. No doubt about it, she was very good. In fact, she would have made a hell of a spy.

"I'm not certain I understand your meaning," she said.

"I mean your departure through his lordship's study window—a rather unusual way out, especially considering the drop to the ground. I'm sure you can understand that my curiosity only increased when I learned that it was the room where Malloran and his footman were found dead only several hours after your exit."

Silence, thick and tense, swelled between them. Finally, she said, "Surely you do not believe I had anything to do with their deaths."

"Why wouldn't I think that? Your actions are, at best, highly suspect."

"If you believed me guilty of murder, you'd have reported me to the authorities."

"What makes you think I haven't?"

There . . . an unmistakable flicker of something in her eyes. But it wasn't guilt. No, it looked like fear—understandable given how she'd spent her time at Vauxhall. London jails were notoriously unpleasant. She hiked up her chin a notch. "No one has questioned me."

"Then it has clearly escaped your notice that that is precisely what *I* am doing."

She appeared completely nonplussed. Then a sound of disbelief passed her lips. "You have no authority to do so."

"No. But I did see you leaving through that window. Very interesting, especially as Malloran and his footman were found poisoned soon after."

Her eyes widened with shock too genuine to be feigned. "B . . . but I thought they'd been bludgeoned. All the gossips said—"

"Yes, they were coshed. But after they were poisoned. Apparently to make the murders look like a robbery. It's also interesting that the poison used is believed to be prussic acid."

She frowned, appearing genuinely confused. "What is prussic acid?"

"An odd question coming from the wife of a rat-catcher, as prussic acid is commonly used by men in your husband's profession to kill the vermin."

She went perfectly still, then as the color slowly seeped from her face, he said softly, "A rather damning coincidence, made more so by the fact that you lied to me about where you lived. But when I searched your rooms, I not only found no evidence of poison. I also found no evidence of a husband."

In a flash he pushed from the wall and stepped toward her. She gasped and moved back, her retreat halted after a single step when her hips hit the desk. Less than an arm's length separated them. He could see the cinnamon flecks in her eyes, the gilded freckles marching across her nose. And the flicker of apprehension in her eyes.

"So why don't you tell me, *Madame* Larchmont, why

I shouldn't believe that you poisoned Lord Malloran and his footman? Give me a reason why I shouldn't immediately report my suspicions to the magistrate."

She licked her lips. "Why haven't you already?"

Because in spite of what I saw, in spite of what I know about you, my gut tells me there's another explanation. "I wanted to hear your explanation first. I learned the hard way that things aren't always as they appear."

Her gaze shifted downward, riveting on his hand, and he realized with a jolt of annoyance that he was unconsciously kneading his sore thigh. He immediately stopped, and her gaze rose to again meet his. Ignoring the questions lurking in those chocolate brown depths, he said, "I'm listening, Madame. I suggest you begin talking."

Alex looked into his eyes, at his implacable expression, and knew there was no point in not telling him the truth about what she'd overheard, although it wasn't necessary to tell him it was *his* unexpected presence that had precipitated her untimely escape from the drawing room, which had ended with her seeking sanctuary in Lord Malloran's study.

After drawing a deep breath, she began, "I was fatigued after so many readings and went in search of a quiet haven in the hopes of finding a moment of sanctuary." She then calmly related how she'd come to the study, the conversation she'd overheard, then the note she'd left for Lord Malloran, concluding with, "As I feared discovery should I be found in the corridor, I decided the window was my safer exit option. Unfortunately, I wasn't aware you were lurking in the bushes."

"I wasn't lurking. I was standing." His brows bunched into a frown. "You're quite certain that one of the persons you overheard was Malloran's now-dead footman?"

"Yes. I didn't see the other person, but I would know

that voice again." After a quick internal debate, she added, "I heard it again, last night."

His gaze sharpened. "When? Where?"

"At the Newtrebble soiree. Just before I left my fortune-telling table for the night, as I leaned down to retrieve my reticule."

"Did you see who'd spoken?"

"No. There were too many people to tell who'd said it. I listened, but didn't hear it again."

His gaze searched hers. "That's why you were so pale."

She offered him a half smile. "I'd been listening all night, but hadn't really expected to hear it since it was a whisper, as opposed to someone's true voice. I'm afraid that hearing it gave me a bit of a turn."

"Do you recall whom you saw?"

"Of course. I wrote down the names as soon as I arrived home so I wouldn't forget." She closed her eyes to visualize the groups. "Walking past me were Lord and Lady Barnes, Lord Carver, Mr. Jennsen, Lord and Lady Ralstrom, and their daughter, Lady Margaret. Standing nearby were Lord and Lady Whitemore, their daughter Lady Alicia, Lady Malloran's distant relative, Lady Miranda, and Lords Mallory and Surringham. There were also two footmen nearby."

He moved around her and pulled a piece of vellum from the desk, then dipped his pen into the inkpot. She watched him quickly write the names she'd just recited, her gaze riveted on his hands. Such strong, yet elegant hands. Hands that only hours earlier had touched her with a breath-stealing combination of gentle strength and heated impatience. Hands she wanted to feel touching her again, with a need that confused and frightened her.

"You have a good memory. And you're very observant," he said, setting down the pen, then moving to stand in front of her once again.

She blinked away the thought of his hands caressing her. "Remembering people, watching them . . . it's a habit of mine."

His gaze probed hers, then he asked quietly, "What is in the knapsack you take to The Broken Barrel each day?"

His question halted her breath, then she fisted her hands in an attempt to control her anger. "You followed me there as well. I suppose I shouldn't be surprised."

"I suppose not. What do you bring there?"

"Why didn't you ask the barkeep?"

"I did. Mr. Wallace declined to tell me, in spite of my offering a substantial bribe. I won't bore you with the details, but his next words involved various threats of bodily harm should I bother you."

"Jack is very . . . loyal."

"A conclusion I reached on my own." He studied her intently for several seconds then asked, "What is he to you?"

"A friend."

"Nothing more?"

She considered lying, telling him Jack was more so as to erect a barrier between them that she badly needed. But instead she shook her. "Nothing more."

"What's in the knapsack?"

"It's none of your business."

"I agree. But I'm asking anyway. Tell me." His eyes searched hers, then he added softly, "Please."

That single word, spoken in that quiet voice, combined with his green-eyed gaze resting so seriously on hers, conspired to wash away the anger she couldn't quite seem to summon. Where had it gone? Trying to resurrect it, she lifted her chin and said, "Even if I tell you, you won't believe me."

He remained silent, and she grudgingly credited him for not offering false reassurances. "Biscuits," she finally muttered. "And orange-flavored muffins." When he still said nothing, she blew out a breath, then said in a rush, "My friend Emma and I bake biscuits and muffins every day. She sells them, along with oranges, near Covent Garden and Drury Lane. Jack buys a sack every day to give to the children who beg for food near The Broken Barrel. They get something to eat, and in return don't steal from him."

He nodded slowly. "I see. So that is why you always smell of oranges."

"We use whatever oranges Emma didn't sell that day in our baking. We also distill orange-scented water from the rinds. I'm very fond of the scent."

"It is . . . unforgettable. Thank you for answering my question."

Did that mean he believed her? Before she could decide, he said, "Now I would like to know about the fictional Monsieur Larchmont."

She heaved an inward sigh. Obviously, there was no point in prevaricating with him any longer. "I don't like to lie—"

"Which is why, I'd wager that your ratcatcher of a cat is named Monsieur." Clearly her expression indicated he was correct for he added, "A very ingenious way to assuage your conscience."

Botheration, the man was too clever by half. She wasn't certain if she was more impressed or irritated. Curling her fingers over the edge of the desk, she said, "Inventing a husband affords me freedoms and safety that I would not otherwise have. I don't need to fear for my reputation as an unmarried woman would, and I always have an excuse to reject unwanted advances. It gives me a measure of security that people know there is a protective husband awaiting me at home. And, of course, the title *Madame* adds a nice mystique to my fortune-telling enterprise."

"Indeed it does. But what if you decided you actually wished to marry?"

"In truth, I've not given the matter any thought as I've no desire to marry. My time and efforts, my heart and passion lie in my work."

"Telling fortunes?"

"No. That is simply a way for me to earn money to fund my passion."

"Which is providing a safe haven for children like Robbie."

She lifted her chin. "Yes. If I had a real husband, I would be legally obligated to answer to him. To obey him. He would own everything that I've worked for— an arrangement that would not in any way benefit me or my cause. Given that my pretense hurts no one, I would ask that you not reveal my true marital status."

"Your secret is safe. However, you should have immediately reported to the magistrate what you overheard in Lord Malloran's study."

She couldn't very well tell him that her former life as a criminal had prevented her from doing so. "There are some people who look askance at the way I earn my living, believing it is, at best, havy cavy. I feared it more likely that I would be looked upon as a suspect rather than a witness."

"Do you know Lord Wexhall?"

"Not well, although we've been introduced. He engaged me to tell fortunes at his upcoming party."

"I am well acquainted with him, and he is completely trustworthy. I would like you to tell him what you've told me."

"So he can tell the magistrate," she said, unable to keep the bitterness from her voice, "so that the magistrate can accuse me of murder. A crime you obviously believe I committed."

He reached out and clasped her upper arms. Even

through the wool of her dress, his touch ignited sparks. She attempted to step back, but with her hips already pressed against the desk, she was trapped. His gaze searched hers, looking, for what she didn't know, but she met his probing regard steadily. Finally, he said, "I believe everything you've told me. I do not doubt your account."

An unfamiliar feeling washed through her, something she couldn't name, that felt like a swirl of relief and gratitude and surprise. She almost asked him *why* he believed her, but instead merely said, "I . . . I'm glad."

"You sound surprised."

"I suppose I am."

Again his gaze searched hers. "You are not accustomed to your words being accepted as truth."

It wasn't a question, and an odd sensation shivered through her. Forcing a lightness she was far from feeling into her voice, she said, "It's common in my profession. Some people believe what I say, others think I simply make things up for entertainment."

He nodded, then said, "I understand. But Lord Wexhall must be told. The murder is to take place at his home next week, and he has the resources to take precautions to hopefully prevent it from happening." His fingers tightened on her upper arms. "You must realize that because you overheard this plot, you, too, are in danger."

"Sadly, I have considered that possibility."

"I'd say it's more than a possibility. You require protection."

"I'm perfectly capable of taking care of myself."

"Under normal circumstances, I'm certain you are. These, however, are not normal circumstances. Have you noticed anything unusual? Has anyone said or done anything that felt threatening in any way?"

His thumbs brushed over her sleeves, shooting heated

tingles down her arms. Very distracting heated tingles. And he was standing very close . . . close enough to see the fine grain of his clean-shaven skin. She licked her suddenly dry lips. "I felt as if someone was watching me, following me, after both the Malloran and the Newtrebble soirees, but as it turns out, it was you. I experienced the same feeling both yesterday and today as I made my way here. Other than that, nothing unusual has occurred."

He frowned. "As you made your way here? Do you mean from your rooms, or from The Broken Barrel?"

After considering for several seconds, she said, "From my rooms both days. From The Broken Barrel only today."

His frown deepened. "Are you certain?"

"Yes. I strongly sensed I was being watched." A shiver ran through her at the memory of feeling someone's eyes upon her. She attempted to hide her discomfort with a small smile. "If I'd looked closely, I gather I would have seen you lurking behind a nearby tree."

"No. I did not follow you here today. Which, if you're correct, means that someone else did."

Ten

Colin stared into her chocolate brown eyes, and felt as if something inside him shifted. He'd wanted to know if she was still a thief, and part of him had secretly hoped she was, as he could then easily dismiss her and talk himself out of this unreasonable attraction.

But this facet of herself she'd revealed, this person who devoted her time and earnings and heart to helping children . . . this person had honor. And integrity. Was loyal and brave. Traits he greatly admired. And to which he found himself strongly drawn. A mere physical interest he could walk away from. But an attraction that engaged more than his body, one that touched his heart and mind . . . he wasn't quite certain how to dismiss or talk himself out of something like that.

Other than to give in to his desire to know more.

To know everything. To uncover each fascinating layer of her personality and discover exactly who she was, and how she'd come to be this woman who so captivated him. Her eloquence, the polite manners with which she deported herself . . . how and where had she learned such things?

Was she still a thief? His instincts now told him no. His suspicions that her fortune-telling enterprise was merely a ruse to steal from the wealthy people in whose homes she conducted her readings appeared unfounded, especially as he'd heard no reports of anything being stolen.

He'd been fully prepared to disbelieve everything she told him, but he couldn't.

"You need protection," he said, forcing himself to concentrate on her eyes and not look at her mouth, which beckoned him to taste, to explore its lush fullness. "We must figure out the best way to provide it."

"I'm not a sheltered Society miss, my lord. I've taken care of myself for a long time."

An image of her, that night in Vauxhall, her face dirty, the scent of despair and desperation clinging to her as she lifted his pocket watch, flashed through his mind, filling him with an ache he couldn't name.

"And have clearly done an excellent job," he said, his voice rough with an emotion that was part pity and part something else he feared examining too closely. "However, now we are dealing with someone who has most likely already killed two people, in a very bold manner, and is planning to see someone at Lord Wexhall's party dead. The fact that you felt you were being followed when I wasn't doing so shouldn't be ignored. And you must consider that any danger directed toward you might carry over to your home. And to those you're trying to protect."

Her eyes widened at his words, then narrowed with clear resolve. "I won't allow anything to hurt those children. Or Emma."

"Then I think it best that they be warned and that you stay away from them until after Wexhall's party and this is resolved."

She moved her hands in a helpless gesture. "A fine

plan, but I've nowhere else to go. I cannot afford—"

"You can stay here. With me."

His words hung in the air, and she went perfectly still under his hands, which still clasped her upper arms. His inner voice admonished him to release her, but he ignored the warning, instead listening to the louder, compelling need to touch her.

Damn it, he wished she weren't so skilled at hiding her feelings. Her expression gave nothing away.

Finally, she said, "While I appreciate your offer, it would present problems for us both. If I took up residence in your home, everyone would assume I was your mistress. The members of Society who currently employ my services would surely be scandalized and no longer seek me out. I fear that your offer, while perhaps providing for my physical safety, would prove the death of me both financially and socially. And then there is the matter of your bride."

"My . . . bride?" he repeated, feeling uncharacteristically bemused. He'd lost his entire line of thought after she said the word *mistress.*

"Yes, your bride." Clearly he sounded as befuddled as he felt for she clarified, "The woman you came to London to find? The woman you're going to marry and bring back to Cornwall?"

"Er, yes. What about her?"

She blew out a clearly exasperated breath. "Even if such an arrangement as you've suggested didn't prove disastrous for me, having people believe that you are openly living with your mistress certainly wouldn't help in your search for a bride."

Finding a bride . . . yes. That's what he was supposed to be doing. But instead all he could think of was the fact that she'd said it again—that thought-destroying word. *Mistress.* He instantly recalled the dream he'd had of her, walking toward him wearing that daring negligee, her eyes glittering with sensual intent. The way a mistress's would. An image flashed through his mind, of her in his bed, naked, aroused, waiting for him. Wanting him.

He suddenly became very much aware of how close they stood. The warmth seeping into his palms from where they rested on her arms. The subtle sweet scent of oranges teasing his senses. He shook his head and frowned, appalled at how easily she could make him lose his concentration.

Deciding it was best to put some distance between them, at least until after their discussion was concluded, he released her and moved to the window. Golden ribbons of afternoon sunlight rippled through the panes, beckoning him outdoors.

Which is where he should be. Riding through Hyde Park, chatting with marriageable young ladies of impeccable breeding who, at this time of day, would be visiting the park with a parent or chaperone, making the most of the fine weather to further acquaintances. Unfortunately, he had no desire whatsoever to chat with any of those marriageable young ladies. The only woman he had any desire to talk to stood ten feet behind him.

But at least now that he wasn't looking at her, wasn't touching her, wasn't absorbing her scent, his thoughts once again fell into alignment. After a moment of consideration, he turned to face her. And as it always seemed to when he looked at her, his breathing hitched. As if he'd sprinted across the room.

"I've arrived at a solution," he said, forcing himself not to move closer to her. "You shall stay at Lord Wexhall's town house, which is very close by. You'll be safe there, and as my brother and his wife are currently in residence as well, there will be no question of impropriety."

A look of pure confusion passed over her features.

"Why would Lord Wexhall agree to such an arrangement?"

"Because we are close friends."

"But if I am in danger, I could be placing his entire household in jeopardy."

"If you are in danger, there is no safer household in England than Wexhall's. He and his staff are well trained in such matters. As is my brother. And myself."

Her brows shot upward. "Trained in such matters? Three gentlemen? You make it sound as if you are all spies or some such nonsense."

"*Were* spies. But old habits die hard. Believe me, you're in capable hands."

Her inscrutable mask fell away, and she looked at him with pure disbelief. "You're joking."

"I'm not. You wondered how a gentleman would know anything about picking locks, and that is how. In fact, Lord Wexhall was my first lock-picking teacher. While you're staying with him, you might want to ask him for a pointer or two."

She folded her arms over her chest and looked at him askance. "Lord Wexhall? That genial, absentminded man? Now I know you're jesting."

"I'm not. Until his retirement several years ago, he was in service to the Crown. My brother and I both reported to him."

"Your brother the doctor."

"Who is also an expert decoder—and retired. And the only brother I have."

"You're telling me you're a spy—"

"*Was* a spy. I, too, retired from active service four years ago."

"Why?"

"Why was I a spy—or why did I retire?"

"Both."

"Wexhall approached me originally with a plan to

station one of his spies on my family's estate in Cornwall, because of its strategic location in relation to France. I agreed to his plan, with the proviso that he take me on and that I be the spy. Knowing my brother's affinity for puzzles and codes and such, I recommended him as well."

Confusion flitted across her features. "But why would a man like you want to involve yourself in such a dangerous enterprise?"

"That is the second time you've said 'a man like you.' What, precisely, do you mean?" He clenched his jaw, irritated at himself for allowing the question to pass his lips. Especially when he knew exactly what she meant. She meant—

"A titled gentleman, of course," she said.

A titled gentleman. Of course. He swallowed the humorless sound that rose in his throat. Well, he certainly couldn't deny the accuracy of her words—that was indeed the sort of man he was. Unfortunately, to most people, that's *all* he was. A title. He'd thought himself long since immune to the hurt that had accompanied that youthful realization, but based on the undeniable sting from her words, clearly he was mistaken on that score. She saw him only as most everyone else did.

Pushing aside his ridiculous disappointment, he drew a deep breath and cast his mind back, to the unfulfilled young man he'd been eight years ago. "Growing up, my entire existence revolved around my duties to my title and estates, and by my twenty-first birthday, my father had taught me everything I needed to know. I took great pleasure in the work, but Father enjoyed—no, *needed*— to fill his lonely days with running the estates himself. I didn't have the heart to ask him to do less so I could do more and thus deny him what he needed. As such, I wasn't doing anything a steward couldn't do. I felt . . . restless. Unnecessary. Empty. And basically useless.

Nathan had his medical profession, but I had nothing other than the usual country gentleman pursuits, which, while enjoyable, were of little use or value."

He paused, vividly recalling his growing discontent. "I'll never forget the day when I'd finally had enough of being nothing save, as you so aptly described me, a titled gentleman. Nathan told Father and me about how he'd saved a man's life that morning. I listened to his words, heard the pride in his voice, and realized I'd never done anything for which I could be that proud. That awed. Certainly nothing as important as saving someone's life."

The memory washed over him, those feelings of dissatisfaction as sharp as if they'd happened yesterday. "I knew then that I wanted, *needed* to prove to myself that I was more than just a title, but I wasn't certain how to go about it. I considered purchasing a commission in the army, but then Wexhall came along wanting to use the estate for spying purposes, and I saw an opportunity. He was doubtful at first about my spying, but I convinced him to give me a chance to prove I was up to the task. Turned out I was, and that I possess a talent for picking locks and gaining entry to places where I wasn't supposed to be. Very handy for a spy."

"Yes, I imagine it is. Did you enjoy spying?"

He considered, then said, "Yes. I enjoyed serving my country. Making a difference. Doing something important. Being useful. I loved the challenge." He didn't add that there were a number of assignments, one in particular, he hadn't enjoyed at all. That had taken deep physical and mental tolls on him. "Looking back, I'd have to say it was the happiest time of my life."

"Why did you retire?"

He pressed his palm against his thigh and decided to tell her the simple version. "I was injured."

"How?"

"I was shot."

Her gaze flicked down to his thigh. "Does it hurt?" she asked softly.

He shrugged and moved his hand, crossing his arms over his chest. "Sometimes." He offered her a half smile. "More when I'm forced to sprint through London's back alleys while in pursuit of fortune-tellers."

She nodded toward the locked drawer. "You could pick that lock?"

"Of course. And in far less time than it took you to get caught at it. Which is only understandable, as you would not, naturally, have lock-picking experience." He inwardly chuckled at the flash of outrage that glittered in her eyes. It clearly galled her and required a great effort on her part not to correct him, for in truth, before he'd made his presence known, he'd noted she'd been about to open the drawer, and it had taken her less than a minute to gain access. Very impressive. It occurred to him once again that she would have made a hell of a spy.

"Are you willing to provide a demonstration?" she asked.

For an answer, he handed her the key. "Why don't you make certain it's securely locked. I wouldn't want to have any unfair advantage."

"Delighted," she said with a smile that didn't quite reach her eyes. After she finished, she stood and handed him the key, which he slipped into his waistcoat pocket.

Instead of kneeling before the desk, however, he stepped closer to her. Alarm flickered in her eyes and she backed up, halting when she bumped into the desk. He moved closer still.

"Wh . . . what are you doing?" she asked in a breathless voice that instantly made him want to do something to render her even more breathless.

With his gaze steady on hers, he reached out and deftly plucked a pin from her hair. Smiling, he held his prize aloft. "I can hardly pick a lock on my passable good looks alone."

Her gaze roamed over his face, lingering on his mouth in a way that tensed his every muscle. "I suppose not," she said in that same breathless voice. "What did you do when there wasn't a woman nearby from whom you could conveniently pluck a pin?"

Bloody hell, it required a Herculean effort not to reach out and touch her. Instead, he shot her a jaunty wink. "I always carry my own."

Dropping to one knee, he made a show of first cracking his knuckles, then rubbing his hands together. Finally, he looked up at her. "Ready?"

"I've *been* ready," came her dust-dry reply.

Without further ado, he delicately inserted the hairpin into the lock, jiggled the device twice, then withdrew it. *"Voilà!"*

"Don't be ridiculous. That drawer isn't unlocked . . ."

Alex's words trailed off as he slowly slid the drawer open. She had to clench her jaw to keep it from hanging agape in utter amazement at his dexterity and skill. She caught sight of what looked like a shiny black box, but before she could see more, he slid the drawer closed, inserted his key, and locked it. Then in a single fluid motion, he stood and tucked the key away in his pocket.

Reaching out, he gently slid the pin back in her hair, and said softly, "Not only did I pick locks, I was also an expert pickpocket."

His nearness, the gentle touch of his hands in her hair, the barest elusive whiff of his clean scent all conspired to render her speechless. After clearing her throat to find her voice, she said, "Pickpocket? Were you good at it?"

He lowered his hands from her hair, stepped back and smiled. "I think the fact that you need to ask proves

I was. And still am." He held out his hand. "I believe these belong to you."

She gaped at the bronze silk-wrapped bundle resting in his palm, then her hand flew to the deep pocket in her gown where she kept her cards. Her *empty* pocket. By God, he *was* good. And by God, she would know. He would have made a hell of a thief.

"Very impressive," she said, unable to keep the admiration from her voice. "I'm amazed."

"Thank you." Mischief kindled in his eyes, impossibly making him even more attractive. "It's merely one of my many talents."

Heavens, she didn't doubt for an instant that he possessed dozens. Certainly kissing a woman until she was breathless and aching, desperate and hot—

"Impressed *and* amazed," he said, yanking back her thoughts which had run horribly amok. "I believe that makes you . . . *imprazed.*"

She couldn't help but smile. "I suppose it does."

"Yet I'd wager you say that to all the titled gentleman pickpockets you know."

Unable to resist his teasing, she matched his light-hearted demeanor, casting her gaze downward, then looking up at him through her lashes. "Oh, dear. You've discovered my deepest secret."

"Have I?"

Before she could toss off a breezy reply, he reached out and brushed his fingertips over her cheek, stealing what little bit of breath he hadn't already robbed her of. Unmistakable heat flared in his eyes, melting all traces of amusement. "I suspect you have other secrets," he said softly, his fingers slowly tracing her jaw.

Her better judgment demanded that she move away from him, from his touch that seemed to ignite fire under her skin. But the woman in her, who knew everything about survival yet little about living and who had remained ruthlessly locked away until he'd opened the door with his kiss, refused to move, unable to restrain her uncontrollable curiosity and desire to know what he would do next.

Heart pounding, she moistened her lips, then said, "Everyone has secrets, my lord. Even you."

Something bleak and haunted flashed in his eyes, disappearing so quickly she wondered if she'd imagined it. "I cannot disagree about that." His fingers drifted along her jaw to lightly circle the shell of her ear. "Although, I firmly disagree with something you said earlier."

"What is that?"

"That you've nothing to be vain about." The pad of his thumb drifted over her lips, arrowing heat down to her toes. "You're beautiful."

A huff of stunned laughter escaped her. "And you're daft."

The corner of his mouth twitched. "I'm also much more complimentary than you are."

"I own a mirror. Beautiful? I'm nothing of the sort."

"You may own a mirror, but you don't see yourself clearly." He tilted his head first left then right, as if assessing her and giving the matter great thought. "Actually, you're right. You're not beautiful. You're exquisite."

That description was even more ludicrous, but his talented fingers made her *feel* exquisite as they continued their delicious exploration, meandering down her neck. Dear God, it was nearly impossible not to close her eyes and lean into his caress, much like her cat, Monsieur, when she petted him. She'd never known a man's touch could be so gentle. So unequivocally delightful yet at the same time so very . . . stirring.

"Have you been drinking?" she felt compelled to ask.

"No." He cupped her face in one palm and brushed his thumb over her cheek, while his other arm encircled her waist, drawing her closer. "There's no need. *You* intoxicate me."

His touch, the intensity in his gaze, made her tremble and feel as if she were melting from the inside out. Her breasts brushed against his chest, and in spite of the layers of clothes separating their skin, she caught her breath at the stunning contact. His eyes seemed to darken, and even if her life had depended upon it, she couldn't have looked away. *Kiss me. Please kiss me . . .*

The words echoed through her mind, demanding to be spoken. Anticipation, so intense it resembled pain, cut through her. Just when she didn't think she could stand it another instant, he bent his head and pressed his lips to the sensitive skin behind her ear.

Her eyes drifted closed at the heady, delicious sensation of his body touching hers from chest to knee. Even as her inner voice warned her to stop, to step away, her hands crept up and grasped his broad shoulders.

"You have no idea how glad I was to discover you weren't married," he whispered, his voice velvety, seductive against her neck, his warm breath eliciting heated tingles that skittered down her spine.

"It was very bad of you to enter my rooms. I . . . I'm . . . most angry with you." Unfortunately, the sigh of pleasure that escaped her in no way matched her words.

"Then I shall have to endeavor to work my way back into your favor."

God help her, he was doing a masterful job. The sensation of his lips leisurely exploring where her neck and shoulder met turned her knees to porridge.

"Yet even if I hadn't seen the lack of evidence of a husband in your rooms," he continued, "I'd still have known you weren't wed."

"How?" The word came out on a breathless sigh as he kissed his way across her throat.

He straightened, and she mourned the loss of his lips

against her skin. She dragged her eyes open, and her heart skipped a beat at the fire burning in his gaze. "Last night, in the carriage," he said, tracing her lips with a single fingertip. "Your kiss. You were too inexperienced to have been married."

All the tingling warmth was extinguished as effectively as if he'd tossed cold water upon her. She couldn't recall the last time she'd blushed, but there was no mistaking the hellfires of mortification burning her cheeks. She squirmed against him, wanting nothing more than to escape, but he tightened his embrace, holding her with an ease that only added to her humiliation.

"Don't be embarrassed," he said, touching her flaming cheek. "I meant it as a compliment."

A humorless sound escaped her. "Compliment? First beautiful, then exquisite, and now compliment? How many more lies do you intend to utter this afternoon?"

"I haven't lied. Perhaps *you* don't think you are exquisite, but I do. Since the first time I saw you, your face has haunted me. As for the way you kissed me . . . I found it enchanting. Exciting. And incredibly arousing, as I'm certain you could tell." His gaze turned questioning. "Or couldn't you?"

What she lacked by way of personal experience, she more than made up for in what she'd witnessed and heard in London's back alleys. Lifting her chin a fraction, she said, "I may be inexperienced, but I am not ignorant of the workings of the human body. I could tell." And God help her, it had thrilled her in a way she'd never anticipated.

"And you're a quick learner. I've thought of little else but you." His gaze searched hers. "Have you thought of me?"

Where, oh where, was the dismissive cold stare she could always call upon at will? The one she'd used to warn off every other man who'd so much as looked at her? Where was her anger? Her resolve to avoid this knee-weakening temptation? They stood no chance under the spell he seemed to cast upon her, evaporating under the blaze of his beautiful green eyes—eyes she'd vowed to blacken if he attempted to kiss her again. Instead, she wanted to experience the magic of his kiss again so badly she trembled.

Have you thought of me? He only filled every crevice of her mind. A lie hovered on her lips, but in light of his honesty, refused to be spoken. "Yes."

"In the same way I've thought about you, I hope."

With an effort, she pulled herself together and cocked a single brow. "I'm not certain. Had you thought about coshing me with an iron skillet?"

One corner of his mouth quirked upward, and he shook his head, while his hands skimmed down her back, pressing her closer against him. "No. I thought about touching you." He leaned forward and brushed his lips over hers. "Kissing you," he whispered against her mouth. "I thought about how warm and sweet and delicious you taste. How much I want to taste you again."

Her heart pounded at his words, spoken in that husky whisper. He ran his tongue along her bottom lip, and her lips parted on a sigh. But instead of kissing her, he raised his head. Cupping her face between his hands, he looked into her eyes, studying her as if she were a puzzle to solve.

"Were your thoughts anything like mine?" he asked softly.

Since the moment you ignited my imagination and fantasies four years ago in Vauxhall. She couldn't have denied him the truth if she'd tried. "Yes."

"Thank God." His words whispered past her lips, then he slanted his mouth over hers, kissing her with that same magical perfection as he had last night.

Only this kiss was . . . more so. Deeper. Fiercer. More

intense and demanding. More passionate and urgent. More exquisite. His tongue swept into her mouth, and she mimicked his every gesture, employed every nuance he'd taught her last night, anxious to learn more and not allow her ignorance to disgrace her.

Wrapping her arms around his neck, she explored the silky heat of his mouth with her tongue. A low growl sounded in his throat, and without breaking their kiss, he turned them so he leaned against the desk. He spread his legs and pulled her into the V of his thighs, pressing his hardness against her. Heat washed through her, and a pulse throbbed between her legs.

Wrapped in his strong arms, she felt completely surrounded by him. Safe. Warm. Protected. A thrilling sensation unlike anything she'd ever experienced. A sensation she greedily craved more of. Heat emanated from him, and she breathed in his clean, masculine scent. Aching, she squirmed against him, shooting jolts of pleasure through her.

With a groan, he widened his stance, then splayed one hand low on her back, urging her tighter against him, while his other hand came forward to cup her breast. She gasped against his mouth, and he broke off their kiss, trailing his mouth down her neck. Her head fell back limply, and she clung to his shoulders, trying to absorb the barrage of delightful sensations, but they bombarded her too quickly. Her nipples tightened, and she arched her back, pressing her aching breast into his palm.

"Oranges," he whispered against the base of her throat. "Delicious." And then he kissed her again, a long, slow, deep kiss that stole her breath, while he palmed her breasts. The secret place between her thighs felt heavy and moist and achy, and it pulsed in tandem to the drugging thrust of his tongue in her mouth. A delicious languor stole over her, and she melted against him. Her hands grew bolder, running up his broad chest, skimming over his strong shoulders, sifting through his thick, silky hair.

She lost all sense of time of place, allowing herself, for the first time in her life, simply to *feel*. Everything faded away except the increasingly desperate need to experience more of his strength. Taste more of his delicious flavor. Touch more of his warm, firm skin. She strained closer to him, her insides trembling, wanting, needing more, knowing only he could put out this inferno he'd lit inside her.

Coolness touched her leg, but before she could fully grasp the implications, his warm hand ran slowly up her thigh, separated from her skin only by the thin layer of her drawers, the sensation shocking her, thrilling her. His hand wandered higher to draw slow circles over her buttocks, and she groaned, craving more of his intoxicating touch. How could such a leisurely caress make her pulse race so?

An insistent tapping sound penetrated the fog of desire engulfing her, and clearly he heard it, too, for he lifted his head. Dazed, she opened her eyes. Their gazes met, and her breath caught at the fiery desire burning in his eyes. The tapping sounded again and with a start she realized—

"The door." His voice sounded low and rough, and he looked flatteringly displeased at the interruption.

Reality returned with a thump, and she gasped, stepping unsteadily from his embrace and putting several feet between them. Her hands flew to her heated cheeks. "Oh, dear." What had she done? Immediately, her inner voice answered, *You enjoyed yourself. More in those few minutes than you ever have before.*

"Don't worry. No one will come in." Without taking his gaze from her, he called out, "What is it, Ellis?"

"Dr. Nathan is here, my lord," came the butler's muffled voice through the door. "Are you at home?"

Before he could reply, another voice, deeply masculine and highly amused, came from beyond the door. "Of course he's at home, Ellis." Then louder, "Greetings, brother dear. I come bearing gifts and will await you in your study. Don't be too long, or I'll eat all the marzipan without you."

Lord Sutton muttered something that sounded suspiciously like *bloody damn pest*. The icy glare he leveled upon the door was surely meant to freeze the oak panels. Indeed, he looked so wholly and thunderously displeased she had to press her lips together to hide her sudden amusement. Clearly she wasn't successful, for his eyes narrowed upon her.

"Are you *laughing*?"

"Me? Certainly not," she said, with a haughty sniff.

"Because if you *were* laughing . . ."

The heated look in his eyes scorched her. "What would you do?" The breathless question popped out before she could stop it, appalling her.

"An interesting question. One upon which I shall have to ponder because you make me want to do so many things." He reached out and took her hand. When his warm fingers wrapped around hers, she recalled with a start that she wasn't wearing her gloves. She looked down and saw the lacy fingertips peeking out from under the desk.

Embarrassment suffused her, but before she could snatch her hand away, he'd lifted it and pressed his lips against her palm. One of her callused, work-worn palms that she was always careful to hide from the wealthy members of Society.

He lowered her hand, then slowly stroked his thumb over the spot he'd just kissed. Another wave of embarrassment rolled over her as he looked at her hand, knowing he'd see the nicks, old scars, and healed-over burns from years of hard work. She tried to gently extricate her hand, but he wouldn't let her.

"You work hard," he said, brushing his finger over a callus.

"Some of us have to."

The instant the words left her mouth she wished she could yank them back. But he didn't seem offended. Rather, he nodded gravely. "You're right." Raising her hand once again, he pressed her palm against his cheek. "I like the feel of your skin on mine. The touch of your hands . . . without your gloves."

A tremor tingled up her arm from where her palm rested against his clean-shaven face. "My hands are . . . not pretty."

"You're correct. Like you, they're exquisite." He smiled. "Have I mentioned that I think you're exquisite?"

Dear God, her mind insisted she stop this flirtatious banter. But it was impossible when her frantically beating heart refused to obey. "Not in the last five minutes."

"A terrible oversight. One I shall correct as soon as I send my brother on his way." He released her hand and, after a quick assessment of her attire, reached out to make a minor adjustment to her bodice and skirt, then brushed a stray curl from her forehead. "Perfect," he murmured.

After tunneling his fingers through his own hair, upon which her hands had wreaked havoc, he tugged his jacket into place and extended his elbow. "Shall we?"

She blinked. "Shall we what?"

"Retire to my study where my brother awaits."

"Surely he wishes to see you privately."

"As he interrupted us at an extremely inopportune moment, I'm not particularly interested in his wishes. You said you wanted to read my cards in a different room, and my study would provide a new location." A half smile tilted his lips. "And I'm certain I can talk Nathan into having a private reading there as well. One for which you'll charge him an exorbitant fee. Heh, heh, heh."

A smile tugged at her lips. "That is a positively *evil* laugh, my lord."

He ran a single fingertip down her arm then entwined their fingers, a breath-stealing gesture that felt warm and delightfully intimate. "Colin," he said.

His name reverberated through her mind, then she repeated softly, "Colin," savoring the taste of his name on her tongue. "My name is—"

"Alexandra."

"How did you know?"

"I asked Lady Malloran. I've a book on name origins which I consulted after her party. Alexandra is of Greek origin, and it means protector of mankind. Given the cause so close to your heart, it appears you were aptly named."

"What does Colin mean?"

"I've no idea, but if I had to guess, I'd say it means 'man who wants to kiss Alexandra again.' "

She stilled. Lord knows she wanted him to. Far too much. Which unsettled and frightened her. She knew where another kiss would lead—a road that would be most foolhardy for her to travel. Especially with a man who, given their divergent stations in life, would never be able to offer her anything more than a quick tumble.

Her lack of control, the way she'd abandoned her resolve, confused and irritated her. Normally she was very levelheaded. Disciplined. Yet a moment in this man's company seemingly robbed her of her common sense. Well, there would simply be no more kissing. She'd not make the same mistake twice. *You've already made that mistake twice,* her inner voice reminded her.

Fine. She'd not make the same mistake *three* times.

He leaned forward, clearly intending to kiss her, and she forced her feet to move away, pulling her hand free from his. "Your brother is waiting."

He nodded slowly, regarding her through serious eyes. "Yes. This is neither the time nor place."

"Actually, there is *no* proper time or place, my lord."

"Colin. And what do you mean by that?"

"A single kiss was one thing, but repeating it today was . . ." *Delightful. Incredible. Unforgettable.* ". . . not wise. Doing it again would be foolhardy indeed."

"Why?"

Because with only two kisses you've made me want things I shouldn't. Things I can't have. "Surely you don't need to ask."

"No, I don't," he said quietly. "I feel the deep attraction between us. The question is, what are we going to do about it?"

"Nothing," she said quickly.

"I don't believe that's going to be an option."

"We'll simply ignore it."

"Again, I don't believe that's going to be an option."

Silence swelled between them, and she felt an overwhelming need to fidget under his quiet, steady regard. Finally, he said, "I suggest we both think on the matter, to see if we can arrive at any other solutions. In the meantime, let's see what my brother wants and apprise him of your situation. Since you'll be staying at Wexhall's, it's important Nathan know everything so as to be on guard."

Not trusting her voice, Alex merely nodded and allowed him to escort her from the room.

There was no point in thinking on the matter, because the only other option would be for them to continue their intimacies and eventually become lovers.

And she simply wouldn't, couldn't do that. The risk to her reputation, not to mention her heart, was too great. No, she simply wouldn't, couldn't consider becoming his lover.

Liar, her inner voice sneered.

She managed, with a great deal of effort to ignore it.

Almost.

Eleven

The first thing Colin saw when he entered his study was Nathan, sprawled in his favorite overstuffed chair, his none-too-clean boots propped on his favorite leather ottoman, popping a piece of his favorite marzipan—an orange—into his mouth. The second thing he saw was B.C., sprawled on his favorite Turkish hearth rug, fast asleep, one plate-sized paw resting over what appeared to be one of his favorite boots.

He pressed his fingertips to his temple in an attempt to hold back the onset of a throbbing headache.

Upon seeing Alexandra, Nathan's eyes lit up, and he jumped to his feet and brushed his hands together, clearly to rid them of the sugary remnants of Colin's favorite confections.

"Is that my boot?" Colin asked, jerking his chin toward the sleeping B.C.

"Yes. But it's the same one from earlier today, so I didn't think you'd mind."

"How delightful." He turned to Alexandra. "Madame Larchmont, my brother, Dr. Nathan Oliver and his boot-chewing dog, B.C. Nathan, may I present Madame Larchmont, the renowned fortune-teller."

Nathan made her a formal bow, and Colin noted how avidly his brother's sharp gaze roamed Alexandra's face. "A pleasure, Madame Larchmont."

Alexandra, who'd retrieved her gloves before leaving the drawing room, extended her lace-covered hand, and Colin inwardly frowned at how badly he wanted to peel off that glove and caress her fingers. "Likewise, Dr. Oliver."

"I've never met a fortune-teller before."

"And I've never seen such a huge dog," she said with a smile, nodding toward the hearth rug. "He's beautiful."

"Thank you."

"He's a menace," Colin muttered, eyeing his ruined boot.

"But a friendly one," Nathan said. His gaze bounced between the two of them, then a speculative gleam glittered in his eyes. "Would your first name be Alexandra?"

Bloody hell. Colin shot his brother a dark look that Nathan blithely ignored.

"Why, yes, it is."

"I suspected as much." Nathan smiled. "I've heard of you—"

"He reads the *Times*," Colin broke in, shooting Nathan a glare meant to incinerate him on the spot. "Cover to cover. Obsessively." Without giving Nathan the opportunity to refute his assertion, he quickly continued, "Actually, Nathan, I'm glad you're here—"

"Yes, that is *patently* obvious—"

"—As there is something important we need to discuss." He indicated the grouping of chairs around the fireplace. "Let's sit. I'll ring for tea."

He turned toward Alexandra, who stood in a pool of

golden sunlight slanting in from the wall of windows, and instantly realized why Nathan had guessed her name. While nothing in her dress or demeanor indicated they'd shared a passionate embrace, someone as observant as Nathan wouldn't miss the lingering rosy flush of arousal that colored her cheeks. Or the deeper rose of her just-kissed lips. Damn it, one look at her, and all he could think about was yanking her into his arms and—

He shook his head to clear the erotic image of her entwined around him. In his bed. Naked. Aroused. Holding her arms out to him—

Later. He could think of that later. After his far-too-observant brother departed. Clearing his throat, he said to her, "Would you prefer chocolate instead of tea?"

Her gaze met his, and he actually had to clench his hands to keep from reaching out to touch her. "Chocolate would be lovely," she said softly.

"Yes, chocolate would be lovely," Nathan echoed. "And some of Cook's biscuits. Extra biscuits, as you're sadly now out of marzipan."

While Nathan and Alexandra settled themselves near the fireplace, Colin pulled the bell cord, and after telling Ellis what they wanted, joined them. He noted that Nathan had strategically chosen the chair opposite the settee where Alexandra sat—a spot where he could fully study her face and reactions. Certainly it's where Colin would have sat if he'd been his overly curious brother.

After sitting next to Alexandra on the settee, he said without preamble, "I have reason to believe Madame Larchmont is in danger." He turned to her, and said, "Please tell him what you told me."

She drew a deep breath, then related the story of the overheard conversation and the fact that she'd heard the same voice again at the Newtrebble soiree to Nathan, who listened intently and without comment.

When she finished, Colin told him everything about Lord Malloran's and the footman's deaths.

At the end of his recitation, Nathan frowned. "I wonder if the intended victim at Wexhall's party might be Wexhall himself?"

Colin leaned forward. "Do you have a reason to believe he's in danger?"

"He told me earlier today that he was attacked outside his club last week. He fought off his assailant, who then escaped, and regarded the incident as a random robbery."

"But perhaps it was more," Colin mused. "Did he see who it was?"

"No. It was dark, and the man wore a hoodlike mask."

Colin nodded slowly and sat back. "Wexhall is certainly someone whose death would 'give rise to inquiries.' And over the years I'm sure he's made enemies." He withdrew a piece of vellum from his waistcoat pocket.

"These are the names of the people who were standing nearby last night when Madame heard the voice again."

Nathan unfolded the paper, then frowned as he studied the names. "With the exception of the servants and Mr. Jennsen, who I've heard is very wealthy, all are very well respected members of the peerage."

"I suppose it's possible," Alexandra said with a frown, "that someone may have been able to leave the room quickly before I looked up from retrieving my reticule under the table. I'm afraid the shock of actually hearing the voice again stunned me for several seconds."

"Perhaps," Colin said. He briefly closed his eyes to visualize the Newtrebble drawing room. "There was an alcove situated close to where your table was. There was also a grouping of potted palms that could easily have concealed someone."

"Then that list is useless," she said, her voice tinged with frustration.

"Not at all," Colin said quickly. "There is merely a *chance* someone else might have been present. We know for certain that these people were." He returned his attention to Nathan. "I'd appreciate it if you'd show that list to Wexhall. He might know something about someone on there that we don't. Also warn him the attack last week might not have been a random incident."

Nathan tucked the vellum into his pocket. "All right."

"Madame Larchmont must be protected while we try to discover who is behind this plot and ascertain who the intended target is. I think the safest place for her is Wexhall's town house."

Nathan nodded slowly. "Yes, I agree."

"Good. Victoria can issue Madame the invitation to stay at the house until the party. Her visit can be explained with some story about her wanting to prepare the house for the spirits' arrival or some such talk. Between you and Wexhall and his staff on the spot, and me only down the road and escorting her everywhere she goes, she'll be safe. We'll make certain one of us is always nearby during the soirees scheduled from now until Wexhall's fete, in case she hears the voice again."

Nathan nodded, then looked at Alexandra. "This plan is amenable to you?"

"Yes, as long as it is amenable to Lord Wexhall."

"Have no fear on that score," Colin said. He turned to Nathan. "After our reading, I'll escort Madame Larchmont home so she can gather whatever essentials she needs while you return to Wexhall's to apprise him of what's going on and make the necessary arrangements for her arrival."

A knock sounded on the door. Colin called out, "Come in," and Ellis entered, bearing a silver tray which he set on the low cherrywood, rectangular table in front of the settee. The delicious scent of warm chocolate and fresh biscuits filled the air. After thanking then dismissing Ellis, he said to Alexandra, "Would you pour while I prepare the plates?"

"Of course."

While they were busy with their tasks, Nathan asked, "What did you mean when you said 'after our reading'?"

"Card reading. I prevailed upon Madame to give you a private reading. As her services are much in demand, such a session doesn't come cheap, but it's worth every penny."

"*You've* had your cards read?"

"I have indeed. Twice. And I'm having them read again today."

Colin recognized all too well the deviltry gleaming in Nathan's eyes. "One can only marvel at your sudden attraction for things of a mystic nature," Nathan said. His gaze shifted to Alexandra. "Tell me, Madame. Were you able to discern any of his deep, dark secrets?"

"I don't have any deep dark secrets," Colin said, a bit more sharply than he'd intended.

"Pshaw. He hasn't always been the proper, priggish, stick-in-the-mud you see before you now, Madame."

Colin shoved back the memories that threatened to intrude, then looked at Alexandra and heaved an exaggerated sigh. "Do you see what I've had to put up with my entire life?"

Clearly hiding a smile, she asked Nathan, "What do you mean?"

"He used to slide down the banister."

"How shocking, my lord," she said, slanting her gaze toward Colin, her lips twitching.

"*And* steal the stablemaster's clothes every Wednesday when the man bathed in the lake."

"You say that as if you didn't help," Colin said mildly. He added another biscuit to Alexandra's plate and grinned at her. "Besides, we didn't *steal* his clothes—we merely relocated them."

"When we were lads, this supposedly upstanding peer of the realm," Nathan said with a dramatically injured sniff, pointing at Colin, "used to toss me in the lake."

"Only when you deserved it," Colin pointed out.

"Surely I didn't deserve it *every day*."

"That's what *you* think."

"He finally stopped when I began pelting him with eggs," Nathan said to Alexandra in a smug tone. He leaned forward and confided, "I have fiendishly accurate aim."

"Those eggs *hurt*," Colin said, involuntarily rubbing the back of his head where'd he'd been hit more than once.

"How much could an *egg* have hurt?" Alexandra asked, clearly amused as she handed him and Nathan their cups of chocolate.

"You have no idea. And the mess. Especially after it hardened." He made a face, and she laughed. Then he smiled. "But I had my revenge. I made up a batch of special eggs by carefully making a small hole in the shell and removing the insides. I then inserted money inside."

"*My* money," Nathan chimed in. "That he'd stolen from me."

"If he'd hidden it in a cleverer spot, I wouldn't have been able to find it," he said, ignoring Nathan. "I made myself an easy target and he ended up throwing all his money at me. Last time he pelted me with eggs."

"Very clever," she said.

"I'm a very clever fellow."

Bloody hell, her lovely eyes smiling into his damn near lulled him into a trance. Pulling himself together, he handed her her plate, then Nathan his.

"Why did I only receive *one* biscuit?" Nathan asked, eyeing Colin's and Alexandra's plates, both of which held four biscuits.

"Because you saw fit to eat all my marzipan. Countries have gone to war for less provocation."

Nathan shot him a glare. "Just for that, I'm inclined not to give you the gift I brought."

"Good. Because knowing you and your penchant for accepting animals of all sorts into your home, your gift is likely of the barking, meowing, quacking, or mooing variety."

Nathan's expression turned innocent—*too* innocent, instantly igniting Colin's suspicions. Before he could question his brother further, however, Nathan turned his attention back to Alexandra. "Tell me, Madame, do you have any brothers?"

"I'm afraid not."

"Consider yourself fortunate. Any sisters?"

"No, but I live with my dearest friend, Emma, who is the sister of my heart."

"And is Emma a fortune-teller as well?"

"No. She's an orange girl." She lifted her chin a fraction, as if expecting a rebuff given her friend's lowly occupation, but Colin held no fear on that account with Nathan.

True to form, Nathan nodded in an approving manner, then said, "My wife is very fond of oranges. Could you arrange for your friend to come to the Wexhall town house so I may purchase some for her?"

She hesitated, and although her expression gave nothing away, Colin sensed her surprise. "I'd be delighted."

"Excellent. Now, tell me, how do we go about conducting this card reading? I'm fascinated."

"First you must pay the fee up front," Colin said, enjoying himself thoroughly, then taking a large, deliberate bite of biscuit. After swallowing, he said, "Then you ask Madame a question. Then she'll deal the cards and tell you all sorts of interesting things about yourself. It's quite the craze this Season."

"I'm ready to begin," Nathan said, scowling at his empty plate. "As I only had one biscuit and all."

After he and Alexandra had finished their drinks and biscuits, Colin called for Ellis, who removed the silver platter. Alexandra slipped her silk-wrapped bundle from her pocket, then said to Nathan, "Given your kindness in arranging for my safety, Dr. Oliver, I cannot charge you for your reading."

"Of course you can," Colin insisted. He doubled the figure she'd charged him, added a bit more, then tossed out the number to Nathan, reminding him, "Payable in advance."

His brother's eyes widened at the ridiculous sum, but he dutifully retrieved the money from his waistcoat pocket without comment and passed the money to Alexandra, who, appearing embarrassed, slipped it into her pocket. Mollified—and smug—that someone had paid more than he, Colin leaned back in his chair and waited.

Instead of shuffling, however, Alexandra looked at him and raised her brows. "Dr. Oliver paid for a *private* reading, my lord."

Nathan waved his hand. "I've no objection to his staying." He grinned. "Especially as I have every intention of remaining for his."

She inclined her head. "Very well." While she shuffled, she said, "I will tell you something of your past, present, and future. What do you wish to know?"

Nathan pondered for several seconds, then asked, "How many children will my wife and I have?"

She nodded, then after the cutting and dealing of the cards, she studied them for a full minute, her expression serious. "The cards representing your past show that you followed the path you'd chosen for many years, but then several years ago a life-changing event occurred. Something that brought harm to people you loved and caused you to . . . lose your way. Forced you to start over. I see estrangement from those you cared about. It was a very lonely time for you. But you finally found your way home again."

An odd feeling gripped Colin's gut at her accurate words, and Nathan's gaze flicked over to him. It was clear in that quick look that his brother erroneously believed he'd told her about his past.

"Go on," Nathan with a smile.

"In your recent past, I see both great happiness and great pain. The happiness is clearly due to love, giving and receiving. The pain is due to loss. The loss of a child." She looked up at Nathan. "Your child."

The tension gripping Colin dissipated, and he barely held back a snort at her ridiculous statement. Nathan didn't have children. Relief rushed through him. For a moment there, he'd actually believed some of this nonsense. Although he inwardly cringed at the sudden somber turn of the reading. Bloody hell, this was supposed to be an entertainment. Couldn't she make up things that were less . . . morbid?

He glanced at Nathan and stilled. His brother's face had gone visibly pale, and he was staring at Alexandra intently, his hands gripped together so tightly his knuckles showed bone white beneath the skin.

"Go on," Nathan said, his voice rough, almost harsh.

"Your present is consumed with your marriage and is filled with love. Happiness. And the prospect of fatherhood. You are extremely concerned for your wife's current delicate condition"—she indicated the last grouping of cards—"but your future indicates all will be well. You've nothing to fear." She smiled at him. "Would you like to hear my prediction as to whether the child will be a boy or girl?"

Nathan swallowed, then nodded.

"A girl. Followed by three more children. Therefore, to answer your question, you are destined to have four children." She picked up the cards from the table, then turned to Colin, and asked, "Are you ready, my lord?"

But Colin's gaze was riveted across the table on Nathan, who tunneled his fingers through his hair, then dragged his hands down his colorless face. He met Colin's gaze, and the look in Nathan's eyes stilled him. Before Colin could question him, Nathan nodded slowly.

"It's true," he said, his voice soft, gravelly. "Victoria miscarried four months ago. We just confirmed last week that she's expecting again."

Colin simply stared. "I . . . had no idea. I'm very sorry for the loss you both suffered."

"Thank you. As we hadn't yet told anyone we were expecting, we decided there was no point in mentioning the miscarriage. We planned to tell everyone about this pregnancy once she was further along." He looked at Alexandra through very serious eyes. "Your skills are . . . formidable, Madame."

"Thank you, but I merely interpreted what the cards indicated."

Nathan smiled. "Skilled and modest. A formidable combination."

An unsettling realization crawled through Colin. If she'd been so unerringly correct in Nathan's reading, then all the dire things she'd predicted for *him* might be accurate as well. They certainly mirrored the dark feeling of foreboding that had consumed him over the past weeks.

Forcing his thoughts back to the conversation, he turned to Nathan and extended his hand. "Please accept my congratulations to both you and Victoria on your impending parenthood."

Nathan clasped his hand tightly between both of his. And in the space of a single heartbeat, Colin read in Nathan's eyes both joy and fear. "Thank you. I'd prefer if you keep the news to yourself for now . . . Uncle Colin."

A lump of emotion formed in his throat, and he coughed to clear it away. God willing the heavy weight of gloom he felt surrounding his own future would lift and he'd see Nathan's child born. And perhaps one of his own.

As if reading his thoughts, Nathan said, "I'd be delighted if you'd return the favor and make me an uncle."

"That's why I'm here. To find a bride and make that happen." *Before it's too late.*

"Perhaps Madame can tell you who your bride will be."

"I've asked her that very question during my two previous readings, but all she's so far discerned is that apparently the lady has dark hair."

"If you recall, my lord," she said, "my saying that your bride was dark-haired was at your request and merely for Lady Newtrebble's benefit. I've seen nothing in your cards about your future wife."

"Well, perhaps today's reading will reveal all. I'm ready whenever you are, Madame."

Instead of picking up her cards, she regarded him steadily. "Given the nature of my previous predictions, perhaps it might be best if we rescheduled our appointment."

Colin shook his head. "I appreciate your discretion, but I'd prefer Nathan be here."

"Was there some problem with your previous readings?" Nathan asked, his gaze turning sharp.

"I'm afraid they weren't filled with sunny predictions for my future. We're hoping for better results this time." He turned to Alexandra. "Let us begin."

"As you wish, my lord." Reaching into her other pocket, she withdrew a different, smaller deck of cards. After completing the shuffling and cutting, she slowly dealt them, laying them out in a different pattern than she'd used before.

After studying the cards at length, she looked at him through troubled eyes. "I'm afraid I see the same things as I did in your previous two readings, with death and betrayal showing an even stronger presence than before—both in your past and in your future. It appears that the betrayal in your past is somehow related to that in your future."

She glanced back at the cards, and her frown deepened. "The inner turmoil I saw earlier is now more profound. You're experiencing great confusion and conflict, yet there is also a growing sense of urgency, a fear of things you will not be able to do. Of responsibilities left undone."

The accuracy of her words tensed his every muscle, cramping his insides. The intensity in her voice, in her eyes held him spellbound. "What of the dark-haired woman you previously saw?" he asked.

She hesitated, then pointed to the cards. "She is still there. Closer to you than before. Indeed, it is her location that concerns me the most."

"What do you mean?"

She looked up, and her gaze met his. Again she hesitated, looking distinctly troubled. Finally, she said, "Her card remains at the center of the danger and deceit and is the only thing standing between your card and the death card. Which means she will either save you or—"

"Be the death of me?" he suggested, keeping his tone light.

But her expression remained utterly serious. "Yes."

"What of my future wife?"

"As in the previous readings, I'm afraid I see no mention of her here, my lord."

His gaze roamed over her face, taking in her serious eyes and lush lips, then coming to rest on the long, shiny tendrils spiraling down toward her collarbone. Long, shiny tendrils of dark hair. And a feeling of unshakable surety slapped him. There was no doubt in his mind.

She was the dark-haired woman.

Twelve

Alex looked at Colin from across the space of his luxurious carriage and, for the dozenth time since they'd departed his town house, wondered what he was thinking. He'd been preoccupied ever since she'd completed his reading, silent during the ride to her rooms.

Was he thinking, as she was, about their kiss? About where it might have led had they not been interrupted? She desperately wanted to believe she would have regained her senses, would have emerged from the sensual world in which she'd been lost even without the knocking on the door, but there was no point in entertaining such a patent falsehood.

The shockingly delicious sensation of his hand beneath her skirt, the heat of his palm cupping her bottom . . . never had she imagined anything so arousing. Just thinking about it set up that insistent throb between her legs.

Her thoughts were interrupted when they arrived at her building, where Colin and his footman accompanied her upstairs. While she gathered her meager belongings into a worn leather portmanteau, Emma arrived. After quick introductions, she explained the plan to her friend, whose blue eyes alternately darted looks of distrust at Lord Sutton, and glances of pure admiration at his tall, handsome young footman.

"I hate to leave you," she said to Emma, twisting her fingers together, "but if I brought danger here—to you, to the children—I'd never forgive myself."

Emma grasped her hands and gently squeezed them to stop their fidgeting. "Don't ye worry about anythin', Alex. I'll take care o' the wee ones and the bakin'. Most important thing is you bein' safe." She scowled at Colin. "From *everything*."

Colin inclined his head. "Keeping her safe is my intention, Miss Bagwell."

"I'm sure it is." Emma's chin jutted out. "I'm just wonderin' if it's yer *only* intention."

Alex gasped, stunned at her friend's unmistakable implications and fierce tone. Before she could find her voice, Colin said, "No harm will come to her, Miss Bagwell."

"See to it that it don't," Emma said sharply. "From anyone. Yerself included."

"Emma—" Alex began.

"I will protect her with my life," he said quietly, his gaze steady on Emma's. "And I thank you for your words. I admire plain speaking. Alexandra is fortunate to have such a loyal and steadfast friend."

"*I'm* the fortunate one, havin' her," Emma said, her eyes narrowed. "There's no one finer, and I don't want her hurt. By nobody. In any way."

"Then we are in complete accord."

A heavy silence filled the air. Alex looked at him—a handsome, wealthy, educated aristocrat of impeccable bearing and breeding, dressed in the finest clothing, standing in her humble rooms, on the rough wooden floor covered by the simple handmade cloth rug she'd fashioned from scraps of material. A humorless, bitter laugh rose in her throat at the incongruous picture, a sharp, piercing reminder of who and what she was. And who and what he was. And how those two things would never, could never, intersect in any way.

She cleared her throat, then said to him, "I'm all packed, but I'd like a few minutes alone with Emma, please."

He nodded. "I'll await you in the carriage." The footman lifted the portmanteau and followed him from the room.

The instant the door closed behind them, Emma let out a long breath and fanned herself with her hand. "Bloody hell, I think I've got me the vapors. Weren't that just the most beautiful man ye've ever seen in yer life?"

Before she could stop herself, Alex let out a sigh that matched Emma's and barely refrained from the hand fanning. "Yes," she agreed, fervently wishing she didn't. "He is the most beautiful man I've ever seen."

"Just lookin' at 'im made me forget how to breathe. Stunned me speechless, he did."

"Yes, I know exactly what you mean. Although you seemed your normal outspoken self to me."

"Oh, sure, to that fancy bloke but not to *him*." She breathed the last word with a reverence Alex had never heard from her before. "And speakin' of that fancy bloke—" Emma's word cut off, and her eyes widened. "Why, it's him ye've been speakin' about right along."

Alex blinked, nonplussed. Clearly she and Emma had been talking at cross-purposes. As there was no point in denying Emma's assertion, she nodded. "But his footman is indeed handsome," she added, although, God help her, she'd barely noticed him.

A slight movement of the curtain room divider caught Alex's attention, and she turned. And caught a glimpse

of a dirty face before it disappeared behind the curtain.
"Come in here, Robbie," she said.

Several seconds past, then the child shuffled forward.
After he stopped in front of Alex, he said in a rush,
"That were the bloke I told ye about. The one wot were
here before."

"Yes, I know. I spoke to him about it. He'll not come
uninvited again. I take it you heard everything?"

He nodded, looking up at her with eyes that reflected
both suspicion and unmistakable hurt. "Ye should
have told me ye were in danger, Miss Alex. I'd've protected ye."

Alex's heart contracted, and she crouched down, setting her hands on the boy's narrow shoulders. "I know.
And a fine job you'd do. But I can't risk that someone
might hurt you or Emma or any of the others. I need
you to look out for each other, and for Emma, too. Can
you do that for me?"

He frowned, then jerked his head in a nod. "Ye were
gonna leave without sayin' good-bye," he said in an accusatory tone.

"Robbie, I'm not *leaving*, I'm simply going to stay in
another part of London for a short time."

"The place where that rich bloke lives," he said, his
voice filled with a bitterness at odds with the trembling
of his chin. "Ye'll take a fancy to the good life and for-
git all 'bout us."

Dear God, this child cleaved right through her heart.
Cupping his small, dirty face between her hands, she
said, "I could never forget you. Or Emma. Or the others. I think about all of you *all the time*. You're always
here"—she laid one hand across her heart—"inside me.
Part of me. I'll only be gone a short time. When I come
back, we'll share an entire plate of biscuits—just you,
me, and Emma—and I'll tell you everything that happened."

"Promise?"

"Promise."

He drew a shaky breath, then launched himself into her arms, his thin arms encircling her neck. Alex hugged him tightly, savoring the sensation, for he didn't often allow hugs. He pulled away seconds later, and she let him go.

Chucking him lightly under the chin, she said, "Now take your orange and off with you."

He dashed to the table, where the extra oranges were stacked, and grabbed the top one. Then he walked to the door and opened it. After a final look over his shoulder, he waved, then left.

After the door closed behind him, she and Emma exchanged a look. "I'll look after him, Alex."

"I know."

"About this Lord Sutton . . . he came here before today?"

"Yes."

"So he knows ye're not married." Emma's gaze turned troubled. "I saw the way he looked at ye, Alex. Like ye were a tasty morsel and he were a starvin' man."

She should have been appalled. Instead, her heart leapt with excitement.

"Ye know that a man like him would only take ye, then leave ye. Probably with his brat in yer belly."

"A man like him?"

Emma made an exasperated sound. "A fancy toff. Only after his own pleasures. Mark my words, he's used to gettin' what he wants, no matter the cost to others, and he wants *you*."

"I agree that many people in Society are like that, but there's more to him. So much more." She drew a deep breath, then asked, "What if I told you that I want him, too?"

Emma frowned, clearly considering. Finally, she said, "Ye know yer heart'll get broke."

"Yes."

"Well, then, I guess ye'd just have to decide if ye think it'd be worth the pain ye'd suffer after he tosses ye aside like yesterday's trash. 'Cause ye know that's wot he'll do."

Alex nodded, inwardly wincing at the reality. "Yes. I know."

"Fer me, I'd be terrified of a fancy bloke like that. Strange birds those rich toffs are. But if his footman were to so much as crook his finger at me, can't say as I'd be able to resist. Or want to. And since he works at a fancy house, he'd no doubt toss me aside like yesterday's trash, too—and I'm guessin' it'd be worth the heart-break." Emma squeezed her hand. "Ye do what ye think is best—for *you*. Ye know I'll love ye no matter what. And will help ye pick up the pieces after he's gone."

A wave of love, strong and fierce, crashed over her, and she hugged Emma. "Thank you. Now, about what I wanted to tell you . . ." She quickly gave her friend the direction of the Wexhall town house, telling her about Dr. Oliver's desire to purchase oranges for his wife. "Come tomorrow. If you bring the knapsack for Jack, I'll deliver it."

"I'll be there. With lots o' oranges. And don't ye worry about Jack. I can take care o' his delivery 'til ye come home."

Unable to keep still, Alex began to pace. "But I'm leaving you with all the baking, the children, and what about your reading and writing lessons?"

"They'll all still be here waitin' when ye return. The only thing I want ye thinkin' about is yer safety." Then her eyes twinkled. "And maybe a way fer me to meet up with yer fancy bloke's footman."

In spite of her heavy heart, Alex smiled. "I'll see what I can arrange."

Two hours later, Alex found herself standing in a bed-chamber at the Wexhall town house, in the likes of which she'd never imagined sleeping. Dr. Oliver's beautiful wife, Lady Victoria, who was as gracious as she was stunning, had escorted her to the chamber more than a quarter hour ago, leaving after telling Alex that dinner was served at eight.

But since the moment she'd left Alex alone, all she'd been able to do was gape. Lady Victoria had called the beautiful bedchamber "the garden room," and with good reason. The green color scheme, accented with a thick grass-colored carpet, its border intertwined with leaves and colorful flowers, made it appear as if she stood in a blooming meadow.

Walking slowly around the perimeter of the room, Alex ran her fingertips over the textured silk-covered walls, which were a shade paler than the carpet and admired the groupings of gilt-framed paintings of flowers. An extravagant bouquet of pale pink roses nestled in a crystal vase set on the bedside table filled the air with a delicate floral scent.

Her gaze fell upon the beautiful bed, and her feet moved toward it, as if in a trance. The bed looked so large and so incredibly soft and inviting, like a green satin cloud, that she couldn't resist trailing her hand over the beautiful counterpane and elaborate tasseled pillows. She found herself peeking over her shoulder, unable to shake the feeling that any second someone would burst in and order her from this heavenly room.

She slowly sat on the edge of the mattress, then took an experimental bounce. A quick laugh filled with jubilant wonder she couldn't contain burst from her lips at the delightful sensation. After another guilty peek to make certain she wasn't about to be evicted, she lay down, carefully, so as not to rumple the counterpane.

Her eyes slid closed on a long sigh of pleasure as she sank into the softness. Surely this was what fluffy clouds felt like. Never in her entire life had she rested upon anything so comfortable.

How many times had she dreamed of sleeping on such a bed, in such a room? More than she could count. Every one of those miserable nights she'd spent huddled in doorways or hiding behind piles of garbage, suffering through rain and cold and oppressive heat, although in truth she'd actually welcomed the summer to ward off the cold that never seemed to fully seep from her bones. Sometimes she'd slept inside, but those rooms were invariably dark, dirty, and foul-smelling places where she'd clustered with others like her. When she'd finally stolen enough money to afford to put a solid, albeit somewhat leaky roof over her head, it had been a day she'd never forget.

Realizing it was best to get up before she decided she never wanted to rise, she left the comfort of the bed and walked to the French windows along the back wall, through which ribbons of golden sunshine slanted. She noted with delight that the windows opened to a balcony. She stepped outside, smiling when the breeze ruffled her hair, and looked down at the small garden below, surrounded by a stone wall and tall, perfectly manicured hedges, unable to fully grasp that she was actually a guest here. Not the hired help paid to entertain the partygoers, but a guest.

God help her, she wasn't certain if she were more excited or intimidated. For the several hours' duration of the Society soirees at which Madame worked, she was able, with an effort, not to gawk at her luxurious surroundings. But this . . . being a guest in this fine home where everyone possessed impeccable manners . . . would she be able to behave in a way that wouldn't shame her? Wouldn't give away her disreputable past? After so many years of carefully observing and listening to the Quality, absorbing their speech patterns and mannerisms like a sponge, she'd been confident enough to take her card-reading talent and adopt her Madame Larchmont persona. She'd been determined to stop stealing, to cease trying to make something of herself by taking things that belonged to others. Perhaps the rich people she stole from didn't deserve all their fine things and their money, but the fact that she stole them, in her mind, made her just as undeserving.

But no matter how accomplished her acting abilities, or the fact that she no longer picked pockets, she wasn't one of them. Wasn't a lady. Never would be. And now, standing amid all this elegance, she felt as incongruous as Colin had looked earlier in her rooms. This stay in this fine home with its servants and plentiful food and elegant belongings was merely temporary. And she needed to remember that.

Just as she needed to remember that nothing save heartache would result from allowing herself further personal involvement with Colin. Kissing him again, while incredibly tempting, was a temptation she simply had to resist. There was no room for her in his life and she needed to forget her impossible attraction to him. For her own peace of mind. A liaison with him risked her reputation, which in turn risked everything she'd worked so hard for. A few hours of pleasure were not worth the risk.

Thus resolved, she returned inside and finished exploring the room, noting with embarrassment that her meager gowns already hung in the wardrobe, obviously the work of a maid. Embarrassment turned to a sense of awe. A maid—taking care of her! Wait until she told Emma.

Shaking her head, she walked to the small, feminine-looking desk in the corner and gingerly perched herself on the delicate chair. After a brief hesitation, she pulled her cards from the pocket of her gown and stared at the silk-wrapped bundle, torn between her desire to read her own cards and trepidation at doing so.

She'd never before feared reading her own cards, but now she dreaded seeing something she didn't want to. But she had to know . . .

After drawing a bracing breath, she unfolded the silk and, after shuffling and cutting the deck, slowly turned over the cards. When she finished, she stared. Then began to tremble.

It was all there . . . her cards nearly identical to the ones she'd dealt for Colin. They showed betrayal. Deceit. Death. All revolving around the dark-haired man— the same dark-haired man who'd figured so prominently in her cards for years. And at the center of it all, a dark-haired woman.

The fact that her reading so closely resembled Colin's couldn't be a mere coincidence. But the two questions the phenomena suggested made her heart pound in slow, hard thumps of dread. Was it possible that the danger surrounding Colin meant *he* was the intended victim at Lord Wexhall's party?

And was it possible that *she* was the dark-haired woman?

After leaving Alexandra at the Wexhall town house in Victoria's very capable hands, Colin arrived home and made his way to the drawing room, where he visited his secret stash of marzipan. He selected a piece that looked like a perfect miniature orange, then settled himself and his prize in his favorite wing chair. He was about to take his first bite when a knock sounded at the door.

Barely covering his irritation, he called out, "Come in, Ellis."

The door opened, and Ellis entered. "Dr. Nathan is here, my lord. Are you at home?"

"Yes, are you at home?" came Nathan's voice from just behind Ellis. The butler winced.

"I'm at home, Ellis, thank you."

Nathan strode across the room and sat opposite him. He appeared about to speak, when he stilled, then sniffed the air. "I smell marzipan."

"Yes, I'm certain you do." He held his orange aloft, then with great relish, slowly bit it in half.

"I thought you said I'd finished the last piece."

"I lied."

"Where are they?"

"Heinous torture could not drag that information from me. Now, why are you here—again? I'll be seeing you in an hour for dinner."

"Several reasons. First, have you found the gift I brought you?"

"No—for which I feel suspiciously relieved. And what do you mean by 'found'? Why not simply give it to me and be done with it?"

A crooked smile lifted one corner of Nathan's mouth. "This way is more fun."

"For you, yes. How will I know when I 'find' this gift?"

"Oh, trust me. You'll know."

"Sadly, that's just what I'm afraid of. What other reasons do you have for once again darkening my doorstep?"

"As you had a guest earlier, there was no opportunity for the private conversation I'd come to have, and I don't want to risk being interrupted at Wexhall's later this evening. A conversation I intend to have with you right after you tell me about this Madame Larchmont."

Colin popped the other half of his marzipan into his mouth, then took his time chewing, keeping his expression carefully blank. After he swallowed, he asked, "What do you want to know?"

"Everything."

"What makes you think there's anything to tell?"

"The fact that you kissed her is a fairly good indication."

Bloody hell. Why did his brother have to be so damnably observant? "What makes you think I kissed her?"

"Being an excellent kisser myself—according to my wife—I know the look of a well-kissed woman. It was a look Madame Larchmont wore like a red banner. Since you're clearly not going to volunteer any information, I'm forced to ask. Is she a widow, or merely pretending to be married?"

"What makes you think she isn't married?"

"Because I know you. You're not the sort of man who would trifle with another man's wife."

Damn it, the way Nathan always thought the best of him, never doubted his honor or integrity, humbled him.

"Thank you for that vote of confidence," he said quietly. "God knows it's far more than I deserve."

"If you say that one more time, I swear I'm going to start pelting you with eggs again," Nathan said mildly. "So, which is it—widow or pretending to be married?"

"Pretending."

Nathan nodded. "The illusion of a husband would offer her a measure of safety, security, and freedom she'd not have as an unmarried or even widowed woman. She's clearly very intelligent."

"Yes, she is."

"And obviously enamored of you. Feelings it's clear to me, who knows you so well, are reciprocated."

A blindfold. That's what he needed to give his far-too-observant brother. A bloody blindfold. "I can't deny I find her attractive."

"I suspect it's a bit more involved than that, which does not mesh well with your bride-finding plans."

"No, it doesn't."

"So, do you wish to tell me all about her, or would you rather begin by explaining the reasons behind your sudden decision to get married?"

"I thought we'd agreed to have this conversation to-morrow over breakfast."

"We did. But as we have the privacy to do so now, let's."

As his own feelings regarding Alexandra were so con-flicted, he opted to postpone discussing her as long as possible. Leaning forward, he braced his elbows on his knees and told Nathan everything—the recurring night-mare where he was trapped in a dark, narrow space, knowing death was near. The growing sense of doom, of time running out, and the gut-level yet inexplicable knowledge that something bad was going to happen to him.

Nathan listened intently and, when he finished, asked, "How are these feelings now that you're here in London?"

"Stronger. But that could merely be the result of my visits to unsafe areas while following Madame Larch-mont." He dragged his hands down his face. "I'm hop-ing this is just some aberration brought on by the fact that I'm now the same age Mother was when she died."

"And you think the same fate of dying young awaits you?"

"It's not something I ever dwelled on, but once the nightmares started, I thought of the age similarity, and now, ridiculous as it seems, I cannot get the thought out of my mind."

"I don't think it's ridiculous," Nathan said. "Indeed, it's a phenomenon I've seen in several patients. The fear of death manifests itself as one approaches the age at which they lost a parent or sibling or loved one, and, unfortunately, the anxiety doesn't fully dissipate until the next birthday.

"With you, however," he continued, "given how finely tuned I know your instincts to be, I'm very much inclined to believe that your feelings of impending danger are correct. The question is what sort of danger? Actual physical danger? Or something more benign?"

"Such as?"

Nathan shrugged. "Given your search for a wife, perhaps you are in danger of suffering a broken heart."

"Extremely doubtful, as I'm not planning to make a love match."

"As someone whose own recently unplanned plunge into love caught him totally unawares, I feel the need to caution you that when the heart is involved, plans invariably . . . go astray."

Nathan's words unsettled him in a way he refused to examine too closely, and unable to sit still any longer, he rose and paced the length of the hearth rug. "The nightmare revolves around physical danger, and that's what my instincts are warning me of."

"It's also what your card reading today indicated, and from what I gather, your two previous readings as well."

A frown pulled down his brows. "Yes. I have to admit that I'd lent little credence to Madame Larchmont's predictions before, but clearly what she told you was accurate."

"Eerily so. Had you told her anything about the events of four years ago?"

"No. Nothing."

"Which only makes what she told me all the more eerie."

"While I'm at a loss to explain or understand this talent she possesses, I can no longer dismiss her predictions, especially as they so closely mirror my own sense of danger . . ." His words trailed off and he halted as a thought occurred to him. He looked at Nathan. "I wonder . . ."

"What?" Nathan asked.

"Given the previous attack on Wexhall, we agree he could be the intended victim. But consider that I've sensed danger for myself and the eerily correct Madame Larchmont has predicted the same. Add that she's heard of a plot in which a person of some note, as a peer could be described, is to be killed. This crime is to take place at the home of the man to whom I used to report, at a party I'm scheduled to attend. Then add that I'm acquainted with every name on the list of people who were in the vicinity when Madame heard the voice last night. Is all that merely coincidence?"

Nathan sat forward in his chair. "I'm not a big believer in coincidences."

"Nor am I."

"You're thinking *you* might be the target at Wexhall's party."

"I think it's possible, yes. Don't you?"

"Hearing all those coincidences tells me it's a theory that cannot be dismissed out of hand. But why would anyone want you dead?"

"Surely, given what happened to you only nine short months ago, you don't need to ask."

He stared at his brother and watched the realization dawn in Nathan's eyes. "You think something—or someone—in your past has come back to haunt you."

"The sort of activities I performed for the Crown weren't those that would endear me to everyone," Colin said.

"Do you have any theories?"

"Not yet, as I've barely had a chance to think upon it."

"Any reason why anyone written on that list you gave me might want to see you dead?"

"I'm not certain. What was Wexhall's reaction when you showed him the list?"

"I haven't yet. He's been out."

Colin crossed to his desk and retrieved the piece of ivory vellum where he'd written the names Alexandra had dictated. Running his gaze down the list, he said, "In recent years I've bested Barnes at the faro table, politely turned down the offer of a liaison from Carver's wife, engaged in a liaison with Mallory's widowed daughter, and decided against purchasing a painting from Surringham. Ralstrom, Whitemore, and I attended the races two years ago, and I cleaned them out. Most recently I dashed Lady Whitemore's wishes for me to marry her daughter, Lady Alicia. Lady Miranda and Lady Margaret both seem pleasant and interested in me. I've only just been introduced to Jennsen."

"None of that sounds particularly threatening."

"No, it doesn't. I'll continue to think on it. Perhaps something else will occur to me. And perhaps Wexhall will be able to shed some light on it."

Nathan nodded. "Rest assured that if you are indeed the target, Wexhall and I will do everything in our power to ensure that no harm befalls you."

"Thank you. Or befalls Madame Larchmont."

"Yes." Nathan's gaze turned questioning. "Are you ready to tell me about her?"

"What precisely do you want to know?"

"Everything. Or at least whatever you're willing to tell me. How did you meet?"

Colin hesitated, then said, "We were introduced at Malloran's soiree." Perfectly true, yet so misleading, his conscience slapped him.

Nathan's brows rose. "Which only leaves me more curious. 'Tis clear she's important to you, yet you've only known her mere days."

"Says a man who *proposed* to a woman he'd known little more than a week."

"Untrue. As you well know, I met Victoria years earlier here in London."

"Yes. On *one* occasion. And then didn't see her again for three years." He tunneled his fingers through his hair, the similarities between his situation and Nathan's not lost on him. "And as it just so happens, I met Madame Larchmont on that very same trip to London and didn't see her again until the Malloran soiree."

"I thought you said you were just introduced."

"We were. We were not introduced four years ago."

"Ah. You merely admired her from afar?"

"Something like that."

"Then that trip to London was fateful indeed. For both of us. Where did you see her?"

He set his hands on the mantel, gripped the cool white marble, and stared into the glowing embers of the fire. "Vauxhall."

After a long silence, Nathan asked, "She was telling fortunes?"

He continued to stare into the fire, then finally turned to face Nathan. "No. I caught her picking my pocket."

Suddenly weary, he sat, resting his elbows on his spread knees and clasped his hands. "I caught her in the act, but only because of my familiarity with the skill. She was good. Very nearly relieved me of Grandfather's gold watch. It was quite a shock to see her in Malloran's drawing room."

"You remembered her?"

"Vividly." He explained how she'd seemed to recognize him, how he'd searched for her, his initial suspicions when he'd first seen her at the Malloran soiree and therefore didn't let on he'd recognized her, then what he'd discovered upon searching her rooms.

"These children she helps," he concluded, "I imagine they are living the same sort of life she experienced as a child."

"Has she told you about her childhood?"

"No. And I haven't asked. Yet. But I have no doubt it was grim." His stomach clenched with both pity and anger on her behalf at the horrors she must have faced.

"Do you believe her fortune-telling is merely a ruse to gain access to the homes of the wealthy?" Nathan asked quietly.

"No," he said without hesitation. "I admit I thought it possible at first, but I don't believe it of the woman who helps those children."

"She could be all the more helpful to them using ill-gotten gains stolen at all these fancy soirees."

"True. But I still don't believe it."

"Those children she's supposedly helping could also be stealing *for* her, making you the victim of a carefully constructed story to gain your sympathy."

"Possibly. But again, I don't believe it. My instincts tell me she's sincere and no longer a thief."

Nathan studied him for a long moment, and Colin could almost hear the wheels turning in his brother's mind. Finally, Nathan said in a quiet voice, "Not that I don't greatly respect your instincts, but as you barely know her I'm compelled to ask: Are you giving this woman your trust because she genuinely deserves it or because of some misplaced sense of guilt?"

He didn't pretend to misunderstand, but when he remained silent, Nathan continued, "Please tell me that you're not simply determined to trust her, no matter what, in an effort to correct what you perceive to be a past wrong."

"I *did* wrong you."

"It's over. In the past."

"I know."

"Then let it go. I have. I thought we'd put this behind us."

"We have. I'm just not willing to make that same mistake again. In spite of the fact that I don't know everything about her, about her past, I'm choosing to believe her story. And that she's changed her life. Because everything in me tells me she's sincere."

Nathan didn't reply for a long moment, then he finally nodded. "I'll respect your decision."

"Thank you."

"And pray that it doesn't cost you your life."

Thirteen

Alex sat in Lord Wexhall's elaborate dining room, beneath a sky-blue ceiling adorned with plump, arrow-bearing cherubs floating among puffy clouds, which made her feel as if she were dining in heaven. The air was redolent with the savory scents of delicious foods while servants and the murmur of polite dinner conversation surrounded her. She reached beneath the table and pinched herself on the thigh. Hard. Then clamped her lips together to contain her yelp of pain. Yes, this was real. All of it.

The sparkling crystal and gleaming silver. The ornate china set upon the dark wood table buffed to an almost glasslike shine. The centerpiece of fresh flowers dripping over the side of an oblong crystal footed bowl. The scent of beeswax from the dozens of candles that bathed the room with a soft wash of golden glow.

And the food . . . never had she seen such an array or quantity in one place. Only five people were present, but surely there was enough food to feed a dozen. Perhaps two dozen. It required every bit of her will not to slip slices of ham and bread into her napkin to smuggle out for Emma and Robbie and the others. Course after succulent course, from soup to creamed peas to pheasant to ham to braised carrots were served by liveried footmen wearing pristine white gloves, each course accompanied by a delicious wine the likes of which she'd never tasted.

Instead of relaxing and enjoying all this luxury, however, she felt on edge and tense, speaking little as she concentrated on exactly copying which utensil Lady Victoria, who sat opposite her, used. Fortunately, she was spared from making much conversation, as Lord Wexhall was in an expansive and verbose mood, regaling the table with amusing anecdotes of his spy days. Then Dr. Oliver told of several mishaps with his menagerie of farm animals. Her concentration, unfortunately, wasn't helped by the fact that _he_ sat directly across from her, next to Lady Victoria.

Never in her life had she been so achingly, painfully aware of another person.

No matter how hard she tried, she could not stop her gaze from seeking Colin out. Every time she finished studying Lady Victoria's hands to ascertain she was using the correct utensil in the proper manner, her errant eyeballs strayed to him. And invariably found his gaze resting upon her. Which only served to rattle her composure further.

He looked devastatingly striking in his forest green cutaway jacket, which intensified the color of his eyes. His dark hair gleamed in the candlelight, contrasting with his snowy white shirt and silver waistcoat. No matter where she looked, she still saw him from the corner of her eyes. Felt his gaze upon her. Even when she focused on her plate, she found herself looking up through her lashes, peeking at how his long, strong fingers held his crystal wine goblet or his silverware.

The sound of his voice, the rumble of his laughter,

resonated deep inside her, eliciting tiny pulses of pleasure that captivated and enthralled her. When she caught herself leaning forward, tilting her head in his direction to hear him better, annoyance crept through her. Botheration, she could no doubt sit in a room and watch the bloody man *breathe* and be as happy as a bird in a puddle.

What in God's name had come over her? When and how had it happened? It was as if he'd cast a spell upon her. But at least her preoccupation with him kept her from dwelling on the fact that in spite of wearing her best emerald green gown, she felt woefully gauche and spectacularly unsophisticated in these grand surroundings. It was one thing to put on an act and fit in as an entertaining fortune-teller amongst a crowd, and quite another to share a formal meal with such an intimately acquainted group of the peerage. Tomorrow night she'd invent an excuse to have dinner in her room and save herself this discomfort.

"—Madame Larchmont."

The sound of her name roused her from her thoughts, and she blinked across the table at Lady Victoria, who regarded her with a questioning smile. Suddenly, she felt the weight of four stares upon her and her throat went dry.

After swallowing to locate her voice, she said, "I'm afraid I was so enamored of the meal that I lost the thread of the conversation."

Lady Victoria smiled. "I'll pass along your compliments to Cook. I was wondering what your answer to the question is as I've already stated mine."

"Question?"

"If you could describe a perfect place, what would it be like?"

Alex didn't need to consider—she'd pictured such a make-believe location in her mind every day since childhood. "My perfect place is always warm. And safe. And filled with golden sunshine and green meadows blooming with colorful flowers. It's near the sea, and scented with clean, salt-tinged breezes and filled with people I care about and who care about me in return. It's a place where no one is ever harmed and everyone always has enough money and food and clothing." She briefly considered not listing her final requisite, then decided to do so. "And where I have a wardrobe filled with so many beautiful gowns, it takes me an hour each day to decide what to wear."

For several seconds silence swelled, and again Alex felt the weight of everyone's eyes upon her. Heat suffused her face at her unguarded words, and her gaze flew to Colin, who regarded her with an unreadable expression.

The silence was broken when Lady Victoria said, "Oh, that does indeed sound like a perfect place."

"Not to me," said Dr. Oliver. "What on earth would I do with a wardrobe filled with gowns?"

"Give them to me," Lady Victoria said tartly. "Of course, my perfect place contains plenty of shops."

"And mine contains no shops whatsoever, nor an opera house," Dr. Oliver said, pulling a comical face. "You made no mention of pets, Madame. My perfect place includes lots of animals."

"A terrible omission," Alex said with a smile, forcing herself to relax. "I love cats, and dogs, too."

"My perfect place would have to include excellent brandy, good cigars, and a library filled with fine books," Lord Wexhall said. He nodded toward Colin. "What about you?"

He tapped his finger to his chin, clearly pondering, then, looking straight at Alex, said, "Creston Manor, where I live in Cornwall, is, to me, a nearly perfect place. It is close enough to the sea that you can always catch the salty scent and hear the music of the waves washing upon the cliffs. The gardens are blooming wonders, the grounds alive with trees and meadows and streams." Mischief glittered in his eyes. "And of course there's the lake, which Nathan can attest is quite cold most of the year."

"And the eggs, which Colin can attest are quite messy when broken," Dr. Oliver retorted.

"It does indeed sound like a perfect place," Alex said, unable to pull her gaze away from Colin's. She felt as if everything and everyone in the room suddenly faded away, leaving just the two of them.

"Not quite," he said softly. "There is, I think, one last thing needed to make a place, any place, perfect."

She didn't realize she was holding her breath until she tried to speak. "What's that?"

"The perfect person to share it with. Being alone is so very . . ."

"Lonely?" she supplied.

A quick smile flitted across his lips. "Yes."

"Now that brings up an interesting question," said Lady Victoria. "What traits should this perfect person possess in order to have the honor of sharing one's perfect place?"

"Victoria, of course, has only to look at me to know the answer to that question," Dr. Oliver said with exaggerated smugness. Everyone laughed, then he added, "And my wife is the perfect person to me. Beautiful, intelligent, loyal, and she thinks I'm unsurpassedly brilliant."

Alex couldn't help but notice the look that passed between Dr. Oliver and his wife—a look filled with love and unmistakable desire. A look that filled her with deep yearning.

"As far as I'm concerned," Lord Wexhall said, "the perfect person would be one who I could soundly beat at cards and who could predict the outcomes of all the horse races."

"If you had to pick just *one* trait," Lady Victoria said, "the one you think most important, most admirable, what would it be?" She turned to her husband. "You first."

He thought for several seconds, then said, "Loyalty. You?"

Lady Victoria pondered, then said, "Patience. Father?"

"Bravery."

"What about you, Madame?" Colin asked.

"Compassion," Alex said softly. "And you, my lord?"

"Honesty."

She inwardly winced. How ironic that of all the qualities he could have chosen, he picked the one that she'd buried under a mountain of lies. Not that it mattered, of course. The thought of her as his perfect person was utterly laughable. Depressingly so.

The meal ended shortly afterward, and the group retired to the drawing room, where talk turned to the murders. Clearly either her husband or father had apprised Lady Victoria of what was going on, for she appeared to be well acquainted with the situation.

"Something interesting about one of the names on the list you gave me, Sutton," Lord Wexhall said. "Whitemore. He used to be one of my best men. Did most of his work out of London. Retired from service two years ago. Pity. He was excellent."

"Why did he retire?" Colin asked.

"He'd been at it a decade. Said he'd seen and done enough."

"I never had any dealings with him," Dr. Oliver said. "Did you, Colin?"

"Nothing spy related."

"He was the only person on the list who stood out to

me," Lord Wexhall said. "I'll be certain to keep an eye on him tomorrow at Ralstrom's party." He then rose and excused himself, claiming fatigue.

After he left the room, Lady Victoria asked, "Would anyone care for a game? Perhaps whist?"

Before Alex could plead ignorance of the game, Colin said, "Actually, I thought to show Madame through the gallery, if you have no objections."

Heat rushed into her face at the unmistakable speculation in Lady Victoria's blue-eyed gaze, which bounced between her and Colin. Lady Victoria believed, as everyone else did, that Alex was married.

"I've no objections," Lady Victoria said, although her eyes seemed to lose a bit of their previous warmth. "That will give me a perfect opportunity to trounce my husband at the backgammon table."

"My darling Victoria, I greatly anticipate any trouncing I might receive at your hands."

As they moved toward the backgammon table near the window, Lord Sutton extended his hand. "Shall we?"

Alex debated, torn between the need to escape the tension of pretending to belong amongst people she didn't while feigning knowledge of polite parlor games, and the fear that being alone with Colin would result in another kiss.

Impatience rose within her. Botheration, she was perfectly capable of controlling herself. If he tried to kiss her, she'd simply rebuff him. Firmly and most emphatically. Thus resolved, she placed her lace-gloved hand in his. Heat instantly tingled up her arm—a warmth she firmly and most emphatically ignored.

Tucking her hand in the crook of his elbow, he escorted her from the room, then led her down a dimly lit corridor. It seemed that the pace he set was rather rapid as she nearly had to trot to keep up with him. Surely that was the cause of her breathlessness. It had nothing whatsoever to do with his nearness.

"You were quiet this evening," he said.

"Yes, I suppose so. I was preoccupied."

"About what?"

Drawing a deep breath, she told him about her theory that he might be the person in danger. When she finished, he said, "I think you could be right. Actually, Nathan and I discussed that same possibility earlier."

Dear God, she didn't how she'd bear it if something happened to him. "I hope you'll be careful."

"I will."

"I also wanted to tell you that I think someone was watching me today."

He turned toward her and frowned. "When? Where?"

"This morning when I returned home after my appointment with Mr. Jennsen."

A muscle ticked in his jaw. "Ah. For his private reading."

"Yes. I didn't see anyone, but I felt a . . . presence."

"Why didn't you tell me this earlier?"

"It slipped my mind. And it was nothing, really. Just a feeling I experienced when I stepped from his carriage."

"He escorted you home?" His voice sounded tight.

"Yes."

"So he knows where you live?"

"Not exactly. The driver left me several buildings away."

"I don't want you going out unescorted anymore. It's too dangerous. Either Nathan or I will accompany you wherever you need to go."

"As I've no desire to place myself in danger, I agree." Since he'd claimed that honesty was the most important quality in a person, she decided to give him some. "I was also quiet because I felt rather overwhelmed. And woefully out of place."

"I gathered that, which is one reason why I thought you might like to escape to the gallery."

Embarrassment heated her face. "I didn't mean that I didn't enjoy—"

"I know. But anyone not accustomed to being a guest in a house like this would feel out of place. I can only assure you that you fit in beautifully."

They continued walking, and she cast desperately about in her mind for something to say other than *kiss me*. "Your brother and Lady Victoria are very much in love."

"Yes. Nathan deserves every bit of happiness he's found. Indeed, I find myself envious."

"Of what?"

"The way she looks at him. The way she lights up like a candle whenever he walks into a room. I can only imagine that it's a very heady experience—to have someone care for you that much. To care that much for someone."

"I imagine so. Although surely it's something you've experienced."

"Why do you say that?"

"Surely you are looked at in such an adoring manner with frightening regularity."

"Not to my knowledge. Who, pray tell, would be gazing at me in such a fashion?"

"I would hazard to guess any female with a heart-beat."

He glanced at her, and amusement kindled in his eyes. "Would you? And why is that?"

"You realize, of course, that this sounds like another shameless fishing expedition for compliments."

They turned a corner, entering an even more dimly lit corridor. Large, framed paintings lined the walls on both sides, and she paused before the first picture, leaned forward, and squinted. "The light is not very good. It's rather difficult—"

Her words died with a swift intake of her breath as he brushed his fingertips over her wrist, just above where her lace glove ended, then slipped one long finger inside the material to stroke over her palm. Heat gushed through her at the sensual intimacy of the gesture. And in a heartbeat all her firm and emphatic resolve dissolved.

"It's rather difficult . . . .?" he prompted.

She swallowed to find her voice. *To breathe.* "To see." She bit her bottom lip to contain a moan of pleasure from the slow, hypnotic caress of his finger.

Colin slid his finger from her glove and touched it to her soft mouth, then stepped closer to her, the tension that had gripped him all evening abating only slightly now that he'd finally gotten her alone. Her eyes widened slightly, and she stepped back. Her shoulders hit the paneled wall between two portraits of Wexhall ancestors, and she gasped. Perfect. Just how he wanted her—trapped and breathless.

Setting his palms on the wall on either side of her head, he leaned closer and said softly, "I think that I would very much like to hear a compliment from you, Alexandra."

She raised her chin. "I'm certain you would. However, you are supposed to be introducing me to the Wexhall ancestors."

"Very well." Keeping his gaze on hers, he jerked his head left. "That gentleman is the brother to"—he jerked his head to the right—"that gentleman. Most likely. The chubby fellow depicted behind me is their uncle. Probably."

"For a person who offered to give me a tour of this gallery, you seem remarkably uninformed."

"Ah, but did you not tell me that men rarely say what they mean?"

She moistened her lips, and he nearly groaned. Bloody hell, he had never, in his entire life, wanted to kiss a woman more.

"Are you saying that when you asked me if I'd like a tour of the gallery—"

"I meant something altogether different."

"I . . . see. As you've stated your wish for a compliment, am I to understand that 'would you like to tour the gallery' really means 'I wish to hear nice things about myself'?"

"No. It means 'I want to feel your hands on me.' " He leaned back from the wall, then reached down to clasp one of her hands. Slowly, one finger at a time, he removed her glove. When he finished, he tucked the bit of lace inside his waistcoat and pressed her bare palm against his cheek.

Still holding her wrist, he turned his head and pressed a kiss against her palm. He inhaled the subtle citrus scent of oranges, then reached down to remove her other glove, pleased that she kept her hand against his cheek.

Her fingers slowly explored his jaw, and if he'd been capable of doing so, he would have laughed at his body's swift and powerful reaction to her gentle touch. A touch he craved with a fierceness he was at a loss to explain but which was categorically undeniable. After tucking her other glove into his pocket, he took both her hands and pressed them to his chest.

"If you intend to kiss me—"

"There is no 'if' about my intention to kiss you, Alexandra. I've wanted to touch you, kiss you, since the moment I arrived this evening. I thought dinner would never end."

"I must warn you that if you wreak havoc upon my

coiffure or gown, your brother and sister-in-law will certainly notice."

"Undoubtedly." He didn't bother to tell her that they'd be able to tell they'd done more in the gallery than gawk at portraits anyway just by looking at her, as he intended to see that she was well kissed.

"I don't want them to form a poor opinion of me."

"Why would they?"

"They believe I am married."

"My brother knows you are not."

"You told him?"

"Given that he knows married women are not to my taste, he guessed. I merely confirmed his correct assumption. As for Victoria, I suggest you tell her. She is very discreet. But if it makes you feel better, in the interests of some form of propriety . . ." He again planted his palms against the wall on either side of her head, then leaned forward until their lips nearly touched. "There. I won't touch you with anything but my mouth."

And then his lips were on hers, and he felt as if he were sinking into a dark abyss of pleasure and need where only she existed. Her fingers gripped his jacket, urging him closer, and he fisted his hands against the wall to keep his promise. Her lips parted, and he delved inside, exploring the satin of her mouth. Need, hot and wild, surged through him, and he stepped closer, pinning her against the wall with his lower body. His erection jerked inside his breeches, and he slowly rubbed himself against her softness, a low growl vibrating in his throat. Twining her arms around his neck, she rose on her toes and pressed herself more fully against him, undulating her hips in a manner that peeled away several more layers of his rapidly vanishing control.

He broke off their kiss and buried his face in the warm curve of her neck, his ragged breaths reverberating off her fragrant skin. Bloody hell. What this woman did to him with a single kiss was absurd. He lifted his head and noted with grim satisfaction that she looked as aroused and glazed and dazed as he felt. At least this fierce passion he felt wasn't unrequited.

Her eyelids fluttered open, and she brushed a single, tentative fingertip over his lips. The impact of her slumberous gaze and that gentle touch grabbed his heart and squeezed.

Normally she kept her feelings so carefully hidden, but now they all shone in her eyes. Wonder. Arousal. Curiosity. Anticipation. Vulnerability. Uncertainty. Confusion. Need. He recognized them all so easily because they exactly mirrored his own feelings. But where women were concerned, vulnerability, uncertainty, and confusion were new territories for him.

How in the bloody hell had a simple kiss turned so . . . complicated?

His body throbbed with the overwhelming need to kiss her again, but before he could do so, her eyes widened and filled with panic. With an exclamation that sounded rife with self-recriminations, she pushed him away, then ducked beneath his arm.

"I must go," she said, her voice tight. She turned to leave, and he caught her arm.

"Alexandra, wait—"

She swung toward him, her eyes dark pools of distress. "Please let me go," she whispered. "I don't want . . . I cannot . . ." She drew a deep, shaky breath. "I wish to retire."

"You mean you wish to run away. From me. From what is between us."

The sadness and vulnerability reflected in her gaze nearly undid him. "Yes. Let me do so. While I still can." She laid her hand over his. "Please, Colin."

Releasing her was the absolute last thing he wanted to do, yet he couldn't deny her. His hand slipped slowly from her arm, and the instant she was free, she turned and walked swiftly away.

After she disappeared around the corner, he leaned his shoulders against the wall and tipped back his head, somehow feeling more alone than he'd ever felt in his life. He slipped one of her gloves from his pocket and raising the bit of lace to his face, he closed his eyes and breathed in her delicious scent. And whispered the single word reverberating through his brain.

"Alexandra."

Her name ended on a groan. Damn it, why wasn't there some magic elixir he could swill to obliterate her from his mind? Make him forget how much he wanted her. Erase the memory of how perfectly she fit in his arms and the taste of her from his mouth. Eliminate this pounding hunger to make love to her and the equally strong craving simply to be in the same room with her. Talk with her. Laugh with her.

Never in his life had he experienced such confusing feelings for a woman, not even those to whom he had been deeply attracted or with whom he'd shared a bed. Those encounters had been pleasant, lighthearted, yet without exception ultimately forgettable.

While he certainly found great pleasure in Alexandra's company, *nothing* about his feelings felt lighthearted. No, this felt . . . intense. Vivid—as if everything around him was suddenly in sharper focus, the colors brighter and more brilliant, making it seem that his life had previously consisted only of shades of gray. As for her being ultimately forgettable . . .

A rough sound pushed past his lips. If he lived until the next century, he knew in his soul that he'd never forget her. She'd continue to haunt him as she had for the past four years—before he'd known so much as her name, let alone the taste of her kiss and the feel of her arms wrapped around him.

Her presence was keeping him from doing what he'd come to London to accomplish, yet he was finding it impossible to look for a bride when all he could think about was her. A woman who, given his responsibility to his title, he couldn't marry.

But you could *make her your mistress,* his inner voice whispered.

His conscience, his honor, and his integrity all immediately balked at the idea of an adulterous affair. Once he spoke marriage vows, he would not dishonor them.

You're not married yet, his inner voice reminded him slyly.

He opened his eyes and lifted his head, staring down at the lace glove he held. No, he wasn't married yet. He wasn't even betrothed. He could make her his mistress until that time. They could enjoy each other until he decided upon a wife. They'd be discreet. He'd make certain she was taken care of—her and the cause dear to her heart. Then . . . they'd say good-bye.

His heart raced with anticipation. He was convinced. Now all he had to do was convince her.

Fourteen

Alex lay in the soft, comfortable, warm lux-ury of the magnificent bed in her elegant bedchamber, wishing with all her might for sleep to overcome her. She tried, as she had for the past several hours, to empty her mind, but it simply could not be done. Not while *he* filled every corner.

She closed her eyes but found no relief from the sensual memories bombarding her. Of his strong arms caging her in against the gallery wall. The heat of his body surrounding her. His masculine scent invading her senses. Lowering his head . . .

She vividly recalled the delicious taste of his kiss. The exquisite sensation of his body pressing into hers. One touch was all it had required for him to strip her of all her fine resolutions. One touch is all he'd needed to make her want more. Make her want everything.

A frustrated sound blew past her lips, and, with an impatient gesture, she pushed away the bedcovers and sat up. She stood, then paced the length of the room several times before pausing to stare into the remnants of the fire glowing in the grate. She blew out a stream of air and watched the embers glow brighter and realized that she felt just like those smoldering remains . . . heated, waiting, ready, merely a breath away from flaring into flames.

She knew what went on between men and women in the dark. Had heard it, witnessed it more times than she cared to remember. She knew that much talk was devoted to such things, but from what she'd seen, it warranted little excitement. Indeed, the entire process had always struck her as something messy, to be avoided.

Until Colin had kissed her. His touch made the carnal acts she'd once dismissed ignite into desires she could not quell. Desires she wanted to explore. Desperately. With him.

But did she dare?

The question reverberated through her mind, and she resumed her pacing. If she were to offer herself to him . . . would he accept? Most likely. Men did not turn down such offers—did they? Especially if they knew there were no ramifications or consequences as she was hardly a Society lady bent on extracting a marriage proposal from him. And especially if he knew the liaison would only be for the short duration he remained in London. She would expect nothing from him except the promise to take precautions to prevent her from conceiving a child. It was obvious from his body's reaction when they kissed that he wouldn't be physically averse to the idea. And surely a man in his position, a man who'd spent years as a spy, was well acquainted with discretion.

Did she dare?

Yes, her inner voice whispered. The female inner voice that she'd forcibly muffled all these years, which now demanded to be heard.

No, her common sense countered, reminding her that

she barely knew this man. That he risked nothing while she risked a great deal.

But then her heart chimed in, insisting that even though she'd only spent a short time in his actual company, thanks to her card readings, she'd known about the dark-haired, green-eyed man long before she'd ever seen him in Vauxhall. That man was, without a doubt, Colin, and he'd lived in her imagination, in her heart and soul, for years. He was the man she'd always wanted, and this was her chance—her *only* chance—to have a very small part of him for a very short period of time.

Did she dare?

She closed her eyes and drew a deep breath. *Yes.* Yes, she did.

She would offer herself to him. And with any luck, he would be hers for a brief, magical time.

The instant she made the decision, a sense of relief washed over her. The pondering was done and the decision made. All she needed to do now was act upon her decision. And she intended to do just that the next time she saw him—which would be tomorrow.

Her gaze strayed to the mantel clock, and she realized that it was nearly 1:00 A.M.

Tomorrow had already arrived.

Anticipation curled through her, and she wrapped her arms around herself. No longer able to stay still, she walked to the French windows and looked out on the garden below.

The full moon cast the small garden with an ethereal silver glow. London's ubiquitous fog lay close to the ground, rising from the grass with ghostly, vaporous fingers. In the center of the garden rose a stately tree. As she watched, it appeared as if a shadow near the tree trunk moved.

Alex's gaze riveted on the spot, and seconds later her heart stuttered when she realized that the shadow was a person. Before she could decide how best to raise an alarm in this unfamiliar household, the shadow detached itself from the tree and moved stealthily toward the hedges surrounding the perimeter of the garden. A shadow that moved with a familiar limp.

Her breath caught, and for a brief instant before the shadows swallowed him again she saw him clearly. What on earth was Colin doing here?

She pressed her hands against her chest, absorbing her sudden frantic heartbeat. Was it possible his thoughts reflected her own? That he'd come intending to make her his lover?

She didn't know, but she refused to wait another moment to find out.

Colin stood in the inky shadows cast by the Wexhall town house. From his vantage point he could scan the entire garden area, and thus far in his vigil had seen nothing out of the ordinary. The deep ache he experienced when fatigued throbbed in his leg, but he knew that even if he returned home and climbed into bed sleep would elude him. Indeed, it was for that very reason he was here, patrolling the grounds. The instant he'd closed his eyes, all he could see was Alexandra. Her beautiful brown eyes. Her soft, plump lips. Her teasing smile.

Then his imagination had jumped to life, flashing erotic images through his brain. Of her, lush and aroused. Naked in his bed. Under him. Over him. Of him, buried deep inside her. With a growl of frustration, he'd abandoned his bed and paced. Stared into the fire. Attempted to read a book. Washed down two pieces of marzipan with a hefty swallow of brandy. Anything to make the time pass until he saw her again.

But no matter how many times he'd glared at the mantel clock, time refused to move faster. Nothing erased her from his mind. And bloody hell, nothing relaxed the erection his sensual thoughts of her had inspired. Since sleep was clearly out of the question, he'd decided to at least make himself useful and patrol around Wexhall's town house to ensure her safety. His inner voice informed him that such a patrol also meant he'd be closer to the object of his desires—to which he'd firmly admonished his inner voice to be quiet.

Now, shrouded in the shadows, his gaze again scanned the garden. Everything was perfectly peaceful. Quiet, except for the rustling leaves from the slight breeze, which also swayed the low covering of misty fog.

He raked his hands through his hair, then closed his eyes and massaged his temples. Damn it, he should go home. Drink brandy until sleep came. So he could dream of her until he saw her again. When he'd make her an offer he prayed she wouldn't refuse.

"Hello, Colin."

Bloody hell! At the sound of those whispered words, his eyes popped open, and he jumped a foot. Heart pounding, his hand reflexively flashed down, and he braced himself, clutching the hilt of his boot knife. Then he froze. And stared.

At Alexandra, who stood less than two feet away. Wearing a plain white robe over what appeared to be an equally plain white nightrail, the pair of which covered her from her chin to her toes. Her dark hair, in the form of a single thick braid, cut a line down her pale attire, ending at her hip with a satin bow.

"Are you going to say hello, or do you intend to stab me?" she asked, her soft voice laced with amusement.

Not yet trusting his voice, he released his knife, then straightened—slowly to give his racing heartbeat a chance to return to normal. Bloody hell, he wasn't certain if he was more annoyed or impressed that she'd managed to sneak up on him and catch him so completely unawares. If the murderer had been in the vicinity, he'd no doubt be dead. Clearly his skills had seriously deteriorated since his retirement.

Even in the shadows he could see her lips twitch. "I'm relieved you opted not to stab me."

He cleared his throat to locate his voice. "What are you doing out here?"

"You told me at the Newtrebble soiree that if bumping into you was to be a habit, you preferred the seclusion of the garden. I am merely taking you at your word."

His brain processes stalled in a quagmire of heated lust at the sight of her standing before him wearing nightclothes which, although virginal in the extreme, nonetheless hinted at the luscious curves beneath. Desire walloped him, and for several seconds he merely stared, trying to recall how to breathe.

"I saw you from my bedchamber window," she continued. "Given that I did and the fact that I so clearly surprised you, I think perhaps your spying skills were . . . less than formidable."

The hint of amusement in her voice jolted him from his stupor, and annoyance rippled through him. He crossed his arms over his chest and narrowed his eyes. "I assure you that isn't the case."

"If you say so."

"I do. Now, why are you here?"

"As I said, I saw you from my window. And I wanted to know . . ." Her voice trailed off, and she looked at the ground.

"Know what?"

She drew an audible breath, then raised her chin to look him in the eyes. "If you'd come here for me."

Something in her expression simultaneously heated and stilled him. "I did," he said carefully, watching her closely. "I was patrolling the grounds. To make certain you were safe."

"I see."

Neither her expression nor her voice gave him any indication of her thoughts. Damn it, why did she have to be so frustratingly unreadable? "Does that upset you?" he asked.

She shook her head. "No. It . . . disappoints me."

"Why?"

She drew another deep breath. "Because I'd hoped you'd come to *see* me."

Her words raced fire through him, evaporating the remnants of his fright and annoyance. Indeed, evaporating everything save her. Reaching out, he lightly grasped her upper arms and felt a tremor run through her. "And if I said I *had* come here to see you?"

"I would welcome those words," she whispered.

One instant Alex was speaking, and the next she was in his arms, crushed against his solid length, his mouth on hers in a wild, fierce, demanding, breath-stealing, bone-melting kiss that left no doubt that *he'd* welcomed *her* words.

Relief and elation collided with anticipation, and she wrapped her arms around his neck, straining closer, parting her lips wider to better relish the erotic friction of his tongue mating with hers. His hands roamed down her back, heating her through the thin material of her nightrail and robe. A delighted shiver rippled down her spine, one which increased when he cupped her buttocks and urged her tighter against him. The hard ridge of his arousal pressed into her belly, fluttering the most delicious and wicked sensations through her.

And then, as quickly as he'd yanked her against him and kissed her breathless, he grasped her arms and set her away from him. Thankfully, he retained his hold on her else she would have slithered to the ground in a steaming heap at his feet.

She forced her eyelids open. His eyes glittered, and his breathing was as erratic as hers. Several seconds past, then he said in a rough voice, "You know I want you."

She licked her lips. "To which I can only say 'thank goodness.' "

"I intend to have you."

"To which I again can only say 'thank goodness.' "

His fierce expression relaxed a bit, and he gently pulled her closer, anchoring her against him with one strong arm around her waist. Then he brushed fingers that she noted weren't quite steady over her cheek.

"Yes," he murmured. "Thank goodness."

"I have a request," she said, setting her hands on his chest and absorbing the slap of his rapid heartbeat against her palms.

"You've only to ask."

She stilled, his words echoing through her mind. *You've only to ask*. No one had ever said such a thing to her.

"Don't you want to know what it is I want before you promise to give it to me?"

"No."

"What if I asked for something extravagant?"

"Such as?"

"Diamonds. And pearls."

"Is that what you want from me, Alexandra—diamonds and pearls?" he asked quietly, his gaze so intense on hers she knew he wasn't jesting.

Two images instantly collided in her mind. Of her, wearing an elegant, low-cut gown, a strand of creamy pearls around her neck and diamond earbobs twinkling from her lobes. Then of the price such jewels would fetch—money that would no doubt finance her and her cause for years. And just for the price of what her intuition told her Colin was offering her right now.

His trust.

Emotion clogged her throat. His expression left no

doubt that if she asked for jewels, he'd give them to her. This beautiful man who, with the gift of his trust, would find himself just another of her victims. And when he realized it, whatever attraction and admiration he now felt for her would disappear.

Even though their time together here in London would be only brief, that still was not a price she was willing to pay.

"No, Colin. I don't want diamonds and pearls."

For several long seconds, he said nothing; just slowly traced his fingertips over her features, as if trying to memorize them, while his gaze followed the same path as his hand. She dearly wished she knew what he was thinking. Finally, he said, "Thank you."

"For what?"

"For being the only woman I know who would utter that sentence. You are . . . extraordinary."

"On the contrary, I am extremely common." *So much more than you know.*

"No. You are extraordinary. In every way. In ways you don't even realize." He brushed the pad of his thumb over her lower lip. "As diamonds and pearls are not what you desire, tell me what you do want."

"It is in regard to our . . . arrangement. I need your assurance that it be known only to us. Madame Larchmont is accepted as a married woman, and I cannot risk her reputation being sullied by an affair."

"You have my word I'll protect you. In every way."

"Thank you. I also would not wish to . . ." She hesitated, knowing that a pregnancy would be disastrous for her, but still for one insane instant, unable to banish the image of herself carrying Colin's child.

"Become pregnant?" he said softly.

"Yes."

"I will take precautions to prevent it."

"And our liaison, it will end when you've chosen a

wife," she said firmly. "I could not carry on such a relationship with another woman's intended husband."

"Nor would I shame my wife with an adulterous affair." He brushed a stray curl from her cheek. "But until then, you're mine."

A feminine thrill ran through her at the quiet possessiveness in his tone. "Yes," she agreed. "And you're mine."

"And I'm yours."

Her heart stuttered at his consent, at the mere notion of this man being hers in any way, for any length of time. It was an opportunity she'd dreamed of, but had never dared hope for. And she intended to cherish every minute they spent together.

"Are those your only requests, Alexandra?"

Dear God, the way he said her name sent shivers of delight through her. "Just one more," she whispered. "I want you to put out this fire you've started inside me."

He rested his forehead against hers. "I want that same thing. But this is neither the time nor the place. And if I kiss you again . . ." He lifted his head and his gaze drifted down to her mouth.

Her lips involuntarily parted. "If you kiss me again . . .?"

"As you have a detrimental effect on my control, I fear this interlude will end with me taking you against the wall."

Oh, my. "You make it sound as if that's bad."

"Not bad. But inconvenient when one is without a bed with a lady who deserves one. At least the first time she's made love to." He leaned down and brushed his lips lightly over hers. "Allow me to try to make the first time perfect for you."

"It feels quite perfect right now. Except for my pulse, which is gravely misbehaving."

He flashed a quick, grim smile. "Good. I'd hate to

think that it's only mine which is doing so." He released her, then clasped her hand. "Come with me." He led her around to the side of the town house to the servants' entrance. He extracted a thin piece of metal from his pocket, then leaned over the lock. In less than a minute, the door swung noiselessly open.

"You are *amazingly* good at that," she whispered, the former thief in her experiencing both admiration and an undeniable twinge of envy.

"I believe I once told you, I'm good at many things. This town house is nearly identical to mine. Just follow this corridor until you reach the stairs. Go to the next floor, then turn right and continue down the corridor and you'll reach your room."

Disappointment flooded her. "Alone?"

"Yes."

"But what about . . . us?"

"My sweet Alexandra, as I said, this is neither the time nor place. 'Us' will happen very soon. I promise. Now tell me, how did you exit the house?"

"Through the French windows by the terrace."

"I'll see to it that they are relocked." He leaned down, and she raised her face, but instead of giving her the kiss she craved, he merely dropped a quick kiss on the tip of her nose. "Be off with you. After I close the door, lock it from the inside. And I'll see you again very soon."

Bemused, confused, irritated, and frustrated as well, she stomped across the threshold.

"A bit of quiet would serve us both well," came his amused voice from the darkness. She turned, intending to incinerate him with her best glare, and discovered he'd already closed the door.

She stared at the wood panel, completely nonplussed. She hadn't thought she'd ever offer herself to a man, and now that she had, what happens? She's sent to her room alone. Perhaps he hadn't wanted to take her against the wall, but blast it, that's the way it was done all the time in the rookery. Maybe he didn't want her quite as much as he claimed.

"Aggravating man," she muttered through clenched teeth. She carefully made her way through the dark, silent house, following his directions toward her bedchamber, her frustration growing with each step. Her body felt hot and impatient, the feminine folds between her thighs swollen and heavy. And now nothing save long sleepless hours faced her until she saw him again. Damnation, she'd go mad before then.

When she reached the stairs, she climbed, then turned right and continued down the corridor. So engrossed was she in her irritation, it wasn't until she reached the end of the passageway that she realized she must have passed her room. Frowning, she turned and as her gaze swept the dim area, she realized that this corridor didn't look in the least familiar. That half-moon table with the bouquet of flowers hadn't been there, nor had the ornate oval mirror hanging on the opposite wall.

Botheration. Not only was the man a plague on one's peace of mind, he possessed no sense of direction whatsoever.

Clenching her jaw, she carefully retraced her steps. Once she reached the stairs, she made her way toward the foyer so as to reorient herself. Once she arrived in the marble-tiled entryway, and reassured of her direction, she made her way to her bedchamber. By the time she arrived, she was well and thoroughly vexed. She opened the door, closing it quietly behind her, barely resisting the urge to slam it. She'd steamed halfway across the room when she halted as if she'd walked into a glass wall. And stared.

At Colin. Who'd removed his jacket and waistcoat and stood next to her bed, his shoulders nonchalantly propped against the thickly carved bedpost, arms crossed casually over his chest, his eyes glittering with an unmistakable heat that ignited every cell in her body.

"Now *this*," he said softly, "is what I'd call a much better time and place."

Fifteen

Colin allowed himself a bit of smug satisfaction at her flabbergasted expression and wished she were normally so easy to read.

"How did you get in here?" she asked, eyeing him as if she weren't quite convinced he was real.

"Through the French windows by the terrace you'd left unlocked." He pushed off the bedpost and slowly made his way toward her, halting when only two feet separated them. The urge to drag her into his arms and simply devour her nearly overpowered him. This clawing hunger she inspired truly baffled him. He'd known lust before, but *this* . . . this wild, reckless, primitive need to press her against the nearest wall or bend her over the closest chair and simply take his pleasure was completely unfamiliar. She somehow stripped him of the gentlemanly mien that had always defined every aspect of his life. She made him feel uncharacteristically out of control. In a way no other woman ever had. And without her doing *anything*. Bloody hell, he hadn't even touched her yet. And could wait no longer to do so.

Forcing a calmness he was far from feeling, he

reached out and loosely entwined his fingers with hers, not in the least surprised when heat pumped through him at the casual contact.

"Leaving windows unlocked is most unwise," he murmured, lightly circling his thumbs over her palms. "Very bad men lurk about in the dark."

She appeared to recover herself. "Yourself included?"

"I may be bad, but only in a very good way."

He lifted her hands and brushed a kiss across the backs of her callused fingers. "Actually, I'm glad the windows were unlocked as that helped shave a minute or two off my entry time—which I appreciated, as I wanted to arrive before you."

Understanding dawned in her eyes. "Which is also why you gave me incorrect directions to my room."

"Guilty as charged. I wanted to arrange a small surprise, and as I've told you, I'm accustomed to getting what I want." He stepped closer, until a mere breath separated their bodies, and very much liked the way her eyes darkened.

"That does challenge one to deny you," she said softly.

"Perhaps, but it shouldn't—not when we want the same thing."

He lowered his head and lightly grazed her earlobe with his teeth.

"I believe you're trying to weaken my knees," she said, her words coming out in a pleasure-soaked sigh.

"Is it working?"

"Remarkably well."

"Excellent." He nuzzled the soft skin behind her ear. When his head filled with the delicate, delicious sweet scent of oranges, he groaned and couldn't help but wonder who was weakening whose knees.

"You mentioned something about arranging a small surprise?" she asked. "What is it?"

"Impatient, are you?"

She leaned back and gazed up at him. "Yes," she said in a voice he could only describe as smoky. "Right now I'm very impatient, and normally I'm not. Quite frankly this uncharacteristic state is all your fault, and I want to know what you're going to do about it. Right now."

Releasing her hands, he reached between them to untie the sash on her robe. After parting the thin cotton, he slid the garment down her arms. The material pooled at her feet with a gentle *swoosh*.

"I intend," he said, keeping his gaze on hers while he slowly began to undo the long row of buttons fastening the front of her gown, "to make you even more impatient."

"I'm not certain that is possible."

"Oh, it's possible." He slid the last tiny button through its hole, leaving her still covered but unfastened to the waist. Slipping a single fingertip inside the opening he'd created, he lightly touched the shallow hollow of her throat.

"I want you impatient," he whispered, leisurely dragging his fingertip downward, over her incredibly soft skin, between her breasts, then lower, to lightly circle her navel. "And hot."

Her eyes drooped halfway closed, and she swayed slightly on her feet. "But I'm already both those things. I feel as if I'm going to burst into flames."

"Good. But it's not enough. I want more. More impatient. Hotter."

Unable to deny himself from seeing her for another second, he slipped his hands inside her gown and slowly spread the material, revealing her inch by inch to his avid gaze as he lowered the garment down her arms. Seconds later it joined her robe at her feet.

She stood in the midst of her nightclothes like a gorgeous, night-blooming flower, her pale skin bathed in both the silvery moonlight coming in from the window and the golden glow from the fire's last embers. His gaze tracked slowly down her form, and he had to fist his hands to keep from snatching her against him like a green, randy lad.

High, full breasts, topped with pebbled rosy nipples beckoned his hands and lips. The indent of her waist gave way to the sinuous curve of her hips. His gaze lingered over the triangle of dark curls gracing the apex of her thighs before continuing down her shapely legs to her slim ankles.

"At the risk of being redundant," he said, his voice a soft rasp, "you are exquisite." Reaching out, he untied the ribbon securing her braid, then sifted his fingers through the silky twines of hair. Glossy strands separated and spilled over his hands, and a delicate citrus scent wafted from the soft tresses. He brought a handful of curls to his face, breathed deeply, and groaned. "God. You smell so incredibly delicious."

"Thank you."

Noting the slight quaver in her voice, he asked, "Are you nervous?"

She hesitated, then nodded. "A bit, yes."

"So am I."

Surprise flashed in her eyes. "Why? Surely you have experience in these matters."

"Yes. But you do not, and I've never made love to a virgin before. It's rather daunting, especially as you make me want to do things . . . in ways that would make me forget I must go slowly."

She settled her hands against his chest, and he knew she felt his hard, rapid heartbeat. "It's true I'm a virgin, but I'm not a shy, delicate lady made of spun glass who has lived a sheltered life, Colin. I am fully aware of what will happen between us. And I want it all."

He slowly wrapped a handful of her fragrant hair

around his fist. "How do you know what will happen between us?"

"I've . . . seen things."

"What sort of things?"

"Men taking their pleasure from women. Women on their knees servicing men."

An image of her, on her knees, her plump lips wrapped around his erection, flashed through his mind. Hot blood rushed to his groin, and he swelled against the already strangling confines of his breeches.

Lifting her chin a fraction, she said, "I've always wondered what all the fuss was about as the proceedings seemed rather furtive and, well, rushed. I've managed to suppress my curiosity, but with you, I no longer can. The sensations you make me feel . . . they must be explored."

He untwined his hand, watching her silky curtain of hair unfurl to her waist. "I've no intention of rushing the . . . proceedings, Alexandra. And I certainly encourage you to explore. In any way you wish."

"An invitation not easily taken advantage of, I'm afraid." She shot him a very pointed head-to-toe look. "At least for me as you are not the one standing about with all your . . . *parts* dangling in the air."

He swallowed the bark of laughter that rose in his throat at her disgruntled tone and managed to merely smile. "Would it make you feel more comfortable if my . . . *parts* dangled in the air as well?"

"I certainly think it would be more fair. After all, I want you to be as impatient as I am."

If she had any idea how impatient he already was, how close his control teetered on the edge—without even yet touching her or being touched by her—she'd be more than "a bit" nervous.

"I can assure you there's no worry on that score. However"—he spread his arms—"feel free to have at it."

Interest and uncertainty flared in her eyes. "I'm not sure exactly where to begin."

"My cravat would probably be a good place."

Her gaze fell to his neckcloth. Stepping from her pile of nightclothes, she reached out and set to work on untying the complicated knot. Standing in front of him, wearing nothing save a frown of concentration, she stole his breath. He tried not to touch her, and succeeded—for precisely three seconds. Then, unable to stop himself, he settled his hands on the curve of her waist.

His eyes slid briefly closed as the realization hit him with stunning force—that he was *finally* touching her skin. That this night she would be his, this woman who'd haunted his dreams for so long. He opened his eyes and watched her, his fingers lightly kneading her supple waist, then trailing slowly up and down her smooth back.

"You're not helping my concentration by doing that," she said, her gaze flicking up to his.

"Oh." He slid his palms upward and cupped her breasts. "Is that better?"

Alex gasped at the bolt of pleasure his touch incited, and her busy fingers stilled, then clenched against his shirt. She dipped her chin and watched him tease her nipples between his long fingers until her eyes drifted closed.

"Better?" he asked.

Questions? He expected her to answer questions? "I . . . I'm not certain. Perhaps you'd best do that again."

His soft chuckle blew warmth against her skin, and it took her only a single heartbeat to realize that his hands were magic. They skimmed over her breasts, igniting a trail of fire. Then he leaned down and traced the outer curve of her breast with his tongue.

She gasped, a soft sound that melted into a long moan when he circled his tongue around her nipple, then drew the aroused peak into the wet warmth of his mouth while his fingers continued their magical tugging tease on her other nipple.

Her head dropped limply back, and she arched forward, greedily wanting more. Each drugging pull of his lips curled heat deep inside her. The folds between her legs grew damp and heavy, and she rubbed her thighs together, but the movement brought no relief. Nor did Colin, who switched his attention to her other breast, while his hands skimmed downward to caress her buttocks.

She gripped his shoulders, drowning in sensation, flushed with the conflicting desires to sink further into this abyss of pleasure and to emerge to yank off his clothing. Never in her life had she felt so *alive*. So aware of herself and her body. And so eager to learn and experience more.

"Delicious," he murmured against her breast. "So damn delicious."

Before she could catch her breath, he bent to drag his mouth down the center of her torso, kissing, licking her skin, circling her navel, then delving his tongue inside. Shivers of delight raced through her, and a growl of pleasure vibrated in her throat.

"Look at me," he commanded in a rough whisper.

With an effort, she dragged her head up and opened her eyes. He knelt before her, his lips a mere whisper from her abdomen. His eyes looked dark and burned with a desire so deeply potent her breath caught.

"Spread your legs for me, Alexandra."

Wordlessly, heart pounding, she obeyed him.

"You say you saw women on their knees before men. Did you ever see a man pleasure a woman that way?"

She shook her head, losing her ability to speak when he slipped a hand between her thighs and lightly stroked—a slow, maddening rhythm over sensitive nerve endings that felt . . . so . . . good. She'd touched herself there, in the dark, on nights when her body had cried out for . . . something. But while her own touch was pleasurable, it had never made her feel like *this*.

His other hand meandered lazily up and down the backs of her thighs, around her buttocks, tracing the line between them, drawing a gasp from her.

"I want to see you," he said, his voice like rough velvet. "All of you." His fingers slipped away, and a groan of protest rose in her throat. But before she could voice it, in one smooth motion, he stood, scooped her into his arms, and strode to the bed. With his gaze intent on hers, he set her on the edge of the mattress, urging her legs wide apart with his hands. He then sank to his knees between her splayed thighs and hooked her calves over his shoulders. The smoldering desire in his eyes burned away her shyness, melted her modesty, leaving only curiosity and aching need. Propped on her elbows, she watched his gaze drop to her exposed flesh and he groaned.

"Beautiful," he said, his fingers spreading her wider, then teasing her with light, perfect strokes. "So wet. So silky and hot."

He slipped his hands beneath her to cup her buttocks, then lifted her and leaned forward. She gasped at the first stunning touch of his mouth against her swollen flesh. The shocking sensation of his tongue caressing her, the sight of his dark head between her widespread thighs was the most erotic, arousing sight she'd ever seen. With a long moan of pleasure, she sank back onto the mattress and gripped the counterpane, wallowing in the sensations licking fire through her veins.

Nothing existed except him. His lips and tongue and fingers were relentless, arousing her beyond the impatience he'd wanted. Shamelessly she arched her back, straining toward his mouth, her every muscle trembling.

Pleasure coursed through her, building, coiling low in her belly, tightening, gathering, pushing her closer to something that remained just out of reach. Until he did something . . . something magical with his mouth that concentrated on a spot so exquisitely sensitive she gasped.

Fisting her hands on the counterpane, she arched her back and spread her legs wider. For several breathless seconds it felt as if she stood on a precipice, then she soared over the cliff. Spasms of pleasure gushed through her, pulsing, until, all too quickly, the intense shudders tapered off into tingling ripples, leaving her limp and languid.

She felt him shift, and dragged her eyes open, watching him press a trail of soft kisses up her torso. After a final kiss to the side of her neck, he settled his lower body against hers and propped his weight on his forearms to look down at her. Their gazes met, and she stilled at the fire burning in his eyes.

"Alexandra," he whispered.

He uttered that single word with such heated reverence, her breath stalled. Lifting a limp arm, she rested her palm against his cheek. "Colin."

The feel of him, fully clothed and hard, pressing against her naked softness, rushed a heated shiver through her. Without moving his gaze from hers, he turned his head and kissed her palm. "Are you all right?" he asked, his warm breath touching her fingers.

"I'm . . ." Her voice trailed off, uncertain how to describe this wickedly delicious languor. "Breathless. Speechless."

A crooked smile pulled up one corner of his mouth. "Breathless *and* speechless. I suppose that makes you 'breachless.' "

"Every time I'm near you," she agreed, brushing back a thick lock of silky hair from his forehead.

"Every time I'm near you," he concurred. Then he leaned down and kissed her, a soft, deep, lush, intimate kiss that tasted of him and her and passion. A kiss that reignited the flame he'd just doused.

When the kiss ended, she looked up into his eyes, wishing she could read his inscrutable expression. "Now I know what all the fuss is about," she said softly. "I had no idea I could feel like . . . that."

"The pleasure was all mine."

"I assure you it was mine as well. I now know what melted wax feels like. Very *impatient* melted wax."

"Ah. Impatient. So it would seem I got my way."

"Yes. And now I want mine."

"Impatient, demanding—two delightful qualities in a naked woman. As for you wanting something, I told you earlier this evening, you've only to ask."

She arched beneath him, pressing her belly more firmly against the hard ridge of his arousal. "I want you impatient."

"I assure you, it's done."

"More impatient. And undressed. I'd started on your cravat when you very sneakily distracted me."

"Sneaky tactics—it is the way of us spies. However, I am more than pleased to grant your request."

He dropped a lingering kiss to her lips, then pushed himself up and off her. He extended his hand and helped her to rise.

"I want to please you," she said, eyeing the very obvious bulge in his breeches, "but I'm not certain what to do."

"There is no chance of your *not* pleasing me. As for what to do, I'll help you." Clasping her hands, he brought them to his chest. "Take off my shirt."

She raised her brows. "Do you promise to keep your hands to yourself and not distract me again?"

He immediately cupped her breasts. "No."

She laughed. "Well, at least you're honest."

Raising his hands, he framed her face in his palms and gazed at her through suddenly serious eyes. "Yes, I am. Given the nature of my previous work, I haven't always been. But with you—"

She reached out and pressed her fingertips to his lips to halt his words. Given her dishonesty regarding her past, her conscience balked at hearing any declarations of truthfulness from him. For one insane instant she considered telling him of her sordid past but immediately pushed the notion away. Their time together was fleeting at most. No point in shortening it even further with confessions that wouldn't matter a short time from now.

Stepping out of his reach, she shook her head. "I want you to remain still. Do you agree?"

His green eyes glittered. "I agree to *try*."

She cocked a brow. "If you do not, I feel it only fair to warn you that I'm a very fast runner."

A slow smile lifted his beautiful lips. "I'm faster."

"I doubt it."

"I'm also dressed. The places where you could run to in your present state"—his gaze traveled lazily down then up her naked form, suffusing her entire body with heat—"are somewhat limited."

"You won't be dressed for long," she said, erasing the distance between them and applying herself to his cravat.

Colin remained perfectly still, attempting to cool his burning ardor, but it was damn difficult when she stood only a foot away, her hair rumpled from his hands, her lips swollen and moist from his kisses, her skin glowing from the aftermath of her climax, and her velvety nipples erect from his mouth. The scent of her—sweet oranges mixed with feminine musk—rose between them, and he had to grit his teeth to suppress the need to lean forward to kiss her. She didn't want him to move, and bloody hell, he didn't dare, not with his control teetering so close to the edge.

After what felt like an eternity, she finally finished untying his cravat, and he made a mental note to employ a much less complicated knot next time. Then she slowly slipped the long length of linen from around his neck. Instead of dropping the material to the floor, however, she shot him a mischievous look and looped it around her neck, like a boa.

His gaze riveted on that length of white material, and his imagination instantly took flight, picturing her on his bed, naked, her wrists loosely bound—

His thought cut off when she pulled his shirttails from his breeches and the soft material skimmed over his aching erection. His shaft jerked, and he gritted back a groan. After unfastening the shirt, she slowly separated the sides, exposing his chest, and he had to forcibly relax his tensely bunched shoulders so she could slide the garment down his arms. He'd expected her to simply drop the shirt onto the floor, but instead she pressed the bundle to her chest and buried her face in the material.

"It's still warm from your body," she whispered. She closed her eyes and drew in an audible breath, which she released in a long sigh. "It bears your scent. I never knew a man could smell so wonderful."

He clenched his hands, confounded by the conflicting waves of tenderness and heat that flooded him at the sight of her clutching his clothing to her. Then she surprised him again by slipping on the garment.

"What do you think?" she asked, her lips curved in a playful smile as she turned in a slow circle.

His gaze tracked downward, along the thin ribbon of pale skin visible between the edges of material, lingering on the indentation of her navel before continuing lower to the alluring shadow of dark curls between her thighs. The sleeves covered her hands, and the wrinkled ends dangled midthigh. He found the sight of her wearing his clothes, her tousled hair falling over her shoulders utterly erotic, and his already speeding pulse quickened further.

He had to clear his dry throat to locate his voice. "I think it looks better on you than it does on me."

She flashed a smile, then rolled back the long sleeves while her gaze roamed over him. "I thought it looked very good on you, but I must say, you look even better without it."

"Thank you . . ." His voice trailed off into a low groan as she settled her palms against his bare chest, then dragged her hands slowly downward.

His eyes closed, and he tipped his head back, determined to retain his control and savor her every touch. His muscles contracted with each pass of her fingers over his skin. Her touch, tentative at first, grew bolder with each caress, and a growl of pleasure rumbled in his throat.

"Do you like that?" she asked, brushing her fingertips over his nipples.

"Aaaah . . . I'm not sure. Do it again."

He felt her huff of laughter against the center of his chest, just before she pressed her lips to his skin. Raising his head, he watched her kiss her way across his chest while her hands smoothed over his shoulders and down his arms. When her tongue peeked out to sweep over his nipple, a tremor ran through him, one he knew she felt by the feminine smile that curved her lips.

Bloody hell, she'd barely touched him, and he was *shaking.* How the hell would he survive the rest of this sweet torture?

She flicked her tongue over his nipple again. "I liked it when you did that do me. Do you like it?"

"Yes. If you enjoyed something, chances are very good that I'd enjoy it as well."

"I see." She ran a single fingertip around the skin just above the waistband of his breeches, and he sucked in a breath.

"You're very . . . manly," she said, running her palms upward, over his abdomen to his tense shoulders. "Very muscular and strong."

"At the moment you're testing that strength, believe me."

"Good. How is your patience?"

"Strained."

She smiled. "How can I strain it further?"

"Kiss me."

Without hesitation, she slid her arms around his neck and urged his head lower. He allowed her to take the lead and groaned when she ran her tongue over his bottom lip. She rose up on her toes, pressing herself against him, and his head spun. Her warm skin touched his bare chest, her hard nipples pressing into him, her tongue invading his mouth, and he instantly forgot not to move. His hands slipped under the shirt she wore, skimming down her back to cup the soft curves of her buttocks. And in an instant she was gone.

"You promised to keep your hands to yourself," she said from three feet away, shaking a finger at him.

"I promised to *try*. I did try. You are impossible to resist."

"You need your hands tied to your sides." Her eyes narrowed, then glittered with mischief. "I believe I can help."

"I can't imagine anything you could do that would make me less inclined to touch you."

"I can." With her gaze steady on his, she slowly pulled the length of his cravat from around her neck. "Put your hands behind your back."

He raised his brows even as his erection jerked. "You're planning to actually tie me?"

"Yes."

"Believe me, that will not make me less inclined to touch you."

"But it will render you less *able* to do so."

"You think so?"

"I'm quite good at tying knots."

"I'm quite good at untying them."

Her eyes glittered with unmistakable challenge. "Shall we see who's better . . . unless you're afraid?"

Keeping his gaze on hers, he slowly moved his hands behind his back. "On the contrary, I'm highly intrigued. However, in the interests of good sportsmanship, I feel it only fair to warn you that once I'm free, I shall make no attempt whatsoever to not touch you. I'll touch you however and wherever I please."

"Fair enough. However, I believe you've already touched me everywhere."

"My sweet Alexandra. I haven't *begun* to touch you in the all the ways I intend to."

The heated interest that flared in her eyes at his softly spoken words coiled raw want through him. She might be inexperienced, but clearly she was adventurous. And not a coward. And had spoken the truth when she'd stated she wasn't shy. He'd planned to seduce her and instead found himself thoroughly seduced. Never had a woman captured every part of his mind and body as this one did.

She stepped behind him, and he positioned his hands. When she finished, she said, "That should hold you nicely."

He wriggled his wrists, testing the bonds. "Seems a thorough job." He looked at her over his shoulder. "It would appear I'm quite at your mercy."

"I'm not certain I've ever heard a more provocative statement." She settled her hands on his shoulders, then ran her palms slowly down his back. When she stepped closer and pressed her lips to his skin, he drew in a sharp breath, gritting his teeth to keep from brushing his bound hands over her soft abdomen.

"I believe you're trying to drive me mad," he ground out.

"Is it working?"

"Extremely well."

She caressed him with long, slow strokes down his back and arms while her lips pressed soft kisses along his spine. He closed his eyes, absorbing the gentle exploration, praying he'd be able to maintain his control and not spill in his damn breeches.

She made her way slowly around until she faced him again. Looking down, he watched her fingers glide down his chest. When she reached his breeches, he went perfectly still, in an agony of anticipation.

At the first light brush of her fingers over his arousal, he closed his eyes and groaned. "Again," he said gruffly.

She obliged him, trailing her fingers slowly down his length, then cupping her palm around him. Heat surged through him. Bloody hell, he wanted her hands on him. Now. He raised his gaze and their eyes met. "Open my pants, Alexandra."

She set to unfastening his breeches, and he clenched his jaw to remain still. Finally, after what seemed like an eternity, his erection was freed. The anticipation of her touch was so intense it bordered on pain. When she reached out and brushed the backs of her fingers down his length, he sucked in a sharp breath, and his eyes slammed shut.

"Did I hurt you?" she asked.

"No. God, no. Don't stop."

She stroked him again, more surely this time, and after drawing a deep, shuddering breath, he opened his eyes and looked down, watching her hands glide over him, stroke him, and cup him. Heat poured through him, and his every muscle tensed and quivered with the effort he expended not to thrust into her hand.

"You feel so hard," she said.

He groaned. "You have no idea."

"And so hot."

Not surprising, as he felt as if he were about to incinerate. Her fingertip lightly encircled the swollen head of his arousal. "You cannot imagine how incredible that feels," he said in a gravelly voice he didn't recognize. She wrapped her fingers around him and gently squeezed, and his groin tightened. When a pearly drop emerged, and she smoothed it over the engorged head, he could remain still no longer. His hips flexed forward, and he thrust into her hand.

"Are you impatient?" she whispered.

"Beyond," he growled. Executing a series of well-practiced movements, he quickly freed his wrists, then yanked her into his arms. She made a startled exclamation, which was cut off by his kiss. One hand moved up into her hair, cupping her head to hold her immobile while he kissed her with all the pent-up need and desire ripping through him. His other hand skimmed down and hooked under her thigh, pulling it upward to settle it high on his hip, opening her for his touch.

His palm brushed over the curve of her bottom, then his fingers caressed her feminine folds from behind, finding them already silky wet and swollen. Thank God, for he wasn't certain how much longer he could last.

He forced himself to arouse her with a deliberate lack of haste, trying to decrease his rapid heart rate, but the way she squirmed against him, her belly brushing against his erection, her hands racing over his skin, was not helping to calm him. Knowing the battle was about to be lost, he scooped her up in his arms and strode to the bed, where he laid her on the counterpane with a gentle bounce. His shirt she wore fell open, as did her thighs, and for several seconds he stood, mesmerized by the sight of her, naked, flushed, aroused, glistening wet. For him. The woman he'd waited years for.

He refused to wait another instant.

Without pausing to remove the remainder of his clothing, he settled himself between her splayed thighs and braced his weight on his forearms. The tip of his erection brushed through her curls and over her silky folds. Looking into her eyes, he eased slowly inside her, absorbing the way her wet, velvety flesh gripped him, stopping when he reached the barrier of her maidenhead.

"I don't want to hurt you," he managed to say.

"I'll hurt *you* if you stop now."

If he'd been capable of laughter, he would have chuckled. Instead, he thrust and slid deep inside her. Then groaned.

Bloody hell, she was so wet and so tight and he was so hard and so close to the edge of his control. He fisted his hands and forced himself to remain still, bludgeoning back the clawing need to simply take her with long, deep, hard thrusts.

She was looking up at him through wide eyes filled with both surprise and hesitancy. "Are you all right?" he asked.

She nodded, slowly, then more positively. "Yes. Are you?"

I'm dying. "I'm fine."

"I feel . . . filled. Are all men as . . . *blessed* as you?"

Christ. He was trembling, could barely think, barely breathe, and she expected him to answer questions? "I don't know. Right now, I'd wager I'm the most blessed man in England. And also the most, um, impatient."

"Excellent. Because I want to know everything. There is more, isn't there?"

He huffed out a breath. "Yes. There's more." Unable to remain still any longer, he slowly withdrew, nearly all the way, then sank again into her wet heat, her body gripping him like a silken fist. He continued those long, slow, deep strokes, watching her hesitation dissipate, turning to need as she clutched his shoulders and moved beneath him, awkwardly at first, but still meeting his every thrust. His breathing turned rough and choppy, and every short breath he dragged into his lungs burned. Need scraped him, and his thrusts increased in speed. Her eyes drifted closed, and with her fingers digging into his shoulders, she arched her back, a low cry escaping her parted lips. He thrust deep, embedding himself fully, then stilled, watching her, feeling her climax pulse around him, clenching, squeezing his shaft. The instant he felt her body go limp, he withdrew and gathered her close, his erection pressed tightly between their damp bodies. Burying his face in the warm, fragrant curve of her neck, his release shuddered through him, dragging a guttural groan from his throat.

When his tremors subsided, he lifted his head. And found her regarding him with a dazed, bemused expression. One, he suspected, that perfectly matched his own. He shifted, prepared to roll off her so as not to crush her, but her arms tightened around his shoulders and she shook her head.

"Don't go," she whispered.

A warm tenderness, unlike anything he'd known before, eased through him, and he gently brushed his fingertips over her smooth cheek. "I'm not leaving. I just don't wish to crush you."

"You're not. Your body on mine, your skin against mine, your weight . . . it all feels so lovely. I'm always cold, and now, well, I've never felt so delightfully warm in my entire life."

I'm always cold. An image of her—cold, hungry, dirty, desperate—flashed in his mind and his chest went hollow. He wasn't certain how to respond, indeed, words suddenly felt completely beyond him. All he could do was stare at her, and wonder . . . at how a woman with no sexual experience had managed to please him more than any other woman ever had. And at the unprecedented heart-tugging feelings curling through him.

Before he could speak, she said, "It did not escape my notice that you freed yourself of your bonds. I'd tied you very securely. How did you manage it?"

"Just a little trick I picked up during my spy days."

"I'm impressed."

A smile tugged at his lips. "I'm an impressive fellow."

She breathed out a long, pleasure-filled sigh. "You'll receive no argument from me."

His gaze roamed her face, settling on a stray dark curl resting on her cheek. He stared at that silky skein, then rubbed it between his fingers. According to his card reading, the danger surrounding him concerned a dark-haired woman. And he suddenly realized that *this* dark-haired woman and the way she made him feel did indeed present a danger to him. Not the sort his instincts had been warning him about, but in a way he suspected could prove just as dangerous.

Because she very easily could jeopardize his heart.

Sixteen

Alex came awake slowly, blinking against the shafts of bright sunlight streaming through the French windows. Sunlight? What time was it?

Pushing herself up onto one elbow, she winced at the tenderness between her legs and turned her sleep-heavy gaze toward at the mantel clock. Her eyes snapped open. Nine o'clock? She never slept so late! Never slept for more than a few hours at a time—

Memory returned with a thump, and she swiveled her head to gaze at the empty pillow next to hers. The pillow that still bore the indentation where he'd lain. Leaning over, she closed her eyes and breathed deeply. The pillow that still bore faint traces of his scent.

An all-over blush warmed her naked body, and, with a sigh, she lay back down, clutching his pillow to her. The soft material abraded her sensitive nipples, and her eyes slid closed, vividly recalling the incredible sensation of his hands and mouth caressing her breasts. Sensual memories bombarded her, and she made no effort to push them aside, instead basking in every one. Colin gently cleansing away the evidence of their lovemaking.

Removing the rest of his clothes. Exploring her body with a gentle passion that left her breathless. Teaching her how to touch him, of what pleased and aroused him, then finding endless ways to please and arouse her. Encouraging her curiosity, refusing to allow her to feel in any way embarrassed or inhibited. Then making love to her again, with such intensity she'd collapsed in his arms afterward, limp and sated and boneless in the most deliciously wicked way.

The last thing she recalled was curling against him, her head on his shoulder, her hand resting on his chest and absorbing the slap of his rapidly beating heart, her thigh settled across his, and his lips pressed against her temple, whispering her name. She'd never felt so safe and warm and secure in her entire life.

She certainly now knew what all the fuss was about. Knew that terrible, wonderful need that had to be satisfied. Understood why men and women escaped to dark alleys to assuage their lustful urges.

Yet unlike those back-alley liaisons, there had been nothing sordid about what she'd shared with Colin. He'd been everything she'd known he would be—tender and patient and beautiful. And for reasons she couldn't understand, he clearly desired her—a man who could have any woman he wanted. Why on earth would he want her?

He wouldn't—not for a minute if he knew what you really were. What you'd been. How you'd lived your life.

Hot moisture pooled behind her eyes, shocking and mortifying her. What on earth was wrong with her? She *never* cried. Certainly not since she'd been a child. Not since she'd held her mother's hand and watched the only person she had in the world pass away.

After brushing away the moisture with impatient fingers, she firmly set aside his pillow, then rose. There was no reason to feel so uncharacteristically weepy. She was merely unaccustomed to the intimacies they'd shared. They'd simply touched her heart in a way she hadn't anticipated. Which explained all the foreign feelings and emotions roiling through her, leaving her vulnerable and unsettled. Feelings and emotions she needed to keep tightly reined in, lest the seeds she feared were already planted be given room to grow.

Crossing toward the ceramic pitcher and bowl in the corner, she paused in front of the cheval glass. And stared. At a naked wide-eyed woman with loose, tousled hair, flushed skin, and kiss-swollen lips. To her, there was no missing the knowing, carnal gleam in her eyes that had not been there before. Would anyone else notice? Emma certainly would, but hopefully only because her friend knew her so well.

She studied her reflection for several long minutes, trying to see what Colin saw, why he had singled her out for his attentions, but couldn't figure it out. It wasn't because she was beautiful because she simply was not. Not with her irregular features, and certainly not if compared to the stunning and elegant young women available during the Season. Yet he'd claimed she was exquisite. Perhaps he needed spectacles?

He'd seemed inordinately enthralled with her body, but as far as she could tell, hers did not differ in any way from any other woman's, except that she was perhaps a bit taller than was fashionable. Perhaps he behaved in a similar way with all his lovers—

She squeezed her eyes closed and shook her head, refusing to think of his kissing, touching, making love to another woman. He would be doing so soon enough— to a woman who would not only be his lover but his wife. A woman who would never, could never be her.

So she would simply concentrate on enjoying their brief time together. Of remembering the magical way he'd made her feel. Of how indescribably safe and warm she felt in his arms. And then, she would let him go.

Opening her eyes, she straightened her spine and continued toward the water pitcher. As she approached, she spied a folded piece of vellum near the wooden stand. Her footsteps quickened, then she stared. At the vellum and the small object resting next to it. She reached out an unsteady hand and took the note. After unfolding it, she read the brief message:

> *An exquisite night with an exquisite woman deserves an exquisite treat. Enjoy your surprise for which you were so deliciously impatient. Until later . . .*

She picked up the single piece of marzipan that rested next to the note. The candy looked like a perfect miniature orange. Her heart turned over, then plummeted a bit farther into the emotion-filled canyon from which she despaired of ever retrieving it. *Until later . . .*

God help her, she could not wait.

Colin paced the length of Lord Wexhall's drawing room, impatiently waiting for his brother to appear. "Gift, indeed," he muttered, glancing down at the bundle of black puppy fur asleep in the crook of his arm.

Bloody hell. He should have known Nathan would do something like this. Try to bribe him into taking on one of his menagerie by calling it a gift. Well, he wasn't having any of it. If he gave his overrun-with-animals brother even the slightest encouragement, he'd soon find himself with not only a dog, but cats and goats and pigs and ducks and cows and God only knows what else. The puppy's floppy ears twitched in its sleep, and Colin sighed.

Naturally Nathan wouldn't give him just any puppy.

No, he'd give him an absolutely melt-your-heart adorable, irresistible puppy. But resist he must, for if he didn't, he knew that the parade of farm beasts that would follow this sweetly innocent dog would never end. Therefore, the minute Nathan appeared, he'd pretend total indifference to the puppy and place him right back into the hands that had delivered it. Blasted nuisance of a brother. The only thing that he could say for Nathan's gift was that it had accomplished the impossible by making him think of something besides Alexandra.

Alexandra. An image of her instantly rose in his mind, and his pacing slowed. Alexandra, naked and sated, her soft lips parted, her eyes heavy with sexual languor, reaching out her arms to him. Alexandra, asleep, her pliant body nestled against his. He'd held her close, breathing in the scent of her hair, her skin, brushing gentle kisses against her temple, reliving each moment of their passion until it was indelibly branded in his brain.

Normally after the passions were spent, he took his leave, preferring to put some distance between himself and his partner. But the feel of Alexandra asleep in his arms had suffused his entire being with a sense of peace unlike anything he'd ever experienced. Not until the first mauve streaks of dawn threatened to break through the night sky did he leave her, and even then he'd had to force himself to do so. Only four hours had passed since he'd slipped from her bed, yet it felt more like four decades.

"Good morning, Colin."

Nathan's cheerful voice yanked him from his thoughts. He turned and watched his brother stride toward him. Nathan's gaze dipped to the puppy, and his smile widened. "Ah! I see you finally discovered your gift. I left him with Ellis, who assured me he'd be well taken care of until he delivered him into your hands."

"At a time when you were not around for me to hand the beast back to you."

Nathan's grin was unrepentant. "Precisely. Timing is an art, you know. As is matchmaking. I took one look at that puppy and knew he was destined to be yours."

"I wouldn't dream of depriving you of the beast's company. Therefore, I must return him." But damn it, even as he said the words, somehow his arm remained cuddling the sleeping dog.

"Nonsense. A man who senses danger in his life needs a good watchdog."

"Perhaps. But you cannot possibly believe that *this* is the dog for the job. As far as I can tell, he'd do nothing but lick an intruder. Indeed, all this beast is capable of doing is sleeping, eating, chewing on boots, piddling on floors, and yipping in a deafening fashion. Especially when one is trying to sleep."

"That pretty well describes puppies in general. Which is why they are so incredibly adorable—to offset those other less endearing qualities."

"It is precisely those other less endearing qualities that have prevented me from acquiring one."

"From acquiring one, yes. But not from wanting one."

"I don't want—"

"Of course you do. You're just too stubborn to admit it. Look at how perfectly little Daffodil fits in your arms."

Colin blinked then looked toward the ceiling. "Daffodil? Good God. What sort of name is Daffodil for a boy dog?"

"You are, of course, welcome to save him from a life of shame and rename him. I can only guess that he'd greatly appreciate it."

"You're lucky he didn't gnaw off your arm at saddling him with such a horrendous moniker. But *you* shall have to rename him, as I'm not keeping him."

"Why not?"

"Because I know you. And I therefore know that creatures named Rosebud, Lilac, Hydrangea, Lily, and Chrysanthemum will soon follow, and my home will resemble a farmhouse."

Nathan laid his hand over his heart. "You have my word that no farm beasts named Rosebud, Lilac, Hydrangea, Lily, or Chrysanthemum will follow."

Colin narrowed his eyes, well acquainted with Nathan's tricks. "Or Gardenia, or Larkspur or anything of that sort."

"Agreed. Actually, I gave you Daffodil not only to protect you—"

"—Excellent, as I fear that is a hopeless case—"

"—But also because he will help you secure a bride."

He stared, nonplussed. "I beg your pardon?"

"Bride," Nathan repeated, drawing out the syllable slowly, as if speaking to a small child. "Take Daffodil for a long walk in Hyde Park. Believe me, there is nothing quite like a gamboling puppy to draw female attention. You can narrow your bride search by rejecting any lady who isn't immediately smitten with your darling dog, as she is clearly coldhearted and not worthy of your admiration. And certainly not worthy of being your bride and bearing the title Viscountess Sutton." He spread his hands and smiled. "See how helpful I am?"

"I'm not certain helpful is the word I would use to describe you right now," he muttered.

Bride. Viscountess Sutton. The words lurched through him, reminding him he'd barely devoted a moment's consideration to the very reason he'd come to London. All thoughts of finding a bride had dissolved like sugar in hot chocolate the moment he'd seen Alexandra.

As if the thought of her conjured her up, she appeared in the doorway, standing behind Lord Wexhall's impeccable butler Peters, who cleared his throat, then announced, "Madame Larchmont." The servant withdrew, leaving her framed in the doorway.

Dressed in a plain, unadorned brown day gown, her hair pulled back in a simple chignon at her nape, she stole his breath. Her gaze met his, and he wasn't in the least bit surprised when his lungs ceased to function for several seconds. He swore something warm and intimate passed between them in that single look. The flood of sensual memories that hovered so close to the surface overflowed, filling him with heat and lust and need and the nearly overwhelming desire to stride across the room and drag her into his arms and spend the rest of the day showing her exactly how much he'd missed her.

Missed her. It was utterly ridiculous that he would do so after so short an absence, but there was no denying that he had. It was as if he'd sat beneath a cloud from the time he'd left her until now. But now that she'd appeared, the sun had emerged, warming him, filling him with energy. And a deep longing to touch her. Kiss her. To be close to her.

"Good morning, gentlemen," she said, stepping into the room.

"Good morning," he murmured, knowing that his too-observant brother would note how his gaze devoured her and not caring.

"Good morning, Madame," Nathan said. "I hope you slept well?"

She smiled. "I did, thank you. I just saw Lady Victoria in the breakfast room. She wondered if you planned to join her."

"An invitation I'd never refuse," Nathan said with a smile. "If you'll both excuse me?"

He started across the room, but before he'd made it to the doorway, Alexandra's gaze dipped to the bundle Colin held and her eyes widened. "Oh, my," she said, a smile curving her lips—lips he noted that still looked kiss-swollen. "What an adorable puppy!"

Colin heard Nathan's chuckle from the doorway and when he looked at his brother, Nathan silently mouthed *I told you so*. Then, with a cheery wave, he exited the room, closing the door softly behind him.

Alexandra stopped in front of him, her gaze riveted on the sleeping and unfortunately named Daffodil.

"Who is this?" she asked, running a fingertip over the puppy's midnight fur.

It took him several seconds to answer as his thought processes were disrupted by her nearness. And the fact that she wasn't wearing her usual lacy gloves. The sight of her bare hand warmed him far more than it should have. The scent of fresh soap and oranges rose from her skin, and he stared at her fingers, recalling the feel of them stroking his skin. Tunneling through his hair. Wrapped around his erection.

Instead of answering her question, he said softly, "You're not wearing your gloves."

She lifted her gaze from the puppy, and he was stilled by the impact of her eyes and the delicate blush coloring her cheeks. "You said you liked my hands."

Surely he shouldn't have been so inordinately glad at her obvious wish to please him. "I do," he said, sliding his free arm around her waist and drawing her close. "I also like your lips."

He lowered his head and kissed her, intending to keep the contact light and brief. But the instant his mouth touched hers, she parted her lips, and with a growl of want, he hauled her against him and gave in to his hunger for the deep, intimate kiss he'd craved for hours.

At that moment the unfortunately named Daffodil squirmed, then let out a series of barks. Alexandra leaned back and Colin groaned, and they both looked down at the puppy, whose button eyes were alert and whose pink tongue was searching for something to kiss.

"He's letting us know that he doesn't like being ignored," she said with a laugh, as the puppy set to work kissing her fingers.

"How delightful," Colin muttered. He tried to glower at the wriggling kiss-interrupting bundle of fur, but it was difficult to remain stern when the woman and the dog were so delighted with each other. "Would you like to hold him?"

"Oh, yes," she said, holding out her hands.

Colin transferred the bundle, then watched Alexandra hold the squirming, ecstatic puppy at arm's length and laugh. "You are so sweet," she crooned, drawing in her arms to cuddle the small dog to her chest. When she buried her face in the soft black fur and gently kissed its head, the pup quieted and let out what sounded like a sigh of contentment.

Damn smart dog, Colin decided.

And damned lucky, too.

"He's absolutely wonderful," Alexandra said, looking up to smile into his eyes. "Is he yours?"

"Yes, he is," he said without hesitation. "He's the gift my brother mentioned. As Nathan's offerings always require feeding and care, I wasn't surprised. Indeed, I was relieved that he didn't see fit to bestow upon me a gaggle of geese or a herd of cows."

"Does he have a name?"

He looked at the small dog, curled in her arms, his little head nestled against the generous curve of her breast, and said, "Lucky. His name is Lucky."

"A very fine name."

"And very apt, as he is close to you." He stepped forward and, unable to keep from touching her, trailed his fingers over her smooth cheek. "How are you feeling this morning?"

"A bit . . . tender, but in a very delightful way."

"Delightful . . ." he murmured, leaning down to brush his lips against the side of her neck. "That describes last night perfectly."

"I'm also surprisingly well rested. I do not normally sleep so late. You make a very comfortable pillow."

His fingers glided lower, tracing over her collarbone, biting back the urge to tell her that the simple act of holding her while she'd slept had brought him as much joy and contentment as making love to her had. "Did you find your surprise?"

"Yes, thank you. It was delicious. Had you brought it from home?"

"No. I pilfered it before coming to your room—from the secret supply of sweets I knew Nathan would have. I know all his hiding places."

"You managed to pilfer it during the short time it took me to get back to my bedchamber?"

"I did."

"Heavens, you are talented. In, um, more ways than one."

"Thank you." His fingers glided lower to cup her breast, and she gasped softly. "Would you be interested in another demonstration of my talents?" he asked, brushing his thumb over her nipple, feeling it pebble beneath the material of her gown.

"Wh . . . what did you have in mind?"

For an answer, he reached out and gently plucked the sleepy puppy from her arms. After settling Lucky on the hearth rug, where he promptly yawned and curled into a drowsy ball, Colin crossed the room and locked the door, the quiet click reverberating in the suddenly tense silence.

Turning, he walked slowly toward her, enjoying the way her eyes widened. When he reached her, he didn't stop, just wrapped his arms around her, lifted her off her feet, and continued moving.

"What are you doing?" she whispered, entwining her arms around his neck.

"Showing you what I have in mind."

"Here? Now?"

He reached the wall and pressed her against the mahogany paneling. "Right here," he whispered against her neck, breathing in her luscious fragrance while his hands lifted her skirts. "Right now."

"But what about Lord Wexhall?"

"He's out for the day."

"Your brother and Lady Victoria?"

"They're notoriously slow eaters."

"And if they aren't today?"

"That's why I locked the door."

"But they'll know what we're doing!" Yet even as she protested, her hands fisted in his hair and dragged his mouth toward hers.

"Only if we're not quick. Exactly how tender are you feeling?" he asked, dropping quick kisses to her lips between each word.

"Not nearly as tender as desperate."

"Thank God." He ruched up her skirts to her waist, then hooked her thigh over his hip, opening her for his exploring fingers.

She sucked in a sharp breath when his hand slipped inside the slit in her drawers, a sound that coincided with his groan as he caressed her slick folds.

"You're already wet," he growled against her mouth.

Her hand stroked over his erection. "You're already hard."

"Constantly." He slowly slid a finger deep inside her tight heat. "Entirely your fault. I'm afraid it's going to become an embarrassing problem."

"Consider me more than willing to help."

"An offer I've no intention of refusing." Slipping his hand from her body, he reached between them and freed himself from his breeches as quickly as his unsteady fingers allowed. A small inner voice interjected that he was showing a decided lack of finesse, but dark, fiery urgency shoved the voice aside. He wanted her, needed her, needed to be inside her. *Now.*

The instant he was free, he grasped her beneath the buttocks and lifted. "Wrap your legs around me," he said in a voice he barely recognized. "And hold on."

Seconds later he slid into her hot, wet heat. And lost all semblance of control. He stroked her with long, hard, deep thrusts, gritting his teeth against the swelling need to climax, watching every nuance of her flushed face, her parted lips. Her eyes slid closed and her fingers bit into his shoulders and she cried out, arching her back, her inner walls convulsing around him. The instant he felt her relax, he withdrew from her body and pressed his erection tight against her abdomen. He pressed his face to the warm, fragrant curve of her neck as his release thundered through him.

When his tremors subsided, he raised his head. Her eyes blinked open, and, for several long seconds, they simply stared at each other. He wanted to say something, something light and witty, but light and witty was beyond him. This woman not only robbed him of his control, but apparently of his wits as well. So he said the only word he felt capable of uttering.

"Alexandra."

Then he leaned forward and kissed her, sliding slowly into the velvety warmth of her mouth, savoring the taste of her, the erotic friction of her tongue rubbing against his, the scent of her warmed skin and their shared passion rising between them. His heart thudded against his ribs, and he ended their kiss as slowly as it had begun.

"You are indeed a talented man," she whispered, her head lolling against the wall.

"And you are a delicious woman. I didn't hurt you?"

"Heavens, no. While last night was slow and gentle and lovely, I cannot deny that there is something wickedly delicious about the hard-and-fast approach."

"Duly noted."

One corner of her mouth lifted in a saucy grin. "I can't wait to see what you plan to demonstrate next."

"Based on the way you affect me, you'll find out very soon."

He lowered her gently, and, when she stood on her own, he pulled a handkerchief from his pocket. "You should visit your bedchamber to better freshen up before we leave," he said, gently wiping at the evidence of their spent passion.

"Leave?"

"Yes. I'm here to accompany you on any errands you may have."

"Oh?" She raised a clearly skeptical brow. "And here I thought you were here to have your wicked way with me."

He chuckled. "And now that I have, we can commence with your errands. And mine as well."

"What errands do you have?"

"Well, first, it would appear I have a dog to walk."

Seventeen

Alex walked in Hyde Park, and as she had at dinner the previous evening, she surreptitiously pinched her leg. Hard. Again the pain made her realize this wasn't a dream.

Yet how could it be real that she—Alexandra Larchmont, back-alley rat and former thief of St. Giles—would be strolling through Hyde Park, escorted by a viscount—a man who was not only handsome and intelligent and wealthy, but her *lover*?

She flexed her fingers against the crook of Colin's arm. The hard muscle beneath his very proper midnight blue cutaway coat was definitely real. Turning her head, she looked up at him, and a sigh of pleasure escaped her.

Ribbons of bright sunshine filtered through the leaves of the soaring elms lining the pathway, gilding his thick dark hair and casting his features in dappled shades of gold. Perhaps there existed, somewhere in the world, a more beautiful man, but she couldn't imagine what that man might look like.

Yet it wasn't simply his handsome features that attracted her so fiercely. He possessed every quality she'd fantasized he would when she'd first laid eyes on him at Vauxhall. He was intelligent and amusing. Kind and patient. Sensual and exciting. And when he'd given her his trust, he'd bestowed upon her a gift more valuable to her than jewels or money.

His trust. Guilt pricked her, knowing he wouldn't have given her such a precious prize if he knew her past, if he'd recalled their Vauxhall meeting. But it was a gift she cherished and selfishly refused to give up. He trusted her, and she'd give him no reason to regret that choice.

He must have felt the weight of her regard as he turned his head. The heated, speculative glimmer in his eyes shot fire to her toes, and she was tempted to pinch herself again to prove that she was actually here. With him. And that he was looking at her in that smoldering, intimate way.

"Are you thinking what I'm thinking?" he asked in an undertone, leaning toward her, his shoulder bumping hers.

"I don't know." She debated whether or not to admit the truth, then said, "I was trying to convince myself that this afternoon stroll with my handsome viscount lover wasn't merely a figment of my imagination."

"Hmmm. Definitely not what I was thinking."

"Oh? In what direction were your thoughts wandering?"

"I was wondering how long before we could leave this bloody park so I could strip my exquisite fortune-teller lover naked and make love to her again."

Fire sizzled through her, and she nearly stumbled. "I don't think Lucky would take kindly to having his walk cut short." She nodded toward the enthusiastic puppy, who alternated between galloping as far ahead as his lead would allow, then stopping to sniff at every blade of grass.

"Perhaps not, but I'd wager I'll end up carrying him

before long since he's bound to run out of energy." He tilted his chin toward the chatting couple walking several yards ahead of them. "I don't think my footman would take kindly to having this walk cut short, either. John seems quite taken with your friend Emma."

"I believe the feeling is mutual." She fiddled with the strings on her reticule, then said, "It was very generous of you to purchase Emma's *entire* crate of oranges. She's never finished selling this early in the day."

"It was my pleasure, especially as I've developed a special liking for the fruit. Besides, I saw the way she and John were looking at each other. By making Emma available to join us, not only could they get acquainted, but her presence provides you with a chaperone."

"Do I *need* a chaperone?"

"Definitely. Otherwise, I'd give in to the temptation to drag you behind a tree and ravish you in broad daylight."

"Oh . . . my," she said, rendered breathless by the image his words created in her mind. "And that would be very bad."

"And very likely if you don't cease looking at me like that."

"Like what?"

"In that way every man wants to be looked at by a woman he desires. It's . . . potent. Especially with those big, beautiful eyes. I suppose most other men would compare their color to a topaz jewel. But to me, your eyes look like warm, melted chocolate, sprinkled with cinnamon."

"As you've admitted a weakness for sweets, I'm delighted. Especially as I prefer chocolate to topaz jewels."

He chuckled softly, then discreetly brushed his arm against the outer curve of her breast. "I knew you were extraordinary, but the fact that you would even think such a thing, let alone say it out loud, makes you truly incredible. Hmmm. Extraordinary *and* incredible . . . I believe that makes you . . . incredinary."

They paused while Lucky examined an apparently fascinating tuft of grass, and she smiled up at him, shading her eyes with her free hand. "I like the way you create new words. Have you always done so?"

"No. You're the first person I've ever met who has inspired me to do so."

She was tempted to categorize his words as mere jest, but the look in his eyes, the tone of his voice, made it clear he was serious. Confused pleasure seeped through her. "I'm flattered."

"And special. Which makes you—"

"Splattered?" she suggested, realizing the word perfectly described her thoughts and emotions—like raindrops scattered by buffeting winds.

He laughed, a deep, rich sound she could have listened to for hours. "Splattered," he agreed, his eyes smiling into hers.

Lucky barked, and they both looked down at the black ball of fur whose prancing and tail wagging indicated he was ready to move on. When they started walking again, Colin said, "I meant to tell you this earlier, but I was distracted by your charms and forgot. When I left Wexhall's last night—or rather early this morning—I saw Robbie."

A frown pulled down her brows. "Robbie? Where?"

"Hiding in Wexhall's bushes. Looking out for you, he claimed."

Concern knotted her stomach. "He shouldn't be doing that."

"Precisely what I told the lad. I assured him you were being well cared for and were perfectly safe. And that you would worry about him if you suspected he was lurking about."

"Thank you. I'll speak to Emma—make sure she tells him I'm fine and to stay away and that I'll be home soon."

"The child loves you."

A lump of emotion clogged her throat. "I love him in return. And speaking of love . . ." She nodded toward Emma and John, who were now quite far ahead, strolling with their heads bent close to each other.

"They seem to be getting on famously," Colin said.

"I can't say I'm surprised. The last time I read Emma's cards, they predicted she'd meet a tall, handsome, blond man."

"And what of your cards? Did they predict you'd meet a man with commanding bearing, superior intelligence, and passable good looks?"

She recalled her last card reading, and the danger she'd seen. Not wishing to cast a pall on the afternoon, she said lightly, "Yes, but it might not have been you, as I read nothing about this man having a weakness for sweets."

"On the contrary, I'm certain it was I. I have so many weaknesses, no doubt that one just became lost amongst all the others."

"Weaknesses other than sweets? What are they?"

"I'll tell you—for a price."

"How much?"

Deviltry and heat danced in his eyes. "The price has nothing to do with money."

"And if I refuse?"

"Then you risk never discovering how sensual a game of billiards can really be."

"Billiards?" she repeated, intrigued. "Sensual?"

He settled his hand on top of hers, which was curled in the crook of his arm. Warmth slid up her arm, but then she gasped when he slowly brushed the backs of his fingers over the outer curve of her breast. "It depends entirely upon with whom you are playing."

He continued his slow caress, and the fire racing through her made it nearly impossible to think. She pretended to ponder, then blew out an exaggerated, put-upon breath. "Very well, I agree to your terms, heinous though they are."

"Noted. Mind you, these weaknesses are of a somewhat recent nature. It appears I have a weakness for oranges."

His finger flicked over her nipple and her heart stuttered. "You do?"

"Yes." He halted under the shade of an elm, then turned to face her. Less than two feet separated them, a dangerous lack of space that was so very tempting to erase with a single step forward. "And big, chocolate brown eyes, and dark, shiny hair," he continued softly. "And smooth skin that has just a smattering of freckles right here . . ." He lifted his hand and brushed his fingertips over her cheek, halting her breath. Then his gaze dropped to her mouth, and heat flared in his eyes. "And full lips."

Dear God, surely he didn't mean to kiss her. Right here, in the open, where anyone could see. Her insides trembled, and although her inner voice warned her to step away, she couldn't move.

"You," he whispered, his fingers lingering on her cheek. "I have a profound weakness for you, Alexandra."

"And I for you." The words slipped out before she could stop them, but as they expressed a sentiment so obvious, there wasn't much point in trying to deny it.

The hint of a smile touched his lips. "I'm glad. I care nothing for things that are one-sided."

He leaned forward, and her heart thudded with an anticipation that should have appalled her but instead thrilled her. A quick look around assured her that no one was nearby. Still, the voice of reason inside her head whispered that she risked a great deal allowing him such liberties in public. She shoved reason away and waited for his kiss.

An insistent barking penetrated the fog surrounding her, and he stepped back with a half-troubled, half-sheepish expression. "It appears Lucky is an able chaperone, and clearly you require one, as I nearly forgot myself." He offered his elbow, and after she slipped her hand back into the warm crook of his arm, they continued their slow walk.

After a dozen paces in a silence broken only by the warbling of birds, she couldn't stop herself from saying, "This weakness of yours for me—it truly baffles me."

"Now who's fishing for compliments?" he asked in a teasing voice.

"I'm not. Truly."

"Then allow me to assure you that you are extraordinary. And your beauty is unsurpassed."

"You require spectacles."

He shook his head. "Your beauty is much more complex, and encompasses far more than mere physical attributes. It has to do with your *essence*. Your soul. The extraordinary person you are."

Guilt slapped her squarely in the midsection. "I'm not the paragon you're making me out to be, Colin. I've done things I'm . . . not proud of."

"I'd be hard-pressed to name anyone who hasn't. God knows I've done plenty of things I'm not proud of. But regardless of those things, you've risen above them and turned yourself into someone to be admired. That in itself is extraordinary."

She turned and found him watching her with an unreadable expression, and her throat went dry. His words, the way he said them . . . it almost sounded as if he knew her past was less than reputable. "What do you mean?" she asked carefully.

"I'm guessing you endured some hardships while growing up. It has been my experience that hardships either break people or inspire them, firing them with determination. It's clear to me you've triumphed over any adversities and want to help others, such as Robbie. That says a great deal about you."

Discomfort edged through her at his uncannily accurate assessment. "What makes you think I endured hardships?"

Obviously her tone wasn't as neutral as she'd hoped because he said, "I meant no offense, Alexandra. I tend to study people—I'm afraid that comes with being a spy—and it's simply a conclusion I've drawn based on my own observations. If I'm wrong, I apologize."

"Upon what observations did you base your conclusion?"

He hesitated, then said, "Many different things. Your hands are those of someone accustomed to hard work. The fact that you are so determined to help children like Robbie, whose young lives are fraught with difficulties, suggests to me that you are motivated by a childhood that was likely less than idyllic. When you mentioned your mother died, I had the impression you were young when that happened."

An image of her mother, so pale and ill, trying to smile, flashed in her mind. "I was eight."

"It's clear she meant a great deal to you."

A frown pulled down her brows. "How? I've barely spoken of her."

"The look in your eyes when you've mentioned her speaks volumes. It's a look I recognize."

She nodded with understanding. "Because of the loss of your own mother."

"Yes. What happened to you after she died?"

A wealth of painful memories flooded her, and even though she had no desire to dredge up that part of her life, she suddenly wanted him to know something of her past—at least enough to realize that she spoke the truth when she said she was common.

"I went to live with an aunt," she said. "My father's sister. She wasn't fond of my mother, whom she labeled 'gypsy rubbish' and was less than pleased to be saddled with me."

"What of your father?"

"He was a sailor. He died at sea when I was a baby. I don't remember him at all."

"I'm sorry." He again rested his hand, which held Lucky's lead on top of hers, and gently squeezed her fingers. "Obviously, your aunt provided for your education."

A humorless sound escaped her. "No. She provided only for her son, Gerald, who was two years older than I. I learned by listening at cracks in the doors and by hiding in the bushes beneath the room where the tutor instructed him." She drew a deep breath, and decided it wasn't necessary to add that she'd been kicked out of her aunt's home at the age of twelve after she'd blackened Gerald's eyes for trying to insinuate his hand up her skirt. "It wasn't a very happy place." Neither were the cold, dark, frightening London streets where she'd taken refuge after being tossed from her aunt's house like yesterday's trash. That was when and where her real education had begun.

"Which proves that you are one of the people who is inspired, rather than oppressed, by adversity. Whatever became of your aunt?"

"I've no idea. I haven't seen or heard from her since I left her home. Nor do I care to. For all I know she's dead. I've often hoped she is." She looked at him and raised her brows in challenge. "What sort of person does that make me?"

"Human. Just like the rest of us."

Deciding she'd walked as far down that road of painful memories as she cared to go, she asked, "What sort of things have you done of which you're not proud?"

Colin turned and looked at her, wanting to question her further, but clearly sensing she would not welcome any more queries. He'd hoped she'd confide in him about her former profession, but he understood why she wouldn't. Yet perhaps if he confided in her, she'd do the same. Or perhaps she'd never look at him again with that same admiration in her eyes.

Keeping his expression and tone perfectly neutral, he asked, "Do you really want to know? You may not like what you hear."

"There's nothing you could say that would make me think badly of you."

"A statement you might regret."

"No." Her gaze searched his. "I understand shame and regrets and making mistakes too well to judge anyone else's. But if you'd rather not tell me, I understand that as well."

Her words, the warm compassion in her eyes, flooded him with a plethora of emotions that tightened his throat. That she'd experienced shame and hurt angered him, and filled him with sympathy, along with an overwhelming desire to tell her heartless aunt precisely what he thought of her treatment of her orphaned niece. Her understanding in that she didn't press him to expose every detail of his life rendered him all the more willing to tell her things he'd never shared with anyone else.

"I want you to know." After drawing a bracing breath, he told her about the night he was shot, how he'd betrayed his brother. Of the estrangement that followed.

And of the guilt he still carried. She listened in silence, her brow furrowed in concentration.

When he finished, she said, "The two of you have reconciled."

"I am fortunate that he forgave me."

"Your brother no doubt carries guilt with him as well because you were shot."

"An occurrence that was entirely my own fault. Nathan had never given me a reason to mistrust him, yet I did."

"Why?"

"I spent countless hours asking myself that very question. And I'm ashamed to say that part of me was jealous of him. Envious certainly. He didn't have the responsibilities I had. He was free in ways I never could be." He shook his head and frowned. "I don't mean to sound as if I don't care about my obligations to my title or take them seriously, because I do. A great many people depend on my family's lands for their livelihood, and that is a responsibility I would never jeopardize or compromise. But I cannot deny that there were times, especially when I was younger, when I would have given a great deal to be the younger brother." He shot her the same challenging look she'd issued to him. "What sort of man does that make me?"

"Human. Just like the rest of us."

A small smile tugged at his lips. "Hoist on my own petard." He debated whether to continue, then decided to lay the rest of his cards on the table. "But I've done other things. Things I've never told anyone."

He suspected he must have looked as bleak as he sounded, for she gently squeezed his arm and said softly, "You don't have to tell me, Colin."

But suddenly he wanted to. For reasons he didn't fully understand, other than to know he didn't want secrets between them. "I spent my spying years living a lie," he began. "Even my own father didn't know I worked for the Crown."

"I think secrecy can be forgiven in such matters."

He slowed their pace, then stopped and turned to face her. And uttered the words he'd never told anyone. "I killed a man."

For several heartbeats silence swelled between them. Then she said calmly, "I'm certain you had a good reason to do so."

Her quiet composure in the face of his confession stunned him, yet at the same time didn't surprise him. This woman, his unique Alexandra, wasn't the sort to suffer the vapors and ring for the hartshorn.

His unique Alexandra. The unsettling words reverberated through him like a heartbeat, filling him with a sensation he couldn't name, one he firmly set aside to examine later. "He was a traitor to England."

"Then he deserved to die. Think of the lives you saved by stopping him."

"I do. But . . ." The images he kept so tightly locked away burst through the dam to flood his mind. "I discovered Richard's perfidy quite by accident while we were on a mission together for the Crown. Indeed, if not for a small misstep on his part, I wouldn't have known. I'd considered him a friend. A colleague. A man loyal to England." All the fury and betrayal he'd felt came rushing back, and he squeezed his eyes shut. But that only served to provide a backdrop to the vivid mental images. Of Richard reaching for his knife. Of Colin being quicker. Of the sickeningly smooth slide of razor-sharp metal into skin. Of the rush of Richard's warm blood oozing over his hands. Watching the life fade from the dulling eyes of a man he'd once considered a friend.

"Colin."

He opened his eyes. She stood in front of him, her eyes filled with concern and a fierce determination.

Reaching out, she clasped his hands. "You did what you had to do."

He nodded. "I know. Deep inside I know. But there's another part of me that cannot forget that I took another man's life, regardless of how deserving he was. That I left his wife a widow."

"She was left a widow by the choices *he* made."

"My common sense knows that. But sometimes even when you know you did what you had to do, what was necessary in order to survive, there's still a small part that rejects those actions. A small part of your soul you lose and can't quite get back." His gaze searched hers. "It's difficult to explain."

She swallowed and squeezed his hands. "I . . . I understand."

"Something told me you would," he said gently. "That's why I told you."

"You said no one knows of this. Was his treachery not made public?"

"No. In order to spare his wife the shame of his betrayal, it is assumed by everyone to this day that he died a hero."

"Your brother doesn't know?"

He shook his head. "The only person who knows the true circumstances of Richard's death other than me is Wexhall. And now you."

"You have my word I won't betray your trust."

"I know," he said, lifting her hand to his lips to press a kiss against her fingers. For the space of several heartbeats, she appeared as if she meant to say something, but she remained silent, and they resumed their walk.

Someday, his inner voice assured him. *She'll tell you someday.*

Perhaps. But to what end? Even if they both walked away from Wexhall's upcoming party unscathed, he couldn't stay in London indefinitely. He needed to return to Cornwall.

With a wife.

A woman he needed to choose very soon. A woman he very likely could find tonight at the Ralstrom soiree if he put any effort into the task.

A woman who was not Alexandra.

Eighteen

Alex sat at her card-reading table, just below the balcony of the upstairs gallery in Lord and Lady Ralstrom's very crowded, very elegant drawing room. While conducting her readings, she listened to the voices around her, hoping to hear the raspy whisper she'd overheard in Lord Malloran's study, but so far had heard nothing resembling the sound. The location afforded her an excellent view of the room, and she spent a great deal of time looking at the guests.

Unfortunately, she hadn't liked what she'd seen.

Every time she'd looked, Colin, who'd situated himself by a nearby grouping of potted palms in case she gave him their prearranged signal that she'd heard the voice, had been conversing with a different woman, each one more beautiful than the next. Each one wearing an expensive gown in the latest fashion, their hair and throats and wrists adorned with glittering precious gems. Although she was not close enough to hear their conversations, she occasionally caught the sound of his laughter. When she'd invariably look his way, she'd see him smiling at some wealthy peer's marriage-age daughter, who gazed at him with stars—in most cases *flirtatious* stars—in her eyes.

And who could blame any woman for doing so? With his dark good looks, his powerful, lean frame enhanced by his elegant black formal wear and snowy white shirt, he was, without question, the most attractive man in the room. He would have garnered more than his fair share of female attention even without benefit of his exalted social position. Given his wealth, title, and the fact that he was actively seeking a wife, it seemed as if, like colorful hummingbirds waiting their turn to sample his nectar, every woman in the room hovered near him.

And damnation, she wanted to slap every one of them to the parquet floor. Right now he was speaking to the lovely Lady Margaret. As if she didn't provide enough beauty, they were joined by Lady Malloran's cousin, Lady Miranda. Looking at the two gorgeous women, one a delicate pale blond and the other a dark, rich brunette, she wondered if one of them might be the writer of the rose-scented note signed only "M" that she'd read in Colin's drawing room. The "M" who looked forward to seeing him again. Well, both women were seeing him again now, and viewing him with the sort of calculated speculation a cat would bestow upon a cream-drenched mouse.

Lady Miranda smiled at him, then extended her hand. Alex watched in an agony of unwanted jealousy as he lifted the woman's hand—one she knew was lily white and perfect and bore no calluses or marks of labor—to his mouth and brushed his lips over her fingertips. Even though the gesture appeared perfectly respectable and he released her immediately, Alex had to force herself to remain in her chair and not dash over brandishing a handkerchief to scrub the imprint of his mouth from her damn perfect hand, and the feel of her damn perfect hand from his lips.

Dear God, this was not good. None of these women had done anything wrong. They all had the perfect right to speak to him and flirt with him. Just as he did with them. *She* was the one who needed to recall that he wasn't hers. Would never, could never be hers, except in the most superficial and fleeting of ways. Pulling in a long, slow breath, she pressed her lips together and closed her eyes to banish the painful sight—of two beautiful women who already had *everything* vying for the one thing Alex wanted but could never have.

Colin.

She had no claim on him. Her mind, her common sense knew it. But, oh, God, her heart felt heavy and as if it had sprung a leak. And he hadn't even chosen a wife yet. If she ached this badly now, how would she bear it when he told her he'd chosen the woman he would spend the rest of his life with, whom he would make love to and who would give birth to his children? How would she bear it when he told her good-bye?

"Do I have the good fortune of finding you available for a reading, Madame?"

At the deep-voiced question, Alex's eyes sprang open, and she found herself looking up at Logan Jennsen. A lazy smile curved his lips, and an impudent gleam lit his dark eyes.

Vastly relieved to see a friendly face and have someone else upon whom to concentrate, she offered him a smile. "Yes, I am available for a reading, Logan. Please join me."

"Thank you." He eased into the chair opposite her, and she was relieved to note that his height and breadth effectively blocked her view of the room. Excellent. What she didn't see wouldn't hurt her. Or so she was determined.

"Neither of them can compare to you," he said.

"I beg your pardon?"

"Lady Miranda and Lady Margaret. As far as I'm concerned, next to you they are beige spots on a beige wall."

She couldn't help but laugh. "Spoken like a true friend—but you're a dreadful liar."

"Actually, I'm an accomplished liar, but in this case, I speak the truth." His gaze skimmed over her. "You look lovely this evening."

"Thank you. So do you."

He smiled. "This is the best conversation I've had all evening."

Smiling in return, she reached for her cards, and said, "For me as well. Now tell me, what question would you like answered?"

He spread his hands. "I would be delighted to hear anything you wished to tell me. Especially if it is good news."

"What would you consider good news?"

"That a certain lady finds me as fascinating as I find her."

At her mock warning look, he held up his hands in surrender. "You did ask."

"How about that you're destined to acquire another fleet of ships?"

He flashed a very attractive smile, which creased two deep dimples in his cheeks. "Certainly I wouldn't consider that *bad* news. Is that what's in store for me?"

Forcing herself not to crane her neck to see over his shoulder, she began to shuffle. "Let's see what the cards predict."

Colin feigned interest at whatever Lady Margaret was saying, nodding politely, but the effort cost him. Bloody hell, that American Jennsen was sitting at Alexandra's table. What the hell was he doing? He'd just had his fortune read at the Newtrebble fete *and* at a private sitting. Which meant that the attraction was clearly the card reader rather than the reading itself. *If that bastard says or does anything untoward, I predict he'll meet the bloody privet hedges. Headfirst.*

Of course, he'd felt precisely the same way about the other eleven—not that he was counting—men who'd visited Alexandra's fortune-telling table this evening. She'd smiled at all of them, and he'd gritted his teeth, painfully aware of her while he listened with only half an ear to the women he should have been paying attention to.

Bloody hell. This . . . whatever she'd done to him, whatever spell she'd cast upon him, was not good. How was he supposed to concentrate on finding a bride when the only woman he could think about was her? While he tossed in a comment here, a chuckle there, and nodded a great deal, his attention remained firmly focused on her. But now that big oaf Jennsen blocked most of his view— and damn it, had that bastard just *kissed her hand*?

An unwelcome jolt of pure, undiluted jealousy shot through him, and his fingers clenched around his crystal champagne flute.

"If you ladies will excuse me," he said to Lady Margaret and Lady Miranda, trying, for politeness' sake, to keep the impatient edge from his voice. After offering them a curt bow, he turned and began weaving his way through the crowd, his gaze riveted on Alexandra while he shoved aside his jealousy and concentrated on his concern for her safety. Any of the men who'd visited her table tonight could be the raspy-voiced murderer. Jennsen included.

He'd taken no more than half a dozen steps, however, when he was waylaid by his sister-in-law.

"Finally, a chance to speak with you, Colin," Victoria said, her eyes alight with . . . something. Something he was too distracted to try deciphering. "You've been surrounded all evening."

"Victoria," he murmured. His gaze flicked past her, and he grimly noted that Alexandra and Jenssen were laughing together.

"Might I have a moment of your time?" Victoria asked.

He wanted to snap out *NO,* and continue walking, but common sense prevailed. It certainly wasn't Victoria's fault he felt so damnably frustrated and irritated. Dragging his attention back to her, he forced a smile. "Of course."

"Shall we step outside for privacy?"

Leaning closer, he said in an undertone, "Is that necessary? I don't want to be unavailable should Alexandra hear the voice."

"Nathan is watching her," she said, nodding toward his brother, who stood within sight of Alexandra's table. "He knows the signal. I'll only keep you a moment."

He looked at Nathan, who gave him an imperceptible nod. "Very well," he said, not pleased but unable to refuse her request without appearing churlish.

He led the way through the French windows leading to the terrace. The moon gleamed, a shiny pearl against a diamond-studded velvet sky, casting a silver glow over the flagstones. A warm breeze, delicately scented with night-blooming flowers, rustled the leaves. Halting near a large potted yew topiary he turned toward Victoria and said, "What do you wish to speak to me about?"

"Your bride search."

"What about it?"

"I was wondering how it was progressing."

It's not. "Fine."

Something flickered in her eyes. Doubt? He wasn't sure, but quite frankly, neither was he interested.

"I see. *Fine* as in 'I'm meeting dozens of interesting, fascinating women I find attractive,' or *fine* as in 'I couldn't name one woman I've spoken to this evening because my thoughts are completely engaged elsewhere'?"

Damn it, a group of men paused near the French windows, blocking his view of Alexandra. "Fine as in . . . fine."

"Ah. Splendid. Have you made any decisions?"

"Decisions?"

"You know, ruled out anyone, decided anyone has potential, that sort of thing."

More gentlemen joined the group, further thwarting his view. Didn't these blasted men have port to drink or cheroots to smoke—elsewhere? "Um, no."

"I rather thought not. Which is why I'm prepared to offer my assistance."

Bloody hell, how long were those men going to stand there? "Assistance? With what?"

She made an exasperated sound. "Your bride search," she said very slowly and very distinctly.

Barely suppressing his own exasperated sound, he forced himself to look at her. "What about it?"

She stared at him for several long seconds, her gaze unnervingly steady, her expression indecipherable. Damn it all, when had women become so frustratingly difficult to read?

Finally, she cleared her throat. "I was prepared to offer you my assistance on your bride search, but it appears it's not necessary."

"No, it's not." Something in her tone, in her eyes, set off a warning signal in his brain. "Why isn't it necessary?"

"Because it seems you've already narrowed down your choice."

Out of the corner of his eye, he noticed that the group of men moved, and his gaze shifted back to the drawing room. "I have?"

"Clearly." She hesitated, then said quietly, "I spoke to Nathan. I know she's not married."

"Who?" Damn it, another group now blocked his view.

"Your choice."

Again he dragged his attention back to his sister-in-law, who for some reason was speaking in riddles. "What about her?"

"She's not married."

He pressed his fingers to the throbbing at his temple. "Of course she—whoever she is—is not married. I can't very well choose a woman who's already married." Ah, like a herd of slow-moving cows, finally the group moved on, clearing his view. And he froze.

Alexandra and Jennsen stood next to her table, her hand tucked into the crook of his arm. She was smiling up at him, and his face bore the unmistakable expression of a man who very much liked what he saw. A man who wanted what he saw. He leaned down to say something to her, then they melted into the crowd. Anger, concern, and jealousy collided in him. For her own safety, she wasn't supposed to leave the drawing room. Where the hell was she going?

"Excuse me," he said to Victoria, and without waiting for a reply, strode across the flagstones and reentered the drawing room. He scanned the room and saw them near the punch bowl. Jaw tight, he started forward. And nearly plowed into Nathan who stepped directly in his path.

"She's fine," Nathan said in undertone, blocking his way. "You, however, look as if you require a brandy." He held a cut-crystal snifter aloft.

"What I require," he said through clenched teeth, ignoring the proffered drink, "is to find out what the bloody hell she thinks she's doing."

"It's obvious what she's doing. She's having a glass of punch."

"With that bloody American who, for all we know, could be the person we're looking for."

"Which is why Wexhall is standing near her, ready to intercept if he tries to get her off alone. *She* is perfectly safe. It's *you* I'm concerned about."

Nathan's words penetrated the haze of fear and anger and jealousy engulfing him, and he dragged his hands down his face. "I'm fine."

"No, you're not. You're upset at Jenssen for looking at her like he's dying of thirst and she's a long, cool drink. I don't blame you. I'd feel the same way in your position and probably would have planted him a facer by now. I'll do so if he makes the mistake of looking at Victoria that way."

Colin drew a deep breath, and guilt slapped him. "Victoria . . . I left her standing alone on the terrace."

"She found her way back inside. She's quite resourceful that way. She's chatting with Lady Margaret and Lady Miranda, two *other* women you abruptly abandoned." Nathan handed him the brandy snifter, and Colin took a hefty sip, savoring the burn down his throat.

"They're both beautiful," Nathan said.

"I suppose."

"Do either of them appeal to you?"

Not in the least. "They were pleasant to talk to."

"Indeed? What were you discussing?"

Damned if he knew. And based on Nathan's overly innocent expression, he was well aware of that. "The weather." Most likely.

"Ah, yes, fascinating stuff. But I meant did either of them appeal to you as a wife candidate."

Before answering, Colin tossed back another swallow

of the potent liquor in a useless attempt to drown the emptiness brought on by the thought of marrying either of them. "From a practical standpoint, either would do."

"And from an impractical standpoint?"

A sense of profound weariness washed through him. "Right now the thought of spending the rest of my life with either of them is . . ." *Depressing.* "Difficult to imagine."

"Why do you suppose that is?"

Irritation pricked him. "Because right now I have other things on my mind. Finding a killer. Keeping a murder from happening. Wexhall's party is next week. Hopefully by the time it's over, all the questions surrounding that puzzle will be answered, and I'll be able to concentrate on my bride search."

"You think you'll be better equipped to choose one of these Society diamonds after Wexhall's party?"

"Yes. Absolutely."

Nathan muttered something that sounded suspiciously like "idiotic dolt," then clapped his hand on Colin's shoulder. "I wish you luck with that. I truly do. But as someone who has recently gone through exactly what you're now facing, I can only offer you my deepest sympathy and my best wishes that it works out as well for you as it did for me."

"What the hell are you talking about?"

"The battle."

"What battle?"

"Between your mind and your heart."

"I don't know what you mean."

Nathan squeezed his shoulder. "You will. Good luck."

Alex sat alone at her fortune-telling table, enjoying the brief respite. Her gaze sought out Colin, and she noted he was once again in the company of a beautiful woman. He appeared to be listening to her, but just then his gaze swiveled toward her. Their gazes collided, and Alex felt the impact down to her feet. She tried to look away, but couldn't.

Yet clearly he suffered from no such affliction as his gaze suddenly shifted up, over her head. A frown puckered his brow and his eyes narrowed. Then widened. His gaze jumped back to her and he lunged forward, waving his arms in a shooing side motion.

"Alexandra!" he yelled, running toward her. "Move! *Move!*"

Startled, she jumped to her feet and dashed around the table. A heartbeat later a large stone urn smashed onto the chair where she'd sat only seconds before. The chair splintered beneath the weight, and the urn broke apart, raising a cloud of dust.

Shocked immobile, she gaped at the destruction while shouts rose around her.

"Alexandra," Colin said, his voice low and tense. He gripped her shoulders and gently shook her. "Are you all right?"

"I . . . I'm fine. Thanks to you." She tore her gaze from the broken urn and chair to look at him. "What happened?"

"The urn fell from the balcony."

Dr. Oliver pushed his way through the gathering crowd to join them. His gaze skimmed over Alex. "Were you injured?"

"No." Realization hit her and her knees wobbled. *Dear God, if that stone urn had hit me . . .*

She closed her eyes, and Colin's fingers tightened on her arms. The crowd was pressing closer, the chatter of voices rising.

"Madame was not hurt," Colin said, raising his voice to the guests.

She opened her eyes and their gazes met, his a deep, burning green. "You saved my life," she whispered.

Before he could reply, Lord Ralstrom appeared. He peered at the mess through his quizzing glass, then said, "Extraordinary. No doubt the urn was moved for cleaning and not resituated properly. You have my deepest apologies, Madame Larchmont, and rest assured, I'll find out who was responsible for such carelessness."

She swallowed, then nodded. "Thank you, my lord."

"Is there a quiet room where Madame can recover herself?" Colin asked Lord Ralstrom in an undertone.

"Of course. Follow me."

Several minutes later, ensconced in Lord Ralstrom's private study, under the watchful eyes of Lady Victoria, Dr. Oliver, and Colin, Alex sipped brandy from a crystal snifter.

"I don't think this was an accident," Colin said the moment Lord Ralstrom left the room.

"My father ran to the gallery immediately," Lady Victoria said. "If someone pushed that urn, Father will find him."

Colin crossed to the decanters and poured himself a generous finger of brandy and tossed back the potent liquor in a single swallow. Fire arrowed down his throat, infusing him with a heat he prayed would relax the tension gripping him.

He closed his eyes, and an image of that urn teetering directly above Alexandra besieged him. The sick realization it was about to fall and that he'd never reach her in time. Perhaps someday he might recover from the stark terror of that moment, but today was not that day.

Anger such as he'd never known ripped through him. Whoever had tried to hurt her would pay. He'd see to it.

A knock sounded at the door and he opened his eyes.

Lord Ralstrom's butler showed Lord Wexhall into the room.

"Well?" Colin asked without preamble.

"The gallery was empty," Wexhall reported, "but given the dimness of the area, someone could have pushed the urn without being seen, then escaped through any number of doorways or down the back stairs."

Colin's gaze roamed over Alexandra, who, although pale, appeared unscathed. He'd purposely forced himself to keep some space between them since entering the room so as not to simply snatch her into his arms and never let go. Which is precisely what he itched to do right now. Which meant he needed a task.

"As Alexandra is unharmed," he said, "I'd like to search the gallery myself. I'll let you know if I discover anything."

After a thirty-minute search of the gallery that yielded nothing, he returned downstairs. The instant he stepped into the drawing room, where the party had resumed in full swing, he felt someone's gaze burning into his back. Turning, he found himself face-to-face with Logan Jennsen.

"Is she really all right?" Jennsen asked.

Colin's fingers clenched. "Yes."

The American raised his brows at Colin's clipped tone. "I'd like to see her. Do you know where she is?"

"I do. But as I said, she's fine. There's no need for you to see her."

For several long seconds, tense silence bounced between them. Then Jennsen said in a low tone, "From what I hear, you'll be returning to Cornwall very soon with one of these fancy Society ladies as your wife. I'm a patient man—and Alexandra is worth the wait." He offered Colin a cold smile. "Luckily for both her and I, I'm not a slave to some lofty English title. Good evening, Sutton."

Colin watched him walk away, sick with the knowledge that Jennsen was absolutely right.

Alex forced a smile and bid good night to Lord Wexhall, Lady Victoria, and Dr. Oliver in the foyer of the Wexhall town house, then climbed the stairs to her bedchamber on legs that felt like stone, eternally grateful the evening had finally ended. They'd departed once Colin had returned to the library after his unsuccessful search of the gallery. Between the accident and the hours beforehand, when she'd watched all those women flirt with him, she'd had enough. If she'd been forced to endure watching one more woman batting her eyelashes at him, she would have—

She blew out a long sigh. Done nothing.

For there was nothing to be done. Except swallow her sadness and smile and pretend that it didn't matter, didn't hurt so badly she could barely breathe that another woman would soon have the man she so foolishly and desperately wanted for herself.

Adding to her misery was the fear that their interlude might already be over. He'd said it would end when he decided upon a wife—had he chosen tonight which woman to pursue?

Except for immediately after the accident, he'd certainly avoided her all night. Hadn't approached her fortune-telling table. Hadn't spoken to her. Her gaze had sought him out more times than she cared to count, but as far as she could tell, although he remained close by for safety's sake, he never looked her way. Even when she departed the party with the Wexhall group, he'd merely offered her a formal bow, a polite good night, happiness that she wasn't hurt, and his usual inscrutable expression. He'd made no move to kiss her hand—to so much as touch her—and as much as she tried to convince herself otherwise, his cool detachment hurt deeply.

Where was the man who'd desired her so fiercely just that morning? Who'd been unable to keep from touching her? Whose eyes had burned with want for her? There'd been no sign of him tonight. In his place he'd left an aloof stranger who hadn't looked at her with the slightest sign of desire. Indeed, it had taken an urn's nearly crushing her for him to show any emotion at all.

She walked slowly down the corridor, misery gripping her stomach. Clearly, although still concerned for her, he'd already tired of her. Seeing her in the same room with all those glittering Society diamonds had, of course, shown her up as the paste imitation she was, a comparison clearly not lost upon him.

Emma's warnings filtered through her mind. *Ye know that a man like him would only take ye then leave ye . . . toss ye aside like yesterday's trash. Ye know yer heart'll get broke.*

Yes, she'd known. Known their affair, this fairy tale, would end. She simply hadn't thought it would end so soon. Or that its demise would hurt this horribly. Hadn't considered that she'd have to see him again after they'd parted ways. It was one thing for propriety's sake to pretend at a soiree that there was nothing between them. It was quite another to pretend she felt nothing because their relationship was now . . . nothing. The prospect of maintaining the charade that everything was fine in front of his family, here at the Wexhall home, tied her insides in cramping knots.

Damn it, she wanted to go home. To *her* home. Where everything was familiar. Where she had a purpose. Where she was needed. The Wexhall party was next week. The instant it ended, she intended to go back where she belonged.

She entered her bedchamber, then leaned back against the wood panel. Her eyes slid closed and a weary sigh escaped her.

"Lock the door."

She gasped, her eyes popping open at the soft, deep-voiced command that rose from the darkened corner. Although she couldn't see him, there was no mistaking Colin's voice, and a tremor tingled through her.

Heart pounding, her gaze scanning the shadows, she reached behind her, and fumbled for the ornate key protruding from the keyhole. When her fingers closed around the cool metal, she turned her wrist. The quiet click of the lock slipping into place reverberated through the room. And in that instant the lock she'd kept around her heart opened and a flood of emotion swamped her. Emotion she could no longer deny.

She loved him.

Completely. Irrevocably. And utterly hopelessly.

The words *I love you* rushed to her lips, and she clenched her jaw to silence them. Voicing useless words of love to a man with whom she had no future would do nothing save humiliate her and make both of them uncomfortable.

"Move in front of the fire."

The husky order came from near the wardrobe, but she could not make out his form in the deep shadows. Storing away her newly minted realization of love, she walked slowly toward the fireplace on legs that felt less than steady. The low flame glowing in the grate warmed her back when she halted—a heat she did not need, as it suddenly felt as if fire surged through her veins.

Questions hovered on her tongue, but her throat felt too dry to utter them. She stared at the far corner of the room and watched a dark form detach from the shadows. He walked toward her, slowly, like a predator stalking its prey, stopping just beyond an arm's length away from her.

Her gaze moved down his body, over his white shirt, opened at the throat. Snug black breeches hugged his long, strong legs and were tucked into low black boots. He looked dark, delicious, and more than a little dangerous. Raising her gaze, she looked into his eyes and stilled. His earlier cool detachment was replaced with a glittering hunger that made it instantly clear why he was here.

He wanted her.

Relief nearly staggered her, and she braced her knees, her body and senses leaping to life. She licked her dry lips to moisten them and noted that his gaze followed the movement, his eyes burning like twin braziers at the gesture.

"Colin—"

He touched a single fingertip to his lips. "Shhhh. Don't speak," he whispered. "Don't move."

She swallowed her words and watched him walk to the dressing table next to the wardrobe. He returned carrying an armless, high-backed upholstered chair which he carefully set about eight feet in front of her. With his gaze hot and steady on hers, he sat, in a lazy, lounging position in complete contrast to the tension she sensed emanating from him. He spread his legs and rested his hands on his thighs, drawing her gaze downward. There was no mistaking the outline of his arousal against his snug breeches.

"Take off your gown."

The silky command snapped her gaze back to his. His dark head rested on the pale green moiré chair back, and his hooded gaze burned into hers.

Heat stabbed her, settling low in her belly. The way he was looking at her . . . as if he were ravenous and intended to make her his next meal, pooled moisture between her legs. She raised her hands, noting they weren't quite steady, and unfastened her gown. Everything in her wanted to rush, but she forced herself to move with a deliberate lack of haste, filled with a surge of excitement she'd never before known at his rapt, intense expression.

When she'd undone her buttons, she slowly skimmed the garment down her body to her hips, where she released it to pool around her ankles. Backlit by the fire, she knew he could see every contour of her body through her thin chemise.

"Very nice," he murmured. "Keep going."

A tremor skittered through her, one she now, thanks to him, recognized as arousal. Using the same unhurried pace, she slipped the chemise down her body, where it joined her gown around her ankles, leaving her clothed in only her drawers, stockings, and shoes. Her nipples tightened, aching for his mouth, his hands, and she arched her back toward him.

"Beautiful," came his husky murmur. His gaze flicked to her drawers. "Keep going."

Taking slow, deep breaths to steady her racing heartbeat, she leaned down to untie the ribbons at her knees, then slipped the cotton garment down her legs. Standing before him, his gaze meandering down her form, she felt the hard, heavy pulse of her heartbeat reverberating through her entire body. In her head. In her belly. Between her legs.

"Step away from the clothes."

Her knees shook as she stepped over the poof of material. His gaze tracked slowly downward and she wondered if his next request would be to remove her stockings and shoes.

"Exquisite. Take down your hair."

Reaching up, she pulled the pins from her chignon, dropping the small fasteners onto her pile of clothing. After she removed the last pin, she shook her head and the thick coil unfurled down her back. The ends brushed her bare hips, shooting a decadent shiver through her.

"Touch your breasts."

Heat sizzled through her, setting her cheeks on fire with a combination of embarrassment and titillation.

"Don't be embarrassed, Alexandra," he said in a husky whisper. "Not with me."

Drawing a shaky breath, she raised her hands and cupped her breasts, filling her palms with their weight.

"How do they feel?"

She had to swallow to find her voice. "Soft. Aching."

"Good. Now caress them. As you would want me to."

She brushed her hands over her sensitive nipples, then rolled the aroused peaks between her fingers. Need curled through her, tugging at the heavy, moist folds between her thighs.

"Don't stop," he whispered.

She obeyed him, toying with her breasts, teasing her nipples, basking in the fire burning in his gaze. A fire that dissolved any lingering hesitancy. Her lips parted with her quickened breaths. Never had she felt so wicked, so wanton.

"Slide your hands down."

The heated desire in his eyes, the harsh need in his voice, urged her on, stripping away the last of her inhibitions. Splaying her fingers, she stretched to her full height and slowly dragged her palms down her torso, stopping when her fingertips brushed the curls between her thighs.

"Lower."

She skimmed her hands downward until her palms rested on her upper thighs.

"Spread your legs."

Heart pounding, she did as he asked, knowing what he would ask next.

"Touch yourself."

Scarcely daring to breathe, she slid one hand between the crease of her thighs. When her fingers brushed over the exquisitely sensitive nub of flesh, she gasped softly.

"How do you feel?"

She licked her dry lips. "Wet. Hot." Her gaze settled on the huge bulge between his widespread legs. "Impatient." He made a low sound that resembled a growl. His hips shifted upward in a slow thrust, and her inner walls clenched in response. "Empty," she whispered.

Colin gritted his teeth against his own impatience, which scraped against his every nerve. Greedy, raw need tensed his every muscle. He'd forced himself not to touch her, to wait, knowing the instant he put a hand on her, his tight rein on his control would snap. The sight of her, naked, aroused, bathed in gold from the firelight, her hair a rumpled cloud of shiny curls, touching herself, pushed him beyond the limits of his endurance.

"Come here," he said in a voice he'd never heard before.

A wicked gleam lit her eyes, and she slowly shook her head. "No." Settling her hands on her thighs, she nodded her chin toward his chest. "Take off your shirt."

A rumble of admiring laughter vibrated in his throat even as heat scorched him at her soft command. Without taking his gaze from her, he slowly unfastened his shirt, then pulled the tails from his breeches to spread the material wide. After shrugging the white linen from his shoulders, he dropped the garment to the floor.

"Lovely," she whispered. "That fine line of dark hair that bisects your abdomen is . . . fascinating." He was tempted to thank her, but he seemed to have lost his voice. Her gaze tracked down the center of his torso to his groin, and an image flamed into his mind, of her tracing that same path with her lips. "Remove your boots."

Leaning down, he obeyed, then straightened after tossing the footwear next to his discarded shirt. He pressed his heels firmly against the soft rug to keep from jumping up and simply grabbing her.

"Is there any part of you that isn't beautiful?" she

mused softly, studying his bare feet. Before he could ask the same about her, she raised her gaze to his. "Open your breeches."

With unsteady hands, he unfastened the two rows of side buttons. His erection sprang free, rising up his belly. He felt the lingering, heated look she gave his hard length like a caress. His arousal jerked, and he gripped the edges of the chair in his rapidly losing battle for control.

"Magnificent." Her eyes glittered. "Take them off."

Watching her, he raised his hips and pushed down the snug material. The effort to move slowly cost him, and by the time he finished, he was breathing hard. He leaned back and assumed his previous lazy, slightly slumped position—one that completely belied the tense anticipation gripping him and the fire licking under his skin.

"Spread your legs. Wide." After he'd done so, her gaze met his. "Touch yourself. As you would want me to."

Forcing slow shallow breaths into his lungs, he reached down and touched two fingers to the base of his shaft, then dragged them slowly upward. When he reached the engorged head, he circled the sensitive tip, then slid slowly back down his length.

"How do you feel?" she whispered, her gaze riveted on his lightly stroking fingers.

"Hard. Hot. Impatient." The words came out in a low growl. "Dry."

Her gaze rose to his, and in a single look something passed between them. Something more profound than mere intimacy and desire. Something he couldn't name . . . because he'd never felt it before.

Without a word, she moved toward him, not stopping until her shins lightly bumped the front of the chair. "Dry?" she murmured. "Perhaps I can help."

She lowered herself to her knees, then gently moved

his hand aside. Leaning forward, she ran her tongue up the length of his shaft.

His stalled heart jumped back to life, slamming against his ribs, and he sucked in a hissing breath. His eyes seemed to glaze over, and in a haze of heated lust he watched her tongue circle the head of his penis, capturing the pearly drop of fluid weeping from the tip with a wet flick.

His head hit the back of the chair, and a long groan rattled in his throat. He tunneled his fingers through her hair, transfixed by the erotic sight and sensation of her moist lips closing over him. It was the height of physical intimacy, yet somehow, at this moment, not enough.

"Alexandra . . ." He fisted his hands in her hair, gently lifting her head. "Come here."

Uncertainty flickered in her eyes. "Did I not please you?"

"Yes, God, yes," he managed to say while urging her to her feet then guiding her to spread her legs and straddle him. Not sure how to explain this unprecedented need to feel her skin pressed to his, to touch her deeply, with his entire body, he simply said, "But I want to feel all of you."

When she was poised above him, he grasped her hips and brushed the tip of his erection over her drenched sex. Her lips parted, and, gripping his shoulders, she slowly lowered herself on him, a hot, wet impalement that dragged a ragged groan from his throat. When he was buried to the hilt in her tight sheath, the final tether on his control snapped. Reaching up, he fisted one hand in her hair and dragged her mouth to his while his other hand palmed her breast.

But it still wasn't enough. He thrust upward, every muscle straining, his tongue stroking inside her delicious mouth in tandem to his body's strokes inside hers. She writhed against him, and his entire existence narrowed to where his body was joined to hers. His groin tightened and quickly—whether too quickly or not quickly enough he didn't know—he felt her clench around him. Breaking off their kiss, he leaned back and absorbed the sight of her arching her back, the sensation of her fingers digging into his shoulders, the sound of her low moan as she climaxed. When her spasms subsided, he quickly withdrew, an effort that nearly killed him. His breathing ragged, he wrapped his arms tightly around her, holding her close, heart to heart, and his release exploded through him.

His heart rate had nowhere near returned to normal when she stirred and lifted her head. Opening his eyes, he saw her—flushed, hair in wild disarray, lips moist and parted, a look of sated satisfaction glowing in her droopy eyes.

Something inside him seemed to shift . . . something that told him that while for right now, this moment, this was enough, it would never, could never, be enough with this woman.

Nineteen

Alexandra looked out the window of her bed-
chamber in the Wexhall town house and sighed. The
leaden, heavy sky perfectly reflected her mood, the swirling dark clouds matching the maelstrom of emotions
roiling through her.

Leaning her forehead against the cool glass, she wist-
fully studied the garden below—the last time she'd ever
do so, as this was the last night she would spend in this
house. Lord Wexhall's party was scheduled to begin in
less than an hour, and tomorrow, regardless of the outcome of the evening ahead, she intended to keep her
promise to herself and return to where she belonged.

Had only a week passed since she'd arrived? She
turned, and her gaze panned over her luxurious surroundings. It frightened her how quickly she'd become
accustomed to all this. The quiet elegance. The sumptu-
ous meals. Limitless hot baths. The warm, huge, comfortable bed. Her every need attended to. Her budding
friendship with Lady Victoria, who, in spite of her lofty
social position, was unpretentious and kind, and in
Alex's mind, the epitome of what a lady should be.

While she still suffered pangs of discomfort from the knowledge that she didn't belong in this social stratum, she couldn't deny she'd basked in the pampering and, for the first time in her memory, having someone take care of *her*.

But she couldn't afford to forget where she came from, to where she was destined to return. This brief time here, living this life, was nothing more than a magical, gossamer dream spun of fragile glass. A gift to be cherished and fondly remembered, but not to be confused with reality. As was her time with Colin.

Colin . . .

Her eyes slid closed. Dear God, how was she going to say good-bye to him? The mere thought filled her with an ache so profound, so enervating, she'd forbidden herself even to think about it over the past week. Instead, she'd savored every minute she'd spent with him, hoarding her memories of each treasured day, every new experience, like a miser guarding gold, refusing to acknowledge the constantly ticking clock in the back of her mind that counted down the time until this whirlwind fairy tale would end. When they both went on with their separate lives—lives that, given their divergent situations and social stations, would no longer intersect in any way.

As the week had passed, her love for him had burned brighter, yet so had the heartbreak looming on the horizon. She'd attended three more soirees as Madame Larchmont, but although she'd listened carefully, she hadn't heard the killer's raspy whisper. No one had approached either her or Colin in any manner that could be construed as suspicious, nor had any further accidents occurred. Still, the parties had been torture, pretending she didn't notice the bevy of Society diamonds glittering around the man she loved, one of whom he would choose to be his wife.

She'd seen Logan at all three soirees, and on each occasion he'd accompanied her for a turn around the room and to the beverage table. Colin clearly didn't like the man, his jaw clenching whenever he saw Logan or his name was mentioned. But she liked Logan. He was intelligent, wickedly witty, and she found his company enjoyable and his attentions flattering. Indeed, she could understand why so many women found him so tempting, and if Colin didn't already own her heart, she suspected Logan Jennsen might have had a chance at doing so.

With no further information or clues about the conversation she'd overheard in the Malloran study, the entire mystery seemed as if it had happened in another lifetime, to another person. The week had passed in a blink, a collage of walks in the park with Colin and Lucky, accompanied at a discreet distance by Emma and John, who clearly enjoyed each other's company. Shared meals, long talks, and heart-stopping intimacies.

To her delight and amazement, Colin never seemed to tire of touching her. Smiling at her. Laughing with her. And the things he taught her! Such as how to play backgammon, especially the version where the loser is required to make love to the winner. As far as she could tell, that rendered *her* the winner, but she wasn't going to quibble. He also taught her a simple, yet scandalous tune on his pianoforte, a lesson made even more enjoyable when she suggested they act out the lyrics to the bawdy ditty.

Her favorite lesson, however took place in his billiards room, where he taught her how to play billiards—and the even more interesting "how to make love while bent over a billiards table."

He'd come to her bedchamber every night, indulging her on each visit with a sweet offering of marzipan and iced cakes before indulging her sensual appetites. Sometimes their lovemaking was slow and gentle, other times fast and wild and furious. He was a generous, exciting, and adventurous lover who encouraged—and inspired—her to be adventurous as well.

An image blinked through her mind of last night . . . he'd brought with him a small bowl filled with creamy frosting he'd pilfered from his kitchen. After decorating her naked body with dabs of the sweet fluff, he'd partaken of the treats he'd created, much to their mutual delight. Afterward, she'd been only too pleased to return the favor. Indeed, the night had been the perfect ending to a perfect day . . .

She squeezed her eyes shut, savoring the kaleidoscope of images of yesterday's outing playing through her mind. Colin's early-morning arrival with a crateful of oranges that looked suspiciously like Emma's and the announcement he had a surprise for her. Then the appearance of Emma, with a wide-eyed Robbie, who held an obviously besotted Lucky, in tow. The three-hour ride in his elegant carriage to a destination he refused to reveal. Arriving at a beautiful, stately home, nestled in a verdant meadow.

He called the property Willow Pond and explained he'd purchased it several years ago, although he rarely used it. He hadn't yet visited the house while in London and thought she'd enjoy a day away from Town with her friends. The fact that he knew, understood, how much she missed Emma and Robbie, how in spite of everyone's kindness she still felt out of place in the luxurious Wexhall town house, touched her deeply.

The weather had been glorious and after a tour of the magnificent house and grounds, they'd all shared a picnic lunch along with his footman John in the shade of a massive willow set by a small lake at the far border of the property.

Just before entering the carriage to return to London, she'd looked back at the beautiful house and grounds and remarked how she couldn't imagine owning anything so fine and not using it. That it seemed such a waste. He'd frowned, and had stared at the house for a full minute, then had nodded in agreement. In all the days she'd lived, yesterday had been her very favorite, and she'd remember it for as long as she lived.

But she'd awakened this morning knowing that this magical time was about to end, and all the heartbreaking, unwanted images she'd managed to bludgeon back all week attacked her from every angle. Colin, smiling at his new wife. Laughing with his new wife. Bringing his new wife sweets. Making love to her. Taking her on private picnics at his country home.

She opened her eyes and turned to stare at the bed . . . the bed she'd shared with him, and her insides went hollow. Maybe it would have been better for her never to have experienced the pleasures and wonders she'd shared with him, for she couldn't miss what she didn't know. Certainly it would have been smarter. But such thoughts were useless, and she needed to put them aside. Force herself to concentrate on the upcoming evening.

She, Colin, Nathan, and Lord Wexhall were all prepared and determined to find the killer tonight and stop anyone else from being hurt. And then, tomorrow, she would leave.

And the hurting would just begin.

With his features arranged in a bland expression that belied the tension gripping him, Colin slowly swirled his snifter of brandy, his gaze scanning over the dwindling guests remaining in Wexhall's ballroom. It was nearly 2:00 A.M., and the party was drawing to a close. Alexandra had not heard the voice, and nothing untoward had occurred. Was it possible that the killer's plans had changed? That the plan had been abandoned? Or perhaps only postponed? While he prayed the plan had been abandoned, his gut told him such was not the case.

Bloody hell, he wanted this over. Wanted to know the identity of the killer, stop any further crimes, and have justice served so they could all resume their normal lives.

His normal life . . . An unpleasant sensation cramped his insides. Resuming his normal life meant finding a bride, a task that had grown more unpalatable as each day of the previous week had passed. Casting his eye over the elegantly dressed young women remaining in the ballroom, he was forced to face the fact that not one of them, in spite of their beauty and wealth, their breeding and family connections, appealed to him in any significant manner. Most of them were actually quite charming and any one of them would make an acceptable wife, but none, no matter how long he conversed with them, sparked the interest that Alexandra elicited with a glance.

Alexandra. His gaze shifted to the alcove where she was conducting a reading. This past week with her had been . . . amazing. The happiest days he'd ever spent. And the thought of them ending filled him with an ache he couldn't name. The nightmares and sense of dread that had brought him to London still persisted, but when he was with her, she dispelled all the darkness.

"The party's drawing to a close and so far, nothing." Startled from his reverie, he turned to find Nathan standing next to him.

Irritation rippled through him. "Stop sneaking up on me."

Nathan's brows rose. "Start paying attention. Especially since the night isn't over, and you might be the one in danger."

"Nothing's going to happen to me," he said, filled with grim determination, although his instincts continued to tingle in that same unsettling way they had all evening.

"Not if I can help it," Nathan agreed.

"Where's Wexhall?"

"Foyer. Saying good-bye to his guests. Victoria is with him. As well as a pair of his trusted men."

They stood in silence, watching the remaining guests file from the room. After several minutes, Nathan said, "Lady Margaret is leaving the fortune-telling table. I wonder if her future predicts her upcoming marriage?"

"She's betrothed?" Colin asked, surprised but not particularly interested.

"Not yet. Is she about to be?"

"How the hell would I know?"

"You'd know if you asked her to marry you."

"Why would I do that?"

"Perhaps because you've claimed to be in search of a wife, and she seems to possess all the qualities a man in your position might require? Or have you changed your mind about marrying?"

A frown jerked down his brows. "No, I haven't changed my mind. It . . . must be done. And it's long past time I fulfilled my duty."

"I agree."

"Says the man who would inherit the title should I kick off without an heir."

"Bloody right. The day you shed your bachelor status and get to work on producing an heir, my sigh of relief will rustle every leaf in England."

They lapsed into silence. Several minutes later, Alexandra joined them, and he had to fist his hands at his side to keep from reaching for her.

"It seems our killer may have had a change of heart," she said in an undertone.

"Very possible," he murmured, feeling more relaxed now that she stood next to him. "Especially since it's known from the note you left Malloran that the original plans were overheard. But I suspect the plot would only be postponed rather than abandoned."

"Unfortunately, I agree," said Nathan. "Even more unfortunately, now we have no way of knowing what's planned."

They followed the last of the guests from the room, and a quarter hour later, after the door closed behind the last partygoer, they stood in the foyer with Wexhall and Victoria—the five of them exchanging glances filled with a combination of relief and unease.

"Rather anticlimactic," Wexhall murmured.

"Yes," said Colin. "But I don't think this is over. The next big soiree is the night after next, at Lord Whitemore's town house. We need to maintain our vigilance." He noticed Alexandra stiffen at his words, but before he could question her, Victoria reached out and clasped Nathan's arm.

"If you all will excuse me, I'd like to retire," she said.

Colin turned to his sister-in-law and noted her paleness. Nathan stepped in front of her and grasped her upper arms. "Are you feeling unwell?" he asked, his voice filled with concern.

She smiled, but the effort was weak. "Just very fatigued."

Without a word, Nathan scooped her up in his arms. Victoria let out a mild protest, then simply wrapped her arms around her husband's neck when he headed toward the stairs. "We'll discuss our plans further in the morning," he said over his shoulder.

Wexhall cleared his throat. "I believe I'll retire as well. It's been an exhausting night, and I'm not as spry as I used to be." He looked at the brandy snifter Colin held. "I trust you can show yourself out after you've finished that?"

"I can."

He turned to Alexandra. "Will you be joining Sutton for a nightcap, Madame, or may I escort you up the stairs?

"A nightcap sounds welcome," she said.

Wexhall waved his hand toward the corridor. "There's a fire laid in my study. Enjoy yourselves."

As soon as he'd climbed the stairs, Colin extended his hand. "Shall we?"

She slipped her gloved hand into his and warmth spread up his arm. Five hours and nineteen minutes had passed since he'd last touched her—not that he was counting—and it was far too long. The eleven hours and twenty-seven minutes since he'd last kissed her felt like a lifetime. But he would remedy that the instant they reached the study—as well as the twenty-two hours and four minutes since he'd last made love to her.

After he closed the door behind them and turned the key in the lock, he set down his drink and yanked her against him, covering her mouth with his, his kiss filled with all the pent-up longing and frustration and concern he'd suppressed all evening. And everything fell away except her. The way she felt in his arms. Her delicious scent. Her lush lips. The warm silk of her mouth. The velvet sweep of her tongue against his. The indescribable way she made him feel.

Aching with the need to touch her, his hands slipped down, over her hips, intending to gather up fistfuls of her bronze skirt. Before he could do so, however, she pushed against his chest, breaking off their kiss, and stepped away from him. When he moved toward her, she back away and shook her head.

"That's not why I came here with you."

Something in her voice filled him with unease. Adopting a casual demeanor, he moved toward the decanters. "That's right. You wished for a nightcap."

"I've no desire for a drink. I wish to talk to you."

"Very well." He approached the leather sofa near the hearth rug, noting her rigid stance. "Shall we sit?"

"I prefer to stand."

His unease multiplied. Bloody hell, had she heard something tonight? Seen something? Had someone insulted her? "All right." He moved closer, but sensing her need for space, left the length of the hearth rug between them. "What is it you wish to discuss?"

"Us," she said in a cool voice.

His brows shot upward at her unexpected answer. "What about us?"

"I want to tell you how much I've enjoyed our time together. It's been . . . magical. And lovely. You've been lovely."

An odd, sick feeling rushed through him, tightening his gut. "Thank you. I've enjoyed our time together as well."

"Please know that I wish you every happiness."

"As I wish you." He gave a light laugh that didn't sound nearly as casual as he'd wanted. "Speaking of happiness, I thought tomorrow you might enjoy an excursion to Bond Street. We could—"

"No."

He tried to shove aside the sense of dark foreboding flooding him and failed. "If there's something else you'd prefer to do—"

"I'm leaving in the morning, Colin."

A cold chill passed through him. "Leaving?"

"Yes. It's time for me to return to my own home. To my own life."

"Absolutely not. You could still be in danger."

"Perhaps. Or perhaps not. I cannot disrupt my life any longer for something that may never happen."

He felt as if she'd slapped him. "Is that what this time with me has been? A disruption?"

"No, of course not. But it is time for me to return home. To take care of my responsibilities. Just as it is time for you to take care of yours."

"Keeping you safe this past week was my responsibility."

"You succeeded. And I thank you. But you have other responsibilities."

"Such as?"

"Marriage."

The word echoed in his mind like a death knell, clanging a sensation akin to panic through him. Clearing his throat, he said, "If you insist upon returning to your rooms—"

"I do."

"Then I'll send my carriage 'round there tomorrow afternoon to pick you up, and we can—"

"No, Colin. Obviously I've not been clear. There is no more 'we.' Our time together has ended. I didn't come to this room to arrange our next assignation. I'm here to say good-bye."

It seemed as if his heart tripped over itself. The hell with giving her space. He erased the distance between them in two long strides and grasped her upper arms. "No."

The word came out harsher than he'd intended, but that cool voice, that bland detachment in her eyes, angered, and damn it, hurt him.

"Yes. We agreed that our affair would end after Lord Wexhall's party."

"Actually, we agreed it wouldn't end until I'd chosen a wife, and I haven't yet done so."

"Only because you've been distracted by trying to stop Lord Malloran's killer from striking again. Now that Lord Wexhall's party has come and gone, it's time for you to get on with it." She briefly looked toward the floor, then again met his gaze. "Our affair has also distracted you from choosing a bride. Colin, I understand you must do your duty. We both knew our arrangement was temporary."

He skimmed his palms down her arms to entwine their fingers. "But it doesn't need to end tonight."

"Yes, it does." She slipped her hands from his. "I want it to. I need it to." Her expression remained neutral, but he caught the faint catch in her voice.

"Why?"

She hesitated, then said, "I'm becoming too comfortable, too accustomed to luxuries I can never have. Finding it too easy to depend on someone whose presence in my life is temporary. I fear that if I continue with our relationship any longer, I risk losing a piece of myself I'm not willing to part with. Ending this now is best for both for us."

He clamped his jaw tight to keep from saying something stupid. Like begging her to stay. His mind knew she was right. But his heart . . . bloody hell, his heart *hurt*.

Her gaze searched his, then she asked softly, "Do you understand?"

"You've left precious little room for misinterpretation."

Her obvious relief scraped another layer of hurt over him. "Good. I want you to know . . ." She paused, and for the first time since they'd entered the room, a fissure of warmth seeped into her eyes. "That I don't regret a moment we've spent together. That I hope your life is a wondrous, happy adventure. And that I'll miss you." Her voice dropped to a whisper. "Every day of my life."

Before he could think, move, react, she brushed a fleeting kiss against his jaw, then swiftly crossed the room. Numb, he watched her quit the room, closing the door quietly behind her without looking back.

He stared at the door, frozen in place, feeling utterly

gutted. He raised his hand and pressed it to his chest, to the spot where his heart used to beat. His heart that felt as if it bore a deep, oozing gash.

If he'd been able to move, he would have gone after her, so it was perhaps best that he remained frozen in place. Because if he went after her, he knew he'd beg her to reconsider, a gesture that, given her obvious determination, would only embarrass them both.

She was gone from his life. As quickly as she'd entered it. He was free to resume his life.

And as soon as he figured out what that was, he'd do it.

Twenty

An hour after leaving Colin in the study, Alex paced the length of her bedchamber, determined not to cry. Her body and mind were exhausted, but she simply couldn't bear the thought of lying alone in the bed she'd shared with him.

Colin. The mere thought of his name sliced pain through her. Would it always hurt this much? Would this keen yearning, this profound longing, this terrible ache ever fade? Dear God, she hoped so. Because contemplating this awful hurt for the rest of her life was unthinkable.

A *ping* near the French windows leading to the balcony pulled her from her distressing thoughts and she turned quickly. Seconds later she heard it again. It sounded like a pebble hitting the glass. Her heart thudded. Colin?

She walked quickly to the window then cautiously looked out. A light drizzle misted the panes, and the moon bathed the ghostly fingers of fog undulating near the ground in pale silver. She saw no one. Perhaps she was mistaken—

Something *pinged* against the glass right in front of her nose and she gasped. Reaching down, she made certain her small, sheathed knife was still tucked into her ankle boot. Reassured, she opened the door enough to squeeze out onto the balcony. She took a cautious peek over the stone ledge and froze when a familiar figure emerged from the shadows.

"Miss Alex," came Robbie's hissing whisper. "I needs to talk with ye. Right away."

"What are you doing here?" she whispered back.

"I'll tell ye when ye get down here. Hurry!"

Grateful she hadn't undressed after the party, she hastened from her room. As soon as she stepped onto the flagstone terrace, Robbie materialized from the shadows and grabbed her hand.

"This way," he whispered, tugging her along. "Hurry, Miss Alex. He's hurt."

Her feet stumbled along with her heart. "Hurt? Who?"

"The bloke. Come on!"

Robbie broke into a run, and she lifted her skirts and ran with him, fear gripping her. Her mind conjured up an image of an injured Colin, and she increased her speed. When they reached the far corner of the garden, Robbie pointed to the gardener's shed. "He's behind there. Don't know if he's breathin' or not."

She pushed Robbie behind her then, reaching down, she slid her knife from her boot. She rounded the corner, and froze. Although it was dark, there was no mistaking the man lying on the ground and her heart flew into her throat.

Dropping to her knees beside him, she pressed her fingers to the side of his neck. His thready pulse beat against her fingers and her insides went weak with relief. He was alive. But for how long? How badly was he hurt?

"Lord Wexhall," she whispered, lightly patting his face. "Can you hear me?"

He didn't move, and she gently ran her hands over him, looking for injuries. "What happened?" she asked Robbie, her voice low and terse.

"I were hidin' in the garden, like I done a few times this past week, watchin' out for ye even though ye said not to, when I heard a noise. Real quiet-like, I looked to see wot it were. Saw a cloaked figure hurryin' away from this spot. When I looked, I saw this bloke. Wasn't sure wot to do, so I got you. Is he dead?"

"No."

"Is he a friend or a bad bloke?"

"Friend." Her fingers brushed over an enormous lump on the back of his head—a warm, wet lump. Blood. She jumped to her feet, grabbed Robbie's hand, then ran back toward the house.

"Aren't ye goin' to help him?"

"Yes. I'm summoning a doctor. He's staying at the house."

"Ye don't need me fer that."

"I'm not leaving you out here alone."

After entering the house, she dashed with Robbie to the foyer, then settled her hands on his shoulders. "I'm going upstairs to awaken the doctor. You stay right here." He jerked his head in a nod, but he wasn't looking at her. Instead, he was gaping at the grandeur surrounding him with a simultaneously awed and speculative gaze she recognized all too well, and she gave his shoulders a quick shake. "Do not steal anything."

Disappointment flashed in his eyes, but he nodded.

She dashed up the stairs, then ran down the corridor, stopping at the door to the room she knew Lady Victoria and Nathan shared. She knocked frantically on the wood panel and it opened within seconds, revealing Nathan, who clearly had not yet gone to bed as he still wore his formal breeches and white dress shirt.

The instant he saw her, a muscle jerked in his jaw. "What's wrong?"

"Lord Wexhall's been attacked. Head wound. He's unconscious, in the garden."

"Alive?"

She nodded.

"Wait here." He disappeared into the room, and she heard the low murmur of voices. Then he returned, carrying a black leather satchel and a lit lantern. "Take me to him," he said in a terse tone.

When they arrived in the foyer, Robbie joined them, and as they dashed through the house, then across the yard, she quickly related what the boy had told her.

After she finished, Nathan said, "I told Victoria to awaken the servants and send two footmen to me."

They reached the shed seconds later, and Alex watched him drop to his knees next to the supine figure. Turning toward Robbie, she crouched down and looked into the child's wide eyes.

"Tell me about this cloaked figure you saw," she said, her voice filled with all the fear and urgency gripping her. "Did you recognize the person?"

He shook his head. "Only saw the big black swirlin' cloak in the fog. Whoever it were ran into the mews, then went that way." He pointed toward the left. And everything inside Alex stilled.

Colin's town house was to the left.

She released Robbie, then dashed to Nathan. "The person who attacked Lord Wexhall ran off in the direction of Colin's town house. He could be in danger. I'm going to him."

A muscle ticked in his jaw. "Wexhall needs immediate care. I can't leave here. The footmen will be here shortly—"

"I can't wait."

"You can't go alone."

"You can't stop me. We may already be too late. I have a knife. I'm not afraid to use it. Send the footmen when they arrive." She looked down at Robbie. "Dr. Oliver will need help. You stay here and do what he tells you." Without waiting for an answer, she ran into the mews and headed toward Colin's town house.

And prayed she wasn't too late.

Slumped in an overstuffed chair set before the fireplace in his private study, empty brandy snifter dangling from his fingers, Colin stared into the dancing flames. Unfortunately, the fiery fingers did not appear to harbor the answer to the question swirling through his mind: How was it possible to hurt so much yet feel so bloody numb at the same time?

He couldn't decide which stung more, her actual words or the cool dispassion with which she'd said them. Damn it, how could she say good-bye and walk away like that? So *calmly*. As if they'd shared nothing more than a casual handshake. Under other circumstances he might have admired her unemotional composure—God knows it was a practiced demeanor at which he himself excelled. But for him, nothing about Alexandra felt calm or casual or unemotional or composed. Hadn't since the first time he'd laid eyes on her. Yet she'd dismissed him, the intimacies they'd shared, without batting an eye.

He needed to make financial arrangements for her, a settlement large enough not only for herself but for the children she helped. *Of course, if that bastard Jennsen has his way, Alexandra won't need any financial support from me.*

The rational part of him interjected that he should be glad, even grateful, that the wealthy American cared for her. Would and could take care of her. But damn it, he wasn't. The mere thought of that bastard touching her, kissing her, loving her, dulled his vision with a red haze. No, he was the exact opposite of glad and grateful for Jennsen. Just as he was that she'd ended their affair.

Of course, she'd saved him the awkward task of doing so. Problem was, he hadn't been anywhere near ready to end it. Which only added frustration and confusion to his hurt. He *should* have been ready for them to go their separate ways. The weight of his responsibility to find a wife pressed down on him like an anvil, and he couldn't deny she was right—their affair had distracted him from his obligation. More thoroughly than she even knew. Because he couldn't think of anyone other than her. Because he didn't want anyone other than her. Because he . . .

Loved her.

The realization hit him like a backhanded slap, and he jerked upright, his empty snifter slipping from his lax fingers. He didn't merely desire her, didn't simply admire her, he loved her. Loved everything about her. Her intelligence and wit. Her compassion and strength. The look of her. The scent of oranges that clung to her skin. Her smile. Her laughter. The way she touched him. The way she made him feel. Well, except for this evening when she'd made him feel bloody horrendous, but other than that, she filled him with a sense of deep-seated happiness unlike anything he'd ever known.

Unable to sit still, he stood and paced in front of the fire. There was much to consider, not the least of which was did *she* love *him*? He paused and raked his hands through his hair. He didn't know, but by God, he was determined to find out. And once he knew—

His thoughts were interrupted by an insistent tapping. Frowning, he walked into the corridor and realized that someone was using the brass knocker on the front door. His mind jumped to who could be calling at this hour. Nathan? Wexhall? Alexandra?

As Ellis had long since retired, he strode to the door, bending quickly to touch his boot and ascertain his knife was in position—just in case his caller was foe rather than friend.

Before turning the lock, he looked out one of the slender glass panels flanking the door, then frowned, surprised and confused as recognition hit him. He opened the door.

"Lady Miranda." His surprise turned to concern as the pale candlelight from the foyer spilled onto the threshold. Her hair was in disarray, her eyes wide, and what appeared to be a streak of dirt marred her cheek. Grasping her arm, he drew her inside, then closed and locked the door. "Are you all right?"

"Actually, no," she said, her voice shaking. A visible shudder ran through her, and she gripped his arm. Tears glistened in her eyes. "Footpads . . . around the corner. They accosted my carriage . . . me. Made off with my reticule and jewels. My driver ran in pursuit. I . . . I was afraid to wait alone in the carriage." Her bottom lip trembled. "I'm sorry to disturb you so late—"

"Are you hurt?"

She shook her head, her tangled dark hair spilling over her black cape. "No. Just . . . shaken." She glanced around the foyer. "Your servants have retired?"

"Yes." Supporting her weight, he led her toward his study. "Let me get you settled and comfortable, then I'll see to your carriage and alerting the authorities."

"Thank you, my lord." She looked up at him, and her bottom lip trembled with a wobbly smile. "I'm so relieved you were home and awake."

They arrived at his study and he led her directly to the settee in front of the fire, where she sank down with a grateful sigh. His gaze riveted on the stain on her cheek, which he could now see by the firelight was blood.

"How many thieves were there?" he asked, pulling his handkerchief from his pocket.

"Two."

"What did they look like?"

"Ugly. Dirty." Another tremor ran through her. "Horrible."

Crouching next to the settee, he held his handkerchief aloft and nodded toward her cheek. "There's a bit of blood. May I?"

"Y . . . Yes."

He gently wiped at the smear. "Were you struck?"

She nodded and wrapped her arms around herself. "Yes. Then he grabbed my reticule."

"I'll pour you a brandy," he said, rising. "It will help steady your nerves."

He turned and crossed the room to the decanters, a frown pulling between his brows. His gut told him something wasn't quite right here. He poured the brandy, carefully replaying in his mind the moments since he'd opened the door. His frown deepened. She said she'd been struck, and there was blood on her cheek—

But no cut or mark on her skin.

Realization struck, and he whirled around. But he was too late. The pistol she held was aimed at his chest. He quickly calculated the distance between them. Too far to grab her weapon. His gaze flicked to the door. She'd closed and locked it.

"Put your hands on top of your head," she ordered in a low, terse voice.

He cocked a brow at the gun. "If you shoot me, the noise will awaken my entire household. You'd be caught before you could reach the foyer."

"We both know I'd get out of here before anyone could reach me. And the first thing I'd do is rid this world of your lover, Madame Larchmont. Your brother and Lady Victoria, too." She smiled pleasantly. "I've already killed Wexhall. I might as well take care of the rest of his household." Her smile vanished. "Hands on your head. Now."

Tension and anxiety collided in his gut, but he forced himself to remain calm and not focus on the horrific images her words branded into his mind. He'd survived worse situations than this. He just needed to bide his time, wait for his opportunity to disarm her.

Slowly raising his arms, he said in a bored drawl, "Do you plan to tell me what this is all about?"

"Oh, yes." She jerked her head to the side. "Move to the center of the room. Nice and slow."

He did as she asked, and she moved with him, keeping a steady distance between them. When he stopped, she walked to the decanters. Keeping the gun trained on him, she slipped a small pouch from her pocket, then emptied the powdered contents into the brandy he'd poured for her. After sliding the pouch back into her pocket, she picked up the crystal snifter and slowly swirled the amber liquor.

"Prussic acid, I presume," he murmured, nodding toward the drink.

She inclined her head in acknowledgment.

"A favorite of yours, but sadly, not of Malloran or his footman, Walters."

She shrugged. "Walters would have met his end anyway. Malloran simply got in the way. After his party, I accompanied him to his study, where he found a note." Her lips curved upward in a travesty of a smile. "It took me a while to figure who wrote that bothersome missive, but I finally succeeded."

Sick dread slicked down his spine. Keeping his expression and tone completely impassive, he asked, "Who wrote it?"

"Madame Larchmont, as you well know. She's proven a very annoying complication."

"So you tried to kill her with the urn."

"Yes. Unfortunately, she has the devil's own luck."

"Why Wexhall? Why me?"

Her eyes filled with cold hate. "You killed my husband."

The words, uttered in the raspy whisper he knew Alexandra would have recognized, hung in the tense air between them, and his mind raced with the implication. He'd killed only one man. But she couldn't know that. And he needed to throw her off-balance.

He shrugged. "I've killed many men. Who was your husband?"

A dark flush washed over her face. "Richard Davenport."

"Ah. The cowardly traitor."

Fury flashed across her features. "He was loyal to France."

"Precisely what made him a traitor." His gaze flicked over her in a deliberately insulting way. "His wife's name was not Miranda, nor was she of noble birth. Who are you?"

She raised her chin. "Sophie. His French-born wife."

"I see. Thus his sudden change of loyalties. Your English accent is impeccable."

"Thank you. I'm good with voices and worked hard to perfect it."

"And the real Lady Miranda?"

"Resides in the rural outreaches of Newcastle."

A faint sound reached his ears. Glass breaking? He coughed to cover the noise, but she didn't appear to notice, and continued, "Lady Malloran hasn't seen Lady Miranda since she was a mere child, and was only too delighted to welcome her long-distance, nearly forgotten relative to stay during the Season. My mission would be complete before anyone realized I was an imposter."

"And your mission was . . . ?"

"To kill the man who murdered my husband and the man who ordered you to do so."

"Richard died five years ago. Why have you waited so long?"

Something flickered in her gaze. "When I heard Richard was dead, I was sick with grief. I lost the baby I was carrying. It took me many months to recover. I had much time to reflect. Richard had told me all about his work for the Crown, about Wexhall and you. The mission Wexhall assigned you two together. When he died, I knew you were responsible. And that you would die for taking everything from me. My husband, my child." Her voice shook with hatred. "Once I recovered, I needed to plan. Carefully. It took time." She inclined her head. "And here we are."

"You cannot believe you will walk away from this alive."

"On the contrary, I have every confidence I shall do so. Who would suspect sweet Lady Miranda of such heinous deeds? And even if they did, Wexhall is already gone. You're about to die. Madame Larchmont will be dead by morning. Then, Lady Miranda will simply disappear, and Sophie shall once again emerge." She gave the snifter a final swirl then set it on the table. Stepping away, she jerked her head toward the liquor. "Drink it."

"Thanks, but I'm not thirsty."

"If you don't drink it, I'll shoot you. The poison is a much less painful way to die."

"As you're clearly concerned for my comfort."

No sooner had he spoken than he heard a very faint, very familiar click, and his heart stuttered. A lock tumbler falling into place. Nathan? Or one of Wexhall's men? He prayed it was the latter and not his brother walking into this mess. Hopefully whoever it was, was armed.

Keeping his gaze steady on Sophie's, he moved slowly toward the table, cutting an angle, trying to force her to turn her back to the door in order to keep her weapon aimed at his chest. As he'd hoped, she pivoted, just as the door behind her slowly opened several inches.

"Would you care to join me for a drink?" he asked, nodding toward the decanters. "I'd be delighted to share."

"Just drink it," she snapped. "No sudden moves."

He opened his mouth to respond, but the words died in his throat. For it wasn't Nathan or one of Wexhall's trained men who slipped into the room.

It was Robbie.

Heart pounding with barely suppressed terror, Alex crouched low on the flagstone terrace outside Colin's study, grateful for the protection offered by the sheer curtains pulled across the French windows and praying the moon would remain behind the clouds. While straining to hear the conversation between Colin and Lady Miranda, she carefully manipulated her hairpin in the lock, grim satisfaction filling her when she felt it give. To her ears, the imperceptible click of the lock opening sounded like the crack of a whip, and her gaze flew to Lady Miranda who'd pivoted and now, unfortunately, had a better view of the French windows. But no matter. The door was unlocked, and Alex had the element of surprise on her side. All she and Colin needed was a distraction, and between the two of them, they would be able to disarm her. Reaching down, she slipped her knife from her boot and palmed the warm metal.

"Just drink it," Lady Miranda's harsh words came muffled through the glass. "No sudden moves."

Lower your hands, she mentally instructed Colin. *That's it. A little more . . .*

She gripped the door handle, ready to pounce, when a movement caught her eye. Her gaze shifted away from Colin, and her blood froze.

Robbie crept into the room, one small hand tucked into his pocket, his fingers no doubt curled around some sort of makeshift weapon. Lady Miranda must have sensed something, for she flicked a glance toward the child, but her hand holding the gun at Colin never wavered.

"Whether this urchin dies after I kill you, entirely depends on you, Lord Sutton," Alex heard her say. "Tell him to remove his hand from his pocket and move where I can see him."

"I'll not let you harm the boy," came Colin's tight reply.

"Then tell him. *Now.*"

Alex turned the brass handle and opened the door a crack.

"Do as she says, Robbie," came Colin's quiet reply.

She watched Robbie slide his hand from his pocket, then move forward. Her breathing halted when he planted himself directly between Lady Miranda and Colin.

"Stand behind me, Robbie," Colin said sharply. "Now."

Robbie hesitated for a heartbeat, then ran behind Colin.

"You can't protect him," Lady Miranda sneered.

"With my last breath, I shall," Colin said in an icy voice Alex had never heard him use. "Robbie," he said in a gentler but still firm tone, "if Lady Miranda shoots me, you run. As fast as you can. Don't stop. Just run."

Robbie nodded, his forehead bumping the back of Colin's thigh.

Alex's gaze swiveled to Lady Miranda, who appeared more than a little flustered.

"Drink the brandy," she ordered.

Alex watched him slowly reach for the snifter and knew it was now or never. Drawing what she prayed wouldn't be her final breath, she rushed into the room.

Twenty-one

Colin's fingers had just closed around the brandy snifter when the French windows burst open and Alex, resembling a wild-eyed, knife-toting avenging angel of fury, rushed through the opening with a feral growl. The distraction was all he needed. Crouching low, he unsheathed his knife with one hand and pushed Robbie to the floor with the other, uttering a terse, "Stay down."

In the same instant, Sophie turned toward Alex, her face a mask of frozen surprise. As if in slow motion, he watched her hand holding the pistol swing toward Alex. With a lightning flick of his wrist, his knife flew, burying itself to the hilt in her chest through the black cape just as a pistol shot exploded. For several heartbeats no one moved, the tableau burning itself into his brain. Then the pistol dropped from Sophie's fingers, hitting the rug with a dull thud, followed by Sophie herself.

Colin jumped to his feet and rushed forward. He paused just long enough to ascertain that Sophie was dead, then continued forward.

"Alexandra . . ." She turned toward him, and his

heart froze. Blood, in a rapidly growing stain, marred the front of her gown. Just as he reached for her, her knees buckled. Catching her against him, he gently laid her on the floor.

"Miss Alex!" cried Robbie. He fell to his knees next to Colin. "Is she . . . is she . . . ?"

"She's alive," Colin said, fighting back the panic that threatened to overwhelm him. "Go to the Wexhall home. Get Doctor Nathan Oliver. Tell him Alexandra's been shot." His gaze met the boy's terrified eyes. "Hurry, Robbie."

The boy was gone in a flash. Colin fit his fingers into the blood-soaked gash in the sleeve of her gown and ripped the material open. Blood pumped from a jagged wound and his stomach turned over. Tearing at the fastenings on his shirt, he yanked off the garment, wadded the material and pressed it against the wound.

"Alexandra," he said, his voice breaking on her name. "Darling, can you hear me?"

She remained motionless, her face waxy pale.

"Ellis!" he bellowed. Surely one of the servants would arrive shortly—the pistol shot had to have awakened them. Seconds later he heard rapid footsteps. Looking up, he saw Ellis in the doorway, panting, his hastily tied robe gaping open to reveal a long nightshirt.

"She's been shot," Colin said, shifting his gaze back to Alexandra. "Nathan's on his way. Boil water, get bandages—whatever you think he'll need."

"Yes, my lord."

After Ellis's footsteps faded away, he leaned down, until his lips hovered just above her ear. The metallic scent of blood filled his nostrils, and he squeezed his eyes shut, pretending he smelled her glorious fragrance of oranges instead.

"You are not allowed to die," he whispered fiercely. "Do you hear me? I absolutely forbid it. You know how

I'm accustomed to getting what I want. Of course you know. You're very fond of telling me how vexing it is."

He leaned back, his gaze roaming her face, looking for any sign of consciousness. Finding none. Sick, mind-numbing fear strangled him. His free hand grasped hers, absorbing the sensation of her bare, callused palm touching his.

"Well, how's this for vexing . . ." he could barely speak around the lump in his throat. "I want you to open your eyes. I want you to smile at me. I want to feed you frosted cakes and marzipan. I want to buy you enough gowns to fill an entire room. I want to make every dream you've ever had come true. I want to tell you how much you mean to me . . . how much I love you . . ." His voice broke. "Please let me do all those things, Alexandra." His gaze shifted to his now-blood-soaked shirt, and terror struck him anew. "Please . . ."

The sound of voices and rapid footsteps sounded in the corridor, and he looked up. Nathan, grim-faced, carrying his black medical bag, rushed across the room, followed by a wide-eyed, out-of-breath Robbie.

"She's bleeding from a wound in her upper arm," Colin reported tersely. "Ellis is bringing hot water and bandages."

Nathan nodded, dropping to his knees beside him. "I have bandage strips in my bag. Get them for me."

Colin relinquished his spot next to Alexandra and retrieved the strips Nathan requested. He watched his brother remove the wadded, blood-soaked shirt, and his insides cramped with fear.

"Is she going to . . . die?" He could barely say the word.

After a rapid examination, Nathan said, "I'm going to do everything I can to ensure she doesn't. It's a flesh wound. A bad one, but her injury could have been much worse."

He pressed a fresh strip of linen to the wound, then his gaze shifted to Sophie.

"She's dead," Colin said. "I'll tell you everything later." His hands clenched. "She killed Wexhall."

"No, she didn't. He's alive, but he cracked a rib when he fell, and he'll have a hell of a headache for several days. Good thing he has such a bloody hard head." Nathan calmly exchanged the blood-soaked bandage for a clean one, then said, "You need to get the magistrate."

"I'm not leaving her."

Ellis arrive with an armful of bandages followed by John, who bore two large buckets of steaming water. After they'd set the supplies next to Nathan, Colin instructed John to fetch the magistrate.

That done, he turned and saw Robbie standing in the corner, watching the proceedings with wide, terrified eyes. Bloody hell, he knew exactly how the boy felt. He walked to the child, who tore his gaze away from Alexandra to look up at him.

"Miss Alex will be all right?" the boy asked in a small, quavering voice.

Colin crouched down in front of him and looked into his eyes. "Nathan is the best doctor I know. He's also my brother."

Robbie swallowed. "There's an awful lot of blood."

"I know. But I guess she has a lot more." At least he hoped she did. "You were very brave tonight, Robbie."

Robbie sniffled, then wiped his nose with the back of his hand. "I had to try to help Miss Alex." Then his bottom lip trembled. "But all I did was get 'er shot."

Colin shook his head. "That's not true. You got the doctor here faster than anyone else could have. And your being here tonight saved my life. You have my gratitude. I'm in your debt." He slowly extended his hand.

Robbie studied the outstretched hand for several long seconds, then, after rubbing his grubby palm on his equally grubby pant leg, extended his arm. The boy's hand felt so small in his. A lump lodged in his throat, smote by this child's hesitant touch more effectively than a knife in his gut.

"Ain't never shook hands with no fancy bloke before," Robbie muttered.

He cleared his throat to dislodge the tightness. "And I've never shook hands with such a brave young hero before."

Robbie withdrew his hand, then slipped it into his pocket. "This here's yors," he said extending his small fist. "I weren't stealin' it. I just took it to use fer a weapon, in case I needed it." He unfurled his fingers. A solid crystal egg that normally resided on the table in the foyer rested in his dirty palm.

Colin offered him a smile, and wished he could rumple the boy's hair but suspected it was still too soon to attempt such familiarity. "Very smart," he said taking the egg.

"I broke yer fancy window," he mumbled. "Couldn't pick the lock on the front door." He jerked his thumb toward the door leading to the corridor. "That one were easy."

"And lucky for us, too. Don't worry about the glass, Robbie. Things like that can easily be fixed." His gaze shifted to Alexandra. "By breaking it, you saved something far more precious that could never be replaced."

Twenty-two

Two nights after Lord Wexhall's memorable party, Alex sat across from Colin in his elegant carriage, trying to gauge his mood. He'd been acting strangely ever since she'd awakened early yesterday morning to be greeted by the sight of his pale, whisker-shadowed face and a hellfire of pain burning in her shoulder. Memory had rushed back and, after assuring her that Robbie was unharmed, he'd explained everything. When he'd finished, she glanced around her guest bedchamber at the Wexhall town house, and asked, "How did I get back here?"

"I carried you. Nathan wanted you close by, so he could keep an eye on you, and given our . . . situation I thought it best you not spend the night at my town house."

"Of course," she'd murmured, trying very hard not to feel hurt and failing miserably, which was ridiculous. Their affair was over. And with the murders solved, there was nothing left for them to discuss. Still, his absence hurt her. Nathan, Lady Victoria, Lord Wexhall, even Robbie and Emma had visited her—more than once—but not Colin. When she'd casually asked Nathan about him while he changed her dressing, he'd just vaguely murmured, "He's busy."

Yes, now that there was no longer any threat hanging over him or a lover to distract him, he was no doubt figuring out whom to marry. *Which is the way it should be,* her inner voice reminded her. *The way it* must *be.* But that didn't make the razor-sharp pain any less eviscerating.

Logan Jennsen had personally delivered a magnificent arrangement of red roses earlier today. He hadn't stayed long, but before departing had said, "It's obvious to me there's something between you and Sutton. But know that my friendship is unconditional. And that you have a choice."

His words had touched her, but he was wrong. There was no choice because Colin was not an option. But clearly Logan was. And he was a good man . . .

But then, at four o'clock this afternoon, the largest bouquet she'd ever seen had been delivered to her, along with a note written in a bold, masculine script: *There's something I'd like to show you this evening, if you're feeling up to a short excursion. If so, I'll see you at eight o'clock. Colin.*

She knew she should say no, but she simply couldn't. Not when she wanted so badly to spend one more evening with him. He'd arrived promptly at eight, and although her bound shoulder ached, the pain was bearable, and she was not only desperate to get out of the house, but insatiably curious as to what he wished to show her. Yet after a few polite comments regarding her health and the weather, he'd lapsed into silence and now stared out the window with his usual unreadable expression.

Several minutes later, the carriage stopped, and when she looked out, her breathing hitched.

"Vauxhall?" she murmured.

He pulled his attention from the window and looked at her. His eyes were serious but frustratingly gave no clue as to his thoughts. "I wanted to show you how beautiful the gardens are at night this time of year. The lanterns, the night-blooming flowers. With the weather so perfect, I thought you might enjoy an evening stroll."

"A stroll would be lovely."

Something that looked like relief flashed in his eyes. He helped her alight, very properly, his hand not lingering on hers even a fraction of a second too long, a fact which unreasonably and ridiculously disappointed her. Then, with a courtly gesture, he extended his arm. After she tucked her hand around the crook of his elbow, they entered the pleasure garden.

Hundreds of globe lanterns twinkled in the tall trees, illuminating the moonlit darkness, lending the landscape a fairylike glow. People strolled the paths in couples, families, and groups, laughing, chatting, many heading toward the private booths where the ham was notoriously thin sliced and the wines notoriously splendid.

They walked in silence down the beautiful Grand Walk, lined on both sides by soaring, globe-dotted trees, and Alex's mind drifted back to all the nights she'd spent here, studying the wealthy patrons, deciding which ones would make the easiest marks. So lost in her thoughts was she, she didn't realize they'd turned onto a lesser traveled path until Colin said softly, "This has always been my favorite part of the gardens."

Jerked back to the present, she looked around, and an odd tingle ran through her. This was the exact spot where she'd first seen him.

"Mine as well," she said before she could stop herself.

He stopped, then turned to face her. "If only this very spot was always warm and safe and filled with golden sunshine and green meadows blooming with colorful flowers, it could be your perfect place."

Warm surprise and pleasure suffused her. "You remembered what I said."

He lightly clasped her hands and heated tingles raced up her arms. "My sweet Alexandra, I recall the very first words you said to me. And the last words as well. And all the words in between."

"What were the first words?"

His eyes searched hers. "Don't you remember?"

It's you. "My memory is not as good as yours," she hedged.

"Then you probably don't recall my first words to you."

I'm very fond of that watch. "Do you?"

"Yes." He released her hands, and she immediately missed their warmth. Instead of resuming their walk, however, he slipped his watch from his waistcoat pocket. Even here, on this more dimly lit path, the fine gold gleamed against his palm. " 'I'm very fond of that watch,' " he said softly.

Her gaze jerked up to his. And realization slammed into her. Her knees suddenly trembled, and she actually felt the blood drain from her face. "You know," she said, her shaking voice no more than a whisper. "You *know.* You've known all along."

"Yes. Since the moment I saw you at Lady Malloran's." His gaze bored into hers. "Clearly you've known all along as well."

Hot humiliation washed over her, turning her cheeks to fire. She nodded mutely, then a humorless laugh escaped her. "I cannot believe you remembered me. That you recognized me."

"I never forgot you," he said, his tone and eyes serious. "Your eyes. Your face. Your words. The way you looked at me. I spent hours searching for you that night. And every night I was in London after that. Even on this visit, I spent my first two nights in Town here at Vauxhall, roaming the paths, looking for you—a woman whose name I didn't even know."

She stared at him, stunned. "Why? Why would you do that?"

Reaching out, he brushed a single fingertip over her cheek. "Did you ever come back here and look for me?"

There was no point in not admitting the truth. "More times than I can count."

"Then you know why I looked for you. For the same reasons you looked for me. I wanted to see you again. Wanted to know what happened to you. But most of all, I wanted to give you this." Taking her hand, he pressed his watch into her palm.

She gaped at the exquisite gold timepiece, then raised her gaze to his and shook her head. "I cannot accept this."

"You can." He curled her fingers over the gold, which still bore the warmth from his palm. "I want you to have it. The moment I took it from you, I regretted doing so."

A huff of stunned laughter rose in her throat. "*I* took it from *you*."

"And I should have let you have it. You needed it far more than I. Please accept it now—as a token of my highest esteem and admiration."

A humorless sound escaped her. "Esteem? Admiration? For a thief?"

"Esteem and admiration for the fights you've fought and won to no longer be a thief. You are . . . amazing."

"I'm nothing of the sort."

"The fact that we are standing here, four years later, and you have risen so far from where you were then, proves you are." He touched his fingers under her chin.

"Don't belittle your accomplishments, Alexandra, or the strength and fortitude it required to achieve them. You've done so much, for yourself and the children you're helping. I'm humbled by all you've done. And I'm proud to know you."

Warm, giddy pleasure washed through her at his words. But what he was offering her . . . "Colin, this watch . . . it's too much. I can't—"

"Alexandra, accept my gift." His gaze held hers. "Please."

"I . . . I don't know what to say."

"Thank you?" he suggested with a half smile.

"Thank you. I'll treasure it always."

"I'm glad. Now, will you satisfy my curiosity about something?"

"If I can."

"That night, you looked at me as if you knew me. And your words, 'it's you.' What did you mean?"

Clutching his watch in her palm, she said, "For years, a handsome, dark-haired, green-eyed man has figured prominently in my card readings. When I saw you that night, I somehow knew you were the man."

"Figured prominently in your card readings in what way?"

"That he would play an important role in my future." She offered him a weak smile. "It appears the cards were once again correct."

"I certainly hope so."

She shook her head. "As those readings occurred in the past, our future has already happened. They've already proven correct."

"Oh." He drew a deep breath, then frowned. "There's something I must tell you."

"What's that?"

"I've decided upon a wife."

At his softly spoken words, all the color leaked from

the evening, from the emotional intimacies they'd shared, leaving only drab shades of gray behind. She'd known this day would come, had thought she was prepared, but nothing had readied her for this knee-weakening blow. Pain and desolation, greater than any she'd ever experienced on London's unforgiving streets, gripped her in a vise. "I . . . see."

His gaze searched hers, then he shook his head. "No, I don't think you do." He reached out and folded her hands between his. "I knew I cared about you, but it wasn't until after you ended our affair that I realized how much. And this morning, when I awoke after having spent a long, miserable night without you, wanting you every minute I lay there alone, I realized that I'm going to want you every night. That even if I could spend every minute with you, it still wouldn't be enough. But I want to try."

Everything inside her stilled. Her breath. Her heart. Her blood. "What are you saying?"

"That I've spent the last four years thinking about you. Wondering about you. I don't want to wonder anymore. I want to know. Firsthand. Every day. I am insanely, ridiculously in love with you." To her utter astonishment, he dropped to one knee before her. "Alexandra, will you marry me?"

Colin looked up at her, his heart hammering as if he'd sprinted across England, Vauxhall gravel digging into his knee and waited. Bloody hell, she was staring at him as if he'd sprouted another eyeball. Was that good? It didn't *seem* particularly promising, but what did he know? He'd never proposed before.

Finally, she cleared her throat. "Have you been drinking?"

Definitely not the response he'd hoped for. "Not a drop."

She slipped the watch into her pocket, then gently tugged on his hands. "Please get up."

After he rose, she squeezed his hands, and he detected the sheen of tears in her eyes. "I am touched and stunned by your offer, but you cannot possibly consider marrying a woman like me."

"A woman like you?"

She made an exasperated sound. "Why are you being deliberately obtuse? You know what I was."

"Yes. And I know what you are. Kind. Caring. Compassionate. Warm, witty, and intelligent. Everything I've ever wanted."

She shook her head. "You could have any woman you want."

"So I always thought. Yet it appears that the one I want doesn't want me."

"This isn't about what I want. This is about what I cannot have."

"Yet I offer myself to you. Me and my title and all my worldly goods."

Her face paled. "I don't want your title or your worldly goods," she said, sounding utterly appalled.

"That is a sentence I'd wager no other woman in England would ever say to me without benefit of a gun pointed at her head. The fact you did, and that I know you mean it, only makes me love you more."

"B . . . but what of your responsibility to your title?"

"It is to marry and produce an heir, an obligation I take very seriously. And one I intend to honor. With you."

"Colin, you are meant for another. For a highborn woman who comes from the same social background as you."

"There was a time when I would have agreed, but no longer. You may believe yourself below those women, but I don't. Your riches are simply of another sort—things that money cannot buy. Character. Integrity. Loyalty. Bravery. I was meant for you, Alexandra. My destiny is *you*."

She was silent for several seconds, then said, "Colin, I lived selfishly for years, taking things that didn't belong to me—"

"In order to survive."

"While that's true, it doesn't change the selfishness of the act. I can't go back to that—to thinking only of me. Your life is in Cornwall. Mine is here. I have responsibilities here. To Emma, Robbie, and the other children. I've made a commitment to them. To myself. I can't just abandon those things."

He raised their entwined hands and rested them against his chest. "I've thought about that, and I believe I have a solution. I was thinking we could spend half the year in Cornwall, then half here. We could use Willow Pond as a training ground of sorts for the children you wish to help—get them away from London and teach them practical skills. How to work in the stables, how to cook, that sort of thing. Prepare them to lead productive lives. Robbie certainly seemed to enjoy his visit there. Perhaps during the months we're in Cornwall, where you'd enjoy the sea, Emma could see to things at Willow Pond."

She appeared stunned. "You would do that?"

"I would do *anything* for you." He leaned forward and touched his forehead to hers. "For years I've felt useless and unnecessary. You, your cause, make me feel needed. I have the resources to help you. I *want* to help you. Let me."

She leaned back, her eyes filled with hope and confusion and trepidation. "But what about your family? Your father? Surely he'd be appalled at your not choosing a peer's daughter to marry."

"Nathan and Victoria have already given me their blessing, and Victoria has promised to help ease your way into Society. As for my father, I'm certain he'll come to love you, but even if he doesn't, it makes no difference. I'll marry you or no one. I've had no more nightmares, and I no longer feel the danger that drove me to seek out a wife at this time. But I want one just the same. You. Only you."

His gaze searched hers. "Do you remember when we spoke about our 'perfect person'?"

"Yes."

"*You* are my perfect person. Is there any hope I could be yours?"

Her bottom lip trembled. "You always have been," she whispered.

He eased his hands from hers and framed her face between his palms—that intriguing face that had captivated him from the first instant he saw it. "Do you love me, Alexandra?"

Huge tears pooled in her eyes. "I am insanely, ridiculously in love with you."

He briefly squeezed his eyes shut. "Thank God." He opened his eyes and a smile pulled up one corner of his mouth. "So you're 'ridiculanely' in love with me?"

She laughed. "I am."

"And you'll marry me?"

"Yes," she said in breathless voice, then laughed again. "Yes!"

Having finally heard the only word he'd wanted to hear for the past half hour, he held her tight against him and kissed her, a long, slow, deep kiss filled with all the wild love and passion careening through him. When he lifted his head, he looked down into beautiful chocolate brown eyes sparkling with love and happiness.

"Tell me," he whispered against her lips. "What does Madame Larchmont predict for our future?"

"Love. Happiness. Children. Marzipan. And lots of frosting."

"Fabulous. Frosting is my favorite. Anything about the billiards room?"

Her laughter warmed his lips. "As a matter of fact . . . yes. Actually, frosting in the billiards room."

"That is very good news, indeed."

"In fact, I'd call it 'increderful'—incredible *and* wonderful."

Laughing, he hugged her against him and twirled her off her feet. "My sweet Alexandra, I couldn't have said it better myself."

Why Do Women Love Inappropriate Men?

*Y*ou know who you are, but perhaps you won't admit to it. You're the wild child drawn to the quiet, bookish guy reading *The Economist*; or maybe you're the reserved society lady who secretly loves nothing better than a ride on a Harley clutching a leather clad biker; or perhaps you're human and he's a vampire . . . But any way you look at it, there's no greater thrill or challenge for you than being with someone you know you shouldn't.

Well you're not the only one . . .

In these four upcoming Avon Romance Superleaders, the old adage that opposites attract never rang more true. Enjoy!

Coming May 2006

THE
Care and Feeding
OF
UNMARRIED MEN

By Christie Ridgway

Palm Springs's "Party Girl" Eve Caruso has finally met her match. "The Preacher," aka Nash Cargill, is in town to protect his starlet sister from a stalker, only to realize that he'd rather "stalk" Eve! But can this granddaughter of a notorious mobster be tamed?

T he rain was pouring down on the Palm Springs desert in biblical proportions the night he stalked into the spa's small bar. He was a big man, tall, brawny, the harsh planes of his face unsoftened by his wet, dark hair. Clint Eastwood minus forty years and plus forty pounds of pure muscle. Water dripped from the hem of his ankle-length black slicker to puddle on the polished marble floor beside his reptilian-skinned cowboy boots.

She flashed on one of the lessons her father had drilled into her. *A girl as beautiful as you and with a name like yours should always be on guard for the snake in Paradise.*

And as the stranger took another step forward, Eve Caruso heard a distinctive hiss.

The sound had come from her, though, the hiss of a quick, indrawn breath, because the big man put every one of her instincts on alert. But she'd also been taught at the school of Never Showing Fear, so she pressed her damp palms against the thighs of her tight white jeans, then scooted around the bar.

"Can I help you?" she asked, positioning her body between him and the lone figure seated on the eighth and last stool.

The stranger's gaze flicked to Eve.

She'd attended a casual dinner party earlier that evening—escorted by her trusty tape recorder so she wouldn't forget a detail of the meal or the guest list, which would appear in her society column—and hadn't bothered to change before taking on the late shift in the Kona Kai's tiny lounge. Her jeans were topped with a honey-beige silk T-shirt she'd belted at her hips. Around her neck was a tangle of turquoise-and-silver necklaces, some of which she'd owned since junior high. Her cowboy boots were turquoise too, and hand-tooled. Due to pressing financial concerns, she'd recently considered selling them on eBay—and maybe she still would, she thought, as his gaze fell to the pointy tips and her toes flexed into involuntary fetal curls.

He took in her flashy boots, then moved on to her long legs, her demi-bra-ed breasts, her shoulder-blade-length blonde hair and blue eyes. She'd been assessed by a thousand men, assessed, admired, desired, and since she was twelve-and-a-half years old, she'd been unfazed by all of them. Her looks were her gift, her luck, her tool, and tonight, a useful distraction in keeping the dark man from noticing the less showy but more famous face of the younger woman sitting by herself at the bar.

Eve placed a hand on an empty stool and gestured with the other behind her back. *Get out, get away,* she signaled, all the while keeping her gaze on the stranger and letting a slow smile break over her face. "What would you like?" she asked, softly releasing the words one by one into the silence, like lingerie dropping onto plush carpeting.

"Sorry, darlin', I'm not here for you," he said, then he and his Southern drawl brushed past her, leaving only the scent of rain and rejection in their wake.

Eve froze in—shock? dismay? fear? *"I'm not here for you."*

What the hell was up with that?

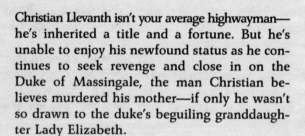

Coming June 2006

Her Officer and Gentleman

By Karen Hawkins

Christian Llevanth isn't your average highwayman—
he's inherited a title and a fortune. But he's
unable to enjoy his newfound status as he con-
tinues to seek revenge and close in on the
Duke of Massingale, the man Christian be-
lieves murdered his mother—if only he wasn't
so drawn to the duke's beguiling granddaughter Lady Elizabeth.

♥

"I have no wish to fall in love," Beth declared.

"Which is exactly why you are so vulnerable
to it."

"Nonsense. That will never happen to me. Beatrice,
you seem to forget that I am far too pragmatic—"

"May I have this dance?" came a deep voice from
behind Beth.

She started to answer, but caught sight of Beatrice's face. Her cousin stood, mouth open, eyes
wide.

Beth turned her head . . . and found herself looking up into the face of the most incredibly handsome man she'd ever seen. He was a full head taller

than her, his shoulders broad, but it was his face that caused her to flush head to toe. Black hair spilled over his forehead, his jaw firm, his mouth masculine and yet sensual. His eyes called the most attention; they were the palest green, thickly lashed, and decidedly masculine.

Her heart thudded, her palms grew damp, and her stomach tightened in the most irksome way. Her entire body felt leaden. What on earth was the matter with her? Had she eaten something ill for dinner that evening? Perchance a scallop, for they never failed to make her feel poorly.

Unaware his effect was being explained away on a shellfish, he smiled, his eyes sparkling down at her with wicked humor. "I believe I have forgotten to introduce myself. Allow me." He bowed. "I am Viscount Westerville."

"Ah!" Beatrice said, breaking into movement as if she'd been shoved from behind. "Westerville! One of Rochester's—ah—"

"Yes," the viscount said smoothly. He bowed, his gaze still riveted on Beth.

Before she knew what he was about, he had captured her limp hand and brought it to his lips, pressing a kiss to her fingers, his eyes sparkling at her intimately.

"Well, Lady Elizabeth?" he asked, his breath warm on her hand. "Shall we dance?"

Coming July 2006

♥

A Bite to Remember

By Lynsay Sands

When Vincent Argeneau's production of *Dracula: The Musical* closes, he suspects sabotage and calls in private detective Jackie Morrisey. He quickly sees that she's more than just a tempting neck, but unfortunately, Jackie doesn't have a thing for vampires . . . that is, until she meets Vincent.

♥

Vincent Argeneau forced one eyelid upward and peered around the dark room where he slept. He saw his office, managing to make out the shape of his desk by the light coming from the hallway. Oh yes, he'd fallen asleep on the couch in his office waiting for Bastien to call him back.

"Vincent?"

"Yeah?" He sat up and glanced around for the owner of that voice, then realized it was coming through his answering machine on the desk. Giving his head a shake, he got to his feet and stumbled across the room, snatching up the cordless phone as he dropped into his desk chair. "Bastien?"

"Vincent? Sorry to wake you, cousin. I waited as late as I could before calling."

Vincent grunted and leaned back in the chair, running his free hand over his face. "What time is it?"

"Five p.m. here. I guess that makes it about two there," Bastien said apologetically.

Vincent scrubbed his hand over his face again, then reached out to turn on his desk lamp. Blinking in the increased light, he said, "I'm up. Were you able to get a hold of that private detective company you said was so good?"

"That's why I couldn't call any later than this. They're on their way. In fact, their plane was scheduled to land at LAX fifteen minutes ago."

"Jesus!" Vincent sat up abruptly in his seat. "That was fast."

"Jackie doesn't waste time. I explained the situation to her and she booked a flight right away. Fortunately for you, she'd just finished a big job for me and was able to put off and delegate whatever else she had on the roster."

"Wow," Vincent murmured, then frowned as he realized what Bastien had said. "She? The detective's a woman?"

"Yes, she is, and she's good. Really good. She'll track down your saboteur and have this whole thing cleaned up for you in no time."

"If you say so," Vincent said quietly. "Thanks, Bastien. I appreciate it."

"Okay, I guess I'll let you go wake yourself up before they arrive."

"Yeah, okay. Hey—" Vincent paused and glanced

toward the curtained windows as a knock sounded at his front door. Frowning, he stood and headed out of the office, taking the cordless phone with him. "Hang on. There's someone at the door."

"Is it the blood delivery?" Bastien asked on the phone.

"Umm . . . no," Vincent said into the phone, but his mind was taken up with running over the duo before him. He'd never set his eyes on such an unlikely pair. The woman was blonde, the man a brunette. She was extremely short and curvy, he was a great behemoth of a man. She was dressed in a black business suit with a crisp white blouse under it, he wore casual cords and a sweater in pale cream. They were a study in contrasts.

"Vincent Argeneau?" the woman asked.

When he nodded, she stuck out her hand. "I'm Jackie Morrisey and this is Tiny McGraw. I believe Bastien called you about us?"

Vincent stared at her hand, but rather than take it, he pushed the door closed and turned away as he lifted the phone back to his ear. "Bastien she's *mortal!*"

"Did you just slam the door in Jackie's face?" Bastien asked with amazement. "I heard the slam, Vincent. Jesus! Don't be so damned rude."

"Hello!" he said impatiently. "She's *mortal*, Bastien. Bad enough she's female, but I need someone who knows about our 'special situation' to deal with this problem. She—"

"Jackie *does* know," Bastien said dryly. "Did you think I'd send you an uninitiated mortal? Have a little faith." A sigh traveled down the phone line. "She has a bit of an attitude when it comes to our kind, but Jackie's the best in the business and she knows about us. Now open the goddamned door for the woman."

"But she's mortal and . . . a girl," Vincent pointed out, still not happy with the situation.

"I'm hanging up, Vincent." Bastien hung up.

Vincent scowled at the phone and almost dialed him back, but then thought better of it and moved back to the door. He needed help tracking down the saboteur out to ruin him. He'd give Ms. Morrisey and her giant a chance. If they sorted out the mess for him, fine. If not, he could hold it over Bastien's head for centuries.

Grinning at the idea, Vincent reached for the doorknob.

Coming August 2006

♥

Never A Lady

♥ **By Jacquie D'Alessandro** ♥

Colin Oliver, Viscount Sutton, is in need of a wife—a demure, proper English paragon to provide him with an heir . . . everything Alexandra Larchmont is not. She's brazen, a fortune-teller and former pickpocket. Clearly they're all wrong for each other . . . Aren't they?

From *The London Times* Society page:

Lord and Lady Malloran's annual soiree promises to be more exciting this year than ever as the entertaining fortune-telling services of the mysterious, much-sought-after Madame Larchmont have been secured. As Madame's provocative predictions are uncannily accurate, her presence at any party guarantees its success. Also attending will be the very eligible Viscount Sutton, who recently returned to London after an extended stay at his Cornwall estate and is rumored to be looking for a wife. Wouldn't it be delicious if Madame Larchmont told him whom it is in the cards for him to marry?

Alexandra Larchmont looked up from the tarot cards she'd just shuffled and was about to deal, intending to smile at Lady Malloran, the hostess for the evening's elegant soiree where Alex's fortune-telling services were in high demand. Just as Alex's lips curved upward, however, the crowd of milling party guests separated a bit and her attention was caught by the sight of a tall, dark-haired man. And the smile died on her lips.

Panic rippled along her nerve endings and her muscles tensed, for in spite of the fact that four years had passed since she'd last seen him, she recognized him instantly. Under the best of circumstances, he wouldn't be a man easily forgotten—and the circumstances of their last encounter could never be described as "best." While she didn't know his name, his image was permanently etched in her memory.

She dearly wished that's where he'd remained—not standing a mere dozen feet away. Dear God, if he recognized *her*, everything she'd worked so long and hard for would be destroyed. Did he normally move in these exalted circles? If so, more than her livelihood was at risk—her very existence was threatened.

Her every instinct screamed at her to flee, but she remained frozen in place, unable to look away from him. As if trapped in a horrible, slow-moving nightmare, her gaze wandered down his form. Impeccably dressed in formal black attire, his dark hair gleamed under the glow of the dozens of candles flickering in the overhead chandelier. He held a crystal champagne glass, and she involuntarily shivered, rubbing her damp palms over her upper arms, recalling in vivid detail the strength in those large hands as they'd gripped her, preventing her escape. Out of necessity, she'd learned at a young age how to master her fears, but this man had alarmed and unnerved her as no one else ever had, before or since their single encounter.

The tarot cards had repeatedly warned her about him—the dark-haired stranger with the vivid green eyes who would wreak havoc with her existence— years before she'd ever seen him that first time. The cards had also predicted she'd someday see him again. Unfortunately the cards hadn't prepared her for someday being *now*.

Looking up, she noted with a sickening sense of alarm that his gaze moved slowly over the crowd. In a matter of seconds that gaze would fall upon her.

Also by Adam Hall

Knight Sinister
Queen in Danger
Bishop in Check
Pawn in Jeopardy
Rook's Gambit

Look for these other titles
in the *Quiller* series

The Quiller Memorandum
The Ninth Directive
The Striker Portfolio
The Warsaw Document
The Tango Briefing

And coming soon

The Kobra Manifesto

Available from
HarperPaperbacks